SETTLED BLOOD

SETTLED BLOOD

Mari Hannah

WINDSOR
PARAGON

First published 2012
by Pan Books
This Large Print edition published 2013
by AudioGO Ltd
by arrangement with
Pan Macmillan Ltd

Hardcover   ISBN: 978 1 4713 3683 6
Softcover   ISBN: 978 1 4713 3684 3

British Library Cataloguing in Publication Data available

Printed and bound in Great Britain by
TJ International Limited

This book is for Mo
She knows why

ACKNOWLEDGEMENTS

I'm immensely proud that this book won the Northern Writers' Award 2010 before it was even sold in the UK. It's a real pleasure to acknowledge the support of New Writing North, Arts Council England and the Leighton group who sponsored the awards.

Many people have contributed to the book since then . . .

Sincere thanks go to my dream team: the entire staff at Pan Macmillan, in particular to my inimitable publishing director, Wayne Brookes; everyone at Blake Friedmann, Literary, TV & Film Agency, especially my fabulous agent, Oli Munson; and my wonderful copy-editor, Anne O'Brien, who kept me right throughout the process.

Huge thanks also to a big mate and all round good guy—ex-army helicopter instructor, now commercial pilot—Dave Willis, for taking this flight with me in more ways than one. His lemon drizzle cake was once legendary in these parts. My loss is Milan's gain, Dave.

And to those even closer: Paul and Chris, Kate and Caroline, who show their support in so many ways; not forgetting special little helpers Max and Frances, for keeping me sane and grounded. And, of course, Mo—partner, mentor and first editor—without whom none of this would've been possible.

PROLOGUE

A slight vibration passed through her body. It took a moment to register that she was no longer on her feet, no longer waiting for her instructor to show. It was dark now. And then she remembered . . . one minute she had been tweeting about her day, the next she was hitting the deck. He hadn't made a sound as he approached. A sharp pain in her shoulder and he was helping her gently to the ground, acting the hero.

What was it he said as she lost control?

'You'll be OK, relax.'

How long ago *was* that?

He was close: she could smell aftershave.

Her eyes searched the darkness but her sight was blurred, extending a few metres in front of her but not to the sides. It was like looking down a tunnel through greasy binoculars. She could just make out a figure, a growth of hair sprouting over the collar of a combat jacket. She tried calling out to him, panic setting in when no words left her mouth.

Her mind was willing but she was otherwise impotent.

Was she having a stroke?

Again she tried speech. But her tongue refused to move, let alone accept instructions or formulate words. With enormous effort she banged one foot on the floor, trying to attract his attention.

He didn't turn round.

Did he even exist?

It took all her strength to lift her leg a second time and bring it crashing to the floor.

Metal?

1

It sounded like a drum . . .
And it was in transit . . .
A lift?
A shipping container?
Christ! Where am I?
A numb sensation began in her chest and crept outward over every part of her. She was neither hot nor cold and her body was shutting down: arms next to go, legs soon after. Her eyelids fluttered, heavy as lead. Then everything went black.

*　　　*　　　*

She was totally paralysed when she opened her eyes, terror ripping through her as she noticed the straps hanging from the ceiling directly above her head. Were they there before? She must have lost consciousness, but for how long?
A split second?
A minute?
An hour?
A day?
She would have sobbed had she been able.
It was impossible to see if her clothes were intact. And she couldn't decide if she was tied down or just pinned to the floor by her own dead weight. She couldn't feel a draught on her skin but she could see its effect as her blonde hair whipped round her face. And still she couldn't move . . . Except she *was* moving. Her world tilted, ever so slightly at first, then more acutely, tipping her body to the right. And now she was sliding sideways, like a side of beef being dragged across the ground in an abattoir, staring at her fate: a bloody black hole.
Oh God! NO!

1

The Senior Investigating Officer failed to notice the sun as it crept over Sewingshields Crags, or the stunning aerial view as the police helicopter descended on Housesteads Roman Fort. Her attention was firmly focused on a handful of hikers crossing Hadrian's Wall in both directions, each one a potential witness or suspect to a serious crime.

A little to the west, a police constable in a yellow fluorescent jacket stood guard outside a crime-scene tent. He held on to his hat as the chopper made its descent, its rotor blades whipping assorted debris high into the air. Jumping out, Daniels felt a stab of pain in her right shoulder as she hit the ground and ran clear. The pilot returned her thumbs-up gesture and lifted off again, banking steeply before turning back towards Northumbria Police HQ.

As curious hikers began heading her way, Daniels turned to the waiting officer. 'I'm DCI Kate Daniels, murder investigation team. Where the hell are the lads from Area Command?'

The PC shrugged. 'I was just told to wait here.'

He was tall, fresh-faced and built like a tank, someone she'd want on her side in a sticky situation. But he was no more than a kid. He looked really uncertain—really spooked.

'This your first one?'

He nodded his reply.

'Then do exactly as I say and you'll be fine. CSI are on their way. Until then, it's just you and me . .

3

.' Daniels gave a reassuring smile. They were two strangers, miles from anywhere. In remote areas, it had always been necessary for police officers to carry equipment their urban counterparts wouldn't know what to do with. The young PC had done well. She pointed at the tent. 'You erect this all by yourself?'

'Me and my shift sergeant, ma'am.'

'Good job.' She nodded at the advancing crowd. 'Now get on the radio. I want these people shifted.' She waited for him to move. 'Er, today would be good.'

'Can we do that, ma'am? I mean, the fort *is* a world heritage site.'

'I couldn't care less if it was the birthplace of Julius Caesar!' She glared at him. 'I want them out of here. Now move it!'

Lifting the flap of the tent, she went inside. A young woman lay face up on the ground, her body splayed out awkwardly like a discarded rag doll. She had long blonde hair and perfect skin. A green scarf round her neck matched the colour of her eyes exactly. There were signs of blood loss from her left ear, a pool of which had dripped down and settled on the grass directly beneath her. One shoe was missing but she was otherwise fully clothed.

Daniels could hear the PC on his radio urging the control room to hurry things along. As she crouched down beside the body he arrived at her side, being careful to use the tread plates so as to preserve forensic evidence.

'Anything strike you as odd?' she asked.

'Ma'am?'

'She looks more quayside than hillside, don't you think?'

4

The PC stifled a grin. Newcastle Quayside was the pulse of a party city some thirty miles away. He watched the DCI take a pen from her pocket. Carefully, she hooked one end under the ankle strap of a high-heeled patent leather shoe which was lying on the grass a few feet from the body.

'With these on, I doubt she walked very far . . .' Daniels studied the five-inch stiletto, holding it up in front of her face, swivelling it round so she could examine the state of the heel. 'In fact, it's a wonder she could walk at all!'

'If you don't mind me asking, what are you looking for?'

'Any damage that might tell us whether it was ripped off or fell off.'

'And which is it?' he queried.

'My guess would be the latter, but don't quote me on that.' Daniels tried to figure out how the girl had got there. They were a fair way from a main road. It had rained the night before and there was no mud on the high heel. Curiously, there were no drag marks on the ground surface either and no tyre tracks outside. The crime scene wasn't telling her anything and that unsettled her. 'Get me a pool car, would you? And while you're at it, have someone check Housesteads car park for any abandoned vehicles. I can't imagine—'

But the young constable had already left to carry out her instructions. Daniels smiled. The lad was keen, might even make a detective one day. Checking her watch, she stood up, hoping the pathologist wouldn't be long. She followed the PC outside, lifting her hand to the glare of early morning sun. There was activity on the horizon. A bunch of uniforms were up at the fort rounding up

5

her growing audience, their deadpan faces turned in her direction, all desperate to know what was going on. Figures wearing white hooded overalls were leaving the car park. Behind them, right on cue, a familiar Range Rover appeared. Tim Stanton, Home Office pathologist, got out carrying a black forensic evidence case and trundled across rough ground heading straight for her.

Daniels looked sideways as the PC spoke.

'I noticed boot prints over there, ma'am.' He pointed to a thin mound of grass a few metres away. 'They're definitely not mine, but they could belong to the guy who found her. He's in the gift shop café waiting to talk to you.'

Stanton had reached them. He was already suited in white forensic clothing, his trousers tucked into a sturdy pair of green wellington boots. He acknowledged them both with a cheerful good morning then turned his attention to the SIO.

'When was she found?'

'An hour ago . . .' Daniels pointed towards his car. 'Spotted from the ridge by a guy out walking the Wall—'

'Did he touch the body at all?'

'No, we got lucky. He's ex-job and had the good sense not to. He's my next port of call.'

Stanton looked tired this morning and Daniels knew why. This was his third call-out in as many hours, according to Pete Brooks in the control room. She stood aside, allowing him to enter the tent alone, comforted in the knowledge that he'd take as much care with his subject as any regular doctor would had the girl still been alive. She'd known him for several years and they had worked together often. His scientific background

6

complemented her intuitive approach perfectly. She never got in his way—or he hers.

The breeze was picking up. Sweeping hair away from her face, Daniels lifted binoculars to her eyes, panning around three hundred and sixty degrees. Other than the tent and hill-top fort, as far as the eye could see there was only the most spectacular countryside, dotted here and there with tiny slate-grey cottages. She wasn't a religious woman—not any more—but the sight was almost spiritual, as if a higher authority had been at work. It wasn't hard to imagine what life was like here when legions of soldiers toiled in all weathers to build the Roman Empire's most northerly defences and a garrison to house eight hundred of their number just metres from where she was standing.

She sighed, taken in by a dramatic wilderness she'd seen many times before.

'Unreal,' she said.

The PC looked at her. 'Ma'am?'

Daniels nodded towards the tent. 'Such an ugly scene in such a stunning location.'

'S'pose. I'm from round here . . .' He pointed off into the distance. 'Just over that ridge, to be precise. Guess you never see what's been on your doorstep your whole life.'

Daniels looked around her. She couldn't imagine taking this place for granted. Moving away from him, she made a call. Newcastle city centre was too far from the crime scene to run a murder enquiry, at least for the critical first few days. Her second in command, Detective Sergeant Hank Gormley, was out searching for a suitable place for a temporary incident room and she was relieved to hear he'd

7

found one.

She wrote down a place name—High Shaw—
then hung up.

Stanton emerged from the tent, bagging his latex
gloves, nodding to the binoculars hanging round
her neck. 'You can put those away, Kate. If I'm
right, you're going to need some divine inspiration
to solve this one.'

Daniels eyed him warily. He was not a man given
to riddles.

'Meaning?' she asked.

'That young woman in there was dropped from a
great height.'

She looked up at a cloudless sky . . .

2

The Mobile Police Incident Unit was visible from
half a mile away. It looked out of place in its
surroundings, almost dwarfing High Shaw, a
single-storey farm cottage bordered by a dry-stone
wall. Daniels drove towards it along a narrow
country lane and managed to squeeze her pool car
alongside.

She got out, removing a TO LET sign tied
loosely to the gatepost. Laying it flat on the
ground, she placed a heavy stone on top of it to
prevent it blowing away. In this part of the world,
particularly on high ground, gale-force winds were
commonplace; what wasn't securely nailed down
often went walkabout.

The pretty front garden was awash with spring
bulbs in pots made out of spent tyres. There was a

child's swing in the garden and a gravel path leading up to the front door.

Daniels pushed it open.

'Don't shoot!' Detective Sergeant Hank Gormley yelled, holding his hands in the air.

The DCI grinned as members of her team fell to the floor clutching their chests, writhing around in agony as if they'd been mortally wounded the minute she'd walked through the door.

'Get up, you idiots. We've got work to do,' she said.

Setting her briefcase on the floor, Daniels found herself surrounded by officers keen to welcome her back to duty. Although touched by their enthusiasm and good wishes, she didn't want a fuss. Taking a man's life, albeit in self-defence, still gave her nightmares. It wasn't something she'd ever be proud of—even when the man in question was a dangerous psychopath.

Turning her attention to her current case, she instructed her team on how she'd like the place arranged. DCs Maxwell and Brown began clearing the floor space for computer desks, moving a heavy sofa out into the wooden garage at the rear of the cottage. DS Robson fetched a drywipe whiteboard from his car and positioned it at the far end of the room. It would act as a makeshift murder wall during their stay. DC Carmichael brought in her laptop, and was logging on within seconds.

It was an incident room—of sorts.

DS Gormley's face lit up as Daniels walked towards him.

'We're dealing with another mean bastard then.' His tone was grim.

Daniels nodded, handing him a set of Polaroids taken at the crime scene.

He sifted through them, sickened by what he saw. 'Suppose we should look on the bright side . . . if the body hadn't been found when it was, the scene could've been crawling with bloody tourists, all with souvenir snaps of their own to take home. It would've been a nightmare. What piece of shit would lob a young lass out of a plane?'

'We don't know that for sure,' Daniels warned. 'Not until Stanton confirms it. If and when he does, we keep it to ourselves. We don't go public— not yet, anyway. This is God's country, Hank. Folks round here don't even lock their doors at night. They won't know what's hit them.'

Gormley handed the photographs back. They helped themselves to a mug of tea being offered on a plastic tray by a community support officer drafted in at short notice. Daniels thanked him, her eyes scanning the room, her mind drifting back to her childhood when she lived in a former gamekeeper's cottage much like this one. She felt at home at High Shaw, decided right there and then that she'd stay over for as long as they needed to use the property. There was no point driving backwards and forwards to the city every day. There was no one at home waiting for her—hadn't been for months.

The ache in Daniels' heart subsided as Detective Constable Carmichael walked towards her, a requisition sheet in her hands, a smile on her young face. Lisa had impressed everyone since joining the murder investigation team and she was fast emerging as their in-house technical expert.

'Sorry to interrupt, boss. The BT lads are here to fix up the comms.'

'OK, Lisa, you better let them in.'

As Carmichael wandered away in the direction of the front door, Daniels took another sip of tea and turned to face Gormley. 'This has got to be the prettiest incident room I ever worked in, Hank. How come you found it so quickly?'

Gormley tapped the side of his nose. 'I know people who know people. Mate of mine's brother-in-law is an estate agent in Hexham. This place is a holiday let normally. Cancelled at short notice, so the owner tells me.'

'I want to know why and by whom, soon as you can.'

'Already taken care of . . .' Gormley gave her a disparaging look. 'Place was booked by a Norwegian guy for a fortnight. Poor bugger had a heart attack and couldn't travel. And before you ask, he's in hospital in Stavanger. I checked.'

Daniels grinned. She should have known better than to ask. Hank Gormley was a skilled detective who knew the risks of taking things at face value. He always had his wits about him, had never let her down.

'You OK?' He eyed her over the top of his bifocals as she massaged her right shoulder. 'I wasn't expecting you back so soon.'

'I'm fine.'

'How did the hearing go?'

Daniels knew he was worried about her. She also knew she wasn't looking her best following a close encounter with a serial killer. But it was time to put all that behind her and concentrate on her job. She'd never been the type to sit around and mope.

As far as she was concerned, you just had to get on with it. She'd done that when her mother died and she'd do it again now.

'Piece of cake . . .' she said finally. 'No case to answer.'

'What time's the briefing?'

'It'll have to wait. Finish setting up and get things rolling. I've got to nip back to HQ and pick up my car.' She rolled her eyes. 'The guv'nor wants to see me. I hope to God he doesn't want chapter and verse on the Professional Standards enquiry. It was a complete waste of time and money. There's nothing to tell.'

Gormley led her to a quiet corner and dropped his voice a little. 'It's none of my business, but shouldn't you still be on leave? You look like shit!'

She made a face. 'So what's your excuse?'

'You need to take it easy, Kate. You've had a tough time of it lately.'

'Back off, Hank. And stop acting like my minder; I'm a big girl now.'

'Nice to see your brush with death hasn't softened you up any.'

'I told you, I'm fine . . .' She patted his upper arm. 'Don't fuss!'

She left him to it, heading outside with his words ringing in her ears. He wasn't alone in thinking she'd returned to work too early: her doctor, her father, her ex-boss—Detective Chief Superintendent Bright—all thought the same. Then again, Bright was master of the art of do-as-I-say-not-as-I-do. He'd recently lost his wife and had point-blank refused to take compassionate leave. So why should she? She was still thinking about him as she turned left on to the Military

12

Road and put her foot down.

Her phone rang as the pool car picked up speed. Tim Stanton had completed the post-mortem and his preliminary findings were not what she wanted to hear.

'Are you sure?' she asked.

'There's absolutely no doubt. Just about every bone in her body was broken. Estimated time of death around three a.m., give or take . . .' He sighed heavily, his tone of voice harder than before. 'And there's something else . . .'

Whatever it was, it wouldn't be good news.

'Tim, what is it?'

'I'm sorry to have to tell you this, but she was alive when she hit the ground.'

His words made Daniels' whole body shudder. She'd seen death in all its grisly forms in her years at the sharp end, but this MO was a first; a despicable act of cruelty and inconceivable even for the most hardened of professionals to take on board. Stanton's voice faded in and out, partly due to a weak satellite signal, mostly because she was imagining the horror of a young girl falling through the air and landing on open ground with a dull thud.

Organs rupturing on impact.
Bones splintering.
Death.

Daniels swallowed hard. 'Is it possible to calculate the height she was thrown from? I assume crime scene investigators took a cast of the ground?'

'They did indeed. They're doing the maths and will give you a call.'

A horse rider up ahead required Daniels' full

attention. She depressed her brake, slowed to a crawl and gave the rider a wide berth. The young woman turned her head slowly, acknowledging her courtesy with a wave. As their eyes locked, Daniels' car nearly left the road as the dead girl's face stared back at her.

'Kate? You still there?'

'Yeah, sorry. Any evidence of sexual assault?'

'None.'

'News on her ID?'

'Yes and no. Hang on a second . . .' The phone went down on a hard surface. Daniels could hear the rustling of papers. She assumed Stanton was looking for something. Then he picked up again. 'I found a receipt in the pocket of her jeans. It's from Durham University Bookshop. If her reading material is anything to go by, I'd say she was a med student.'

3

The PC knocked hard. The door to the farmhouse was in need of a lick of paint and the cast-iron knocker was falling off. An elderly lady in a floral patterned dress and a deep blue cardigan opened the door. On her feet she was wearing one blue wellie, one green one. She had a round, liver-spotted face and piercing blue eyes, permanent rosy cheeks and a mop of cotton-wool hair in dire need of a trim.

Mary Fenwick was a fixture in this part of the world.

'Fine day, Billy.'

'For some it is, aye.'

'How's your mother?' The old lady didn't wait for a reply. 'Haven't seen her since our Florence's wedding up at High Barns. What a do that was! I've never seen anything like it.'

'Me mam's fine, Mary.' The PC puffed out his chest, suddenly remembering he was an officer of the law. 'This isn't a social call today. I'm here on police business.'

'Oh, it's like that, is it?' Mary was too long in the tooth to be impressed. She looked past him, checking he was alone. 'Too busy to chew the fat with an old woman who damn near brought you into this world, are you? Well, maybe I'll be minding my neb next time your mam needs my help. You best be off then, if you're about the Queen's business.'

The young policeman blushed. He felt guilty now. He'd heard the story of his birth many times before. How an ambulance had slid off the road in deep snow on the steep incline leading to his mother's cottage. How Mary had run half a mile across the top field to fetch her tractor, then driven back and pulled the ambulance and their shaky crew out of the dyke on Hagg Bank. Blue he was by the time they reached the War Memorial Hospital in Haltwhistle, and lucky to survive—or so he was told.

As she began to shut him out, he tucked his foot in the door, thinking it best to placate her before things got out of hand. Salt of the earth she may be, but Mary Fenwick was prone to go off on one if riled.

'It's the Queen that needs your help this time, Mary,' was all he could think of to say. 'There's

15

been a bit of bother up at Housesteads through the night.'

'What kind of bother? If them young uns have pulled my fence down again—'

'A girl's been found dead. Suspicious circumstances, too.'

'Never!' Shaken by the news, Mary adjusted her hearing aid as if she'd heard him wrong, the skin around her eyes and on her forehead forming into deep creases as she looked up at him in disbelief. She stepped back inside the hallway. 'Come in, lad. I'll put on the kettle. A local girl, was it?'

He ignored the question, a trick his sergeant had taught him when he was a probationary constable. 'If someone asks you a question you don't want to answer, ask one back, lad,' he'd said. 'It works every time.'

'No time for tea,' he said. 'Did you hear or see anything unusual last night?'

A look of disapproval crossed Mary's face. The policeman suddenly felt like a little boy about to get a scolding for his cheek. No doubt Mary would have a word or two in his mother's ear next time they met.

'You'd best ask your Ronnie,' she said. 'He's in the bottom field with the horses.'

She was referring to his cousin who worked on her farm, a strapping lad who looked a lot like him. Rumour had it they might even be brothers.

The officer touched his police helmet. It was almost a salute. 'Thanks for your help, Mary. You'll be locking your door, just in case?'

The old woman gave him an odd look. 'I would, if I could find my key.'

16

He knew she meant it. Her door was never locked.

'Can't you come in and tell me all about it?' she pushed. 'Your mam'll have my guts for garters if I don't offer you something to eat. Big lad like you needs plenty bait inside him, working all hours on them funny shifts.'

'I've been told I can't discuss the case with anyone.' He found himself apologizing, a frequent occurrence whenever he was in her presence. 'I'll get myself away now and report back to the SIO. That's the Senior Investigating Officer, in case you didn't know. A lady detective chief inspector! She's a bit of all right, too.'

Mary Fenwick giggled.

Turning to leave, the young constable regretting having no time to sample her famous scones, kept warming in the range in case of a visitor. He knew fine well they'd be thrown out for the birds, if unused. Remembering a question he should've asked, he glanced over his shoulder. Mary was gone but the door was ajar. Then suddenly she reappeared with a lumpy bundle in a Christmas napkin, nearly five months after the event.

She held it out to him, smiling through smoker's teeth.

He thanked her, stuffing the scones in his pocket for later.

'Any campers on your land I need to know about?' he asked. 'Any family staying up at the old farmhouse?'

Mary fiddled with her ear again.

'Campers, Mary? Do you have any strangers staying just now?'

'Aye, there's no need to shout, son. I heard you

17

the first time.' She pointed away from the house. 'We have one or two in the cow pasture. I'll get my stick and walk with you.'

4

The XJ Portfolio had dark privacy glass in the windows and sumptuous cashew leather seats. In the rear of the vehicle, Adam Finch folded his *Financial Times* neatly and used a touch-screen remote control mounted in the centre armrest to select BBC News 24 on his digital TV. He checked his watch and smiled. He'd catch the headlines at the top of the hour.

Ten minutes later, the Jaguar turned left off the main road and passed sedately through cast-iron gates with a name inscribed upon them in bold gold lettering: *The Mansion House*. The familiar sound of tyres on gravel caused Adam Finch to look out of the window in time to see his gardener extinguish a cigarette, pocketing what was left of it.

Adam Finch hated filthy habits. He had banned smoking on his estate and made a mental note to hit Townsend where it would hurt the most—in his next pay packet. Warmed by this thought, he relaxed back in his seat for a further hundred metres along a narrow driveway bordered on either side by willow trees planted by his great-great-grandfather. The Jaguar glided gently to a halt directly opposite the front door of his Georgian country house. Finch waited for the rear door to open.

'Will I be required later, sir?' the chauffeur

asked him as he emerged from the car.

'No, Pearce. That'll be all for today.'

Finch's housekeeper arrived to greet him, a little out of breath. 'Welcome home, Mr Finch,' she said, taking his coat and umbrella.

'Thank you, Mrs P.' He didn't make eye contact with the woman, just strode off into the house, scooping his mail from a silver tray on the hall table on his way in. Pausing a second, he moved a blue flower vase a centimetre to the left before proceeding along the hallway, shouting over his shoulder as he walked. 'I'll take my tea in my office.'

'Very good, sir,' came the reply.

Finch's leather-soled shoes squeaked as he moved swiftly across the highly polished parquet flooring, through a set of double doors and into his study. He sat down at his desk, scanning the surface carefully, making minor adjustments to favoured items: repositioning a photograph of his late wife, Beth, and daughter, Jessica, a little further away; an inkwell a tad nearer; his fountain pens more evenly spread. His eyes slid over each item. Then he turned the pen clips until all four were exactly in line with one another. Only when he was perfectly satisfied did he log on to his computer.

Finch spent half an hour reading and replying to emails and then turned his attention to the post he'd collected on his way in. Using an antique paper knife Beth had bought him on their fifth wedding anniversary he slit open the first envelope and took out the letter contained inside. The news wasn't good. His investments had tumbled to an all-time low. An annual statement from his stockbroker confirmed his worst fears.

The recession was still not over.

Finch didn't look up as Mrs Partridge arrived with his tea. She set the cup and saucer down on a coaster, turning the handle to a precise angle so that he could easily pick it up. As she left the room again, he sat back in his chair, a man with all the troubles of the world on his shoulders. In his entire life, he couldn't remember a year quite like this one.

A small brown envelope caught his eye. It looked conspicuous among the rest of his mail, the address rudely handwritten in thick green pen. Finch set his cup back down and lifted the envelope off the desk, turning it over and over in his hands, disgusted by the childlike writing, by the sheer audacity of whoever had sent it. Probably a local from Kirby Ayden; most definitely nobody he knew.

Finch bristled. He'd received several ill-considered pleas for employment on his estate in recent months. Nothing short of begging letters he tore up the moment they arrived. He was about to disregard this one too when Beth's voice jumped into his head: 'Adam! Don't be so mean . . . we must embrace the locals, not push them away.' Her face beamed out from the photograph on his desk, her eyes teasing him. 'Your ancestors have employed people from the village for hundreds of years on the estate. What harm would it do to show a little humanity?'

Poppycock!

But Beth's smile seemed broader than ever.

Finch sighed. He still missed his wife terribly, had remained celibate and sober since her death many years before. Even from her grave, she could twist him round her little finger, persuade him to do the *right* thing. And, as always, he relented. Slicing through the envelope flap, he shook out the contents. A frown formed on his brow as a jagged piece of paper fluttered out, landing face down on his desk. He flipped it over with the knife. What he saw made him reach for the phone.

5

Detective Chief Superintendent Phillip Bright was on his knees searching his waste-paper basket when the phone rang. He hauled himself off the floor and fumbled with the receiver, cursing his new civilian clerk. Ellen was a spirited woman who took no shit from anyone—especially not him. They hadn't quite gelled as a team and he was wondering if they ever would.

'Didn't I tell you to hold all calls?' he barked.

'So you did, but this is urgent apparently. One of your golfing pals?'

'Which one?' Bright took a deep breath. No reply was forthcoming. 'Ellen? Who is it, *please*?'

'A *gentleman* called Adam Finch.' Ellen had made her point. 'He sounds rather anxious. Said he's sorry to interrupt you, but it really can't wait.'

The line clicked and she put him through.

Bright listened for a long time, his stomach in knots as he heard the news. After a short conversation he ended the call. He was about to contact DCI Kate Daniels when he saw her through his office window, fifty metres away and charging towards him. He hung up the receiver and waited.

'We have a problem,' he said, as she entered the room.

'So you said, guv. That's why I'm here.'

'No, I mean another one.'

'Guv, I'm up to my neck in it.' Daniels was parched. Her eyes scanned his new office and found the water cooler. As she walked towards it she heard yelling from the office next door. It reminded her of the last time she'd been in that room, before Assistant Chief Constable Billings took over. His predecessor, ACC Martin, had completely lost his temper and shown her the door. She smiled at the memory, feeling Bright's eyes upon her. 'I'm sorry, guv . . .' She still had her back to him. 'But our only witness wants to leave the area. I've told the poor sod his holiday's on hold and I'm about to take his statement so he can get on his way. He's ex-job? Can it wait?'

'No, it can't. The daughter of one of my closest friends is missing and I'd like you to handle it personally.'

'I'm sorry to hear that.' The water was taking its time to dribble into the white plastic cup. 'Can't you send a uniform?'

'She's a Durham University student, Kate.'

Daniels turned towards him, all ears.

'Five ten. Blonde hair. Green eyes. Ring any bells?'

'Shit!'

'Her name is Jessica Finch. Her father, Adam, owns half of North Yorkshire. You may have heard of him.'

'Can't say I have.'

22

'I've known him for many years. He's not a guy to panic easily. Before he called me, he called the university and found out that Jess has missed lectures. She hasn't slept at her halls for the past two nights. Nobody he spoke to has seen or heard from her. He was told she may have moved out, but he doesn't know where. University staff don't know either. He's frantic, Kate. Look at this—'

Bright turned his laptop round to face her. On the screen was an email message from Adam Finch with a scanned document attached. Daniels leaned forward, opened the attachment and found a hastily scrawled note mounted on a shaded background to make it stand out. The paper was un-lined and had been torn from a much larger sheet. She read the message twice. It was brief and to the point: STAY BY THE PHONE—CONTACT THE LAW AND I'LL SEND YOUR DAUGHTER HOME IN BITS.

'When did he receive this?' Daniels asked.

'It came in this morning's post. It was waiting for him when he got home shortly after ten. He's been away on business and only got back today.'

Daniels studied the note.

For the second time that day, the circumstances of a crime didn't seem to fit. 'That doesn't make sense,' she said.

Bright just looked at her.

'Assuming our dead girl and Jessica Finch are one and the same, why would her kidnapper risk the pay-off by killing her?'

'Maybe they panicked—'

'*Before* making a demand?'

Bright hesitated. 'Maybe she tried to escape? Or they roughed her up and—'

23

'No.' Daniels shook her head. 'Stanton told me her injuries are all consistent with the fall. There are no restraint marks and nothing to indicate a struggle.'

'Perhaps they gave her too many drugs and she died. They lost control and dumped her, hoping to score financially before her body was discovered. That's probably why they chose such a remote spot. It could just be Sod's Law that she landed where she did. Otherwise it might've been months, years even, until someone stumbled across her remains. If they ever did.' He paused for a moment, gathering his thoughts, meeting her eyes across his desk. 'You know how these things pan out, Kate. Abductions often go horribly wrong. The snatch was planned, I agree, but her death could've been accidental.'

Bollocks! Bright was clutching at straws. 'She was alive when she hit the ground, guv. There was *no* mistake, believe me.'

Her words hung in the air between them.

'Is Finch aware we found a body?' Daniels asked finally.

Bright's expression was grim. 'He soon will be.'

6

Daniels was troubled by thoughts of yet another linked incident coming straight off the back of the most gruelling murder investigation of her police career. But somehow it didn't surprise her that her new case was more complex than first it appeared. She didn't know why, but her guts had been telling her that right from the start, from the moment she'd stepped inside the crime-scene tent with a rookie PC breathing down her neck.

Her victim had died at Housesteads, but the question Daniels was asking herself was this: was the disposal site accidental or deliberate? She needed to find the answer at the earliest opportunity. The why of the case appeared to be a little clearer now. Monetary gain had been a motive for many a mindless and futile murder since the beginning of time. So why did she still feel as if her detective nose was out of joint, pointing in the wrong direction?

Three uniforms she knew vaguely passed her in the corridor. Acknowledging them with a smile and a nod, Daniels made her way through a set of double doors and out into the sunshine towards the car park where she'd left her car. She was pleased to be getting her Toyota back. The pool car she'd been driving was a piece of shit: smelly on the inside, uncared for on the out, in dire need of a service if the noise of the engine was anything to go by.

Pulling her phone out of her pocket, she keyed in the number for the mortuary. The call was picked up almost immediately by a young woman with a pleasant but distinctive Welsh accent.

'Mortuary, Sam speaking.'

Daniels didn't recognize the voice at all. 'Sam, this is Detective Chief Inspector Kate Daniels. I'm the SIO for the murder up at Housesteads Fort. I'd like to arrange a viewing of the victim for identification purposes.'

'No problem. What time would suit?'

Daniels looked at her watch. She'd offered to

drive down to Yorkshire to collect Adam Finch, accompany him on his painful journey north. But he'd saved her the trouble, insisting that he'd get there under his own steam. She estimated that it would take him an hour and a half at least. She didn't want to rush him, but neither did she want him hanging around waiting when he arrived.

'About twelve thirty?' Daniels suggested. 'Sorry not to be more specific, Sam. The man we think may be the IP's father has a long way to travel. I'm meeting him at headquarters and I'll let you know as soon as he arrives. His name is Adam Finch. I'll accompany him, as will Detective Chief Superintendent Bright.'

Daniels completed the arrangements and hung up. She had reached her Toyota. Opening the door, she took off her coat and threw it on the passenger seat before climbing in. The inside of her car smelled fresh and clean. She started the engine, but didn't immediately move off. First she dialled Gormley's mobile. It went straight to voicemail so she tried Robson instead, this time with more success. She gave him a quick update on developments and asked him to pass the information on to the rest of the team.

'I'll be off the radar for a while,' she said. 'Any problems, text me.'

Robson told her there was absolutely nothing doing up at High Shaw. He asked if there wasn't something more useful he could do, his resentment reaching her down the line.

'Be patient, Robbo. Let's take it one step at a time, shall we?'

She hung up.

Engaging first gear, she drove away from

headquarters and out on to the main road heading for Etal Lane in Westerhope, Newcastle Area Command. It was only a short journey, a distance of four and a half miles, give or take a few hundred metres. Passing the airport on the way, she wondered how much detail air traffic control might hold on light aircraft movement.

Parking the Toyota in a bay reserved for the Area Commander, she got out and locked it, hoping it wouldn't be clamped by the time she returned. As she rushed into the building, there were many questions running through her mind in relation to her victim's cause of death. The man who'd found her had been transported to the station in a patrol car and had been made to wait for over an hour.

He looked bored as she entered the interview room.

'Mr Bull, I'm so sorry for having kept you . . .' Daniels held out her hand. 'I'm Kate Daniels, Senior Investigating Officer. I had no idea I'd be this long.'

'Pleased to meet you.' Frank Bull sat back in his chair and yawned. Holding up a foot in a thick green woollen sock, he explained that Forensics had seized his footwear to take a cast of the sole for comparison with boot prints they had found at the scene. He was red in the face and dressed for hiking, had too many layers of clothing on to be contained in a centrally heated office block. 'It wasn't smart, finding your body, was it, DCI Daniels? Should've kept walking, shouldn't I? Instead, I've been walking down memory lane.' He yawned again. 'Excuse me! I'm not used to being inside for very long these days. In my former role as a police officer, I spent many an hour in rooms like this one.'

Daniels phone rang: BRIGHT CALLING.

Bull saw a look of frustration cross her face before she had time to hide it.

'Better order lunch then.' He smiled, accepting that she was about to ask him to wait even longer. 'Grub still as bad as ever?'

'I'm so sorry. I wish I could be in two places at once, but I can't. I'll call Hank Gormley, my DS. Ask him to take your statement immediately. Then you can get on your way, as long as you leave a contact number so I'll be able to reach you.'

*   *   *

The viewing room of any city morgue is grim at the best of times. For Adam Finch, this was the worst of times. His near-perfect life had fallen apart spectacularly in the past few hours. He looked small and insignificant standing beside a corpse covered with a green sheet, flanked on either side by Bright and Daniels.

The DCI spoke softly, not wanting to pressure him. 'Are you ready, Mr Finch?'

Finch nodded. Anxiety seemed to have aged him in a matter of minutes. Daniels lifted the sheet exposing the dead girl's face and took a step back as Finch leaned over the body. He shut his eyes but said nothing. She thought he was praying and allowed him a moment of silence. When he opened his eyes, a single tear ran from his eye and dripped off the end of his nose on to the girl's cheek, making it look like she was crying too. That was when he fell apart.

28

Daniels exchanged a concerned glance with Bright. He placed a steadying hand on his friend's shoulder and guided him from the room into the corridor beyond.

'I'm so very sorry, Adam,' Bright said as they left the room.

'No . . .' It was almost a sob. 'It's not her. It's not Jessica.'

7

The Jaguar sped off with Daniels' Toyota following close behind. The fiasco at the morgue had riled Bright, so much so that he'd ordered her to accompany Finch home in return for access to his daughter's room. For all that abduction was a very serious offence—if indeed that's what it was—Daniels wasn't too chuffed with the arrangement. In fact she was really pissed off. She was an SIO with a murder enquiry to run. Besides, Adam Finch had told them that this wasn't the first time his daughter had taken off and on previous occasions she had always turned up safe and well. She'd been living away from home for eighteen months now, and they weren't in regular contact.

Fuck's sake: he didn't even have an address for her!

As the miles rushed by, Daniels' frustration grew. She wondered if she were on a wild-goose chase when she ought to have been concentrating her efforts on finding the identity of a woman lying in a freezer in Newcastle. Passing a sign for Yarm, her phone rang. Stanton had faxed his preliminary report to the incident room and an officer had called him back confirming receipt of it. But he never left anything to chance and wanted to let her know personally. It was as he'd feared: the dead girl had hit the ground with incredible force.

Daniels thanked him and hung up.

She tried Gormley's mobile.

This time he answered.

'You manage to interview Frank Bull?' she asked.

'Yep . . .' His voice was breaking up a little. 'He seems genuine enough to me, but his evidence hasn't taken us any further forward.'

'Where are you now?'

'Heading back to High Shaw.'

'You sent Bull on his way?'

'Yeah, conditional on daily contact until you tell him otherwise.'

'Good. You know what to do, Hank. Start with the local airports: Newcastle, Carlisle, Sunderland. If necessary we can fan out from there. I want details of all private airstrips and military establishments within a fifty-mile radius, plus a large-scale map of the area. Make sure it's detailed enough to show us all we need to know. Get Robbo to help too and put Lisa on missing persons, liaising with Durham Uni. Tell her we're looking at med students in particular and keep the uniforms busy 'til I'm back. I could be a while.'

Half an hour later, Daniels followed the Jaguar as it turned off the main road leading to Finch's estate. Pulling up behind it at the front door of the Mansion House, she could see that a glass partition separated Finch from his chauffeur. Sensing her interest, Pearce glanced in her

30

direction. Checking his rear-view mirror, he mouthed something to his boss before cutting the Jaguar's three-litre V6 diesel engine. Pearce took off his cap as he got out of the car and placed it under his left arm, military fashion. With a gloved hand he opened the rear passenger door and waited for Finch to emerge.

As Daniels climbed out of her own car she heard a mobile phone bleep twice.

Finch went for his pocket as his housekeeper appeared through the panelled front door. She ran up to him, waiting to take his coat. He waved her away and she turned tail and went back inside. As they followed her in, Daniels registered the man's coldness. There was something about him she didn't like. She studied him closely as he fumbled with his specs, relief replacing concern on his face as he peered at the tiny screen.

His tone was more annoyed than reassured. 'I seem to have wasted your valuable time, Chief Inspector.' He held up the phone. 'Text message from my daughter.'

Daniels swore under her breath but was taken aback when Finch suddenly handed her the mobile and rushed from the hall, retching. The chilling message had only six words: **I TOLD YOU TO STAY PUT!** *Finch was being watched.* Daniels looked around her, waiting for the businessman to resurface. Although elegant, the house was formal, silent, and bloody cold inside. Dog-leg stairs led up to the floor above, to Jessica's room and possible clues to whoever was holding her against her will. From the plethora of art on the walls, she formed the impression that Finch was definitely old money, not new.

Had his inherited wealth made him a target for blackmail?

Her eyes fell on the open library door. Beyond it, a portrait of a beautiful young woman hung above a fireplace large enough for a small person to stand up in. Finch rejoined her, looking ashen but composed. Apologizing for leaving her alone, he offered her something to drink after their long journey south.

Daniels declined. She had to get on.

Finch nodded. 'Of course.'

'Can I call someone for you?'

Finch shook his head and turned away, pressing a bell-push on the wall, mumbling something she didn't quite catch.

'I need to keep this.' Daniels held up his mobile. 'Do you have another you can use?'

Finch nodded. 'It's obvious they're watching me. What the hell do they want?'

The housekeeper arrived in the hall. She hung back, waiting for instructions. Finch ignored her as if she wasn't there. He was deep in his own dark thoughts. Daniels glanced again at the portrait in the adjoining room and asked if she might take a look. The library was a magnificent room furnished with antiques and several thousand books. Some of the larger volumes looked ancient. Daniels figured there would be first editions among them, a treasure trove of history dating back to who knows when.

On closer inspection, the portrait above the fireplace was stunning. It was painted in oils and mounted in a heavy gilt frame, the like of which Daniels had only ever seen hanging in an art gallery. It was probably worth a small fortune, as was the exquisite piece of jewellery around the subject's neck. The artist had signed and dated the portrait not so very long ago, with a flamboyant *FF*. Making a mental note to follow that up, Daniels asked Finch when the painting was commissioned.

'Before she went to university . . .' Finch said, eyes fixed on the painting. 'Getting her to sit was hopeless. My daughter is a wonderful free spirit, but wilful to the point of being downright obstinate at times. No sense of ancestral history, I'm afraid, unlike her mother.'

Daniels knew he was a widower. Bright had told her as much. She couldn't help wondering what had happened to the late Mrs Finch, but decided that now was not the time to pry into his personal affairs. In the past few hours, Adam Finch had faced a parent's worst nightmare. He didn't need her adding to his grief, reminding him of the wife he'd once had. There would be time enough for questions later, and every reason to hope that his daughter was still alive.

For now.

Looking up at the painting, Daniels said, 'She's very beautiful.'

'And very like the young woman I saw earlier,' Finch said.

His jaw bunched, his eyes growing cold. It was as if he'd read her mind.

'Yes, I'm so sorry we put you through that.'

'I've work to do, DCI Daniels.' It was a dismissal. He pointed towards the door where his housekeeper was still waiting. 'Mrs Partridge will show you to my daughter's room.'

8

Daniels woke early, unable to sleep, and spent the next half-hour on her new treadmill, feet pounding, giving it her all—heart monitor showing she was at the peak of fitness.

A digital clock clicked forward a notch—06:00.

She killed the machine, ending her workout, and walked back to her bedroom undressing as she went. There was a pile of neatly folded clean clothes on a chair by the door put there the night before; shoes and briefcase on the floor beneath; a banana, a bottle of water and car keys on her bedside table in case of a call-out during the night.

Thankfully there hadn't been one.

Daniels jumped in the shower, deliberating the day ahead. It came as no surprise that there was too much to do in too little time. That was the reality of being an SIO. She would spend the day prioritizing actions, house-to-house, forensics, press, TV, public relations, liaison with HQ and dealing with scene issues. Both ends of the enquiry would be tricky and time consuming. Searches of areas surrounding Housesteads and the Mansion House involved outbuildings, difficult terrain and woodland, taking up valuable resources, financial as well as human.

Please God nobody call in sick.

She dressed quickly, a pair of black pants and a silk blouse, the top button left undone. She dried her hair, tied it up and applied a little make-up. A last check in the mirror and she was ready for anything.

High Shaw cottage was shrouded in early morning
mist. Without knocking, she opened the door to
the Mobile Incident Unit and came face to face
with Police Constable Kevin Hook. He was around
thirty years old with a great body, much of which
was on display. He'd cut himself shaving in two
places, was only half dressed and was holding a
steaming mug of coffee.

'Too early for you is it, Constable?'

'A little . . .' Hook stuck out his hand. 'Name's
Kevin, ma'am.'

Daniels accepted the greeting. 'I won't shake it
too hard, Kevin. I'm worried about that towel. Is
anyone else here?'

'Only DS Gormley . . .' Hook grinned. 'I thought
you were staying on here last night, ma'am? Or
that's what I was led to believe, anyhow.'

'I was late back from Yorkshire.'

They both turned to the sound of a vehicle
approaching. Seconds later, a rusty old Ford Fiesta
limped up the lane. The car was full to bursting, its
suspension unable to cope, DS Robson and DC
Lisa Carmichael in the front, DCs Brown and
Maxwell in the back. They all got out and trooped
inside the cottage, Daniels following them in.

The team set about unpacking what they'd
brought with them, all the usual paraphernalia
they needed to run a murder enquiry efficiently.
Documentation included: action forms, forensic
submission forms, overtime requests, house-to-
house questionnaires, various maps of the area.
And there were other essentials too: coffee,

35

cartons of fresh milk, Fudges Belgian Dark Chocolate Florentines and, most important of all, lemon drizzle cake supplied by Carmichael's aunt.

Someone quickly made tea. They all gathered round for their morning briefing, listening intently as Daniels updated them on developments: Adam Finch's failure to identify the body, the threatening message received from his daughter's mobile, the fact that the enquiry was back to square one.

'Poor sod!' Gormley said. 'Finch must be demented.'

'He is, and the guv'nor's not too thrilled either.' Daniels glanced at the murder wall, her eyes finding the photograph of the unidentified girl. 'He and Finch go back a long way, apparently.'

'It could've been worse . . .' Carmichael logged on to her computer, keying in 'MISSING PERSONS' as she spoke. 'The dead girl might have *been* his daughter. All the same, it's a horrible experience for anyone to go through.'

'Bright wants us to run a parallel enquiry with this one.' Daniels' comment drew sceptical faces and expressions of concern all round. 'I know it's going to be tough, but we have no choice. The guv'nor wants our very best team on it and that happens to be you guys.'

She caught Robson's eye. Aware that his future hung in the balance, he dropped his head. During their last murder enquiry, his loyalty to Daniels and the team had been questionable. He'd admitted passing information to Assistant Chief Constable Martin, a senior officer who had himself withheld information relating to the murder of an innocent man.

Martin had since resigned from his post.

Thank God!

As far as Daniels was concerned, there was only one downside to his departure and that was the subsequent reshuffle that had taken place in its wake: promotions for Chief Superintendent Billings to Assistant Chief Constable; Detective Superintendent Bright to Detective Chief Superintendent—Force Crime Manager—a role he'd coveted for years.

Losing her guv'nor was a big blow. His replacement had not yet been approved and the uncertainty over the appointment was worrying, to say the least. She wondered who it might be, concerned that the dynamics in the team might change if the wrong person arrived to take charge. Bright could sometimes be a bully, but she'd walk over hot coals for him. He'd taught her everything she knew and they understood each other perfectly.

Better the devil you know.

A vibrating mobile interrupted her thoughts.

'DCI Daniels.'

'Kate, how's it going?' It was Detective Superintendent Ronald Naylor of neighbouring Durham Constabulary, a colleague for many years, a friend for nearly as long.

'Run off our feet. And you?'

'Word is you have an unidentified body of a young woman on your patch.'

'Bad news travels fast.'

'Care to share a description?'

'Care to tell me what it's got to do with you?' Daniels' eyes scanned her depleted team. They were waiting patiently for her to get off the phone. But curiosity took over. Naylor's call obviously wasn't a social one. 'Hold on, Ron. I'm going to take this outside.' She covered the speaker with her free hand. 'Carry on, Hank. I'll be back in a second.'

She got up and walked away from the others, brilliant sunshine blinding her as she opened the front door.

'Kate?'

'Yep, still here. What's your interest?'

'I've just interviewed a couple whose daughter hasn't come home.'

Daniels wondered why a Detective Superintendent had involved himself in a misper case. Ninety-five per cent of missing persons turned up safe and well eventually. As Naylor talked, she wandered down the garden, amazed at how quickly the early mist had cleared. She parked her bum on a drystone wall, on the other side of which a newly dug veggie patch was losing its war to keep weeds at bay from the adjacent unploughed field. A low-flying military aircraft—the vibration of which she could feel through her feet—screamed across the sky above her, drowning out Naylor's voice.

'Can you repeat that, Ron? I'm being bombarded by UFOs.'

'Yeah, I heard.' Naylor shuffled papers at the other end. 'I said she was a student. Twenty-one years old.'

'Studying at Durham?'

'As it happens.'

The portrait of Jessica Finch flew into Daniels' head, a young woman at the prime of her life with everything to live for. 'Pretty blonde girl? Very tall?'

'You psychic now?'

A second wave of military aircraft passed overhead.

'We need to meet,' she said.

9

Detective Superintendent Ron Naylor turned up at twelve thirty, as planned, at a pub not far from the Northumbria/Durham force border. Daniels had been there ten minutes already, having fought her way through a myriad of smokers at the front door, and used the dead time to scan the morning's papers and order a coffee at the bar.

The room was busy when she arrived, with people spilling in from offices on the high street looking for a quick bite to eat before heading back to work. The music was too loud for the time of day, many of the tables set for dining. The aroma of food from the kitchen made her hungry. A banana for breakfast hadn't been sufficient to carry her through to lunch.

Ron Naylor tapped her on the shoulder. He was around six feet tall with bright eyes and a winning smile, going a bit thin on top. He looked really smart in a dark suit, pinstriped shirt and striped tie, a combination that suited his switched-on personality.

'Got an appointment with your bank manager?' Daniels grinned. 'Good to see you, Ron.'

She leaned forward and gave him a friendly peck on the cheek. They'd known each other since training school and had worked together often, mostly on joint training initiatives, but occasionally on enquiries that straddled the two forces. They ordered more coffee and had a quick chat before setting off. The missing girl's house was just a few minutes away.

Daniels was still curious to know why someone of his rank had involved himself in the case of a missing girl. Different if he knew she was dead. Naylor explained that a rumour circulating at his station had become fact. Some nasty individuals were encouraging students into prostitution, preying on their financial hardship in order to get them on the game. A group of worried parents, one of whom he knew personally, had begged him to nip it in the bud.

'You made any arrests?'

'I'm working on it.'

They had reached the house: a part brick, part pebble-dashed 1960s mid-terraced, situated on a quiet tree-lined street on the outskirts of Durham City. Amy Grainger's mother let them in, showed them into the living room and sat down on the sofa. Her husband stood nervously by her side, his right hand on her shoulder. The man was unshaven and unwashed, having been up all night at his wife's request, searching every place he could think of where their daughter might have gone.

'As I've already explained to Superintendent Naylor, Amy hasn't been home the last couple of nights. Mind you, she's done this before. But she usually sends a text saying she's on her way home and we're not to worry.' Mr Grainger looked down at his other half. Mrs Grainger sat rigid and upright, her arms folded across her chest. They

40

had obviously had words. 'I told my wife we should've waited, not wasted your precious time.'

Daniels could see that the couple were beside themselves with worry.

'You're not wasting anyone's time,' she said. 'Do you have a recent photograph of Amy I can look at?

'Will that one do?' Mrs Grainger pointed at a photograph on the mantelpiece.

Daniels twisted in her seat. As soon as she clapped eyes on the girl, a fist closed around her throat, keeping tight hold until she could hardly breathe. She stood up, went over to the fireplace to examine the photograph more closely, hoping she was wrong, knowing she wasn't. As she handed it to Naylor, a message passed between them, leaving him in no doubt whatsoever that it *was* her unidentified victim.

Daniels sat back down. 'Mr and Mrs Grainger—'

'My husband is right, Detective. We're—I'm probably jumping the gun. You watch, our Amy will come breezing through that door any minute now, large as life, wondering what all the fuss is about.' Mrs Grainger forced a smile. Her eyes darted from Daniels to Naylor and back again, picking up on their concern and fighting hard to disregard it. 'That was taken on her first day at university. We were ever so proud, weren't we, Terry? She's doing really well, according to her tutors.'

She stopped talking then and fixed the officers with a cold, hard stare.

Daniels' mouth was dry, her heart racing a little, as it did every time she had to tell a murder victim's loved ones the worst possible news. There was no way round it; they had to be told.

'I'm so sorry. The body of a young woman fitting Amy's description was found in Northumberland yesterday.'

Mr Grainger collapsed on to the arm of the sofa, his legs unable to hold his weight. Daniels expected his wife to break down. Instead she smiled broadly, completely ignoring what she'd just been told.

'Who'd like a nice cup of tea? I was forgetting my manners. I know you've come a long way.'

It took another half an hour before Mrs Grainger would accept the possibility that her daughter may be dead, another to persuade her husband that identification was necessary, even though Daniels was in no doubt. Then they put on their coats and followed the detectives from the house.

*   *   *

Only Amy's head was visible above the sheet. She was very beautiful with bow lips, perfect skin and extremely long eyelashes. Apart from broken veins on her face due to the impact of hitting the ground, she could almost have been in a deep and peaceful sleep. Daniels shut her eyes as a strangulated wail filled the air, the sound of a mother's pain that seemed to go on and on for ever. Then it stopped as suddenly as it had begun and the room was plunged into an icy silence that was almost as difficult to bear.

'She was the first one in our family ever to make it to university . . .' Mr Grainger was crying now, unable to hold on to his sorrow any longer. 'She worked so hard to get there, never missed a day off school. She was top of her class every year.'

Mrs Grainger bent over her daughter. Cradling her head in her arms, she began to sob, her whole body wracked with grief. Mr Grainger looked on, not knowing what to do, how to act. He took a handkerchief from his pocket, wiped his eyes, then passed it to his distraught wife, apologizing to Daniels.

'We'd like to see the place, the place where Amy—'

'Of course,' Daniels said gently. 'But first I need to ask you some questions, if I may. There's no hurry. You take your time and let me know when you're ready.'

Daniels stepped back to the door, not wanting to intrude, wishing she could leave them alone with their daughter, knowing it wasn't the done thing. They left the viewing room a few minutes later and walked along the corridor to a quiet area set aside for grieving relatives. Daniels gave them time to compose themselves, offering them a cup of tea, some water.

She sat down beside them. 'When did you last have contact with Amy?'

'When she left the house the night before last,' Mr Grainger said.

'On Wednesday?' Daniels wanted to be sure.

'Yes.'

'What time was that?'

'Seven thirty,' Amy's mother said.

'Do you know where she was going?' Daniels probed. 'Who with?'

Mrs Grainger glanced at her husband. Daniels caught a look of guilt cross her face. Something

43

was troubling her. Something she didn't wish to share with her husband in the room. He'd noticed it too.

'What, Jen? What is it?'

Daniels took Mrs Grainger's hand in hers. 'I know how very difficult this is for you both, but it's vital you answer my questions as best you can. If I'm to have any chance of catching those responsible for taking Amy from you, you must understand that I need to establish her whereabouts in the hours leading up to her death.'

Mrs Grainger gave a little nod. 'She was catching the bus to Durham City, I think. Some friends were celebrating something or other. It may have been a birthday, I'm not sure.' Mrs Grainger made eye contact with Daniels, her voice faltering. *Another guilty look?* 'To be honest with you I, I wasn't really listening. Isn't that awful? What kind of a mum am I? The last time my daughter speaks to me and I . . . was too busy . . . I was too busy because *Coronation Street* was coming on. She said she wouldn't be late though, I do remember that much. I think she said she had a seminar early the next morning.'

'That's right,' Mr Grainger nodded in agreement.

'And she never made it home?'

Mrs Grainger was struggling to go on.

Mr Grainger answered for her. 'No. We didn't worry at first, but then we found out Amy never made it to her seminar either. A friend called yesterday to see if she was all right. Emma, I think her name was.'

'And she's not been in touch since, by phone, text, email?'

They both shook their heads.

10

It was tanking down when they parked at Housesteads car park and made the short, grim journey across fields to where Amy Grainger met her death. The crime-scene tent was now gone. In its place, officers from MIT had left a discreet bunch of flowers to mark the spot. Under a large umbrella, Mr and Mrs Grainger held hands for a few moments of solidarity and quiet contemplation before returning with Daniels to her car.

The Toyota sped south as the rain began to ease. Daniels was worried about her passengers. Amy's mother was in a severe state of shock, eyes fixed straight ahead, hearing and seeing nothing. Almost catatonic. Mr Grainger had his arm around her. He was staring blankly out of the window at countryside so beautiful it took your breath away, even on such a dull, damp day. Unmoved by the stunning landscape, he was a broken man, a torn soul. He may as well have been peering into hell, or so Daniels thought as she glanced at him in the rear-view mirror.

'Amy would have loved it here . . .' He returned her gaze. 'Did you know she was studying the countryside?'

'No, I didn't know that.'

Daniels fell silent, taking in this new information. If Amy was not a med student, why then had she bought a medical textbook? *Principles of Anatomy and Physiology*, according to

45

the receipt Stanton had found in her jeans pocket, retailing at around forty-five quid.

'Environmental something or other.' Mr Grainger was really losing it now.

Eyes back on the road, Daniels spotted a lay-by up ahead. She signalled her intention to pull over and steered towards it, parking the Toyota as far off the road as she could get. She cut the ignition and turned to face her passengers. Mr Grainger took his wife's limp hand in his and again looked out of the window. It was brighter now. The rain had stopped, the sky was less threatening and there was a hint of blue appearing in between empty clouds.

'Amy loved the outdoors,' Mr Grainger said wistfully. 'Even as a kid we could never get her to come inside. She loved plants, animals. Life was one big adventure for her from the day she was born. What I don't understand is why she was here, so far from home. Like I said, she never missed a day at school. She wouldn't wag off, I know she wouldn't.'

'I'll need to speak to her pals.' Daniels was grateful that one of her passengers felt able to talk. She'd known times when neither parent of a murder victim could find words. Others raged against the injustice of having lost a loved one; unable to keep it together, unable to assist investigators in the vital hours following the discovery of a body. She needed to piece together Amy's last movements, find out who the last person was to have seen her alive—and where. 'Was Amy close to anyone in particular at university?'

'Nobody special.' Mr Grainger rubbed at the

46

stubble on his chin. 'She had lots of girlfriends, though. She was a typical student . . . liked to party, but was otherwise a hard worker.'

Daniels nodded her understanding. 'Did she work—outside of her studies, I mean?'

'A part-time job at the students' union bar. Said she didn't want a loan, didn't want to get into the debt trap, or freeload off Jen and me.'

Mrs Grainger broke down again and buried her head in his shoulder.

'She sounds like a lovely girl,' Daniels said.

'She is, was . . .' Mr Grainger bit his lip. 'The best.'

He patted his wife's hand and forced a smile. Daniels asked if he was up to continuing with the journey. He said not. He asked to sit for a while longer, said he felt closer to his daughter here. He would visit this place in years to come. Daniels knew he meant it. She turned her back on the couple, trying to make herself invisible, allowing them a few quiet moments of reflection.

'Did you find Amy's mobile phone?' The words stuck in Mr Grainger's throat as they came out. 'She was never off it, was she, Jen? You'll find details of her mates in there, no doubt.'

His comment hung in the air.

Daniels turned back to face him, forced to explain that no mobile phone had been found on Amy's body. No bag either. Mr Grainger suddenly got angry, began raging over the fact that the person responsible for her death still had his daughter's private things. They had no right. What kind of animals were these people?

A good question.

'Did Amy ever mention a student friend studying

47

medicine?'

'No, I don't think so. Why d'you ask?'

'We found a till receipt for a medical textbook in the back pocket of her jeans.'

'She wasn't wearing jeans,' Mrs Grainger said softly. 'She never wore jeans.'

11

A man in a blue uniform waved the Fiesta through an air-side security gate of Newcastle International Airport. Passing a sign—authorized personnel only—DS Robson parked at the gable end of a single-storey building on the right. As he took his key from the ignition, another man in plain clothes approached the car, holding up ID.

Robson got out and did likewise.

'DS Robson,' he said. 'Thanks for seeing me at short notice.'

'John Hobbs. Pleased to meet you. Come this way.'

Hobbs' office was basic, cube-shaped with windows: a desk, two chairs and a filing cabinet, the top drawer of which was hanging open. He sat in silence as Robson explained the reason for his visit and the need to keep their discussion strictly confidential. 'Specifically, we're investigating an incident that occurred the night before last.'

As Robson carried on, Hobbs' face paled. From the look of him, he heard only bits of sentences. It wasn't the first time Robson had seen this happen when people were given shocking information. It was as if their brains weren't wired properly. Not quite connecting as they should. Unable to cope with the morbid data that police officers dealt with on a daily basis. The result? They took in snippets of facts they couldn't altogether grasp: young woman . . . fallen or pushed . . . aircraft . . . odds of finding those responsible . . .

'Mr Hobbs?'

Hobbs emerged from his trance. 'Sorry, what were you saying?'

'I was asking what the odds were of finding those responsible.'

'That really depends whether the pilot is licensed or not. Are you absolutely sure of your facts?'

Robson cocked an eyebrow. *Like I'd be asking if I wasn't!*

Hobbs blushed. 'Yes, sorry, I can't get that shocking image out of my head.'

Robson tried to move him on. 'What about radar?'

Jet engines revved outside, drowning out Hobbs' voice. He looked out of his window as a 747 began taxiing for take-off along the nearest runway. Robson hated flying and the noise alone made him cringe. Just driving into the airport had set his heart palpitating. Thankfully, the man opposite hadn't noticed his discomfort.

The noise subsided.

'Radar?' Robson repeated. 'Is there likely to be a record?'

' 'Fraid not. There'd be no audit trail if he didn't use his radio during flight. All we'd see this end is a blip on the screen.'

'That's what our Air Support Unit told me. What about if we found the plane?'

'You know for sure it was a fixed wing?'

Robson shook his head. 'Wouldn't it be more difficult to control a helicopter and push a body out at the same time?'

'More difficult, yes. But not impossible with a bit of know-how.'

'Even without an accomplice?'

'It's feasible, provided the victim was unconscious. She was, wasn't she?' Hobbs waited for Robson to confirm or deny this was so. When the detective did neither, he continued, 'A skilled pilot could do it easily from a few hundred feet. It would simply be a case of slowing it down below, say, thirty knots over the drop zone, reaching across and unlatching the door. A little shove and roll the helicopter at the same time and—'

'Gravity takes care of the rest?'

Hobbs nodded. 'Quick roll the other way to pull the door back in and back to blighty for tea and medals in the mess. It'd take about twenty seconds.'

'You're ex-military?'

Hobbs gave a friendly salute. 'Yes, I am.'

'What would an aircraft tachometer tell us?' Robson stopped talking mid-sentence as the windows began to rattle. He almost ducked as a budget aircraft with a distinctive orange tail took off a hundred or so metres away. 'Assuming that's what they call them in your industry?'

'Only the number of hours flown,' Hobbs offered, 'not where it was flown, direction, altitude and so on, which is what I suspect you're after. Most helicopter flights going from A to B would probably fly at no more than two thousand feet, dictated by the fact that helos are unpressurized. Give them oxygen and they'd be able to fly much higher.'

'You fly yourself?' Robson asked, his nausea returning.

'You must be joking!' Hobbs leaned back in his seat and crossed his arms over his chest. 'I just work here, mate. I get vertigo from my seat at the match. But I've spent a lot of time with and around pilots.'

Robson felt less of a wimp but still couldn't get out of there quick enough.

12

On the way back from the crime scene Amy's parents were utterly lost. They sat in silence, unable to communicate with each other; a scene all too familiar to Daniels. She called ahead, instructing the exhibits officer to meet her in the quiet interview room next door to the Major Incident Suite and to bring along the evidence box relating to the case.

It was unnecessary to tell him which one.

He was already there when they arrived, as was Gormley. They stood quietly to one side as Daniels ushered the bereaved parents in, offering to fetch refreshments at the end of their distressing journey. They both declined. Identification of their daughter's belongings would be equally harrowing and they were keen to get it over with, an action made imperative now there was doubt over what she'd been wearing when last seen.

According to Mrs Grainger, Amy had left home in a red mini-dress, leggings and ballet pumps and carrying a large canvas shoulder bag.

Daniels wondered if the latter was to hold a change of clothes.

The exhibits officer was getting impatient. It was unusual, though not unheard of, to remove evidence from the security of his exhibits room. But he was nervous about it and insisted on Daniels' signature in the log he was holding out to her. She led him out of earshot, explaining why she wanted Amy's clothing brought to the family rather than the other way round. His office on the floor below was a sterile, windowless room, wedged between two noisy offices on either side, constantly disturbed by the sound of foot traffic— not to mention laughter and chatter from the busy corridor beyond. It had sickly green paintwork and burns on the lino where staff had extinguished cigarettes before the ban on smoking was introduced.

'. . . hardly conducive to the solemn occasion facing them now, is it?'

'I agree.' He pointed at the log, indicating where she should sign it. 'But it's my neck on the line if any or part of this evidence goes missing.'

'It won't, I promise you. I don't blame you for covering your back. In your position, I'd have done the same. Only difference is, I would have done it with more sensitivity.' Daniels scribbled her name, timing and dating her entry. She dropped her voice to a whisper. 'Now piss off and let me do my job!'

Shutting the log, the exhibits officer quickly left the room. The DCI waited for him to shut the door. She nodded in Gormley's direction, indicating her readiness to begin. He in turn had a quiet word with Mr Grainger, who seemed

52

reluctant to leave his wife, even for a second. Daniels stepped forward, reassuring him that the procedure wouldn't take long. Eventually, he let go of his wife's hand and moved gingerly towards the evidence box.

Before opening it, Daniels suggested quietly that he take his wife to see her GP.

Mr Grainger nodded. 'Just as soon as we get Amy home. There are arrangements to be taken care of, lots of people to contact, her grandparents of course . . .' He hesitated, pained by thoughts of what he might say to them. 'Then there's her godparents, her friends . . .' He looked at Daniels. 'Do you think Bardgett are the best funeral directors? I need to choose a suitable casket. And flowers . . . white lilies . . . Amy loved lilies.'

Daniels and Gormley exchanged a look.

They both knew it might be a long time before the poor man could have his daughter back. An inquest would have to be opened and most probably adjourned. There could even be a further post-mortem. Any defence lawyer worth his salt would ask for one. Daniels tried to find the words to convey that information without distressing Mr Grainger too much. He was fast picking up on her reticence.

At moments like these she wanted to run away and hide.

'It isn't possible for you to take Amy home yet, I'm afraid.' She scanned his face, making sure that what she had said was sinking in. 'I know how difficult this is for you to accept, but we can't release her for burial until the coroner—'

'She's my daughter!'

'I'm so sorry—'

'You can't keep her! Why would you want to?' Mr Grainger choked back a sob and looked at his wife. She was staring blankly at the floor, too traumatized to react to the discussion taking place just feet away. He gave a resigned nod. 'My apologies, Detective Inspector, I wasn't thinking.'

'I promise I'll keep you informed of developments as and when I can. And as soon as we're done here, I'll get someone to take you home.'

Mr Grainger seemed to be ageing with every passing second. But he wasn't done yet, Daniels could see. She braced herself for the question he almost couldn't bring himself to ask.

'How did she . . . ?' He didn't finish.

'We've carried out a post-mortem. We know exactly how Amy died . . .' Daniels chose her words carefully. 'I can tell you with certainty that she didn't suffer. There was evidence of a large amount of drugs in her system—'

'No, I don't accept that!' He shook his head vigorously and lowered his voice so his wife wouldn't hear him. 'Amy would never take drugs. She was dead against them, always has been.'

Daniels nodded. 'It's my belief and that of the pathologist that these drugs were administered by a third party. Obviously, we can't be one hundred per cent certain, but that is the assumption we are working on.'

'I see . . .' Amy's father seemed to draw some comfort from that. He looked down with dread at the evidence box on the counter, then back at Daniels. 'Please continue. You've been very kind to us. My wife and I appreciate that more than you will ever know.'

54

Daniels reached into the evidence box. She took out a cellophane bag containing the first item of clothing: a green scarf, according to the label. She laid it down flat on the counter, allowing Mr Grainger a closer look.

'That's *not* Amy's!' Mrs Grainger almost spat out the words. Her husband turned towards her. Daniels did too. Supported by Hank Gormley, the woman rose to her feet and walked over to them, pointing at the evidence bag. 'That's *not* our Amy's!' she repeated.

The DCI searched for confirmation from Mr Grainger and found it.

'Jen's right. It's not hers.'

'Are you absolutely sure?'

The man nodded, putting an arm around his wife.

'Perhaps she borrowed it . . .' Daniels said. 'Young women often—'

'It's possible I suppose, but not likely. She was—'

Mrs Grainger rounded on her husband. 'No!'

His eyes found Daniels, an apologetic expression, she thought.

'Our Amy is very fussy about what she wears, obsessive almost. She would never swap clothes. Never!' Mrs Grainger pulled away from her husband. 'You should know that, Terry. She's your daughter too!'

It wasn't difficult to see how this tragedy might blow this couple apart. Daniels had seen it happen over the years to a number of parents of murdered children, even those she regarded as particularly close. Blame, guilt, past indiscretions were often raked up at the point of crisis, used like bullets to fire at one another until there was nothing left.

Divorce was high among parents of homicide victims. Just the thought of it made her sad.

Returning to the box, the DCI lifted other items free: a pair of size-ten skinny Giorgio Armani jeans, a blue shirt with three-quarter-length sleeves, a pair of high-heeled shoes. On each occasion, Mrs Grainger's lips bunched tight shut and she shook her head vehemently. Daniels expected the same response when she removed a bag containing underwear, but, much to her surprise, the woman nodded this time.

Registering this development as significant, Daniels' eyes found Gormley. With Amy's parents present, it was inappropriate to indulge in speculation. So she filed away the troubling thought and showed them the final exhibit, a bag containing the last item: a delicate necklace.

Daniels missed the couple's response to it. She was too busy coping with a reaction of her own. As her eyes fixed on the necklace, the hairs on her neck stood up.

Something was very wrong.

Picking up on her preoccupation with the item of jewellery, Gormley looked on curiously as she pulled the exhibits log towards her and scrolled down the list with her index finger, dwelling on the last entry: *Item of jewellery removed from the neck of Nominal One—unidentified female found near Housesteads Roman Fort.*

'Why would she be dressed in someone else's clothes?' Mrs Grainger asked.

Daniels hadn't heard her.

Gormley answered for her. 'We don't know, is the honest answer. But we *will* find out. There are things we can't tell you at the moment, but as soon

56

as we can, we will.'

Daniels was back. 'You have our absolute word on that. In the meantime, I must ask you not to talk about Amy's death to anyone, in particular the fact that she was wearing another girl's clothes. Reporters will use every trick in the book to get you to talk. But I urge you not to. It might help the perpetrator escape justice if you do. And I know you wouldn't want that.'

'But whose clothes are they?' Mr Grainger asked. 'Why would—'

'You think another girl's been taken, don't you?' Mrs Grainger was talking now. A good sign, Daniels thought. 'You do! I can see it in your eyes. What are you not telling us? Oh my God! Terry, what's happening? I can't bear the thought of another family going through . . .' Her voice trailed off as something caught her eye.

Carmichael had arrived in the nick of time.

Gormley opened the door, inviting her to step inside. 'This is Lisa,' he said.

Daniels' stomach was leaden as a flicker of life appeared on Mrs Grainger's face. It was almost, but not quite, recognition. Lisa Carmichael was not unlike Amy Grainger to look at: she was fairly tall with long blonde hair and a youthful, cheery face. Not the most appropriate officer to be around right now. From the looks on their faces, Gormley and Carmichael had spotted her reaction too.

'Lisa will see to it that you get an escort home,' Gormley hurried on.

'Or if not home, somewhere else . . .' Carmichael smiled. 'A relative perhaps?'

Mrs Grainger managed a weak smile. 'It's OK,

Lisa.'

She'd said it in a way they all understood.

Daniels repeated her condolences, advising the couple that a Family Liaison Officer would be in touch, a person designated to answer any questions they might have about the case, and whose job it was to keep them informed of developments as and when they occurred.

Carmichael eased the couple out into the corridor. As she closed the door behind them, Daniels blew out her cheeks and breathed a hefty sigh of relief.

'What?' Gormley pulled a face. 'What did I miss?'

'Get the exhibits officer on the phone, right away.' Daniels held the necklace up to the light. 'I've seen this before, Hank. Jessica Finch was wearing it in a portrait hanging in her father's library. We need to get over there, first thing in the morning.'

13

'It's a one-off Cartier piece which belonged to her mother,' Adam Finch said. 'I don't like Jessica wearing it because of its monetary value. But you can't tell them, can you? My daughter thinks of it in purely sentimental terms. Her mother died when she was four years old. It's the only thing she remembers her wearing.'

They were in the Mansion House library standing in front of the cavernous fireplace, Adam Finch with his back to it, Gormley and Daniels

58

facing him. He was dressed more casually than when she'd seen him the day before yesterday: brown corduroy slacks, a fawn cashmere sweater and a pair of brogues on his feet. Under the circumstances, she thought he looked far too rested. She'd expected more of a reaction when she showed him the necklace. But the man didn't flinch. If he was nervous or even curious as to how she came by it, he certainly wasn't letting on.

Gormley scanned Jessica's portrait. 'She wears it all the time?'

'Never takes it off,' Finch said. 'May I ask where you found it?'

'I'm sorry to have to tell you, but it was taken from the young woman you were asked to identify at the morgue.'

Daniels watched for a reaction but there was none. 'Her name is Amy Grainger. She was also a Durham University student.'

Finch swallowed hard and didn't speak for a few seconds. 'I told Jessica time and again that someone would lift the damn thing one day. But, as always, I was wasting my breath. This *girl,* this . . . Amy, did you say her name was? She was obviously up to no good. She's probably in cahoots with whoever sent me those dreadful threats. Perhaps now one of them has come to a sticky end, they'll stop tormenting me. Even if they don't, I will not be blackmailed!'

'Has your daughter ever talked about Amy Grainger?' Gormley asked.

Finch shook his head.

'She was studying Environmental Management,' Daniels said. 'Same intake year as Jessica. If they were mates, perhaps she loaned the necklace to

59

Amy.'

'No.' Finch fixed on Daniels. 'My daughter may take financial risks, but she's got her head screwed on properly when she chooses her friends. She would never associate with a bad crowd. She's got too much to lose. She stands to inherit a substantial fortune one day. Anyway, I hardly think this girl would be her type. She's a medical student, not some tree-hugger.'

Daniels' jaw went rigid.

Finch was acting like a prat with no thought for anyone but himself. She could already imagine the tirade that would follow from Gormley on the way home. Eyeballing Jessica's father, she didn't bother to hide her disgust. 'A young girl is dead, Mr Finch. A girl you saw with your own eyes lying on a slab in the mortuary. Her parents are beside themselves too, so perhaps you'd care to show a little respect.'

Finch made no comment.

'There's something else I need you to look at.' Putting a hand in her pocket, Daniels pulled out her car keys and gave them to Gormley. 'Will you get the box from my car?'

Gormley's expression conveyed a clear message: *It'll be my pleasure.* He left the room, passing Mrs Partridge who was on her way in with a tea tray. She poured Finch some tea and handed it to him. He sat down at a partner's desk near the window, saucer in his left hand, cup in his right. Then Gormley was back, carrying the same evidence box they had shown the Graingers the day before. He set it down on a chair, took out six bags and placed them in a line on Finch's desk, the items clearly visible through cellophane windows: a pair of

60

jeans, a blue top, a green scarf, underwear and a pair of shoes—left and right in separate bags.

'Are you able to identify any of these?' Gormley asked. 'You can pick them up, but I can't allow you to break the seal.'

Finch looked at him as if *allow* was not a word in his vocabulary.

Daniels gave him a nudge. 'If you wouldn't mind, sir. It's very important.'

Finch shifted his gaze to the bags. 'I recognize the shoes. Jessica has a pair just like them, though I couldn't say for sure they're hers. Jeans are jeans, aren't they? Frankly, I wouldn't know one pair from another. I hate the things. My daughter's underwear is not something I'm privy to.'

'And the scarf?' Gormley asked.

'Is identical to one I bought for her last Christmas when we were in Milan.'

Finch sat back in his chair avoiding eye contact with them both. Daniels detected a chink in his armour. He didn't say anything, but his hand shook as he put down his tea. She gave him a moment, assured that he'd already worked out what was coming next.

She hated saying it. 'These are the clothes we took from Amy Grainger's body.'

'Then she must've stolen them!' Finch snapped.

The man was in denial, a normal reaction under the circumstances. He didn't want to believe that his daughter was in danger. *Or worse.* Why should he? It was unimaginable for any parent to contemplate.

The DCI chose her words carefully. 'We know nothing of Amy that would suggest she's anything other than a lovely girl who tragically met her death wearing Jessica's clothes. I'm so sorry.'

Finch broke down.

Picking up the evidence bag containing the scarf, he held it to his chest and wept.

'Sir, we'd be lying if we told you that we're not worried. Of course we are. We all are. But we'll do everything we can to find her.'

The man's bluntness was shocking. 'Dead or alive?' he asked.

'My officers are the very best, sir.' Their eyes locked as Daniels tried to reassure him. 'They'll work day and night to find Jessica and I'll personally keep you updated on all new developments. I assume you've had no further contact, from anyone?'

Finch glared at her. 'Don't you think I'd have said?'

Gormley had had enough. 'We will, of course, need to search the house and grounds.'

Finch rounded on him. 'Why?'

'It's routine in cases like these . . .' Daniels said. 'We must be absolutely sure we've covered every possibility. I'd also like a word with the artist who painted Jessica's portrait. I imagine they'll have talked a lot during the time they spent together. I'd be grateful if you would point me in the right direction.'

'No stone unturned, is that it?'

'Something like that.' Daniels didn't want to row with him. In fact she just wanted out of there, the sooner the better. 'I'll also need to interview your staff. If we could have a list by morning, that would be helpful.'

'You'll have it within the hour,' Finch said.

Opening the desk drawer, he removed a business

card and handed it over with the name and studio of the artist in question, a woman named Fiona Fielding. They thanked him and went off to look around the house for clues. Their search was unproductive. Two hours later, Mrs Partridge showed them out. Daniels felt the woman's eyes on her back as she walked to her car, keying in Robson's number before she reached it. The Toyota's lights flashed and the door locks clunked open.

Robson picked up. 'What's up, boss?'

'What's not? I want you to arrange an emergency meeting of the squad for four o'clock sharp. Also, give Bright a bell and tell him it's confirmed: Amy Grainger *was* wearing Jessica Finch's clothes and jewellery. I want the Major Incident Suite made ready. This is now a linked incident and we can't run it from a cottage in the wilds of Northumberland. We're going to have to make other arrangements. I'll let the guv'nor know we're moving back to town as soon as possible. Except you. I'd like to leave you up there for a few days to coordinate things that end.'

There was a short pause.

'Robbo? You OK with that?'

'No problem. You want everyone at the briefing?'

'If humanly possible, yes . . .' She started the engine and moved off with Finch watching from his library window. 'And just for your information, the motive wasn't financial. That necklace was worth a mint.'

Daniels hung up. If robbery wasn't the motive, then what was? Someone was threatening Finch, but for what purpose? No demands had yet been made.

'You're thinking again,' Gormley said. 'I can hear the cogs turning from here.'

'The lack of contact from Jessica's abductors worries me.' Daniels slowed as the gates to the Mansion House opened, allowing them to move off the estate. 'There's only one reason I can think of for that. Amy Grainger was chosen in order to send a graphic warning to Finch.'

'Some warning!' Gormley said.

'Someone must really hate him. We find out why and we'll find our man.'

Gormley settled down in his seat, making himself comfortable for the drive to Newcastle. They hadn't yet spoken about Daniels' absence from work, the unease she felt at being back, the confidence she'd lost. In fact they'd seen little of each other at all in the past few days, which was unheard of in the normal course of a week's work.

For her part, Daniels was aware Hank had his own problems to sort and she didn't want to add to them.

She glanced at him. 'How's Julie?'

'Why d'you ask?' It was almost a grunt.

'Just making conversation. You heard from her?'

'Nothing civil.'

'Ryan?'

'What is this, Twenty Questions?'

When Gormley's sense of humour went walkabout that usually meant he didn't want to talk. Daniels wondered what was going on. It wasn't like him to be secretive and she hoped his silence wasn't an indication that things had gone from bad to worse at home. She shouldn't have mentioned his wife and son. Any minute now her

64

DS would cross his arms, shut his eyes, and hang like a bat from his seat belt so she couldn't quiz him any more.

'I'll take that as a no then, shall I?' She accelerated round a bend in the road.

'Why don't we talk about Jo instead?'

Daniels clammed up. He was referring to criminal profiler, Jo Soulsby. The last thing she wanted to do was talk about her. When last they'd spoken, it had felt more like a therapy session with a professional counsellor than a conversation between mates, let alone ex-lovers still attracted to one another. She missed Jo more than she cared to admit, even to herself. She missed her smell, her laughter, her touch—just breathing the same air.

She wanted to stop loving her and make the pain go away.

A sign pointed off to the left. Daniels took the slip road on to the A1 heading north, hoping Gormley would change the subject.

He didn't disappoint. 'Finch is an arrogant bastard. I'm not surprised he has enemies.'

'Don't be too hard on him, Hank. He's under so much stress he probably doesn't know what he's saying half the time.'

'Sympathy sits between shit and syphilis in the dictionary.'

She grinned. 'Don't get me wrong. I'm not suggesting he's someone I've warmed to a whole lot, but I think we should give him the benefit of the doubt, don't you?'

'The man's a prick, Kate.'

Gormley took off his bifocals, put them in his breast pocket and shut his eyes. Conversation over: at least for now. Within seconds, he was sending the zeds up. He didn't wake until she stopped to refuel at Washington Services. They grabbed a quick bite to eat, the atmosphere between them thawing a little, and then got back in the car. Traffic was unusually light and they made good time. At Corbridge, Daniels turned north on the A68 and cut up on to the Military Road, reaching High Shaw at three forty-five.

14

PC Kevin Hook walked towards the Toyota as Daniels parked in the only space available. As they got out of the car, he handed her a message from the forensic science laboratory and stood by waiting for further instructions.

'Matt West said it wasn't urgent, but he'd appreciate a call back.'

Daniels thanked him and made a mental note to return the call. 'Any news from the house-to-house while we were gone?'

Hook shook his head. 'Nothing so far.'

Gormley spoke over his shoulder as they walked away. 'Keep us posted.'

The murder investigation team were ready and waiting as they entered High Shaw. It was standing-room only with the whole squad crammed into the tiny cottage. They were on starter's orders, the buzz of a new enquiry filling the air. Robson had been busy. Photographs of Jessica Finch and Amy Grainger were pinned to the whiteboard, alongside their details: height, build and eye colour. These photographs were the focus of everyone's attention, the similarity between the two glaringly obvious.

'OK, listen up!' Daniels sat down surrounded by her squad. 'It won't have escaped your notice that Amy Grainger is a dead ringer for Jessica Finch, which means that our priorities have now changed. I'm not suggesting for one minute that we forget about Amy. This *is* a murder enquiry. But our main concern must be on finding Jessica Finch while there's a chance she's still alive.'

'Did they know each other?' Robson asked.

'Not according to either of their parents,' Gormley said.

'Yeah, but what do parents ever know?' Daniels said. 'Mine were on a different planet, hadn't a clue what I was up to. It's like that for most kids, surely.' Her eyes found Carmichael. 'Lisa, when we're done here, get over to the university and find out what you can. I need an address for Jessica and I need it now. Her father was under the impression she was living at halls, but she's moved out. Someone must know where she lives. Be careful what you say though. We don't want to spook the students.'

Daniels had worked on many high-profile cases but this MO somehow seemed more macabre than all the rest. It was an exceptionally cold method of sending anyone to an early grave and calculated in its intent. It brought to mind Jonathan Forster, a serial killer who'd recently terrorized northern Britain—payback for an abusive mother. A deranged psychopath, he'd killed many times, once by placing a gun into a toddler's hand, pointing it at the child's grandfather and pulling the trigger.

Equally gross.

Daniels' left hand stroked her right shoulder, injured by the same bullet that had glanced off her clavicle before imbedding itself in Forster's heart—killing him instantaneously. Her memory of his killing spree was drowned out by Carmichael's voice.

'So what are we looking at, a kidnapping?'

'Yes, but as I've said, it may not be motivated by money. The necklace I showed you earlier was worth a small fortune, enough to keep your average arsehole going for months. This offence is personal—someone *really* wants Adam Finch to suffer.'

'So what happens now?' Carmichael asked. 'We run the two cases as one?'

'Theoretically, yes, but under no circumstances does that fact leave this room. I don't want the press finding out we have yet another linked incident on our patch. They'll have a field day.'

'So we're the lead force again?' Robson was referring to the case the DCI had just been thinking about. Three forces had been involved but Northumbria Police had taken control of the investigation. 'There's going to be no involvement from Durham?'

'For the time being, at least,' Gormley said. 'We had a conversation with Ron Naylor on the way back here. He agrees that's the best course of action. So keep up the good work, boys and girls. You know what to do.'

The team scattered.

Daniels pulled out her phone to call Matt West. As the number rang out she imagined him eighty-five miles south, puzzling over some sample or other, his eyes permanently fixed to the lenses of his microscope. After several rings he picked up.

'Matt, it's Kate Daniels returning your call.'

'How you doing?' He sounded preoccupied.

'You got something for me?'

'Maybe . . . that sample I took from your victim's shoe—'

'Hold on . . .' Daniels nodded as Gormley walked in from the kitchen holding up a china mug. Then she switched the phone to loudspeaker so he could listen in on her call. 'OK, shoot. I want Hank to hear this too.'

'I've found a slight mineral deposit. I thought it was glass at first, but it isn't. I'm not going to commit myself until I've completed my research, but I'm fairly sure I've never come across it before.'

'Can you be more specific?' The DCI had detected excitement in his voice. But Matt being Matt he was always cagey until he was sure of his facts. All the same, she had every reason to think that he might be on to something. 'Those test results are vital now. Another girl's gone missing. It looks like the same guy has taken her.'

'The only thing I can say for certain is that it didn't come from the area where the body was found. Not a chance. In fact, I'm looking at it now . . .' There was a slight pause in the conversation. 'I've been testing it for a good few hours. It's so unusual it might determine *exactly* where your victim was held before she met her death. You find that, chances are you'll find your missing girl.'

Daniels locked eyes with Gormley.

It didn't get much better than that.

15

Somewhere deep within the North Pennines, Jessica Finch opened her eyes wondering if she was still asleep, her terror and confusion part of a bad dream. She tried to focus, tried to make out where she was. She could hear a noise she couldn't immediately identify, the same sound that had woken her. The drip, drip, drip of liquid as it plopped heavily into the moving body of black water she was standing in.

Jessica moved her head to the left, her eyes following the dim pool of light reflected on the wet wall opposite. Her only source of light was coming from the cap lamp attached to the hard hat on her head, the chin strap of which was hanging loose around her neck.

Something slithered past her right calf.

She was sure it was nibbling at her skin.

A rat?

Something worse than a rat?

Jessica struggled but the shackles held firm. She screamed at the top of her voice, trying to look down without knocking off the hat, her terrified eyes searching the water below. Whatever it was, it slithered past again and she screamed even louder, her voice echoing in the chamber beyond . . .

HELP!

And then she noticed something else. Something even more terrifying than whatever was swimming around her in the water below. It was the colour that caught her eye, one she'd hated all her life. To some it signified triumph, courage and determination. To others, danger, rage, malevolence . . . blood. To her it was the colour of nightmares since the night her mother passed away. At first she thought she was seeing things. Fear did that to people, didn't it? Surely her mind was playing tricks. But as she strained her eyes to look again, she realized she was right. Her dress. No . . . not *her* dress. Someone else's.

Why?

And why hadn't her abductors gagged her?

There could be only one possible explanation.

She was in a place too remote to be heard.

16

Daniels glanced through the open door hoping to catch a few minutes with her former boss. Detective Chief Superintendent Bright hung up as she entered the room, tapping on the door on her way in.

Ellen Crawford smiled as she walked in.

'Am I interrupting?' Daniels asked.

'No, I was just leaving.' Ellen made a show of looking at her watch. 'As soon as Phil signs his mail, which has been sitting on his desk for hours.'

Bright smiled at her. 'Don't suppose you could organize a cup of tea for DCI Daniels before you go? One for me too, if you're boiling the kettle; I know how you love to save the planet.'

'I'm your PA, not your tea lady.' Ellen's eyes flashed, warning him not to push his luck. But she was smiling when she turned to Daniels. 'What's he like? How on earth you've put up with him all these years is beyond me, it really is!'

Bright scribbled his name on various documents. As he handed them to Ellen, Daniels' eyes slid over her. She was a woman of indeterminate age; mid to late forties, Daniels guessed. She had the body of someone half her age, good skin and perfect teeth, her own, not manufactured in some laboratory. She had great hair too, red to match her fiery personality.

'How about that tea?' Bright made a begging gesture. 'Just this once?'

'It's fine, Ellen,' Daniels said. 'I can make my own tea and so can he.'

Ellen relented. 'Milk, no sugar?'

'You sure?'

The PA smiled.

Daniels took a seat as she left the room.

Bright spoke up as she shut the door. 'What have *you* got that I haven't?

'Appreciation might do it.' She grinned. 'It usually works a treat, guv.'

'You any further forward? Adam must be desperate for news.'

'Well, he's going to be disappointed.'

'How's he holding up?'

Daniels shrugged. 'As well as can be expected, I suppose.'

'House-to-house come up with anything?'

'Have you seen his place? It's miles from the nearest village, not a neighbour in sight— thousands of acres of land accessible from all points on the compass. It's a bloody nightmare.'

'I meant around the crime scene.'

'That's even worse! Open countryside. Big sky. Sheep. And not a lot else. There's hardly any

72

CCTV from Greenhead in the west all the way to Heddon-on-the-Wall in the east. I've got officers with local knowledge helping us, but it isn't going to be easy. There are only forty or so buildings within a four-mile radius. Some of those are derelict. I'm having them all checked out, but my guts are telling me we're wasting our time up there. You *do* know it's also a military training area?' She didn't wait for an answer. 'That means low-flying exercises at all times of the day and night. Aircraft noise—fixed wing or helicopter—isn't something the locals would notice a whole lot.'

Daniels' eyes fell on his new desk, in particular on his most prized possession: a photograph of his late wife Stella posing in the foyer of the city's Malmaison Hotel. She had her glad rags on and high-heeled shoes, her shapely dancer's legs on show for all to see. Next to her photograph sat a card with Daniels' name on it.

Damn! He'd remembered it was her birthday.

She hoped he wasn't planning anything. She was supposed to be having dinner with her father, who was trying his best to make things right between them. He'd booked a table at Bouchon, a French restaurant in Hexham she'd heard good reports of. Friends had been there and had raved about the food. She looked at her watch. It was far too late to cancel. *But what choice did she have?* It would cause a row, she knew that much. Her father, a stickler for protocol and good manners, would take it as a personal affront if she allowed her job to come first again. The irony was not lost on her. The fact of the matter was, her chosen career had driven a wedge between them from the moment

73

she had signed on the dotted line all those years ago.

It hadn't always been like that.

Ed Daniels was an affectionate, hard-working man with a great sense of humour. At least, he used to be, until the miners' strike put him out of work and closed his pit. They had been close back then. But years later, when she left school with above-average grades and a burning ambition to join the police force, he saw her career choice as a personal betrayal and from there on things began to slide downhill.

Her mother's premature death hadn't helped.

Daniels sighed.

Her father had a strong moral code. He'd encouraged her always to do the right thing, taught her the importance of devotion and commitment, nurtured those qualities as she grew up. He'd given her the foundation Bright had later used to mould her into the impressive officer she was.

Ellen was back with her coat on, a pot of tea and two mugs.

Bright watched her set it down. 'You're a darling, you know that?'

'And you're a sexist pig!' Ellen left the room without another word.

Daniels laughed out loud. 'Looks like you met your match, guv.'

She meant it too. Ellen Crawford was just the sort of woman to put Bright back in his box. He was a great bloke, an excellent mentor, but a law unto himself. He was often overbearing and occasionally downright rude to his staff. Her included. Ellen had nailed him the minute she set eyes on him. They were made for each other.

'How well do you know Adam Finch?' she asked.

'He's a mate. We play golf together now and again. Why?'

Daniels met his eyes over the rim of her mug.

'Remind me, guv. How did you say you met him?'

'I didn't.' Bright opened his desk drawer and pulled out a packet of his favourite biscuits. He offered her one, but she waved it away.

'Well, now I'm asking. How *did* you meet?'

'You're barking up the wrong tree, Kate.'

'Humour me.'

'He was my commanding officer in the army.'

'What regiment?'

Bright took a bite of his garibaldi. 'Army Air Corps.'

'You *are* kidding?'

17

The restaurant was candlelit, an intimate space done out in a rich wine colour that made it feel warm and cosy beneath an open beamed ceiling. Daniels wished she'd made more of an effort to dress for the occasion. But she didn't intend to stop long. She was there under sufferance and was keen to get back to High Shaw where she planned to spend the night. It was closer to home and she could get an early start in the morning.

Her father was sitting directly opposite, smart as a pin in a navy suit with a waistcoat, a spotted tie and pocket handkerchief to match. In many ways he reminded her of Bright. In fact, the more she thought about it, the more convinced she became that they were two of a kind. Immaculate on the outside but flawed when it came to the personal stuff. She'd argued with Bright before leaving his office. His failure to disclose Finch's obvious flying experience bothered her still. When they had parted she was angry, a mood that only got worse when her father rang her to confirm arrangements for dinner, refusing to take no for an answer.

Sensing she'd gone to another place, Ed Daniels smiled at the women on the next table even though they were strangers. Daniels hated his fake charm. As long as he didn't know you, you had his undivided attention. They were halfway through their meal, trying hard to ignore the atmosphere between them. Though the seared mullet on her plate was beautifully cooked and smelled delicious, somehow she couldn't summon up the appetite.

Ed Daniels tucked into his rib-eye, oblivious to his daughter, or so it seemed. He put down his knife and fork, dabbed his mouth with a napkin and lifted the wine bottle. Daniels shook her head, regretting her decision not to cancel. He'd gone to great lengths to celebrate her birthday and she hadn't had the heart. Recent events had put things into perspective. He was all the family she had now. She owed it to them both to give it a go. But nobody said it would be easy.

'Can't you have *one* glass?'

'Not even one. I told you I couldn't make a night of it.' She looked at her watch. It was gone nine. 'I've still got stuff to do.'

'It's your birthday!'

Daniels looked at him. Was he really too dumb to understand what it was like doing her job? Or was he merely pretending to be? He did that sometimes, just to wind her up. Her terms and conditions as a Detective Chief Inspector and SIO on this particular murder investigation didn't recognize family occasions of any description.

'I've got a lot on.' She wasn't telling any lies, although she knew fine well that her squad would've knocked off by now, gone home to recharge the batteries and get some kip for a few hours at least. 'Think yourself lucky I made it at all.'

'I'm surprised you did.' Ed picked up his wine. 'I heard you were busy.'

Daniels bristled. 'Hank still spying on me, is he?'

'He has your best interests at heart, Kate. Don't be so hard on him.'

'I'm not!'

'That's not what it sounds like.'

'Well, tough!' Daniels glared at him.

'Why are you so angry?' Ed looked at his half-eaten dinner, put down his wine glass and picked up his knife and fork. Daniels watched him slice into the meat, blood-red and cooked to perfection. He didn't bother to look up. 'Is it because of Jo?'

Daniels folded her napkin and put it on her side plate. It was a warning not to go any further, advance notice that she was about to leave. When she'd first told Ed of her relationship with Jo Soulsby he hadn't wanted to know. He certainly didn't care that it was over. In fact, if anything, he was glad. Did he really expect her to confide in him now? Well, it wasn't going to happen.

'I've got to go.'

'Touchy subject?'

'We'll do this some other time.'

'The conversation or dinner?' He just wouldn't leave it alone.

The women on the next table glanced in their direction. Her father smiled at them again. To save his blushes, Daniels got up and walked round the table. She gave him a peck on the cheek, made her apologies, promising to make it up to him. On the way out of the restaurant she paid the bill, an action she regretted before she'd pinned her number.

Her father would be furious.

Another thing for him to complain about.

She left the restaurant and walked quickly to her Toyota. She drove away, suddenly feeling lonely and upset. What a way to spend a birthday! She put on some music, a Dixie Chicks album Jo had bought her when they were still together. Track five was playing: 'You Were Mine'. The lyrics got to her and she turned it off again.

She glanced at her watch, an idea forming. Taking her left hand off the steering wheel she pressed the talking-head icon on her touch-screen Bluetooth device and said:

'Dial Jo Soulsby.'

The machine said: 'Pardon?'

Bollocks. 'Call Jo.'

'Call Jo, general?'

The Bury device was beginning to annoy her. 'Yes!' she said.

The number rang out and then switched to voicemail.

'Jo, it's me. I need to speak to you. Can you call me when you get in?'

She hung up.

Almost immediately, the phone rang and the Bury kicked in. 'Incoming call.'

Daniels could see from the display screen that it was Jo calling. She'd obviously ignored the house phone, then had second thoughts. Or maybe she just hadn't got there in time. Daniels pressed the receiver icon.

'Ringing me from your police number now?' Jo said cheerfully. 'Wow! Things have moved on!'

She was teasing. There was a time when they only used pay-as-you-go unregistered mobiles to ring each other, a must-have item for those who dealt in deception. It had been Daniels' idea to keep their relationship private—*secret*—for fear that coming out would hamper her chances of promotion within the force. Putting ambition before Jo had been a fatal mistake.

'Happy birthday, by the way.' There was hint of sadness in Jo's voice now. 'You doing anything nice? Didn't have time to buy you a card. Anyway, I know how you hate all that hearts and flowers stuff.'

At least she'd remembered to forget.

'Didn't expect one.' Daniels tried to sound upbeat. Jo could've picked up the phone. *If she'd wanted to.* 'You in for the rest of the night?'

'It's a bit late, isn't it?'

'Sounds like you're still up.' Daniels could hear music in the background. Jackson Browne, one of Jo's favourite artists. 'I need to talk to you.'

'About?'

'Work! What else is there?'

'Thought I was about to get lucky,' Jo said.

Daniels' heart skipped a beat. She still craved a close relationship with this woman and yet she was her own worst enemy in achieving it. She knew she'd said the wrong thing. *Again.* She also knew she'd have to up her game if she stood any chance of a reconciliation.

Was this a come-on?

Or wishful thinking on her part?

'I could be there in twenty . . .' Daniels hesitated after saying that. She could hardly breathe and felt much like a fifteen-year-old trying to arrange a first date. She turned right, heading east along the A69 towards Newcastle. 'It would be great to see you.'

'Just being friendly,' Jo came back. 'I have Kirsten here.'

Hearing those words was like a knife in the guts. Daniels felt like a fool. She did a reciprocal at the Styford roundabout and floored the accelerator, heading in the opposite direction.

'Kate? You still there?'

'Yep, traffic's a nightmare, sorry.' Daniels lied.

There wasn't a soul on the road.

'Is it urgent?' Jo asked.

'No, I'll call you in the morning.' Daniels hung up. She looked at the talking-head icon. 'And you can fuck off too!' she said.

18

Switching on her main-beam headlights, Daniels turned off the road and entered a narrow country lane, a thick blanket of cloud above and dense hedgerows on either side. A few minutes later, she saw a light in the distance: the Mobile Police

Incident Unit. She drove towards it, cut her lights, got out of her car and went straight to the caravan to let the duty officer know she'd arrived. She tapped on the door and it opened immediately. For some reason, Hook was working a double shift.

'Oh, it's you, ma'am,' he peered beyond her into the darkness.

'Who were you expecting—Madonna?'

He grinned. 'I should be so lucky.'

'I think you'll find that was Kylie.'

Hook grinned.

'Just letting you know I'm back.'

'Want me to see you in?' Hook nodded towards High Shaw.

His comment amused her. She glanced over her shoulder. The cottage was in darkness. Had she been wearing a blindfold it would have made little difference to what she could see. In this part of the world there were no streetlights to guide folks home. They weren't necessary. It was as safe as houses round here, according to the parish council—not a single violent incident for almost forty years.

Until now.

Taking a pencil torch from her pocket, she switched it on, said goodnight to Hook and turned away. He wasn't to know she'd grown up in the countryside and was well used to the silence and the darkness. He remained at the caravan door watching her back as she picked her way through the garden gate and up the path. She looked round as she reached the front door and gave him the thumbs up. He waved back and disappeared inside. But as Daniels put her key in the lock and pushed open the door, she wished he hadn't.

There was someone inside.

She could feel it.

Adrenalin pumped through her veins as she called out to Hook. When he didn't come running she braced herself for an attack. She fumbled for the light switch and heard a small explosion which damn near gave her a heart attack.

'Surprise! Surprise!'

Party poppers ignited and trumpets blew. The light came on and a curtain of streamers floated gently to the floor in front of her. Gormley, Brown, Robson, Carmichael and Bright held up their glasses, the work hard, play hard mentality returning to her squad. Reluctantly she accepted a glass of champagne. It had been a very long day and she needed a party like a hole in the head.

19

Mist hung like a veil over the grass. Detective Chief Superintendent Bright was standing outside High Shaw looking out at the scenery wishing Stella could've seen the place. She'd have loved it. Last night had been the first time since her untimely death he'd truly enjoyed himself surrounded by his former team, his other family. Stella couldn't have kids.

Hank Gormley joined him, mug in each hand, muttering a husky greeting. He needed a shave and was clearly hung-over. Handing Bright a coffee, he leaned back against the metre-thick stone wall of the cottage.

Bright took a slurp. 'Shit, that's hot!'

'It's made with boiling water, guv.'

A grunt was all Bright managed in reply.

Gormley yawned. 'Suppose I should clear out the troops before the world and his wife get up. What the hell happened to Lisa? She didn't hang around long.'

'Try the caravan.'

Gormley's gaze shifted to the Mobile Incident Unit.

When he looked back, his former guv'nor was grinning.

'Nah.' Hank shook his head. 'Fiver says you're wrong.'

Bright stuck a hand out. 'Fifty quid says I'm right.'

Gormley didn't shake on it. They stood for a while, taking in the view, enjoying the silence. Then the door to the Mobile Incident Unit opened and DC Lisa Carmichael emerged. She was clearly half-asleep and didn't notice their eyes upon her.

'Bad choice, Lisa.' Bright didn't even try to hide his amusement. 'Did nobody tell you he's got more patter than Gandhi's flip-flop?'

Gormley stifled a laugh as Carmichael hurried into the cottage.

Within half an hour Bright had returned to headquarters and High Shaw was back to normal with no evidence of the previous night's impromptu celebration. Daniels was sitting in the centre of her squad, stressing that the party was over and from here on in she wanted their minds on the job. Kevin Hook smirked at Carmichael, who looked at her boss with an expression of regret. Daniels felt sorry for her. Most young

83

detectives she'd ever known had been in that particular place. Drink in, wits out—a drunken fuck with an inappropriate other whose name they couldn't and didn't want to recall the next day.

She moved quickly on. 'Adam Finch is our starting point. He was once in the Army Air Corps . . .' She paused to let the information sink in. 'And yes, he *was* a pilot, although according to the guv'nor he currently has no licence. Later today, Hank and I will re-interview him, but I want to run this scenario past Jo Soulsby first, see if she can give us a handle on the person or persons we're looking for. Andy, put in a request to Durham Uni: I want all CCTV footage seized. Tell them we'll be along later in the day—get us an office up there, if you can. If you come up with any leads, feed them back through Robbo, who'll coordinate things this end. Robbo, I want you to get in touch with this artist woman, make arrangements for her to come in and see me.' She handed over the business card for Fiona Fielding that Finch had supplied. 'Kevin, caravan, now! The rest of you can go.'

In the privacy of the Mobile Incident Unit, Hook stood to attention. He was far less cocky than he had been a minute ago as he waited for a dressing down.

Daniels was far from happy. 'Your supervisor tells me you have your sights on a transfer to the murder investigation team. Problem is, we only have vacancies for people who can be discreet.'

'Pardon, ma'am?'

'Don't come the innocent with me, Kevin. I saw that little display in there. Carmichael is a bloody good operator. She doesn't need distractions.

84

Know what I'm saying?'

'Yes, ma'am.'

'Well, if you do want a permanent posting with us, I suggest you think long and hard before notching up any more of my team on your bedpost. Last night didn't happen, got me?'

Hook nodded, his face going red.

Daniels walked out.

After agreeing to meet up with Gormley later in the morning, she got in her car and took the road to Newcastle. Traffic was light and she made good time until she reached Jesmond. At the top of Osborne Road, a diversion had sprung up, re-routing vehicles along St Georges Terrace and then left on to Acorn Road—a nightmare at the best of times.

In a long line of vehicles, she sat tapping her fingers on the steering wheel, concerned that she might be late for her appointment with Jo. Bored waiting, her eyes scanned the parade of shops: a mini-market, a newsagent, a couple of bakeries, a hardware store and Boilerhouse, her favourite hair salon. And soon she was out on to Osborne Road again, an area transformed in recent years. Hotel bars had terraces fronting on to the tree-lined street and, even at this early hour, the café culture was thriving. A few minutes later she arrived at Jo's front door.

She took a deep breath and knocked . . .

20

They kissed gently, a peck on each cheek. Jo
Soulsby looked relaxed. She was dressed in a pair
of jeans and a deep pink shirt, a hint of cleavage
on show. Daniels followed her into the house and
through into the kitchen where she made coffee
and left it to percolate. Daniels went to use the
bathroom. She found Jo in the living room a few
minutes later, curled up on the sofa cradling a
cup of coffee in both hands. The Dixie Chicks
were singing about a Travelin' Soldier in the
background.

Daniels sat down, watching Jo.

It was difficult not to.

She couldn't help wondering if Jo and her friend
Kirsten Edwards were intimate and, if so, how
serious the relationship between them was. They
had known each other since university. Kirsten was
Irish, stunning and a successful businesswoman—
former North East Woman Entrepreneur of the
Year. Daniels had Googled her more than once in
the past few weeks.

'What's wrong?' Jo asked. 'Something happening
on planet Kate?'

Daniels blushed. Her ex had always been able to
read her.

Jo waited patiently for an answer.

'How's Kirsten?' Daniels asked, regretting the
words the second they were out of her mouth.
Asking such a personal question made her sound
like a jealous teenager, unable to cope with the
thought that another girl had taken her place.

86

She'd met Kirsten during her last case, could smell the woman's distinctive perfume as soon as she'd entered Jo's bathroom.

'Kate?'

'Sorry?'

'I said, I'm not going there again.' Jo held up the briefing notes Daniels had sent her before leaving the MIR. 'I thought you were here to discuss this? I also thought we were past all that.'

'We are! Hey, I'm cool with it. Doesn't mean I'm not interested in how you're doing.' *Quit digging.* 'I didn't mean to pry. It's just, well, you and Kirsten seem to be spending a lot of time together lately.'

'Depends how you define a lot—'

'She was here last night!'

'That makes once.'

Daniels grinned. 'Last Tuesday, Wednesday and Friday.'

Jo's eyes blazed. 'You're keeping obs on me now? D'you know how insecure and weak that makes you seem?'

'God, you make it sound like I'm stalking!'

'Are you?'

Daniels looked away. The room temperature seemed to have dropped several degrees. Jo felt it too. She silenced her iPod, then leaned across and lit a flame-effect gas fire to take the chill off the room. The sun would flood in later in the day, but Daniels would be long gone by then. Jo sat up straight and quickly changed the subject.

'How's the shoulder?' she asked.

'Good.' That was a lie. Daniels pointed at the briefing notes. 'You've read those?'

'Yes, poor Amy . . . Any news on Jessica?'

Daniels shook her head.

Jo pushed a pile of Sunday newspapers on to the floor, placed a cushion behind her back and made herself more comfortable, crossing one long leg over the other. She was wearing Havaianas. Her toenails were painted to match the exact colour of her shirt. She was good at that: outfit and nail polish carefully chosen and worn with style, making it look like she hadn't tried too hard—hadn't tried full stop.

Daniels pushed on. 'First impressions?'

'Not good, I'm afraid,' Jo warned. 'As you well know, staging a crime scene is usually done to suggest a false motive. In this case, it seems to me that your offender has done the exact opposite.'

'I agree. He's trying to draw attention, not deflect it. And he's doing it to scare the hell out of Adam Finch . . .' Daniels went over what she knew so far, telling Jo she too had a nasty feeling about the case. The offender had gone to a lot of bother. He'd been very thorough, selected a perfect body double in Amy, dressed her in Jess's clothes and dumped her in a remote spot, miles from home. 'Mission accomplished, once that happened: Finch is forced into the worst corner possible, viewing a dead body at the morgue. It might not have been his daughter on the slab, but it was the knife going in. His agony goes on . . .'

'What's your opinion on motive?' Jo asked.

'Well it isn't about extortion, which was our starting point when we thought the dead girl was Jessica Finch. Bright floated the idea that her abductors might've been spooked into getting rid of her, hoping to cop a ransom before she was found. But that doesn't make sense in light of what we now know to be true. No, whoever took Jess and killed Amy is callous and loathsome. They want to make Finch suffer in the worst possible way.'

'I think you're right.

'I think so too. Question is, am I looking at the case arse first?'

'What d'you mean?'

'Amy was discovered in the middle of nowhere, right? What if our man, assuming it is a man, manipulated discovery by a third party? I mean, dumped Amy's body near Hadrian's Wall not so she *wouldn't* be found, but so she *would*? Doesn't this smack of some macabre game to you?'

'Yes, it does. One the killer wants to win.'

'He's taken huge risks to show absolute contempt for Finch; as a punishment, I suspect. How am I doing so far?'

Jo smiled. 'Can you hear me arguing?'

'But why, Jo? What would drive someone to such lengths? What God-awful thing did Finch ever do to elicit such hatred from his tormentor?' Daniels hardly stopped for breath. 'And another thing. What self-respecting offender would leave a very valuable piece of jewellery at a crime scene?'

'You think that was deliberate? Some sort of message?'

Daniels shrugged. 'It was a one-off piece, easy for us to identify.'

They sat for a long time deep in thought. They had worked many cases together over the years but this one sank to a new low. Allowing Jo time to process her theories, Daniels' eyes travelled round a room she felt entirely at home in. She'd spent many happy moments there.

Many intimate moments.

She looked back at Jo. 'There's something else; something not quite gelling with me. If Amy's parents had come forward to report their daughter missing before Finch did, then the killer's efforts would've all been in vain. Unless—'

'Unless he's manipulating you too,' Jo said, interrupting.

'How d'you mean?'

'The way I see it, he made sure that wouldn't happen. He waited until the eleventh hour to take Amy Grainger. In your report, you said Finch was under surveillance. There are only two certainties here, Kate. One—' Jo held up a thumb—'this is a highly organized offender you're up against. And two—' she added a forefinger—'there's absolutely nothing haphazard about this abduction.'

Daniels had been afraid Jo was going to say that. She rubbed her right temple, trying to ease the pressure in her aching head. 'Recidivist, d'you reckon?'

'That's impossible to say.'

'But he's been in risky situations before?'

'Yes, and he's not afraid. He's in control and he's really fucked up. But . . .' Jo glanced at the papers in her hand. 'Not a sexual predator, I see—'

'Apparently not. Amy's underwear was intact. There were no signs of sexual assault and no defence or restraint marks. I'm assuming she was drugged very early on. At least, I'm hoping she was.'

'I was making an observation,' Jo said. 'Not asking a question.'

'I'm sorry?'

Jo held Daniels' gaze for a beat, making sure she had her full attention. 'The underwear issue could

90

be hugely significant. Or, and this is vitally important, it could have no relevance at all.'

'That's helpful.' Daniels' frustration was beginning to show. 'And your point is . . . ?'

'It wasn't part of the killer's master plan. Think about it. Swapping the outer clothing alone has put the fear of God into Finch. In my humble opinion, we have two scenarios here. Either the offender was simply running short of time, or leaving the underwear intact actually mattered to him. In my view, it's the latter. He's letting us know he's no pervert.'

Daniels almost laughed out loud, but Jo's grim expression stopped her. 'You're seriously suggesting that he's so fucked up he's prepared to kill Amy but not to take away her dignity by making her strip?'

'And in doing so he's made a big mistake.'

Daniels frowned. 'I'm not with you.'

'He's given away more than he planned to. He didn't want to degrade her, Kate. Just use her to hurt someone else.'

'You're not telling me he cares! He threw her out of an aircraft at approximately two hundred feet!'

'I get that. Make no mistake, this man is unhinged. He's playing to his own set of rules. Even the most dangerous offenders have a line over which they will not cross.'

'He's way past that, surely?'

'Not necessarily.' Jo was quiet for a while. 'Some prostitutes will shag anyone for money, right? Give their clients a hand job, a blow job, whatever turns them on. What won't they do?'

'Allow their clients to kiss them on the lips.'

Jo nodded. 'Because?'

'It's too personal. That's their bottom line and it keeps them in control.'

'Exactly. So what does that tell you?'

Daniels was silent for a moment. And then she suddenly realized where Jo was heading. Her next question was one she felt compelled to ask: 'You're telling me he's a father?'

'I'd bet my job on it.'

Jo's words hung in the air between them.

Daniels' mobile rang, startling them both: Hank calling.

Ignoring it, Daniels said, 'Hank doesn't like Finch.'

'That'll make him guilty then!' Jo was being ironic.

They both laughed, not because it was all that funny, but as a way of releasing the tension. Jo had grown to like Gormley during the time they had spent together at a safe house when it was thought that she'd unwittingly become the target of one of her clients, a man who'd killed several times. It wasn't until later that the murder investigation team found evidence that it was actually Daniels he'd been watching. And *she* certainly didn't need reminding of his name.

Joining Jo on the sofa, Daniels opened the murder file. Inside there were crime-scene photographs, statements and criminal records checks on Adam Finch and key members of his staff: Pearce, Townsend and Mrs Partridge. 'There's nothing recorded against any of them,' she said. 'Apart from a spent conviction of urinating in a public place when Pearce was eighteen years old.'

'And the Graingers?'

'Bloody snow white . . .' Flipping pages, Daniels reached her notes on the bereaved family. 'Not so much as an unpaid bill or a row with the neighbours. They come across as a lovely couple on paper and in person. They're totally devastated by this.'

'Adam Finch is the only pilot among them?'

Daniels nodded. 'Claims he hasn't flown for years, hasn't even got a licence any more. It lapsed a long time ago.'

'Doesn't mean he can't still fly.'

'That's very true.'

'May I?' Jo pointed at the file.

As she leaned over to take it, her hand brushed Daniels' lap. They hadn't been this close in months and it made Kate's heart race.

'It can't be Finch,' she said, trying hard to focus. 'I'm certain Amy was killed to punish him.'

'I am too, unless . . .' Jo didn't finish.

Daniels looked at her. 'Unless what?'

Jo didn't answer.

'Go on, what were you going to say?'

'If it is Finch, then he's lost the plot completely and the whole thing is even more elaborate and contrived than I first thought. However, if you're right and it's someone else, someone who's prepared to kill to get back at him, then this goes way beyond anger. This is hateful rage. The suffering is all part of it, Kate. And I'm betting it's someone he knows personally.'

This close to Jo, Daniels felt both uncomfortable and stimulated at the same time. She valued her opinion and, what's more, Jo had a point. Most murders were domestics, offences carried out on the spur of the moment: people losing their rag or getting pissed. There were some notable exceptions: one or two cases Daniels had been involved with that had been underworld or gangster-related, where an element of planning was involved; another where a serial killer had tracked down a long list of victims in order to get back at his mother. But as far as the modus operandi was concerned, the case she was now dealing with was definitely out there on its own.

21

At High Shaw, spring sunshine flooded the room and fresh country air wafted in through the open front door. But the ambience of the place wasn't lifting DS Robson's foul mood. Daniels had left him alone there with a huge pile of statements to read—meaningless statements at that. He looked up as a dark shadow crossed his face. PC Hook was on the threshold with a farm labourer in tow.

'This is Ronnie Raine, Sarge. Says he has something important to tell you. Is it OK if I leave him with you?'

Robson nodded.

Hook set off for the mobile unit, leaving Raine alone in the doorway. Casting his eye over the lad, Robson beckoned him inside. He was a giant, six four at least, with sandy-coloured hair, a ruddy complexion and bright eyes. At a guess, the DS figured he was around twenty years old and yet he looked as though he'd worked on the land for years. Unlike the detective, who was longing to get back to the city, he seemed entirely comfortable in his surroundings.

Raine stepped forward, stooping to get through the door. Robson offered him a seat but he declined, pointing down at mucky boots that smelled markedly of horse manure.

'Suit yourself,' Robson said. 'What was it you thought I should know?'

'It might not mean anything, sir.'

'True. But I won't know 'til you tell me, right?'

'My cousin Billy is the local constable.' Raine waited for some recognition from the detective but none was forthcoming. 'He asked me and some other young farmers if we'd seen anything, anything out of the ordinary in the last few weeks.'

'And have you?'

'Maybe.' Remembering his manners, Raine took off his cap. Crushing it in huge, dirty hands he continued. 'Very early one morning—I mean *really* early—before the tourists usually arrive, I seen this car parked up at Housesteads with nobody in it.'

'How long ago was this?'

' 'Bout three weeks.'

'What were you doing up there?'

'Going for the sheep, like I do every day. When I came down from the pasture I saw a man and a young blonde lass arguing. When they saw me, they hurried back to the car. This was very close to where Billy said you found the young girl's body.'

'Who's Billy?'

'My cousin, the polis!' Raine frowned. 'You listening to me?'

'Last name?'

'Raine! Same as me. Cousins, aren't we?'

'Of course, how stupid of me.'

'You taking the piss? Cos if you are, I've got

better things to do.'

Robson felt guilty and dropped the attitude. It wasn't Raine's fault that his police career was on a downward spiral, and he certainly couldn't afford a complaint against him—especially now. Already mired in the kind of trouble that could cost him his job, the odds of him rescuing his good reputation were slim to say the least.

'Sorry, it's been a long day. No offence meant.'

Raine accepted the half-hearted apology and carried on. 'I seen them again on Tuesday. Same pair. I think she must've hurt herself because he was helping her across the field. I was going to give them a hand, but the man waved me away so I left them to it. Didn't want to stick my nose in. Wasn't my business, was it?'

'S'pose not,' Robson said. 'You sure it was Tuesday?'

'Aye, it's market day in Hexham. I was sellin' stock at the mart later.' Raine seemed in no doubt. 'Like I said, it might be nothing. But Billy said I should let you know about it just in case. He said people should come forward and help in any way they can.'

'He was right. I'll need your address and a contact number.'

Robson picked up his pen. As Raine reeled off his details, he began writing them down, hoping he hadn't sounded as hacked off as he felt. Being left alone at High Shaw when there was very little going on was not his idea of fun. One local smelling of horse shit was the only person he'd seen all day, apart from PC Hook, who was manning the caravan next door.

And he was an irritating prick!

Robson was a team player, not a one-man band. He'd been stewing all morning, aware that he alone was to blame for his predicament, for slipping spectacularly to the bottom of the pecking order in the murder investigation team. He'd made mistakes on their last enquiry. And when Daniels had given him a second chance, then a third, what had he done? Fucked her over good and proper, that's what!

A one-time loyal member of her team, he'd disgraced himself by passing insider information to Assistant Chief Constable Martin, a hate figure within the Northumbria force. In return for very little—or so it seemed at the time—Martin had promised him the recognition he deserved both within the squad and beyond. Robson had only agreed to talk because his wife and new baby son deserved a bigger house, a new car, a holiday, none of which he could possibly provide having got into debt playing online poker. So when Martin offered 'fast-track promotion' he'd grabbed it with both hands.

Doddle.

End of problem.

Except Martin was now history, leaving Robson out on a limb, having to explain his behaviour, distrusted by his mates and the one boss he had any time for. His colleagues were good people. They didn't deserve a grass in their midst, making their difficult job even more so. No matter how he dressed it up, he had to admit he'd made a complete mess of things. Borrowing heavily against his house in order to keep his wife from finding out had been the worst decision he'd ever made. And now it was payback time.

Daniels had every reason to be pissed off, but she'd taken it really well.

Jesus! She'd even offered to help.

'When you're on the bottom,' she'd said, 'the only way is up.'

Wasn't that the truth?

Checking the statement over, Robson pushed it across his desk, asking Raine to read it through and sign the caption at the bottom certifying its accuracy. But the lad hadn't heard him, or if he had he was too preoccupied with goings on outside the cottage to respond. Robson looked out of the window too. He could see nothing of interest, just miles and miles of boring bloody countryside and an angry grey sky to the south.

'Mr Raine?'

Raine gave his attention.

Robson pointed at the statement. The big lad leaned over the desk. After a moment of scanning the document, he scribbled his name on a line marked with a blue cross. Then he stood up and asked if he could go; the beast in the field beyond required his attention.

'We might need to talk to you again, sir.' Robson thanked the lad for coming forward and smiled at him for the first time since he'd entered the room. 'You're not planning on going away on a holiday anytime soon, are you?'

The lad seemed baffled by the question.

Robson tapped the statement. 'This could be very important or entirely innocent, but we'll definitely check it out. You did right coming in.'

Raine put on his cap and turned to go.

'Just one more thing,' Robson said before the witness reached the door. 'The man you saw? He

98

was definitely helping the girl, not dragging her?'

'Could've been doing either.' Raine thought for a moment. 'It was hard to tell. I was a good way off, wouldn't like to say for sure.'

22

Dr Matthew West swivelled his chair round so he was facing the window, his phone held between cheek and shoulder as he waited for Daniels to pick up. His office was on the second floor of the forensic science laboratory where he'd worked as a Civil Servant for the past twenty-three years. He'd never had any other job since leaving university with a first-class Honours in Chemistry. Hadn't wanted one either. He was happy doing exactly what he was good at: crime-scene examination and analysis. Trace evidence cases, to be more precise. He'd already worked his way up to department head and was now so respected in his field of expertise he'd even published articles and books on the subject.

He had ambitions to go further.

Matt looked round his laboratory. Colleagues in white coats, some with masks on, some not, sat pensively at their stations poring over microscopic particles of glass, paint and explosives, pausing occasionally to detail physical and chemical properties, or to consult one of several databases when identification proved difficult. The report on Matt's computer screen was but one page long, a detailed analysis of trace evidence taken from the heel of a shoe worn by Amy Grainger on the day she died. Analysis he fully expected to present at court at a later date, to defend orally under cross-examination no doubt.

He was proud to be an expert witness.

The ringing tone ceased in Matt's ear.

'Daniels.'

Matt smiled. She was out of breath. 'Someone's busy,' he said.

'Sorry, Matt. It's crazy here. Tell me you have good news.'

'Put it this way, you owe me one.'

'Really? I knew you wouldn't let me down.'

Was it any wonder she sounded over the moon? Matt's work usually began after the event, usually in cases involving sudden or violent death at the hands of another. So far as Amy Grainger was concerned, the only use for his microscopes and scientific knowledge would be in assisting the police to compile evidence that might lead to the apprehension of an offender. In other words, bring him or her to justice with good old-fashioned proof. But this current case was different: it involved a second missing girl. His identification of the sample could pinpoint a search area with accuracy. It might help Daniels find her before it was too late.

A living victim not a dead one.

He willed it to be true.

'The mineral deposit I found on Amy Grainger's shoe is definitely green fluorspar,' he said. 'There's absolutely no doubt about it.'

'In layman's terms, what does that mean exactly?'

'It means you just got lucky.'

There was an intake of breath at the other end of

100

the line. Daniels stayed silent, waiting for him to tell her more. Despite their physical distance, he could feel her excitement down the line.

'Green fluorspar is unique to the North Pennines area. It isn't found anywhere else.'

23

'Guv, I need a word.'

Bright was looking out of his office window, deep in thought.

He looked at his watch. 'I'm late for an appointment, Kate. Can it wait?'

'It could, but there have been developments I think you should know about.'

'Concerning . . . ?'

'Several things. First, I need your authorization for a press release to trace a couple of potential witnesses seen around Housesteads in the past few days and weeks.'

'Knock yourself out. You're the SIO. As far as I'm concerned, until they find my replacement you can do what the hell you want, within reason.'

'Good. Then that solves my next problem.'

'Which is?'

'I meant to tell you this last night. I've decided to leave Robbo up at High Shaw and move the rest of the squad back to town first thing in the morning. As soon as enquiries dry up at Housesteads, we'll pull out altogether and haul him back here too.'

'This got anything to do with him serving a penance?'

'Why d'you ask?'

'He seems to have drawn the short straw, that's all.'

'Better than no straw at all.' Daniels meant it.

'You pulled him?'

'Oh yes.'

'And he coughed?'

Daniels nodded soberly, remembering how angry she'd been with Robson for letting the team down. But since having it out with him she'd mellowed. The man clearly had his problems and, as his direct supervisor, she saw it as her duty to help him solve them.

Bright was waiting. 'Well! What did the bastard say?'

'It's complicated, guv.' She didn't want to get into it with Bright. They were bound to end up arguing. He'd tell her she was an SIO, not a bloody social worker. Then he'd have words with Robson himself. And he wouldn't hold back. 'Let's just say I'm handling it, shall we? We came to an understanding. Robbo has renewed his commitment to the team and, as far as I'm concerned, that's the end of it. I've got more important things on my mind.'

'Such as?'

'Matt West called to say—' She stopped talking as Bright lost his balance momentarily, the blood draining from his face, sweat pouring from him. She went to his aid but he fended her off using his desk to steady himself. She got him a beaker of water and made him sit down. 'Guv, what's wrong?'

'Bit of a migraine that's all.'

Daniels wondered what kind of a migraine had him plaiting his legs. He'd been drinking heavily since Stella's death but last night, up at High Shaw, she'd noticed he'd refrained from alcohol, apart from a half-glass of bubbly to toast her birthday. *Unheard of.* The door opened and Ellen walked in. Odd that she too was working on a Sunday. Now Daniels knew something was up.

'Your car's on its way, Phil.' Ellen set a printed note down on his desk. 'And your appointment at the Conrad Clinic has been confirmed.'

Bright glared at her.

Daniels eyeballed their boss. Ellen had dropped him in it on purpose and now he had some explaining to do. A weekend appointment at the prestigious private clinic, especially in the evening, would not only cost a bomb but it would suggest something really quite serious. That assumption was confirmed by the worried look on Ellen's face. She made a quick exit, leaving them alone to talk. A few minutes later, the DCI walked Bright to his car, telling him off for having kept her in the dark.

'Sure you don't want me to come with you? I'm happy to?'

He shook his head, got in the car and gave instructions to his driver before turning back to face her. 'You mentioned Matt West,' he said.

'It'll keep, guv. I'll speak to you tomorrow. You take care.' He opened his mouth to speak but before he could say anything she shut the door. As the car moved off, she called Gormley. 'Hank, any chance you can meet me at my place in half an hour?'

24

About four miles away, Gormley was dining with his wife and son. They'd been back for less than a week and already he was thinking that their last-ditch attempt to repair their broken relationship wasn't going to work. Julie was irritated with the interruption to their evening meal, but an urgency in Daniels' voice prevented him from putting down the phone.

'Sure,' he said. 'What's up?'

'I'll tell you when you get here.'

Daniels hung up, unaware he had company, which suited Gormley perfectly. Julie's decision to give their marriage another go had been sudden, almost as sudden as her decision to leave in the first place. He wasn't about to queer his pitch at work by letting Kate know that his domestic circumstances might get in the way of a murder enquiry.

He looked at Julie across the table. 'Sorry, love. I have to go out again.'

'For God's sake, Hank. You only just got in!'

Julie clashed down her cutlery and glanced at their son. Fearing a row brewing, Ryan kept his head down and went back to his dinner. For the next five minutes he was the referee in his parent's points-scoring routine, each of them too pig-headed to back down.

'. . . and while we're at it,' Julie said, 'maybe you could tell me where the hell you *were* last night?'

Gormley chose silence. It had been Julie's idea to try again. She'd promised him she could handle the demands of his job, not just the professional but the social too. And already she was going back on her word. Ryan had had enough. He murmured something sarcastic about true love and left the table, taking his dinner with him. They waited in silence until he'd cleared the room, his father wincing as the door slammed shut.

'You happy now?' Gormley said, shoving his plate away.

He got up from the table, put on his coat and left.

*　　　*　　　*

A presenter on TV warned of flooding due to heavy rain in Cumbria. It was the third year running this had happened. Residents right across the county—some of whom had barely moved back into their homes since the devastation caused the year before—were experiencing major disruption again. Hundreds of people were in temporary accommodation, their homes, schools and businesses under almost three feet of water.

Gormley shook his head, saddened by the tragic death of PC Bill Barker, a heroic Cumbrian officer who'd lost his life when the Northside bridge collapsed in Workington in 2009. He'd been trying to save others by directing motorists away from the bridge when chunks of masonry fell into the swollen river, taking him with it. Many had lived because of his bravery.

The man was a hero.

'They must wonder if it's ever going to end,' Gormley said.

'It's dreadful, isn't it?' Daniels appeared in the

living room with a glass of wine in each hand. She glanced at the set just as Gormley turned it off with the remote. 'Julie let you out to play then?' she said, without looking at him.

'How the fuck did—'

Daniels grinned. 'Jungle telegraph. Pete saw her in Waitrose yesterday. I'm pleased for you. How are things?'

'Tell you the truth, I was dying for an excuse to get out of the house.' He practically threw back his drink. 'She was spoiling for a row.'

'Can't say I blame her, the week we've had.' Daniels met his eyes over the top of her glass. 'My birthday bash have anything to do with it?'

Gormley blushed. 'As good a reason as any to give me earache.'

Daniels grimaced. 'Things are no better then?'

'It's over for us, Kate.'

'I'm sorry, I shouldn't have called you.'

'Don't be daft.' Gormley knew where he'd rather be right now. 'It was a mistake to think we could make it work. It's not fair on Ryan to drag it out any longer. Anyway, I didn't come here for marriage guidance. What's going on?'

'The guv'nor's not too well. When I left him tonight he was on his way to see a neurosurgeon at the Conrad Clinic. Apparently he's been having violent headaches and intermittent double vision.'

'He gets that every night in the Bridge.' Gormley grinned.

The Bridge was a public house close to the station that neither of them liked very much. It had recently become popular among police personnel following a major refurb. And not before time.

'Not funny, Hank. They want him to have a brain scan.'

Gormley's grin disappeared.

25

Jessica Finch was in a state of semi-consciousness, blood dripping from her wrists where the shackles dug into her skin. Moving her head to the right, she stared at the black hole at the end of the hollow chamber. There was no doubt in her mind that she was below ground. She wondered how he—or was it they?—had managed to get her down here, why they'd taken her and how long they planned to leave her there alone.

Jessica shivered as a ghost walked over her skin. In these extremely cold conditions she knew she could only survive for a few days without liquid. She moistened her lips, driven crazy by the sight of water running down the opposite wall.

Dehydration: the silent killer.

As a med student, she'd seen both sides of the medical debate: those that thought that death by dehydration was serene, that it could, and should be, used in a voluntary capacity to end a life; others who thought the process unimaginably painful and cruel. The awareness of what would happen to her body if she were to remain in captivity without sustenance made Jessica cry tears she could ill afford to waste. In a fight for survival she would suffer extreme thirst, dizziness, severe stomach cramps, hallucinations, shut-down of the circulatory system as the body pushed blood to vital organs in order to keep her alive.

Coma.

Death.

Serene?

She didn't feel serene.

Her mouth was parched, her saliva thick, her head pounding. How long before she couldn't speak? Couldn't cry because her tears had dried up? She urged her captors to return and yet feared what they might do to her. The sound in the chamber was torturous. Constant and hollow, enough to drive a sane person mad.

Drip.

Drip.

Drip.

Quicker now?

Water rising?

It was raining outside—SHIT!

The bulb in the miner's lamp flickered . . .

And went out.

26

Ellen Crawford showed Daniels into the room, then retreated to her own office, closing the door behind her. Bright was sitting at his desk engrossed in his work, highlighting text in a report.

'Take a seat, Kate.' He didn't look up. 'I'll be with you in one second.'

Daniels couldn't figure what mood he was in. He seemed relaxed and she assumed his appointment with the consultant had gone well. She sat down, crossed her legs and glanced around the room, wondering if she'd ever occupy the rank and post that came with it.

Force Crime Manager.

She liked the sound of that.

Signing off on his document, a modest signature that didn't quite fit with his colourful personality, Bright put down his pen and sat back in his chair. 'What's up?'

'I was just passing, wondered how you went on last night.'

'Since when does a ten-mile detour qualify as "just passing"?' he asked, appreciating her concern. 'The scan was clear. I'll live, apparently.'

'That's great news, guv! I can't tell you how relieved I am.'

'I'm touched.'

'You should be ecstatic!'

'Except the consultant hasn't got a bloody clue what's causing the headaches. Not yet, anyway.' A frown formed on his brow. 'You know what the cheeky git asked me?'

Daniels waited.

Bright made a crazed face. 'Was I under any stress?'

Daniels searched his face. He looked very tired and she was concerned he was doing too much. Stress was cumulative. Dangerous even. It crept up on people when they least expected it to, silent symptoms, like a charged bomb waiting to explode.

'What?' Bright said. 'You're making me nervous.'

Daniels drew her chair a little closer to his desk. 'I know you don't want to hear this, but I'm going to say it anyway, guv. You've had a hell of a time the last six months, one way or another. Stella's death . . .' She could see he didn't want a lecture.

'Well, let's face it, you feel responsible, even though you're not. That's bound to have an effect on your general health. Your headaches are probably the result of that and of carrying this department under difficult circumstances for far too long. Trouble with you is you're too stubborn to seek professional help. If you want my honest opinion, the consultant you saw is probably spot on.'

'You quite finished?'

Daniels spread her hands. 'It needed to be said.'

'And if you repeat it outside of these four walls, you and I will fall out big time!'

'C'mon, guv. You know me better than that. You're doing two jobs at a time when you should be—'

'What? What *should* I be doing, Kate?' Bright was angry now and it showed. He was like a coiled spring, tapping his fingers on the desk. 'Relaxing with my feet up? Going out of my mind with boredom in an empty house I can no longer bear to live in?'

'I was talking about the job, guv. Delegate some of your stuff to me. Let me take the weight off you for a bit, at least until they've found your replacement. And if the headaches continue, then at least you'll know it isn't work-related.'

'No. You've got enough on your plate already.'

'Then I'll give Hank more responsibility. He's up for it. What harm can it do?'

'No. This stays between me and you, understood?'

'He's your mate, for Christ's sake!'

'You already told him, didn't you?'

Daniels looked out of the window.

27

The door was marked Major Incident Suite. Kate Daniels swiped her warrant card to gain access. She entered the room to find the briefing already underway with Gormley holding the fort. He was standing beside a state-of-the-art digital screen. It was in pause mode, showing a crime-scene photograph on one side and details of the deceased, Amy Grainger, on the other.

He raised a questioning eyebrow as she approached. Turning away from the others, he dropped his voice and asked, 'How is he?'

'Just as awkward as ever,' she whispered.

Gormley grinned. 'I'll get worried when he starts being civil.'

Andy Brown arrived in a panic, his face matching his strawberry blond hair when he realized they'd started without him. There'd been an accident on the southbound carriageway near the Angel of the North, forcing him to make a five-mile detour to get into town. He apologized, asking Daniels if there was any chance he could swap with Robson. Grinning, he peeled off his coat.

'I much preferred it at High Shaw,' he said as he sat down.

Someone made a vulgar joke about sheep-shaggers and everyone laughed.

Daniels was keen to move on. She looked at Gormley. 'You told them yet?'

He shook his head and sat down too, signalling for the squad to pay attention.

'I have some very good news.' Daniels informed

the squad that Matt West in Forensics had come up trumps again. 'Trace evidence on the shoe Amy Grainger was wearing is unique to the North Pennines. We find out exactly where and there's a good chance we find Jessica Finch.' There was a ripple of excitement in the room, everyone conscious of how significant a lead that was. 'Dave Weldon, one of Hank's many mates, actually heads up the Fell Rescue Team. He knows the area like the back of his hand and we think he'll be able to act as an advisor.'

'I tried his mobile,' Gormley said. 'No joy. Coverage up there is pants.'

'Send a car right away. We need him down here.'

'Quicker if I go myself,' Gormley said. 'I know exactly where he hangs out and you need a bloody compass to find it. It'll only take me an hour to get there and I can brief him and pick up any detailed maps we might need.'

Daniels hesitated, telling him she'd planned for him to accompany her to the Mansion House to interview Adam Finch's staff. Carmichael sprang up, volunteering to go instead, a pleading look in her eyes.

It made sense.

'OK, you're on.' Daniels turned back to Gormley: 'Meet back here at two?'

28

The old Methodist Chapel looked frozen in time, unchanged since it was built in the 1800s. There was a sign on the door: BACK AT 10.30 but there was no one around. Gormley took a seat on the stone steps out front, checking his watch as a Land Rover Defender 110 drove round the side of the building. It had a long wheelbase, perfect for driving over rough terrain, and lettering on the side: North Pennines Fell Rescue. Dave Weldon, a man in his mid-fifties, turned off the engine and jumped down, pointing at Gormley's dusty car. On the offside door, someone had drawn the bumbling cartoon character, Mr Magoo.

Weldon smiled broadly. 'Someone's trying to tell you something, old man.'

The two friends embraced with a hearty slap on the back.

'You're looking good, mate,' Gormley said. 'Fit as ever, I see.'

'Better than you, anyhow,' Weldon's eyes fixed on Gormley's expanding waistline.

The DS inhaled, grinning. 'I need your help, not your diet plan.'

'Thought as much. Howay in.'

Weldon led the way towards the chapel. Inside, Gormley explained the reason behind his visit and the urgency of getting his friend on board. Ten minutes later, armed with detailed maps of the area, they got in the car and drove off down a narrow track and out on to the main road again.

'How's Frances?' Gormley asked.

'You didn't hear?'

Gormley kept his eyes on the road. 'Hear what?'

'She left me for one of them IT types, a dot.com millionaire in fact. Some guy she met on a business trip to Hong Kong.'

'Shit, man. I'm sorry.' Gormley wondered if anyone he knew was capable of holding down a

113

relationship these days. 'Is she still working for HSBC?'

'Yep.'

'She still with him?'

'Nope. He promised her the world and the silly bitch fell for it. Six months later, he dumped her right on her tight little arse.'

Weldon laughed; a little too loudly, Gormley thought. Turning right, he followed a sign for Allenheads, picking up speed on a straight stretch of an otherwise winding road. 'Do you still see her?'

'Nope. I've got plans and she isn't part of them.'

Weldon waved at the driver of an identical Fell Rescue vehicle travelling in the opposite direction. The driver stuck a thumb in the air as he drove by. In his rear-view mirror, Gormley saw brake lights. The Land Rover slowed but he drove on. There wasn't time to stop and chew the fat with one of Weldon's team. He needed to make it to the MIR by two. Besides, Weldon had left a message on the chapel door explaining where he'd gone, letting his own team know he'd be off the radar for a good few hours and what action he wanted them to take.

'I'm emigrating,' Weldon said after a long period of silence.

'Yeah, pull the other one.'

'I'm serious! Soon as the paperwork comes through I'm taking my bike, my boat and my pension and I'm out of here.'

'Where the hell to? Thought Durham was the centre of your universe?'

'The States. I'm setting up a business running motorcycle tours over there: bikes, route maps, the whole nine yards. It's time I lived a little.'

'Sounds like the dog's bollocks,' Gormley said wistfully. 'I hope it works out.'

'To be honest, I need a bit more cash and a partner to set it up properly.' Weldon glanced sideways. 'You don't fancy putting in some of your hard-earned and riding off into the sunset? I assume you're still riding?'

'Not for years,' Gormley said, with some regret. 'Julie insisted I give it up in case Ryan got interested. I felt I had no choice.'

'You are joking!' Weldon went quiet again.

The image of Kate Daniels' Yamaha Fazer popped into Gormley's head. The last time he'd seen a motorcycle, it was hers. It was parked on its own at Hartside Pass in the depths of winter, a trip she'd taken during a particularly difficult case. He glanced at Weldon, trying to shake the image from his thoughts.

Gormley felt that an explanation was warranted. 'I'd never have forgiven myself if anything had happened to Ryan. Maybe Julie had a point.'

Weldon disagreed. 'Bloody women! I tell you, if I had to make a choice between my bike and a lass, any lass . . .' He twisted an imaginary throttle. 'No contest, mate. The bike wins, hands down.'

'My boss rides.' Gormley's thoughts were back at Hartside.

'Maybe I should ask him to join me,' Weldon said. 'Is he close to retirement?'

Gormley shook his head and kept on driving.

29

Daniels heard the distinct sound of a lawn mower as she wandered through patio doors and out into the sunshine. The view from the impressive terrace was spectacular, with gardens designed to perfection: geometric lawns bordered with clipped hedges; paths leading the eye through a variety of plant-rich shrubberies; sculptures, water features including a perfectly symmetrical manmade lake with a fountain in the middle, the tip of its spout just touching the horizon.

It was timeless.

A middle-aged gardener glanced up in her direction as she sat down next to Adam Finch at a table in the shade. He was staring off into the distance, seemingly unaware of her presence. Or so she thought.

'You want him to stop?' Finch didn't look at her.

'No, that's not necessary. I'll speak to Mr Townsend shortly, along with the rest of your staff. First I'd like to talk to you about Jessica.'

'What about her?'

'Were you close?

'For God's sake!' Finch turned, his eyes boring into her. He rubbed at his temple, apologized for his quick temper. 'What the *hell* are they waiting for? Why don't they make further contact?'

'You think there's more than one person involved?'

'He, they, what difference does it make?'

'Can we concentrate on what we *do* know for a second.' The DCI tried to sound sympathetic even though deep down she didn't trust him. 'All crime investigations begin with a study of the victim, sir. It's important that I get to know Jess, and I can only do that through you.'

'Her name is Jessica!' he barked. 'And with all due respect, this isn't getting us anywhere. Shouldn't you be out there searching instead of asking me bloody silly questions?'

'Well, therein lies the problem. It's a question of where we start looking.'

Daniels wondered if the trace evidence Matt West had identified as green fluorspar would give them a clue as to Jessica's whereabouts. The North Pennines was a massive area and searching it would be a nightmare. Surreptitiously, she glanced at her watch, hoping Gormley had made contact with Dave Weldon. Adam Finch got up and wandered away from the table. He spoke with his back to her.

'There are no skeletons in my cupboard, DCI Daniels. Ask your boss.'

Daniels intended to do just that. She was convinced Finch wasn't being honest. Then again, what father would admit to a rift with their only child under the circumstances he was facing? For all his faults, she knew hers wouldn't.

Carmichael appeared in the doorway. Daniels held up a hand, spreading her fingers, indicating five more minutes. She needn't have bothered. Adam Finch couldn't think of anyone he'd made an enemy of, anyone at all who'd wish him or Jessica any harm. In fact, nothing he said took her any further forward.

Leaving him on the patio, she wandered down into the garden to speak to Townsend. She was

117

halfway along the path when Carmichael caught up with her.

'Any luck?' she said.

'None . . .' Daniels spotted movement in a semi-shaded area off to their left. She steered Carmichael towards it, their feet crunching across the gravel as they walked. 'He's either deliberately being evasive or he's simply too preoccupied with the threats to answer a straight question. For the moment, I wouldn't like to say which.'

The estate gardener had stopped mowing and was now busy cutting back tree peonies that stood either side of a gated entrance to a walled garden, so a wooden sign proclaimed.

'Brian Townsend?'

'Who wants to know?' The man didn't look up.

'Detective Chief Inspector Daniels and Detective Constable Carmichael. Can we have a word?'

Townsend stood upright, running his eyes over the detectives. He was a well-built man with chiselled features and deep-set eyes. He was wearing a tool belt around his waist and a red peaked cap with a faded *Coke Is It* motif on the front.

'You're here about young Miss Jessica, I take it.'

Daniels nodded.

'Terrible business.'

It surprised Daniels to learn that Adam Finch had warned his staff she was coming, much less confided in them the details of his daughter's disappearance. Maybe she'd misjudged him. Maybe he wasn't such a frosty man with people he knew well.

'How long have you worked here, Mr

Townsend?'

'Far *too* long, ma'am.'

Daniels registered the man's cynicism. 'Mr Finch is an exacting boss, is he?'

'None of us minds hard work, ma'am.' His eye strayed to a rogue branch above their heads. He raised a pair of secateurs and clipped it off. 'A little kindness and respect now and then wouldn't go amiss. We ask no more than that.'

'Are you telling me—'

'I'm telling you nowt, ma'am. And that's all I know—nowt! Now, I must get on.'

They detained Townsend from his work for a while longer, establishing that he hadn't seen Jessica Finch since early January, when her term began. They told him they might want to speak to him again and then went up to the big house. They found Mrs Partridge ready and waiting in the kitchen. It was a massive room with a cast-iron cooking range in the centre of a wall covered in white brick-shaped tiles. Above the range a collection of brass cooking pots hung on hooks in order of size, tapering off with the smallest on the left. To the right of them, steam rose from a double Belfast sink where Mrs Partridge had just finished washing up. She hadn't been wearing gloves and her hands were red raw when she lifted them out of the water, her engagement ring glistening through the suds.

Mrs Partridge dried her hands on a dishcloth and hung it above the range to dry, telling them she'd been housekeeper there for several years since her predecessor finally hung up her apron and moved on. Daniels' eyes were drawn to an old-fashioned tapestry hanging on one wall with the words *Home*

119

Sweet Home written on it. When she turned back, the housekeeper was pouring tea from a large aluminium pot and Carmichael was eyeing a plate of sultana scones that were fresh from the oven.

'Help yourself,' the housekeeper said.

Carmichael took one, inhaling as she lifted it to her nose. 'Mmm, haven't smelled grub like this since I lived with my aunt.'

The housekeeper pushed a pot of home-made raspberry jam in her direction. She handed Carmichael a solid silver teaspoon.

Daniels pointed at a photograph of a young girl on the opposite wall to the tapestry.

'Granddaughter?' she said.

'Daughter,' Mrs Partridge smiled. 'I have no grandchildren.'

'Bet she appreciates your cooking . . .' Carmichael didn't look up. She was too busy biting her scone and washing it down with a gulp of tea. 'You should try one, boss. They're excellent.'

Daniels gave her a look: they were there to work, not chat.

Taking her cue, Carmichael wiped crumbs from her lips and asked, 'How long has Tom Pearce been the chauffeur?'

'About four years, give or take.' Mrs Partridge thought for a moment. 'It could even be five, come to think of it. He knew Mr Finch from when they were in the army together.'

'And how long ago was that?' Daniels wanted more. Finch's association with Bright still bothered her. She couldn't understand why her former guv'nor had chosen not to disclose their regiment the minute he'd found out about the MO in the Amy Grainger case. Mrs Partridge's answer

120

interrupted her chain of thought.

'Must be a good ten years since Mr Finch resigned his commission.'

'And he'd kept in touch with Pearce all that time?' Carmichael asked.

Mrs Partridge giggled as if the question had been daft. 'Oh no, dear. Mr Finch is an important man, the landed gentry if you will.' She looked around, making sure she couldn't be overheard. 'Dear me, no. If I remember correctly, Tom saw an article about Mr Finch in the local paper and wrote to him asking for work. He was down on his luck, you see. Yes, I'm sure that was it. Mr Finch had just lost his driver and, well, it was fortuitous for them both as it turned out.'

Daniels asked, 'Have you seen or heard of Jessica since she left for university?'

The housekeeper looked at the floor.

'Mrs Partridge?'

'I've had a text or two.'

Daniels' interest grew. 'Can you recall when you last heard from her?'

'It was a few weeks ago. But that's not unusual . . .' Mrs Partridge began to fidget, wringing her hands in her lap. 'Mr Finch doesn't need to know, does he? I'm not sure he would approve, you see. In fact, he definitely would not. He spends a lot of time away on business and I've been like a mother to Jess over the years. We get on well and she always remembers birthdays, sends me Christmas cards, that sort of thing. She's a very thoughtful girl. I do hope she hasn't come to any harm.'

An image of Amy Grainger lying on wet ground in the middle of nowhere popped into Daniels' head, every detail etched on her brain: her green sightless eyes, a pool of settled blood beneath her left ear, one shoe missing. Daniels knew it was a long shot, but she was hoping that the discovery of an unusual mineral in the heel of that shoe was the key that would eventually unlock the door on the enquiry. A definite clue. Something she could work with.

Half a chance at least of saving Jessica's life.

Mrs Partridge had picked up on her anxiety. The woman was staring at her now, no doubt fearing the worst. Daniels forced a smile, wondering how close the housekeeper really was to Jessica and whether she might know things others were keeping quiet about.

'Does Jessica have a boyfriend?' she asked.

Mrs Partridge glanced again at the open kitchen door. 'Rob, his name's Rob.'

'Surname?'

'Lester. But please keep me out of this. I need this job. I can't afford to lose it.'

'Do you know where Jess is currently living?'

Another guilty look. 'I'm aware she moved out of halls, but no more than that.'

'Is Rob Lester with her?'

'I'm not sure.'

'She didn't want her father finding out? Is that it?'

Mrs Partridge made no comment.

'Am I at least getting warm?' Daniels pushed.

A resigned nod followed.

They thanked the housekeeper and left via the servants' entrance. Outside, the sun was shining and it was really warm for the time of year. Summer was on its way. They passed through a pretty gateway, its uprights covered with budding

122

clematis, then out of the rear courtyard and along a path Mrs Partridge had told them would lead them back to their car. Daniels looked at her watch. There was enough time to find Rob Lester before meeting Gormley at two.

30

Durham University School of Medicine and Health was located at the Queen's Campus in Stockton, around twenty miles south-east of Durham City itself. Daniels parked the Toyota right outside on double yellow lines and asked Lisa Carmichael to wait in the car.

'Move it if necessary. I don't intend being long,' she said.

She got out and stood for a moment looking up at the building. John Snow College—named after the nineteenth-century Yorkshire obstetrician to Queen Victoria—was a modern, purpose-built affair with a waterside location on the south bank of the river Tees. Impressive too, Daniels thought, as she walked through the front door.

Inside the main entrance, Jessica's personal tutor was waiting to greet her. Maria Wilson was a lady nearing retirement age. She had funky, spiky, dyed red hair peeping out from a purple and blue headscarf which she had tied with a bow at a natty angle, floppy ends hanging loose over her brow. Very cheerful and arty. Much like the woman herself. She was anxious about Jessica and keen to assist in any way she could.

'I was horrified to learn she'd gone missing, and

so soon after the death of poor Amy Grainger.'
Maria told Daniels that the whole university
community had been stunned by recent events.
Her peers were holding their collective breath that
Jess hadn't suffered the same fate. 'If there is
anything we can do, anything at all, just ask.'

'Do you happen to know who her close friends
were?'

'I'm sorry, I don't. Jessica was a sociable girl, I'm
sure, but her dealings with me were purely
academic. I'm certain no student, or indeed staff
member, has heard from her though, or they'd
have come forward by now. We put a poster up
with the telephone number of your incident room
in case anyone wanted to ring you in confidence.'

'That's really kind.' Daniels wished the public
were always this helpful. 'Was Jessica the type to
go off without telling someone first?'

'I wouldn't have said so.' Maria Wilson sighed.
'She always struck me as such a level-headed
student. It's in the genes, I guess. I take it you've
met her father. He's a formidable man, if ever I
saw one.'

Deflecting her away from Finch, Daniels asked
about the boyfriend. 'I've been led to believe
Jessica was close to a fellow student, though I
gather it wasn't common knowledge. I'd like to
speak with Rob Lester as a matter of urgency. It's
possible he may have been the last person to have
seen her before she disappeared. If you could see
your way to supplying his contact details, I'd
appreciate that.'

The woman left the room and came back a few
minutes later with a sheet of paper in her hand.
Daniels took it from her, scanning the document,

noting a mobile number in a box on the right.

She pulled out her phone, began entering it into the keypad.

'If you want to speak to him now,' Ms Wilson interrupted, 'I'll point him out to you.'

Daniels stopped dialling. 'You know where he is?'

Maria glanced to the left. 'He's right outside.'

She led Daniels to the window. The campus grounds were full of students taking time out on perfect lawns, enjoying unseasonably good weather. Some were reading, others sleeping, Robert Lester in their midst. He was a handsome young man with exquisite skin. He wore dreadlocks, collar-length, tied at the nape of his neck, one or two shorter braids hanging loose around his face.

Daniels thanked Maria Wilson and left the building immediately. Seconds later, she approached a group of four students and held up ID. 'Rob Lester?' She smiled as he looked up. 'Could you spare a moment?'

Robert Lester put down his book: Graham Poll, *Seeing Red*. On the front cover was a photograph of the author holding up his right hand, whistle at the ready—a warning look on his face. Seeing red was something Daniels knew a lot about. In her years in the police force she'd witnessed the descent of the red mist on numerous occasions, more often as not from violent offenders and occasionally from those charged with bringing them to justice. It was hard not to let the job get to you sometimes.

Lester's friends made themselves scarce. Picking up their belongings, they scarpered to the edge of the freshly mown lawn where they gathered in a huddle, just far enough away to allow Daniels space to do her job but near enough to hear every word being said. The DCI sat down in the space they had vacated, feeling the warmth of the sun on her back.

'I'm sorry to interrupt your break.' She gestured towards a triangular cellophane packet on the ground. 'Don't mind me if you want to finish that. I'd like to ask you some questions about Jessica, if that's OK, purely for information purposes, nothing at all for you to worry about. I gather you haven't seen or heard from her for some time. Is that right?'

A slight nod—almost imperceptible.

Lester pushed away the half-eaten sandwich.

His eyes grew sad.

'When exactly did you last see her?'

'About eight o'clock, Tuesday.'

'The fourth?'

Lester nodded.

'Night or morning?'

'Night.' He wiped a tear from his cheek and cleared his throat. 'I'm sorry, we both had a free afternoon so we went for a walk down at the river and a bite to eat. Then I took her home to her place. We had a quick coffee and I left pretty much straight away. I had revision to do, y'know, stuff I'd been avoiding.'

'And you didn't call her after that?'

Lester shook his head. 'She was getting an early night.'

'What kind of young woman is she?'

Lester raised his head, light filling his bloodshot eyes. 'She's brilliant. Not just academically but a brilliant person too. We're on the same med course. You think something awful has happened to her, don't you?'

'That's what I'm trying to find out. The more information I have, the quicker I can get on with it.' Daniels tried not to sound alarmist. 'Would you describe Jessica as happy?'

'Now she is.' The student hesitated. 'She was a bit withdrawn when she started her course last year, wasn't really sure what branch of medicine she wanted to study. This term she really got into it though, said she could see herself being a regular doctor, making a difference in the Third World. She has plans to go to Africa, but her father doesn't approve. He wants her to be a surgeon like his father was.'

'You're more than just good friends?'

'Yes, we are. Something else her father disapproved of.'

'Why was that?'

'Isn't it obvious?'

'You're suggesting he's a racist?' Daniels said, considering motive.

Lester was struggling for composure now. He looked away and didn't answer. His fellow students were still keeping watch, their fingers hovering over their mobiles. Daniels had to be careful not to give anything away that might make a social media network and queer her pitch. She asked Lester to walk with her. When they were out of earshot of the others, they danced around the subject of Adam Finch until the young man finally lost his cool.

He didn't even try to hide his contempt. 'The guy's a control freak. We've had to keep our relationship a secret. You have no idea what that's like.'

Daniels knew exactly what it was like. 'Is that why she moved out of halls?'

Lester nodded.

'You have a key to Jess's accommodation?'

'I've told you, she's not there!'

'I believe you, Rob. All the same, I must check it out. I take it nothing's been touched in her digs since she disappeared?'

'No, nothing, as far as I can tell,' he said, his voice softer than before.

'Is it far from here?'

'She commutes from Durham, unless she's staying over with me.' He dug deep into his pocket and pulled out a bunch of keys, removing one from a VW key ring. Handing it to the DCI, his eyes misted over as if he were about to cry. 'She was happy in halls until her father stuck his nose in. He thinks we've split up.' He took in Daniels' nod. 'She loves Durham. She loves the cobbled streets, the shops. She's really into the history and culture of the place. We spend a lot of time there.'

Daniels took down the address, a flat in Old Elvet. She thanked him, saying she'd be in touch, and walked briskly back to her car.

31

Twenty minutes later, Daniels entered the Durham City charge zone. The county council had levied a congestion charge between the hours of ten a.m. to four p.m.—a traffic and pollution

128

reduction measure aimed at improving air quality in the heavily pedestrianized streets.

'Or so the blurb would have people believe,' Daniels said.

'It's just another stealth tax . . .' Carmichael moaned. She unclipped her seat belt as Daniels parked the car. 'It's bloody ridiculous. Can't we have one of them exemption permits?'

'What's up with you? It's two quid. We can claim it back!'

'I've got news for you, boss. We didn't even need to be here. You should've turned left back there.'

'I need an ice cream and some fresh air.'

'I bet you know where to get one too.'

Daniels grinned.

Parking on a double-yellow, she chucked a POLICE sign in the window and got out. She waited for Carmichael to follow suit, then locked the car and slipped on her sunglasses against the midday sun. It felt good to have contact with the outside world, to feel the warmth of the sun on her face and the breeze through her hair, to be mingling with civilians for once. She'd spent far too long in her car in the past few days, and she hated the way it made her feel.

She led Carmichael down some steps to the riverside, then they nipped into a shop and bought an ice cream, which they ate as they wandered back up the steps, turning left across Elvet Bridge with its cobbled stones.

'Ever been in there?' Carmichael asked, pointing at the Swan and Three Cygnets public house, a great place to sit out and watch the world go by.

'Couple of times.' Daniels took another lick of her ice cream. 'When you work with Hank, you get to see the inside of most pubs eventually.'

At the traffic lights, they crossed the road into Old Elvet. On the left-hand side there was an ancient pub with a tiny front door, so small Gormley would have to duck his head to enter. Jessica's flat was a really old property right next door. They let themselves in, unsure what to expect.

'Bloody hell!' Carmichael said as she walked through the door. 'Is she for real?'

Daniels looked sideways. 'How d'you mean?'

'Well, this!' Carmichael swept her arm around the immacu-late room. 'Have you *ever* seen student accommodation look quite this orderly? Mind you, I'd have thought her old man would've bankrolled a better pad than this one. That Mansion House was something else, wasn't it? I guess this could be construed as slumming it for her.'

'Maybe she wasn't interested in a better pad.' Daniels opened the door to the only cupboard in a room no bigger than a prison cell. Jessica's clothes hung from a rail, all ironed to perfection, dark shades to the left through to white on the right and all colours in between. 'Maybe she just wanted to fit in. Be normal like other students on her course.'

'Yeah, right, like *they'd* be any different!'

'Rob Lester isn't posh. And he's a nice quiet lad, from what I could tell.'

'That him?' Carmichael pointed at a photograph on the wall.

Daniels nodded.

'Well, he might be the exception—'

'Bring that with you. We might need it.'

Carmichael bagged the photograph, set it to one

side, then got down on her knees to look under the bed. There was a suitcase underneath and she began rifling through it: keepsakes mainly, photos, trinkets, letters posted from all over the globe, a pressed daisy chain.

'You don't get many med students from socially deprived areas, not any I've ever come across,' Carmichael said. 'Even though they'll tell you otherwise, there's still a class divide in academic institutions.'

Daniels ignored the comment, too busy with her own search. A mini chest, each drawer packed with clean socks and multi-coloured underwear, pyjamas right at the very bottom. On top of the chest was a course timetable, a medical textbook and a three-ring binder. Daniels opened it. Jessica had typed up all her lecture and tutorial notes and put them neatly in chronological order, the last sheet dated Monday the third of May. Carmichael had gone back to the wardrobe, was moving clothing along the rail and rummaging through pockets.

'Remember that kid a couple of years ago?' she said. 'The brilliant one who had the best grades and applied to Oxford? *She* was turned down. Ended up going to America to study! Now what's fair about that? If I'd been her mother I'd have had something to say about it.'

Daniels moved to the desk.

At last, a junk drawer.

'You listening to me, boss? Or should I shut my trap and get on with it?'

'No, stay on your soapbox, Lisa. I'd hate to cramp your style.' It was a nice way of saying *shut the fuck up*.

131

Daniels smiled to herself, more interested in the contents of the drawer in front of her. She removed it from the desk completely and set it down on the bed. There were various documents inside: an appointment with a dental surgeon for a date in the future, a donor card with Jessica's name on it, detailed information from international, medical and humanitarian aid organization Médecins Sans Frontières and some personal mail from Rob Lester—raunchy stuff that made her blush.

She sifted through some Barclays Bank statements, noting that Jessica received a monthly allowance of one thousand pounds from her father's account, which was more than generous if her balance was anything to go by. On the most recent statement, there were several entries she couldn't immediately identify, quite a large one—five hundred pounds—to an extreme sports organization, a regular transfer to another account in Jessica's name within the same bank, and generous donations to MSF (UK).

As far as she could tell, Jessica Finch spent very little on herself.

Further back in the drawer, Daniels found a neat pile of ATM withdrawal slips securely fastened in a giant paper-clip, timed and dated from a machine she assumed might be close to the university. Pocket money really—no more than a few pounds—enough to keep her going for a day or two at a time. The most recent one, a withdrawal of twenty pounds dispensed at just after nine o'clock on the morning of Sunday, 2 May.

Jessica Finch obviously wasn't keen to carry large amounts of cash around. Neither was she as gung-ho in life as her father would have Daniels believe. No. Her financial accounts drew a very different picture, of a young woman who was not only organized and methodical but cautious and caring too.

32

They arrived back at the Major Incident Room with only minutes to spare. The room was a hive of activity with the majority of the murder investigation team hard at it. Gormley was busy taking a call on his mobile and had left Dave Weldon to fend for himself. The ex-detective had helped himself to a cup of coffee and was standing like a spare part with nothing to do. He stuck out like a sore thumb.

It was unusual to see a civilian in the room.

Carmichael went off to find Harry Graham, the receiver. Daniels watched her go and then moved towards Weldon, extending her hand. 'Dave, I'm Kate Daniels, SIO. Hank's told me a lot about you. Nice to have you on board . . .' She pointed to a rolled-up map he was carrying. 'That our search area?'

' 'Fraid so.' Weldon handed her the map. 'I'm happy to help for as long as it takes.'

'Has he filled you in?'

Weldon nodded.

'Everything?'

Looking up from his call, Gormley put a thumb in the air. Daniels used her hands as winders, urging him to get off the phone. Ignoring her request, he got up from his desk and wandered away in the direction of her office. The call was obviously important, so she decided to begin without him.

'OK everybody, switch off your mobiles and pay attention.' She raised her voice above the din in the room and waited for the chatter to die down. 'I'd like to introduce you all to Dave Weldon from Fell Rescue, an expert in his field. Hank tells me he's worked the search area for almost a decade since he took his bit and packed in a proper job as a police officer.'

There were grins all round.

Someone shouted out: 'Silly bugger.'

Someone else followed with: 'Any vacancies?'

Weldon smiled, enjoying the banter.

Unrolling the map, Daniels attached it to the murder wall so everyone in the room could see it. 'This—' she pointed to a specific place on the map—'is the area we're most interested in based on information received from Matt West.' She turned to face Weldon. 'Assuming we have no other choice but to carry out an intensive search, can you estimate how long it'll take?'

'That's a hard one. This whole area is a honeycomb of tunnels extending to around a hundred or so square miles. Some of the mines are a mile in length and many are flooded. Given the obvious danger of rockfalls it's bound to be a slow process. If the IP is being hidden below ground it could take weeks or even months to find her.'

His reference to the injured party made Daniels' heart ache for a young girl she'd never even met. The atmosphere in the room plummeted as the grim reality of a search in the North Pennines hit home. Through the glass window of her office door, she could see Gormley was now sitting on her desk, still on the phone, deep in conversation.

'How d'you want to play this?' Weldon asked.

'I'm proposing your volunteers work in conjunction with the Tactical Support Group. Your guys have the expertise, after all. We'll take our lead from you.'

'Suits me,' Weldon said. 'I've already left instructions at our base. My team will take note of temporary shelters, signs of life in odd locations, that sort of thing. They're awaiting further instructions.'

Daniels liked his proactive style. Dave Weldon was a man after her own heart, not content to sit back and wait to be told when and how to act. He was a doer, as well as a thinker. It sounded like he was on top of things already and she appreciated that.

'Assuming Jessica is still alive, what are her chances?' Carmichael asked.

Weldon's expression was grave. 'Hard to say. Those mines are wet and pitch-black. If she's far enough in, she could scream until her lungs burst and never be heard. It's a desolate place at the best of times. Temperature below ground, even in summer, is bloody cold. If it continues to rain . . . well, I'm sure I don't need to draw you guys any pictures—'

'Assuming a worst-case scenario,' Daniels interrupted, 'and by that I mean that she's not receiving any form of nourishment at all, how long might she survive?'

Weldon outlined cases where people had somehow managed to hold on for much longer than expected and gave a few examples, the recent Haiti earthquake victims being just one. His comments lifted her spirits and reminded her of the payment reference to an extreme sports organization found in Jessica's room. Privately she began to speculate as to how fit the girl might be. Adam Finch had told her that his daughter was 'a wonderful free spirit, wilful to the point of being downright obstinate.' Hoping that those characteristics would enhance her chances of survival, Daniels turned to face Weldon again, thinking more positively now.

'You know about the trace evidence found at the scene, the mineral deposit on the dead girl's shoe?'

Weldon nodded, but his eyes were on Gormley, who had wandered back into the room with his mobile phone still stuck to his ear.

'Will that help you at all?' Daniels pushed.

'That's beyond my expertise. You'll need a geologist's opinion for that.'

And no bullshitter either.

Daniels knew she and Weldon were destined to get along. Carmichael was already logging on to her computer, her fingers flying over the keys accessing the Crime Faculty database looking for an expert geologist—hopefully one who could narrow down the search area. Maybe it wasn't all doom and gloom. Maybe things were looking up.

Gormley hung up, a sober expression on his face.

'What?' Daniels held her breath.

'He's got another one, boss. Rachel Somers, twenty years old.'

33

The witness was quite clear . . .

'I could tell they didn't know each other by the way he was looking at her.'

Daniels knew exactly what he meant by that.

Gormley did too.

'And you're sure it was Rachel Somers?' Daniels repeated.

Riley Archer nodded, a heavy fringe flopping over slate-grey eyes. He was a pleasant-looking lad: good skin, intelligent eyes, quite small in stature. Not someone who could easily overpower a taller individual, Daniels thought, particularly if that person happened to put up a good fight. Archer seemed relaxed surrounded by officers from the murder investigation team.

Any further laid back and he'd end up horizontal.

He had given detectives a very detailed description, claiming to have known Rachel Somers since junior school. He described her as tall, blonde, a Durham University student. In other words, a dead ringer for Jessica Finch and Amy Grainger. For that reason, and that reason only, Daniels had taken the unprecedented step of allowing her team to hear his evidence first-hand. Time was of the essence and she needed to be sure it was a positive ID. She brought the squad to attention, inviting Archer to tell them all exactly what he'd seen.

'I was sitting in my car waiting for a mate at our usual pickup point close to the Testo's roundabout,' he began. 'Three of us, including

Rachel, car share. Saves a shitload of money we haven't got.'

'And this was Friday—the seventh?'

Archer nodded. 'Rachel rang me earlier, said she wasn't feeling too good, asked if I'd let our course tutor know. Anyway, there was a line of traffic waiting to get on to the A19 and the lorry pulled up right in front of me. I did a double take when I saw her sitting in the cab. I didn't like the way he was looking at her. She seemed kind of shy in his company—'

'Shy, not nervous?' Daniels interrupted. 'There's a distinct difference, Riley. It's critical to be precise.'

'Bit of both, I reckon. But nice nervous rather than unhappy, if you know what I mean. Not like she was agitated and didn't want to be there or anything. Timid is probably a better word to describe her. Y'know, like he was someone she just met.' Riley swept his fringe back off his face. He sighed. 'I'm not explaining myself very well, am I?'

'You're doing great,' Daniels said. 'Did you get a good look at him?'

Riley nodded. 'He was middle-aged. Baseball cap, chiselled face, light V-neck T-shirt . . . stocky, I would've said. Thick neck, y'know what I mean. I only saw head and shoulders, it was difficult to tell.'

Carmichael exchanged a knowing look with Daniels whose mind raced back to the Mansion House, to a gardener's peaked cap and a powerful physique. She logged that thought.

'What colour was the cap?' she asked.

'Red.'

'Was it a plain cap?' Carmichael could hardly

contain her-self.

'No, it was a New York Yankees cap with white lettering. Y'know, the ones with N and Y printed one on top of the other.'

Two red caps and two American motifs. Daniels was getting interested.

'Go on,' she pushed.

But Archer's attention had drifted off. His face drained of all colour and he closed his eyes, suddenly exhausted by all the questions. When he opened them again, he seemed not to have heard a word she'd said.

'Do you need a break, Riley?' Daniels asked.

Archer shook his head. 'His eyes were all over her. I don't know what possessed me, but I sent her a text as he drove away. I got nothing back, so I rang her mobile and it went straight to voicemail. I tried her home number but there was no answer. Her mum works, so I must've missed her. I was about to try Rachel's mobile again when Calum arrived—'

'Calum being the third student?' Gormley queried.

Archer gave a nod. 'He convinced me there was probably an innocent explanation. We drove to Durham as usual, but it bugged me all day. Rachel isn't the type to pull a sickie. I got home around six. At seven, her mother called me asking what time I dropped her off. Rachel had a guitar lesson booked and hadn't come home by the time her music teacher arrived. That's when I knew.' Riley Archer shifted his gaze from Daniels to Gormley and back, a real sadness in his eyes. 'Look, it's all over the campus about the other two girls. I just want to help in any way I can.'

139

Gormley leaned forwards in his seat, elbows on knees, hands clasped together.

'Tell me about the HGV.'

'It was a dark blue flat-back lorry, a Selby firm according to the blurb on the side. Conrad Couriers Limited—'

'You seem quite certain about that.'

'I am. Conrad is my brother's name.'

'And you are *absolutely* certain it was Rachel?'

Archer nodded. 'And no one's seen or heard from her since.'

You could hear a pin drop in the Major Incident Suite. Daniels nodded to Carmichael, who got up and wandered over to her work station to begin making enquiries. Not one member of MIT could believe their luck. Witnesses like Riley Archer were few and far between; a godsend to any murder investigation team. The focus of several pairs of eyes, his expression darkened as he took in the excitement building around him.

Daniels' pulse was racing. 'Do you recall what time you called her on Friday morning?'

'Exactly eight forty-seven.' Archer dug his mobile out of his pocket and offered it to her. 'You can check the sent message details on the phone, if you like. You want the vehicle registration number too?'

*   *   *

Riley Archer was almost bundled out of the MIR. Before the door closed behind him, Carmichael hit the keyboard, typing in Conrad Couriers in an effort to identify the man last seen with Rachel Somers. Carmichael studied the company profile closely as the rest of the team gathered round, the DCI included. They ran a heavy goods delivery service and their head office was in Selby. Daniels could see from the website what type of fleet they used: ordinary lorries with open backs.

'Get them on the phone, Lisa. I'll be in my office.'

Daniels walked away, Gormley following close behind. He was like a coiled spring, desperate to jump in the car and lock the fucker up. But he was nervous too. Painfully aware that another girl's life might be at stake. The phone rang before either of them sat down.

Daniels snatched up the phone.

'This is them,' Carmichael said. 'Guy on the other end is called Alistair.'

The line clicked.

Daniels sighed. *It was time to make up the truth again.*

'Alistair, thanks for your time.' Her tone was casual, friendly. 'This is Gateshead traffic department, Northumbria Police. We've had a complaint that a metal drum fell off the back of one of your lorries on Friday and hit a car. There wasn't much damage and no personal injury, so it's not too serious. But I'd like to know who the driver was, the route taken, et cetera, see if we can clear the matter up.'

She gave the registration number.

The member of staff apologized, went off to check and then named the employee as Mark Harris. That was the good news. The bad news was, Harris was away down south on another job and not expected back at the depot until next morning. Then he had another job up in Stockton.

'Tomorrow, you say?' Daniels winced. She'd repeated it back for Gormley's benefit. 'Any particular time?'

'He's due to leave here at nine. Look, I can't give out Harris's address or anything, not without authorization from my boss. I'd get my head in my hands to play with. You should meet her. She's like a Rottweiler. Always banging on about data protection, but I'm sure you know all about that, doing your job. And I must point out that supplying information in no way constitutes an admission of guilt. What did you say your name was again?'

'I didn't. Listen, you've been a great help. Don't concern yourself over it. I'll give Mr Harris a bell, probably tomorrow night because I'm on shifts. There's no hurry. These things happen sometimes. Whenever he's free is fine. And Alistair . . . I'd like you to keep this between the two of us for now, unless you think I should speak to the Rottweiler.'

The clerk hesitated. 'Is that necessary?'

'You gonna mention this phone call?'

'What phone call is that?'

'That was the right answer.' Daniels hung up.

Gormley was sulking.

'Don't worry,' she told him. 'We'll get the jump on him first thing tomorrow. Harris has no idea he was clocked by Riley in his truck with Rachel. He's hardly going to make a run for it, is he?'

34

Daniels got home late, had something to eat and went straight to bed, a guaranteed recipe for a sleepless night. When her alarm went off at six, she turned on the radio and stumbled into the shower, trying to energize herself for the day ahead. Similarly sleep-deprived, Gormley rang at six thirty. When he offered to pick her up and act as chauffeur for the day, she jumped at the chance.

They made good time. Conrad Couriers was situated close to the A63 Selby bypass. Neither of them could wait to get there and Gormley had committed a number of moving traffic offences along the way. As he began to slow down, Daniels reached into his glove compartment and pulled out a map book.

'Hey, put that away!' Gormley said. 'You'll upset my new friend.'

Daniels smiled as a woman's voice instructed him to turn left. Gormley's new toy was the latest satellite navigation device.

'You know, we're not that far away from the Mansion House.' Daniels found the page she was looking for, her eyes homing in on the exact location. 'We're also close to several major routes: A1, M62 and A19.'

'You still think the guy Archer described could be Townsend?'

'I don't know, Hank. Gardening pays peanuts. He could be moonlighting in his spare time. He's strong enough to have carried out an abduction, that's for sure. And he doesn't like Finch a whole lot either—'

'I'm sensing a "but" coming.'

'He just doesn't strike me as the type. If there is a type.'

They sat in silence for a few minutes. Journey time was often thinking time. Daniels had spent the majority of the last six days on the road, driving back and forth across three counties: Northumberland, Durham and Yorkshire. That's the way it was sometimes. Every lead had to be followed up, every detail checked, no matter how long it took or what cost to the incident budget—which in this case was a joke. She'd have to tell Bright they needed more cash.

'You think Rachel's heading for the same fate as Amy?'

Daniels didn't answer. She bloody hoped not. The woman's voice was back, instructing Gormley to turn left. He completed the manoeuvre. Seconds later they arrived at their destination, the secure car park of a modern industrial unit on a new-build business park, the company name emblazoned on the gable end in italic writing. There was a large service yard out front and a loading bay surrounded by a chain-link fence at the side. A sign directed heavy goods vehicles to an entry point further down the road.

Gormley drove up to the main gate, pushed a button on the entry console. He ID'd himself. A barrier lifted and he moved forward, parking as close to the front door as he could. They got out of the car and made their way inside.

The integrated office space was contemporary. Advertisements for the company adorned the walls, along with an impressive number of plaques:

business awards for excellence in the service sector. The Rottweiler turned out to be the firm's managing director, Cynthia Beecham, a smartly dressed, petite, thirty-year-old. She ushered them into the boardroom and closed the door, offering them privacy from the corridor beyond. She waited until they'd taken their seats before following suit, a consignment schedule already open at the appropriate page on the table in front of her.

'His name is Mark Harris,' Cynthia Beecham said.

Daniels was impressed. Alistair had kept his word.

Cynthia Beecham slid a driver's log across the table towards the detectives. 'He's been with us since we formed the company and he's never put a foot wrong.'

'Is he a full-time employee?' Gormley asked.

'No, he's sessional only. He turfs up if and when we're particularly busy. He has other work, I believe.'

'Doing what exactly?' Daniels asked.

'Is that relevant?'

Daniels ignored the question. 'He was your only driver in that area on Friday?'

'No. Several of our fleet cover the north east. It's a large area and many of our big clients are sited there.'

'I see . . .' Daniels thought for a moment. 'Is there any chance that Mark Harris was not driving the vehicle with the registration number I gave you on the phone? People swap shifts occasionally, don't they?'

'Not a chance. Our transport manager, Allen Amos, installed a fingerprint-recognition entrance controller that links directly to his office, so he no longer has to stand at the gate and personally check drivers in and out of the depot. It's foolproof. We also have CCTV. You can check it, if you like.'

This was getting better and better. Daniels could see a point in the future where such technology was commonplace and thought how much easier it would make her job. Looking at her watch, she couldn't help but feel excited that they were closing in on a prime suspect.

Cynthia Beecham was far less happy. 'Can I ask why you want to know?'

Gormley answered. 'We believe he may be able to help us with our enquiries.'

'Into what exactly? I need to know . . .' Cynthia Beecham wasn't about to be fobbed off by the vague answer she'd received. 'Given you're both detectives, I take it this is not a speeding offence. If it's a serious matter, our company has a repu—'

'It is a serious matter, Ms Beecham,' Daniels cut in. 'One that requires us to get a move on, so please answer our questions. There's no need for you to concern yourself with the detail, not at this stage anyway. Is Harris here now?'

Cynthia Beecham looked at her watch. 'He should be in the loading dock.'

'You need to delay his departure without telling him why,' Daniels said. 'I have to speak to him now.'

Cynthia Beecham made the call. Then they made their way from the boardroom to the loading shed, a huge hangar-like structure sectioned off into areas marked alphabetically. In one corner, an elderly man was allocating work to three drivers, one of whom—according to Cynthia Beecham—was the man they had come to see.

None of them was Townsend.

Cynthia Beecham stopped short of the group. 'Do you mind if I get him? He's an excellent employee and I'd like to give him the benefit of the doubt until you tell me otherwise.'

'We'll wait here,' Daniels said.

'Mark?' The MD walked on, high heels clicking on the concrete floor. 'Can I have a word?'

Harris turned round, his expression changing when he saw she was not alone. As she led him away from the others, Daniels couldn't help notice his obvious discomfort. Cynthia Beecham took them across the yard to a side office: a small, windowless box. Mark Harris couldn't look Daniels in the eye as his boss left the room, closing the door behind her, having given him the bad news.

Daniels came right to the point. 'Do you know why we're here?'

Harris shrugged. 'I've got a bloody good idea.'

'Tell us then.' Gormley's tone was harsh.

'I didn't mean to hurt her—'

His words hung in the air. Daniels felt sick and elated at the same time. The man had guilt written all over his face and she couldn't wait to hear more.

'Who?' she asked. 'Who didn't you mean to hurt?'

Harris looked at the floor.

Gormley was getting impatient. 'Mr Harris?'

Harris lifted his head. 'Rachel, Rachel Somers.'

'Where is she?' Daniels fought hard to keep her temper in check. 'What have you done with her?'

147

'Nothing!' Harris looked *really* worried. 'Nothing, I promise you!'

'We have a witness who saw her in your cab.' Daniels eyeballed the man, letting him know he was in big trouble. 'Nobody has seen or heard from her since. We think we know why.'

'Then you're a mile wrong,' Harris snapped back. 'I don't know what she's told you, but all I did was talk to her. That's all, I swear. Then I dropped her in Durham on my way to Northallerton.'

'Course you did.' Gormley glared at him. 'And we're supposed to believe that?'

'Believe what you like, it's the truth!' Harris suddenly became defensive, puffing out his chest like he was ready for a fight. 'Hey, I don't know what it is you think I've done, but I'm telling you nowt 'til I see a solicitor.'

'Fine.' Daniels cuffed him. 'Hank, lock him up and get him in the car.'

35

The journey back to Newcastle was uncomfortable. It seemed to take for ever, but thankfully it was nearly over. Riley Archer's information had been spot on. As far as Daniels was concerned he deserved a commendation and would get one from a judge eventually if she had anything to do with it, assuming the case ever reached a court of law. But that was still a long way off.

Glancing over her shoulder, she wondered if the man in the back seat was responsible for Amy Grainger's death and Jessica's disappearance. Not

148

to mention Rachel. Her suspect had made absolutely no comment whatsoever since his arrest. Harris glared back at her from under the peak of his red cap. Not one word had passed his lips in over two hours and she was relieved when they finally turned into the station car park.

Gormley parked as close to the back door as he could. They got out and took their prisoner straight to the custody suite, booked him in and handed him over to the custody sergeant, who put him in a cell to await his solicitor.

Back in MIR, Daniels went directly to her office, picked up the phone and made arrangements for Harris's fingerprint image to be entered into PNC database for comparison. Cynthia Beecham hadn't argued about handing it over. *Protected data could prove innocence as well as guilt,* was how she'd put it. Daniels couldn't argue with that. In the end, it drew a blank. Harris had no criminal record, not as much as a speeding ticket. With no time to dwell on that, the DCI lifted the telephone receiver to call Laura Somers. Rachel's mother was anxious for news, understandable given the recent death of Amy Grainger. Updating her on developments, Daniels arranged for a family liaison officer to visit, hesitating when she heard a knock at the door.

She covered the speaker with her free hand.

Carmichael poked her head in. 'Harris's brief has arrived,' she whispered.

Miming a thank you, Daniels went back to her call, apologizing to Mrs Somers for the interruption. 'Has Rachel ever mentioned someone called Mark to you, now or in the past?'

'I don't think so.' There was a short delay, some

149

noise at the other end of the line, then Laura Somers was back. 'Sorry, Inspector, I dropped something. Who is he?'

'We have reason to believe that a man called Mark met with Rachel on Friday morning. I'll be speaking to him shortly. I thought I'd run it by you first in case you knew anything about him. I'll keep you informed if my enquiries come to anything.'

Daniels rang off.

Mark Harris and his brief were waiting in the interview room when she and Gormley walked in. The solicitor wasn't known to them. He was relatively young, around thirty years old, very good-looking but with a deep red scar which ran from his hairline down his forehead and through his left eyebrow as if he'd recently had an argument with a car windscreen. Unless, Daniels thought, one of his clients had taken umbrage at his instructions. Either way, it looked painful.

Harris was sitting back in his chair, arms folded across his chest. A little smug, Daniels observed, but nervous too, if the perspiration on his brow was anything to go by. He looked right through her as if she wasn't there. Noticing the exchange between accused and accuser, the brief quickly got to his feet and handed over his business card. He smiled broadly, trying his best to take the heat out of the situation.

'I'm Alec Walton, Bradley, Walton and Associates. I'll be acting for Mr Harris. I don't think we've met.'

'DCI Daniels.' She pointed to her left. 'My colleague, DS Gormley.'

They all sat down. Gormley turned on a recording device housed in a recess in the wall,

150

reintroduced all four for the benefit of the tape, adding the time and date, reminding Harris he was still under caution and had been arrested on suspicion of the abduction of Rachel Somers.

'Do you understand?' he said.

The suspect sighed. 'Yes.'

Daniels leaned her elbows on the table. 'Would you please tell us where you were between eight a.m. and ten a.m. on the morning of Friday the seventh, and what exactly you were doing?'

Harris looked at his brief and received a nod in return. 'I was at work.'

'In what capacity?' Gormley picked up his pen.

'I work as an HGV driver for Conrad Couriers.'

'Their head office being where exactly?' Daniels asked.

'On the Access 63 business park. It's near Selby. You should know, you've already been there. Thanks to you, I'll probably lose my job.'

Daniels moved on. 'What time did your shift begin?'

'Four a.m. I had an early delivery to South Shields. Got there around six, dropped my load and grabbed some breakfast—'

'Where?' Gormley stopped making notes.

Harris's brow creased. 'Excuse me?'

'It's a simple enough question.' Daniels met his gaze across the table. 'Where did you eat?'

'In my cab.'

'Packed it yourself, did you?' Gormley asked.

'No. I bought it from a mobile breakfast van.'

Daniels wanted more. 'Which one?'

'Lindisfarne roundabout. It's one I use regularly. Lass called Sheila runs it, does an excellent fry-up, if you guys are ever interested.' Harris grinned.

151

'Ask her if you don't believe me.'

'Oh, we intend to,' Gormley said. 'First chance we get.

'Did you meet anyone else while you were having breakfast?' Daniels asked.

She watched for a reaction and got one. Harris's grin had disappeared. She looked across the table at Alec Walton, wondering what advice he'd given his client, suspecting that she was about to encounter a stone wall. A 'no comment' interview was not what she needed right now. But Mark Harris surprised her.

'I told you, I didn't mean to hurt her. I just . . . I wanted to talk to her.'

'Rachel Somers?'

'Yes.'

'She met you at Sheila's breakfast bar?'

Harris nodded.

'I appreciate your honesty,' Daniels said. 'Had you met before?'

'Only in cyberspace.' The grin was back.

Daniels bristled. The remark was more than irritating. Millions of people around the world had fallen foul of web fraudsters and conmen. Yet people continued to post personal information on social networking sites with total disregard to the consequences, some of which had been fatal.

'I take it you mean the Internet?' she said.

Another nod.

'On which site?' Gormley asked.

Harris hung his right arm over the back of his chair. 'Facebook.'

Daniels waited for Gormley to stop scribbling. Harris was a cool customer. Either he hadn't taken on board the seriousness of the situation or he had a perfectly reasonable explanation for his meeting a girl half his age. But if that were so, why had he refused to speak to them without a solicitor present?

She moved on. 'You told us earlier, you hadn't meant to hurt her. What did you mean by that?'

Harris looked away.

'Answer the DCI's question.' Alec Walton put a hand on his client's arm. 'It's OK, Mark, you have nothing to hide. We discussed this.'

Harris was scared and it showed.

Walton looked at him.

But still he remained silent.

'Could I have a few moments alone with my client?' Walton said.

At such a critical point in the interview, Daniels was annoyed at the suggestion that they should take a break. Her suspect was beginning to lose his bottle and this was no time to take her eye off the ball. Refusing Alec Walton's request, she said, 'Earlier you told me that you dropped Rachel Somers in Durham, Mr Harris. What time was that exactly?'

'No comment.'

The brief spoke next. 'DCI Daniels, if I could just—'

But Daniels was on a roll. 'How long have you been corresponding with Rachel on Facebook?'

'No comment.'

'Suit yourself.' Daniels looked at her watch. 'Interview terminated at 3.05 p.m. Mr Walton, there's no point in you hanging around. This is a major investigation. We've got urgent enquiries to make outside of the area and time is of the essence. Your client is going to be lodged here until those enquiries are complete. If you wish to speak to him, see the custody officer. If he has anything more to say, I'll be happy to listen. I don't have time for this.'

36

Daniels hovered outside the interview room. She was experienced enough to recognize when an interviewee was ready to give up his secrets and, in her considered opinion, any further questioning of Harris at this time was unlikely to bear fruit.

'Lodge him in the cells,' she told Gormley. 'He's giving us fuck all. What time are we meeting Dave Weldon?'

'An hour?' Gormley checked his watch. 'Actually, we'd better get a move on.'

They waited until the custody sergeant had taken charge of Harris. Then Daniels led Gormley out of the station and into the car park. They argued over whose car to take and finally tossed a coin. With a big smile on her face, Daniels unlocked her Toyota and got in—Gormley's new toy would have to wait.

It was a lovely day, bright sunshine and a cloudless sky, and for that Daniels was grateful. A change in the weather might represent imminent danger to Jessica Finch if, as they suspected, she was being held underground. Unclipping her sunglasses from the visor above her head, Daniels put them on and moved off. They had been in the car about half an hour when her mobile rang, a number she didn't recognize. She answered, leaving the phone on loudspeaker.

'DCI Daniels, this is Alec Walton.'

'What can I do for you, Mr Walton?'

'I was hoping to catch you before you left the station. I don't want you to get the wrong impression of Mark Harris—or me, come to think of it. You should know he acted against my advice during questioning.'

'I'm relieved to hear it. Next you'll be telling me that he has a legitimate explanation for his contact with Rachel Somers.'

'I assure you that is the case. He knows about your missing teenagers and he's scared. Understandable, don't you think?'

'Or he's as guilty as sin,' Gormley muttered under his breath.

Daniels dug him in the ribs, lifting a finger to her lips to shut him up. He grinned at her, holding out a pack of gum. She shook her head. He took one for himself then put the packet back on the dash.

Changing down, Daniels negotiated a left hander.

'Watch out!' Gormley yelled.

Daniels braked sharply as two young females stepped off the pavement without looking, one with a mobile stuck to her ear, the other pushing a stroller with a newborn baby inside and a toddler riding a buggy board. The little boy was around three years old with the face of an angel and a mischievous expression in big brown eyes. He waved at her as they passed in front of the car and got a slap from his mother for letting go of the handle straps.

The DCI wanted to stop and give her a piece of her mind but didn't have time.

'DCI Daniels?' Walton's voice cut through her

155

thoughts. 'Is everything OK?'

'Depends, is Harris ready to talk?'

'Ready might be a bit too strong a word—'

'Listen to me, Mr Walton. If your client is going to front up and tell me the truth I'll happily come back and interview him. I've got two missing girls and a dead one. So if he's going to piss me about, he'll have a long wait. By all means relay that message to him and in the meantime the custody sergeant will review his detention.'

Walton didn't respond.

'I'll wait to hear from you then.' Daniels ended the call abruptly.

'That went well.' Gormley grinned. 'It's not like you to be so arsy.'

'Yeah, well, I'm a bit sick of being messed around, Hank. A life is at stake—two potentially— and time-wasting bastards like Harris make my blood boil. He can wait now until I'm good and ready.'

'You think he's our man?'

'He's hiding something.'

'That's not what I asked.'

'Could we be that lucky? I honestly don't know if he is or not.'

They drove on in silence until they reached a signpost: A689 Nenthead and Killhope. Daniels followed it, joining a minor road, very narrow in parts. As they travelled further still, the atmosphere both inside the car and out became heavy and the sunshine disappeared. Daniels looked up at the sky. A huge black mass of cloud had formed up ahead.

'Don't think I'm going to need these any more.' Taking off her shades, she hung them over the visor.

Gormley didn't answer. He'd fallen asleep.

As Daniels drove on, the landscape changed. Rolling hills and valleys were replaced by wilder and more rugged terrain. Snow poles flashed by on either side of the road, testament to the extreme conditions encountered there in winter. And suddenly there was a crack of thunder so loud it damn near shook the Toyota from its chassis.

Gormley snorted, waking with a start.

Daniels switched on the wipers as the heavens opened. But even at full pelt they were hardly able to cope with the water raining down on them. Gormley yawned. Leaning forward, he peered through the windscreen at the sight of lights ahead. A cluster of vehicles—all Land Rover Defenders—were parked off the road about half a mile away. Daniels drove towards them, eventually pulling up alongside. Each vehicle bore the logo of the North Pennines Fell Rescue.

Someone they couldn't identify waved through the steamed-up window of the lead vehicle. He leapt out and ran to the rear of the Toyota, water pouring off him as he opened the rear door and climbed in. Weldon was wearing waterproof combat pants, a red cagoule with the hood pulled tight around his face and a white safety helmet protruding from beneath.

His expression was grave as the hood came off.

Pulling down the heavy zip of his cagoule he revealed a whistle, a GPS and a pair of binoculars round his neck. The latter he handed to Daniels, her side window being the least exposed to the driving rain. Lifting them to her eyes, she brought them into focus. Panning the landscape, her morale took a dive. The rough ground she was looking at was dotted with shaft mounds, spoil heaps and old mine workings as far as the eye could see. Worse still, gentle streams were forming into raging torrents of white water, splashing and bubbling all over the place. Just what she didn't need.

37

Jessica Finch was turning into her own medical emergency. If dehydration didn't kill her, then hypothermia eventually would. Shivering uncontrollably, her core body temperature dropped like a stone as the water rose around her, inch by painful inch. No longer still, its swirling currents lapped about her legs with such ferocity it would have swept her away had it not been for the shackles securing her to the wall.

Move!

Jessica began walking on the spot, trying to stimulate circulation. She had little sense of time: minutes seemed like hours, hours like days and she was beginning to feel disorientated. The pool of light was back on the wall opposite and she couldn't work out why. Had her captors replaced the bulb? Or had she simply imagined the light going out as she slipped into semi-consciousness?

Jessica turned her head to one side but it was difficult to make out what she was looking at. Shadows played tricks on the shiny black wall. One minute she saw a man's figure, still as a statue, the next she wasn't so sure. Whatever it was, it seemed to be moving in and out of focus the more she looked at it.

She tried swallowing but her throat was dry and swollen.

Then she began to hyperventilate.

'Hello? Hello? Hello? Hello?' she called out breathlessly, her weak voice bouncing around in the chamber. 'Who's there? Who's there? Who's there? Who's there?'

Nothing.

'Hello? Hello? Hello? Hello?'

The nibbling at her ankles no longer bothered Jessica. The potential for infection from whatever was swimming around in the water below could never be as bad as the sheer terror she was experiencing right now. She shouted again, her voice echoing down the tunnel. She began to count the drips of liquid that had been driving her slowly insane since waking up in hell. They seemed strangely reassuring now—like the rhythm of a pulse.

Her pulse.

She was alive!

And determined to survive her ordeal.

But as her heart-rate slowed to normal, the air in the chamber suddenly deteriorated and Jessica gagged as the smell of decomposing flesh crept up her nose and into her mouth and the image of half-eaten corpses—mouths frozen open in permanent screams—rushed into her head.

This isn't really happening.

It's delirium.

Hallucinatory.

She tried pushing away those macabre thoughts, but they persisted. She shut her eyes and went

159

back to her counting: one . . . two . . . three . . .
louder now . . . seven . . . *get a grip!* . . . until
exhaustion took over and she was but four years
old with a favourite storybook on her knee. She
drifted off to sleep to the sound of her mother's
voice.

38

'Jesus Christ!' Daniels lowered the binoculars and
looked at the two men. 'Where the hell do we start
the search?'

'Did Lisa locate a geologist?' Weldon asked.

Gormley nodded. 'He has your number. Expect a
call.'

'It was never going to be easy . . .' Weldon's voice
trailed off as he looked out of the window at the
bleak landscape facing them. 'But now the
weather's turned, if we can't narrow the field down
a bit we're going to be too late.'

The comment irritated Gormley. 'Don't be so
bloody negative. You're the fucking expert. We're
expecting you to find her—at least give it your best
shot. You heard what I said yesterday. There could
be two of them now.'

'I'm not a magician!'

'Hey, you two!' Daniels turned to Weldon.
'Hank's right, though, Dave. That kind of thinking
isn't going to get us very far. We need your guys to
be up for this one hundred per cent or we haven't
got a hope in hell of finding Jessica Finch alive.
We know she's here somewhere. I can't bear to
think that Rachel Somers is too.'

'Don't you worry about that.' Weldon gestured to his team, waiting in their vehicles. 'That lot will work 'til they drop, no question, and so will I. You just say the word and we're out of here.'

Daniels noticed the rain was getting worse. 'Any ideas on how to proceed?'

Weldon thought for a moment. 'Bearing in mind your suspect would've had to carry Jessica—either struggling or dead weight if she was drugged—I'd recommend we start with the mines most accessible to this road.'

'Good idea,' Daniels said.

'I disagree,' Gormley cut in. 'If I were hiding her, I'd probably do the exact opposite. He might have flown here, don't forget.'

'He's got a point.' Over their shoulders, Daniels spotted a caravan of vehicles making their way slowly up the hill. Through the binoculars she saw that they were specialist 4WDs, each one carrying the Northumbria police insignia. Headlights were on full-beam, illuminating a strip of tarmac that looked more like a fast-moving river than a road. She glanced at Weldon. 'The cavalry are here. I suggest the TSG search for potential landing sites off-road and your lot cover the areas closer to the main drag.'

Weldon nodded. 'Sounds like a plan to me.'

Daniels mobile rang: Alec Walton again.

Please God he'll have talked some sense into Harris.

161

39

The custody suite was bedlam when they arrived back at the station. Walking through the door, Daniels almost felt like she was tripping. The air was thick with the unmistakable smell of skunk cannabis. Word on the grapevine was that there'd been a big drugs bust that morning with a hundred grand's worth of the stuff seized. What she hadn't quite figured on was sampling the goods herself.

There was a queue at the booking-in desk. The cells were overflowing. Prisoners were yelling for this and that, banging on cell doors, shouting abuse at the custody officer. The noise was deafening. As she made her way through the room, a scuffle broke out and she was forced to step sideways round a well-known local hooker struggling with a rookie policewoman. A feeling of déjà vu hit Daniels as she witnessed the comical scene. Her first encounter with a prostitute had begun in much the same way and had ended in the Royal Victoria Infirmary with two stitches in a head wound.

It bloody hurt too.

'Take my advice and cuff her,' Daniels said as she walked by.

The PC blushed, grabbing her charge and shoving her up against the wall.

'Ow, that hurt!' the girl yelled. 'You broke my nail.'

Entering the interview room, Daniels sat next to Gormley and directly opposite Mark Harris and Alec Walton. Detecting the lingering scent of drugs on her clothing, Gormley glanced sideways, raised an amused eyebrow. Mildly embarrassed, she ignored his smug expression and concentrated on the suspect. Harris looked confident with his arm slung over the back of his chair. Although it was cold in the room, his Conrad Couriers boiler suit was unbuttoned to the waist, revealing a crisp white T-shirt and a fit body beneath.

Daniels let him know she wasn't about to waste any more of her precious time, then nodded to Gormley, who immediately restarted the tape, giving the time and date, identifying everyone in the room. With all the preliminaries complete, the DCI placed her elbows on the table and eyeballed Harris. She didn't need notes to remind her where she was in the proceedings when he clammed up. Where interviews were concerned, she had a brilliant memory. Every 'no comment' answer was lodged in her brain, every question she'd put to him waiting to be asked again.

'OK, Mr Harris. I'm here. You're still under caution. What have you got to tell me?'

'I think Rachel Somers is my daughter,' Harris said quietly. 'I had an affair with her mother when we were both very young. I only found out she existed a few months ago when I bumped into an old friend I'd lost touch with.'

Of all the answers he could have given, this one threw the DCI. She held his gaze until he suddenly became interested in his chewed-off fingernails. 'Earlier you told me that you hadn't meant to hurt Rachel, is that correct?'

His answer came in the form of a nod.

'For the benefit of the tape, the suspect is nodding.'

The brief reminded Harris to answer the question verbally.

'Yes, I did say that but—'

'What exactly did you mean by it?'

'Not what you're implying,' Harris said calmly. 'I wasn't honest with her, not at first—at least, not when I made contact with her on Facebook. I wanted to tell her the truth, but I knew if I didn't handle it right I'd scare her away. It all got a bit complicated. In the end I think Rachel got the wrong idea. She had a different agenda, if you know what I mean.'

Gormley shook his head. Clearly he didn't believe a word Harris was saying. 'And what agenda would that be? You're not telling us she fancied you, a young girl like that. I mean, you're hardly Brad Pitt, are you?'

Harris was smirking now.

'You think this is funny, sir?' Daniels asked. 'I assure you it's not. You see, right now I'm not sure if you're telling me the truth, or if your story is a complete fabrication, a pack of lies designed to mislead us. I'm afraid you're going to have to do better than that or I'm ending this interview right now!'

'I lied to her, I admit it. But I'm not lying now. I'm not proud of myself. I may have given her the impression I was a younger man, but—'

'Impression?' Gormley didn't try to hide his contempt for Harris. 'What exactly did you tell her? No, let me guess: fun guy, mid-twenties, fit, seeking friendship and possibly more . . .'

'Take the piss all you like, mate. I know it sounds bad, but I thought if she knew my age she wouldn't agree to meet with me and I'd never get to

164

see her.'

Daniels looked at Harris's hands. Jewellery was automatically removed by the custody officer when suspects were brought in, but there was no telltale indentation on his ring finger to suggest he ever wore a wedding ring. She couldn't remember seeing one when she'd made the arrest.

'Are you married, Mr Harris?' she asked.

'Fuck's that got to do with anything?'

'Are you?' Daniels waited.

'No! And I'm no pervert either.'

The conversation with Jo Soulsby replayed in Daniels' mind: *He's letting us know he's no pervert . . . he's prepared to kill Amy but not to take away her dignity by making her strip . . . He didn't want to degrade her . . . just use her to hurt someone else.*

And Harris was a father too, or so he'd have them believe.

Daniels sifted fact from fiction. The man she was facing had, by his own admission, met with Rachel Somers. But he had no criminal history and at no time had he attempted to deny having had contact with the girl. In fact, Daniels had no way of knowing if Rachel was alive, dead, or lying low, licking her wounds having been told by a complete stranger that the father she'd known all her life wasn't even a relation. In fact, although Rachel's description was broadly similar to the other students who'd gone missing, Daniels had no proof her disappearance was a linked incident at all.

Yet.

She changed tack. 'If you are telling us the truth then I'm sure you'd want us to find Rachel at the earliest opportunity. Tell me when and where you last saw her so I can make further enquiries and we'll see where that takes us, shall we?'

'I told you. I dropped her off at Durham on my way to Northallerton. That is the God's honest truth, I swear to you.'

Daniels knew the Durham area well, having spent a lot of time at the police headquarters there as part of the collab-orative learning programme for detectives of both forces. Cognitive interviewing was her particular specialism, a skill she was keen to share. She asked Harris to describe exactly where he'd dropped Rachel off.

'At the A1M/Durham junction,' he said.

'Which one? There are several,' Gormley demanded.

'The first one. Get us a map and I'll show you.'

Daniels nodded to Gormley.

He immediately stood up and made a move. She waited for the door to close behind him and then spoke for the benefit of the tape, indicating that Gormley had left the room. Seconds later he arrived back. Daniels announced him to the recorder while he placed a map on the table between the suspect and his solicitor. They both leaned forward, scanning the document. After a few seconds, Harris pointed to Junction 62 of the A1, a road that led on to the A690.

'She said she'd catch a bus the rest of the way.' Harris relaxed back in his seat. 'I was running late by then and didn't have time to take her all the way into the city centre. Anyway, she was upset. Said she wanted to get out. She was yelling at me, freaking out, threatening to open the door while I was still driving. I'd read the papers. What was I supposed to do?'

'Why was she so upset?' Gormley asked.

'Why d'you think!' Harris checked himself, dropping his voice and his attitude. 'I'd just told her I might be her father. So she flew off on one. She went ape-shit in the cab, screaming and kicking. I'd never seen anything like it. She obviously didn't believe me.' He paused. 'And from the look on your faces, she isn't the only one.'

The CCTV camera mounted on the ceiling blinked. Daniels wondered if she should have asked Jo Soulsby to observe the interview. Harris was either innocent or he was an accomplished liar the like of which she'd rarely come across. Daniels had met her fair share of liars and, contrary to popular opinion, had found that most were not very good at it. Most tripped themselves up trying to be too clever. Harris had been careful to say only that he *thought* he might be Rachel's father, not that he actually was. If Laura Somers denied having had a relationship with him, it was her word against his. Only a DNA test could prove or disprove paternity.

Alec Walton sat passively on the other side of the table. The solicitor hadn't said a word during the interview. He'd let his client speak for himself and answer Daniels' questions without interference. She appreciated that. Her eyes shifted from the brief to Mark Harris. He wasn't showing any signs of stress now, and that surprised her. Even if he were entirely innocent she would have expected some anxiety on his part, given the nature of the charge he was facing. Then again, it wasn't against the law to lie about your age. Until she could prove otherwise, that was all he'd admitted so far.

'Did you touch Rachel at all during this journey?' Gormley said.

It was a good question; one the DCI would have asked herself in due course. Harris remained silent. He seemed thrown off guard, unsure of what to say. Daniels wondered if he was playing for time or merely trying to work out what Gormley was implying by the word 'touch'.

'Mr Harris?' Daniels waited.

The suspect just looked at her, his eyes flitting briefly to his solicitor.

The sound of Gormley's pen tapping on the tabletop was evidence of his growing impatience. Daniels understood his frustration. She willed him to exercise some self-control. Slow down. Take his time. This line of questioning was vitally important. If Harris lied now, his answer might prove crucial; especially if, God forbid, Rachel was subsequently found dead with his DNA all over her. A provable lie would cast doubt on the rest of his evidence in a court of law when the time came, even though his defence team would argue that his DNA would be all over the cab of his lorry.

With no time to dwell on that, Daniels moved. 'Answer the question, Mr Harris. Did you or did you not touch Rachel at any time when the two of you were together?'

Harris shook his head.

'You're absolutely sure about that?' Gormley piled on the pressure. 'You didn't shake her hand when you met at the roadside cafe? Help her up into the cab or anything like that?'

'No! I swear! I never touched her, not once!'

'One last question, Mr Harris . . .' Daniels paused, making him sweat. 'What was Rachel wearing when you last saw her?'

'Jeans and a grey jacket—that's all I remember.'

168

Daniels had a call to make. And now was the time to make it.

'Thank you. You're free to go.'

All three men looked stunned.

40

Before they left the interview room, Harris damned near begged them to keep him in custody. Now Daniels was charging down the corridor with Gormley in pursuit and the suspect's words ringing in her ears:

'I'm not going anywhere, not until you clear this matter up. There's no way I'm letting the police come knocking at my mother's door. She's a frail seventy-year-old with dementia. The confusion will probably kill her. I should know—I'm her carer!'

So, that was his other job.

Daniels swiped her warrant card to gain access to the MIR. She'd told Harris in no uncertain terms that she wouldn't authorize his further detention but, if he insisted, he could wait in the reception area while they checked out his version of events. She assumed that's where he was now.

'You know what you just did?' Gormley was out of breath when he caught up with her. 'Or did I nod off during the interview? We've got him bang to rights, boss.'

He nearly ran into her as she did an about turn.

'We've got sod all, Hank. Think about it!'

'We've got enough to hold him, surely!'

'For what? Having a conversation with a student

169

who met him voluntarily?'

Without waiting for an answer, she walked off, leaving her affronted DS standing in the middle of the incident room. Raised voices had drawn the interest of the rest of the squad and Gormley was now the focus of several pairs of eyes.

Daniels busied herself checking the murder wall for any significant progress. It was always her first task on returning to the office. On the right-hand side of the digital screen, the box for flagging up new events stood empty. Frustrated, she wandered into her office and sat down. Gormley followed her in and threw himself down on the chair opposite. On the desk, someone had deposited their dinner in the form of two paper bags from Dene's Deli, a great out-of-town delicatessen the police used a lot. Gormley opened one bag and found a Greek salad box. He grimaced at the sight of feta cheese and olives.

'Yuck, that must be yours,' he said, pushing the bag towards her. Diving into the other, he pulled out a stottie filled with Warkworth ham and Northumberland cheese. He took a big bite and spoke with his mouth full. 'You going to tell me what I missed?'

'We've been wasting our time, Hank.' Daniels lifted the phone and dialled out. 'If I'm right, Laura Somers will confirm it.'

'And if you're not?'

'Trust me, I know what I'm doing.'

Gormley was too busy with his sandwich to care. Getting up, he took one more bite of his stottie and then set it down on the desk. He picked up Daniels' kettle, shook it to check if there was water, then switched it on and placed two level scoops of Harvey Nick's coffee in her cafetière. 'You want it black?' he asked.

'Black's fine.' Still no one picked up.

'Just as well.' He pointed through her door. 'Those bastards have had all your milk.'

The phone stopped ringing. Daniels introduced herself to Rachel's mother. 'You haven't been entirely honest with me, have you?'

'I don't understand,' the woman said.

'Mrs Somers, I'm very busy.'

'I don't know—'

'Cut the crap!' Daniels snapped. 'You know fine well who Mark is, don't you?'

Gormley was back in his seat. He stopped chewing and paid attention.

Daniels rolled her eyes as the line went quiet. 'I haven't got time to mess around, Laura. Tell me the truth or I'll come round there and lock you up for wasting police time. Another girl's life may be at stake.'

The woman began to cry.

'Fuck!' Daniels slammed the phone down.

'Great interview technique.' Gormley swallowed what was in his mouth. 'I take it Harris was telling the truth?'

Daniels nodded.

'How did you know?'

'I was asking myself why Riley, rather than Rachel's family, had reported her missing. The answer was obvious. They knew about Harris all along. I didn't think anything of it at the time, but Laura Somers actually dropped the phone when I questioned whether Rachel knew anyone called Mark. I only remembered when we were interviewing him.'

'Then where's the girl?'

'She'll be back, if for no other reason than to give her mother a mouthful.'

'You reckon?'

'I reckon.'

The kettle began to boil. Gormley got up and began making coffee she knew would be as weak as dishwater. It always was when he made it. In need of a strong one, she told him to add another scoop to the pot and looked at her watch, wondering how the search team were going. It was already quarter to seven and there was only an hour and a half of daylight left.

As Gormley sat down, she slid Harris's file across her desk.

'Put this in for referral, Hank. We've got more pressing matters to attend to. And tell the squad we'll hold a briefing at eight o'clock sharp. They don't get to go home tonight and put their kids to bed, I'm afraid. It's all hands on deck until we work out where we go from here.'

'And where do we go from here?' Gormley asked.

Daniels sighed. 'Fucked if I know.'

41

Daniels forced herself to eat her salad then made a few phone calls: first to the TSG, then to Weldon, to find out how they were getting on with the search. His answer was not what she wanted to hear. The weather hadn't improved any and progress was slow due to the dangerous conditions.

'Mineshafts are waist-deep in water,' he said, forced to raise his voice against driving rain. 'I can't risk anyone going underground until the levels drop, Kate. We're about to call it a day. I'm really sorry. We'll be out again, crack of dawn, I promise you.'

'Did the geologist get in touch?'

'I wish he would. It's vital we narrow down the search area.'

'OK, leave it with me. I'll see what I can do to hurry him along.'

She rang off and then made the call. The geologist wasn't available so she left an urgent message for him to contact her. Deciding that from now on she should run the incident wholly from the MIR and not split between two sites, she called High Shaw. She was expecting to speak with DS Robson, but it was Kevin Hook who answered. There was still nothing doing on the house-to-house. Robson had apparently left and was on his way to attend the briefing. Even better, Daniels thought. She'd give him the good news in person. In truth, she'd missed having him around. She was worried that his isolation up at Hadrian's Wall could trigger more Internet gambling, particu-larly if he was bored with little to occupy his mind. She instructed Hook to clear out High Shaw first thing in the morning and decamp to the city.

'And make sure you leave the place how we found it,' she said finally.

'Will do. Er, before you go, ma'am,' Hook hesitated. 'Any update on my secondment to the murder investigation team?'

'It continues.'

'Really?'

173

'From what I hear, you've earned it. But drop the "ma'am", eh?'

His obvious delight lifted her mood. Glancing at her watch, she ended the call, figuring she had just enough time before the briefing to update Adam Finch on developments and call the liaison officer assigned to Amy Grainger's parents. So many people were relying on her and yet, six days into the enquiry, she was back to square one. There wasn't one tangible lead, apart from Matt West's assertion that the sample he'd examined had come from the area now being searched.

This case would keep her awake tonight.

A large white binder caught Daniels' eye—her Murder Investigation Manual. It was an SIO's bible, a thick strategic document several hundred pages long, covering every aspect of murder investigation. She'd read every page, had committed to memory much of the information contained within it, for all the good it did when there was no crime scene to examine and little intelligence to exploit.

Sometimes an SIO's only way forward was to go back.

Daniels needed to re-examine the basics by using standard analytical procedures, check out her victim's history and associations, past and present, not just Amy Grainger's but Jessica's too. In the case of the latter, the DCI was convinced that someone knew something and wasn't letting on. She would need to review the accounts given by Finch, Pearce, Townsend, Mrs Partridge and Robert Lester; and then there was the artist, Fiona Fielding, she'd yet to interview—the woman with whom Jessica had spent a good deal of time, if the stunning oil on canvas above the fireplace in her father's library was anything to go by.

Adam Finch had implied that the painting had been very expensive to commission. It had taken him many months to find the right artist, one capable of depicting the next generation of the Finch dynasty for display in his ancestral home. In order to capture a true representation, he would have insisted on the traditional painstaking process whereby the subject was required to sit for hours at a time over a period of weeks. There would have been no shortcuts, no copying the likeness from a digital image; Adam Finch was too much of a traditionalist for that.

An awful noise set Daniels' teeth on edge and caused her to look out of her office window. The red-and-white security barrier to the station car was stuck halfway with a rusty old R-Reg Fiesta waiting to gain entry. DS Robson wound his window down manually and stuck his arm out of the vehicle, swiping his warrant card again and again. The barrier shook, then—with the ear-splitting sound of metal scraping on metal—slowly began to lift.

Completely unaware that he was under observation, Robson parked close to the perimeter fence and got out of the car. He opened the rear door and reached inside, retrieving something from the back seat, his baggy suit trousers testament to the fact that he was still losing weight. His personal battle to overcome his addiction was obviously not going well. Daniels felt guilty for not having been around to help him in recent days.

Maybe he'd turn the corner now he was returning to the fold.

Comforted by that thought, she made more phone calls. She'd just hung up when Gormley arrived in her office with Bright in tow. Obviously in a foul mood, the Superintendent announced that he would be sitting in on the briefing.

In other words, he'd rather not go home.

Daniels knew only too well what that felt like.

But that wasn't the only reason he was there. Apparently, Adam Finch wanted answers. He'd been calling in favours from local politicians, demanding that they put pressure on senior brass in the force. And Bright certainly had the look of a man under pressure. His usually immaculate suit was crumpled, his tie askew, the top button of his white shirt unbuttoned. His hair was flat to his head, damp from the rain, and he was sporting a heavy five o'clock shadow flecked with grey. He sat down as a flash of lightning lit up the room, an ominous precursor of what was to follow.

As a mentor, there was no one better than Bright. He'd taught the DCI all she knew about criminal investigation and was largely responsible for her promotion through the ranks. The downside was, he had a tendency to deal with his frustration by giving her a hard time. For more years than she cared to admit, even to herself, she had put up with his vitriol in silence. But not today.

The moment he started poking his nose in where, in Daniels' opinion, it didn't belong, she bit back: 'This is my case, guv. I'll run it how the hell I like. And that means investigating who the hell I like, including Finch. If he wants results, I want full disclosure—I can't afford to be selective.'

'Why are you so hung up about the fact that he can fly?'

Gormley made a face. 'I would have thought that was obvious, guv.'

'Who asked you?' Bright said sourly.

Daniels leapt to Gormley's defence. 'Come on, guv. Don't tell me his being a pilot doesn't cast suspicion on him. If the two of you weren't mates, you'd—'

'*Was* a pilot,' Bright reminded her. 'His licence expired years ago.'

'And that makes him less of a suspect?' Gormley shook his head. 'All it means is he can't hire a plane without forging documents. You know fine well how easy that is if you have the right contacts and the money. You can buy a licence on the net and have it delivered to your door these days with little chance of detection.'

'You've been watching too much TV.' Bright eyeballed Gormley. 'You think he killed a girl and then pretended to kidnap his own daughter? It's ridiculous.'

Daniels began pacing. Her hackles were up and it showed. 'Well, I'm pulling his army records, and those of Pearce and Townsend too. I'm not happy with any of them. Don't you think it's strange that he employed the pair of them after they left the forces?'

'Not really,' Bright said. 'I told you, he's a nice guy. You'd see that for yourself if you took the trouble to look. If you weren't so busy making wild accusations—'

'Now hold on!' Daniels wasn't having that. 'I'm not making accusations, wild or any other kind. I'll be sure to let you know if I do. He lied to us, guv.'

'About what?'

'His relationship with Jessica for a start.'

177

'Says who?'

'Robert Lester for one. And for what it's worth, I believe him.' Daniels watched Bright's colour rise. To avert the risk of him exploding, she sat down—calmed down—until she judged it was safe to continue. 'According to Robert Lester, Adam Finch is a manipulative control freak with a nasty temper. I don't doubt he's charming at the golf club. All I'm saying is he has another side to his character, a side he doesn't want you to see.'

'Seems like you two have a lot in common then,' Bright quipped.

Daniels just looked at him. She'd wondered how long it would take him to raise the fact that she'd misled him on the previous enquiry, failing to disclose a conflict of interest when Jo Soulsby was charged with her ex-husband's murder—wrongly, as it turned out. This time Gormley came to her defence, telling Bright in no uncertain terms that his last comment was a lowballer, uncalled for . . .

'Downright bollocks, in fact.'

'I said he was a nice guy, not a saint.' Bright back-pedalled slightly, realizing he'd gone too far. 'Come on, Kate. His only daughter is missing. He's not about to bare his soul and say they didn't get along, now, is he? Would you?'

'I'm not talking about me!'

Bright looked at his watch. 'I'm out of here. Let me know how the briefing goes.'

'I thought you were—'

But he was already gone.

'Why's he being so defensive?' Gormley asked.

Daniels raised her eyes to the ceiling. 'There's something he's not telling us.'

42

The invitation to supper was sudden and unexpected and her first thought was to reject it. But then Detective Superintendent Ron Naylor's excitement got the better of her when he suggested—no, demanded—that she leave the Toyota at the station, insisting that a taxi had already been sent to pick her up.

Daniels pocketed her mobile, curious to know what he had to say to her that couldn't wait. She scanned the crowded incident room. The review of the case had gone well, given that the murder investigation team were scratching around in the dark. As often happened when enquiries stalled, her staff lifted their game. No thanks to Bright, who'd spat his dummy out and walked off in a huff. In the past hour, several lines of enquiry had been agreed and prioritized and DS Robson had news of the elusive artist, Fiona Fielding, who was in New York for an exhibition.

No starving wretch in a garret then.

'Does she know, or even care, that I need to speak to her?' Daniels asked.

Robson nodded. 'According to one of her understudies, she does. I gather she'll make contact on her return to the UK. She should've been back by now. I'll get on to it first thing.'

It was nice to see Robson back where he belonged, at the core of Daniels' team. She hoped he'd turn his life around and stop buggering about spending money he didn't have. Thanking him, she moved on, asking DC Maxwell to trace and eliminate the couple seen acting suspiciously near Hadrian's Wall in the days leading up to the discovery of Amy Grainger's body. Uniforms were supposed to be following up on responses from the press release but they weren't doing it quickly enough.

'You have my permission to put a rocket up their arses,' she said.

Someone threw in an oddball theory that Jessica Finch may have been caught up in the prostitution ring Durham force were investigating, though how this tied in with the threatening letter Finch had received they didn't know. It wasn't likely, Daniels countered. Jessica was training to become a doctor and was hardly a struggling student short of cash.

'I wouldn't rule it out, boss. People do stuff for kicks, not just for money,' Gormley reminded her. 'If Jessica *was* caught up in something shady, maybe someone's threatening her father with it. Maybe *he's* trying to protect his reputation, his coveted family name.'

'Nothing surprises me any more, Hank.' Daniels took in the clock on the wall. 'I'm due to meet Ron Naylor in around fifteen minutes. I'll run her name by him and see what gives.'

'Bit late to be fraternizing with the enemy, isn't it, boss?' Maxwell was grinning. 'You sure that's the only thing on your agenda this evening?'

He was unable to help himself. Anything salacious in the office and he was always first there. Daniels could have—perhaps should have—put him in his place there and then, but she knew it would only add fuel to the fire. For years, rumours had been circulating about her relationship with Naylor, insinuations and

180

innuendo she'd never really stamped on. If she was being honest, it suited her to let them continue. Naylor wasn't married, had never been, so what was the harm? No. The way Daniels saw it, if people thought they were an item then they weren't looking into her real affairs—*and they were far more interesting.*

Gormley, the only one who truly knew Kate Daniels, gave her a wry smile.

She ignored him in favour of Maxwell. 'Ron Naylor is a mate, Neil. Sorry to disappoint your overactive imagination.'

But Maxwell was off again. 'Nice of you to put that one to bed,' he quipped.

A giggle went round the room.

Keen to get off the subject, Daniels turned her attention to the murder wall. Using a remote, she brought up images of Amy Grainger and Jessica Finch. Looking at them gave her an idea. She turned back to the squad and focused on Carmichael. Her physical similarity to the victims was difficult to miss.

'Fancy a spell undercover, Lisa?' Daniels asked.

As she explained what she had in mind, Carmichael's face lit up. This would be her first time undercover, and it was obvious she couldn't wait to get started. Daniels was transported back a decade or more to her own undercover debut. She had been part of a drug squad team selected to infiltrate a gay club on the beach at South Shields. When she walked up to the bar to order a drink, she was immediately approached by a girl of her own age. 'Watch out if you're looking to score,' she'd said under her breath. 'The place is full of cops.' Later, when the bust went down and she

181

realized her mistake, she'd simply blown Daniels a kiss as she was led away in cuffs.

Wonder where she is now?

Safe from harm, Daniels hoped.

Carmichael was still grinning.

With everyone clear about what they had to do, the DCI sent them on their way, turning her thoughts to Adam Finch. Despite her guv'nor's assertion that she was wrong about him, she planned to put pressure on him first thing in the morning, along with the Mansion House staff.

Leaving the MIR, she went downstairs to the female shower block, putting her hair up as she walked through the door. She took a quick shower, changed her clothes and applied fresh make-up, then stood back to check her appearance in the mirror. Not perfect, but Naylor wouldn't care. It was ten o'clock in the evening and she was coming off a sixteen-hour shift.

A black Mercedes S-Class was waiting outside the station. The driver held the door open while Daniels climbed in. She was absolutely starving when she arrived at Café 21 a few minutes later, her Dene's Deli take-out a distant memory now. The driver got out and did the door thing again, insisting that Naylor had already settled his bill.

Daniels tipped him generously as she stepped from the cab.

Terry Laybourne's stylish restaurant was elegant without being ostentatious, the clientele well-groomed but relaxed as they chatted over background music without having to shout. The aroma of food, cooked to perfection with local ingredients, was to die for, a blend of flavours that whetted Daniels' appetite and let her taste buds

182

know they were in for a rare treat. She'd eaten there only once before—a surprise organized by Jo when they were still together.

Light years ago . . .

High heels clicking on the wooden floor to her left made Daniels turn her head. She was half expecting to see Jo. Instead, a much younger but equally attractive woman was standing there, offering to take her coat and show her to her table. Daniels followed her across the room. Naylor was nowhere in sight but a bottle of champagne was already on ice: Champagne Perrier-Jouët 'La Belle Epoque'.

Wow! Daniels stared at the label. 'Are you sure this is the right table?'

'Yes, madam.' The young woman pulled out a chair. 'Enjoy your meal.'

Daniels sat down, wondering what Naylor was up to. Then he materialized in the centre of the room, shaking hands vigorously with someone they both knew, a retired Divisional Commander whose name was on the tip of her tongue. Sensing her gaze, Naylor turned his head and gave her a winning smile.

Seconds later he arrived by her side. He bent down, gave her a gentle peck on the cheek and whispered something wonderful in her ear, something totally unexpected that filled her with joy. Over his shoulder, the retired commander's interest grew. Daniels almost welled up as Naylor sat down and handed her a menu across a pristine white tablecloth.

'Well, say something! It wasn't that much of a bloody shock, surely?'

Daniels felt choked. For a moment she was

183

speechless. She watched him pour two glasses of champagne. He picked one up and held his glass out, waiting for her to do likewise.

'Ron, you've made me one happy bunny,' she said.

43

The list of potential candidates for the top job in the murder investigation team had been circulating among the rank and file for weeks. And no amount of fishing for information from Human Resources had given Daniels a clue. It was obviously a closely guarded secret. Even her spy in the control room, Pete Brooks, aka 'The Font' (of all knowledge), hadn't been able to enlighten her on that score. And if anyone could wheedle a name from HR, he could.

Bright was always going to be a hard act to follow, but never in her wildest dreams had Ron Naylor's name entered Daniels' thoughts. Why? Because he was highly respected within his own force and there was every reason to believe he'd make chief constable one day. But now she'd had time to think about it, it made perfect sense. All chief constables were required to work in at least one other force at some time during their career. No, Naylor's sideways move was no happy accident. It was part of a calculated, strategic long-term plan to take the top job in Durham Constabulary further down the line. As far as she was concerned, it would be a just reward for a lifetime of service to his community.

It really couldn't happen to a nicer guy.

In all the years Kate had known Naylor, he'd made the most of his life, in and out of work. At training school he'd taken the place by storm, instigating all sorts of shenanigans that rookies with less of a personality would never have got away with. On one occasion, drunk as a skunk, he'd found himself locked out of the accommodation block at three a.m. Undeterred by the final warning he'd received from their senior instructor, he'd scaled a ledge in order to knock on her bedroom window and beg her to let him—only to realize in the sober light of day that he was looking down at a forty-foot drop on to a concrete garage floor.

Mr Invincible, that was Ron—the star of that year's intake.

A broad grin spread across Daniels' face. She'd arrived at the office first thing hoping to break the news, but it seemed the team had already heard. When Naylor followed her in a few minutes later, he was mobbed by detectives offering congratulations, queuing up to shake his hand. Despite their late-night celebration, his eyes were bright and alert, not even the slightest hint that he'd hung one on in spectacular fashion at Café 21. He'd insisted they make a night of it, inviting half the restaurant to join them, including the retired Divisional Commander, his third wife and their guests.

And still Daniels couldn't remember the man's bloody name.

Eventually, the muddle of bodies around Naylor dispersed and Daniels led him away to the privacy of her office. She made coffee, strong and black, before giving him the rundown on the enquiry so far. He listened without interrupting her and seemed satisfied that she was doing all she could to resolve the case. But he was as disturbed as she was by the depressing news that Jessica Finch might be incarcerated underground in some hellhole in the middle of nowhere with little chance of being found.

They were a week into the enquiry and time was running out.

Daniels pushed away that sombre thought. 'Hank floated the idea that our victims were somehow caught up in your prostitution ring.'

'Negative. I ran their names.'

'Figures. You don't miss much, do you?'

'Can't afford to. It's a bloody nightmare and a political hot potato. Councillors from all parties are up in arms demanding we stamp it out. The city doesn't want that kind of slur on its good name. But the operation hasn't produced any arrests yet. Whoever's running those girls is very good at covering their tracks.'

Looking out of the window, Daniels noticed a brand-new Land Rover Discovery passing under the security barrier in the car park below. The 2010 Car of the Year: one she *definitely* would have chosen if she were ready to part with her beloved Toyota. She was shocked to see Jo Soulsby get out the driver's side. The vehicle wasn't her style but was probably a replacement for the BMW she'd written off in an accident that very nearly cost her her life.

Jo opened the back door and reached inside. She looked happy and relaxed as she re-emerged, briefcase in hand. Shutting the door, she peered back through the window and spoke to someone still inside.

Kirsten.

'She's looking good,' Naylor said. 'All things considered.'

'Isn't she?' Daniels changed the subject. 'I don't know if you're aware of this but one of my DCs, Lisa Carmichael, is a dead ringer for Jess and Amy. Amy's mother even thought so, poor woman. Is there any mileage in putting her undercover for a while, see what she can find out? She might pick up some useful information for Durham and for us. She's a clean face, not known in the area. And the scumbag we're after may still be a threat to innocent students, may even attempt to take other girls . . .'

Naylor looked at her, a solid gaze. 'You know, that's not a bad idea.'

Taking a sip of his coffee, his eyes shifted past her, a little to her left. From the wry smile on his lips, she guessed he was looking at a framed poster on the wall behind her. It was a reproduction of Beryl Cook's painting *The Staircase*—used for a national theft campaign with the kind permission of the artist. It depicted two rather voluptuous ladies walking up the stairs of a pub, wine in hand, knickers on show. To the right of the picture was a caption: *Who's giving your bag the eye? Don't let a thief get away with it.* It was an old poster Daniels had found in an unused office. She'd taken a shine to it and kept it for posterity.

Naylor's smile disappeared. 'You're not suggesting we use Carmichael as bait?'

'I'm suggesting she has attributes we could use in the apprehension of a serious offender or

187

offenders. That's what she joined for, a privilege she gets well paid for on the penultimate day of every month, same as we do.'

It was a brutally honest statement. Daniels' new guv'nor was too experienced to have the wool pulled over his eyes. Besides, she had too much respect for the man to lie to him. When *they* had joined the job, all those years ago, there was an expectation that you'd risk life and limb to get the right result. Lisa Carmichael felt the same. Daniels knew it. Now all she had to do was to convince their new boss.

'Don't get me wrong,' Naylor said. 'I'm not discounting it. It's just, I don't know Carmichael very well. And from what I remember of her service record, she hasn't got a lot of time in. I have to admit that concerns me a little. You think she'd be ready for that kind of exposure?'

'Ready and raring to go.' Daniels picked up the internal phone and dialled Carmichael's extension. 'Got a minute, Lisa? Detective Superintendent Naylor would like a word.'

'No problem. Do I need to bring anything?'

'Just yourself.' Daniels was about to hang up. 'Wait! On second thoughts, bring the photographs of Amy and Jessica.'

There was a short pause. Someone else was trying to get Carmichael's attention. Daniels looked over Naylor's shoulder through the pane of glass in her office door. Robson was having a word with Carmichael and Daniels caught a fleeting glimpse of Jo Soulsby entering the MIR.

'Boss?' Carmichael was back on the line. 'Robbo wants you to know that Fiona Fielding is in reception waiting to speak with you. She hasn't got

188

long apparently. She's got another plane to catch.'

'Tell her I'll be straight down.' Daniels put down the phone. 'Can you carry on without me, Ron? I'm needed downstairs.'

44

Daniels peered through the glass pane in the double doors leading to reception. She was excited at the prospect of working with Ron Naylor again, convinced that his timely arrival might trigger a new impetus within the murder investigation team. Morale had been starting to flag a little and she couldn't afford that.

Fiona Fielding was sitting on a hard wooden bench near the entrance to the station with her head buried in a paperback. More attractive than pretty, her outfit was smart but casual, consisting of tight-fitting jeans, high heels and a brown leather jacket over a cream-coloured shirt. A handbag worth more than your average copper's monthly income lay at her feet.

Apologizing for keeping her waiting, Daniels introduced herself. 'I appreciate you taking time out to see me. I'll try not to keep you long.' She led Fielding back through the double doors and along a dreary corridor to IR2, the only interview room presently unoccupied. It wasn't until she opened the door that she realized why—it had recently been redecorated and still reeked of chemicals. 'I'm sorry.' She stepped back out. 'We'll go somewhere else.'

'Paint doesn't bother me, Chief Inspector. And

you apologize too much.' Fielding's voice was low and sexy, like Mariella Frostrup with a sore throat. She swept past Daniels, placed her bag on the floor and promptly sat down, crossing one shapely leg over the other. 'I understand Jess Finch has gone missing. I take it she hasn't yet materialized?'

Daniels shook her head and shut the door. 'Her father is beside himself.'

'Really? Insufferable man. I'm not surprised she went AWOL.'

Daniels usually warmed to people who spoke their minds but wasn't sure if she liked the artist or not. Brutal honesty was all well and good, but, given the circumstances, her comment bordered on insensitive. Then again, Fielding didn't know what *she* knew. She reminded Daniels of another creative type she once knew, a soul singer who used to play in the clubs around town. A woman with real presence who never took anything too seriously, a quality she would have found attractive had she not been in the throes of a murder investigation.

'Ms Fielding—'

'The name is Fiona. Do you have one also, or just a rank?'

'Madam, may I remind you, you're here to help—'

'That sounded like a Mo to me, or possibly a Grace.'

The soul singer again.

A grin played around Fielding's mouth as she locked eyes with the DCI. She was flirting openly. Daniels needed another proposition from a member of the public like a hole in the head. If she had a type, Fielding definitely wasn't it.

'I'm sorry,' she said. 'Can we just get on?'

'There you go again, apologizing.'

'It wasn't an apology.' Daniels glared at her. 'Jess Finch may be in danger.'

Fielding instantly backed off, her turn to apologize for overstepping the mark. Making no more of it, Daniels moved on, asking her about the missing girl, making her aware of the gravity of the situation without giving too much away. Pulling a pen from her pocket, she opened the table drawer and grabbed a statement pad, relieved that her interview was finally getting underway.

'I'm particularly interested in girlfriends, boyfriends, uni mates . . . I'm guessing she didn't tell you she was about to run away from her father because they don't get along?'

Fielding said no. She went on to confirm what Daniels had suspected all along. In the course of painting Jessica's portrait they had spent a considerable amount of time together. Daniels quickly formed the impression that the globe-trotting artist knew the Finch family as well as anyone she'd interviewed so far. As Fielding began to open up, a serious, caring, human being emerged, one who was very fond of Jess and deeply troubled by what she'd been told.

In a different social setting, Daniels knew they'd get along.

'Did Jessica have any special friends? Anyone she talked about a lot?'

'She had lots of acquaintances, but few close friends from what I could gather. She was besotted with Robert Lester though, in spite of her father's disapproval.' A flash of anger lit up Fielding's eyes. 'Adam can be a prize arsehole sometimes. When

191

he found out about the relationship he stopped Jess from seeing the lad. If you ask me, the man needs to drag himself out of the dark ages. He even tried to pay Robert off! Can you believe that?'

Daniels looked up from her note-taking, reminded of her conversation with Robert Lester, his assertion that Finch was a racist. If he'd been offered money to stay away from Jess, was it enough of a trigger to tip him over the edge? 'What form did that take?' she asked. 'I mean, did he meet with the lad, give him a cheque, or what?'

Fielding shook her head. 'Adam's far too clever for that. He'd never involve himself directly in such a transaction. He gave the money to Jessica, in cash I believe. She promised to end the relationship, but, instead of dumping Robert, gave the lot to charity and kept on seeing him behind Adam's back. That about sums her up really. She's fiercely independent. I'm not sure what more I can tell you.'

'Did Adam know they were still seeing one another?'

'I honestly don't know.'

'Was her relationship with Robert the only bone of contention between them?'

Fielding shrugged, hesitated.

There was something else. Daniels could sense it. 'If you know something—'

'I don't *know* anything, not for sure.' Fielding took a long, deep breath. 'If I repeat something Jess told me it's just hearsay, isn't it?'

'Let me be the judge of that.'

'You know that her mother died in a car crash many years ago?'

Daniels gave a little nod.

'Well, Jess is convinced Adam was responsible. She claims that he was pissed at the wheel, but . . . well, to put it bluntly, the police did nothing about it. She swears they covered it up.'

'That's quite an allegation.' Though she didn't like the way the conversation was going, Daniels' interest grew. 'What made her think that?'

'Please bear in mind she was very young at the time.'

Daniels encouraged her to go on.

'To this day she remembers the strong smell of alcohol on Adam's breath when he told her that Beth, her mother, was never coming home. I was convinced she was mistaken at first. Receiving such bloody awful news at such a young age is bound to have been traumatic. I thought perhaps she'd got her memories mixed up and, I don't know, maybe they became fixed as fact in her mind as she grew up. I think that's possible, don't you?'

'And now you've changed your mind?'

Fielding nodded. 'The more she talked about it, the more convinced I became that she was actually reliving a moment she'd played over and over in her head a million times before.'

'People drink when they're bereaved, don't they? That doesn't mean—'

'I totally agree. But Jess said Adam was distraught, couldn't stop crying for days.'

'As I said, it's what you'd expect from someone recently widowed.'

'That's also true. But Jessica swears she'd never seen him like that before or since. You know the man: stiff upper lip and all that crap. Does he strike you as a person who'd wear his heart on his sleeve? It really isn't his style. Anyway, that's all I know.' Fielding looked at her watch. 'Will you have dinner with me tonight?'

Daniels just looked at her.

'Detectives do eat, don't they?'

Detectives do eat, don't they?

Daniels felt her stomach lurch. Jo had used those very words a long time ago when Daniels declined a dinner invitation due to work commitments. On that occasion, she changed her mind and never looked back. Until it all went pear-shaped. Maybe now was the time to move on. For a moment, she envied Fielding. She was a professional in her own right, answerable to no one, confident and successful too—a woman without any baggage by the looks. She enjoyed life. And why not? If her website was anything to go by, she had a great gift, one she exploited to the full. Her talents were in great demand across the globe. It was refreshing to meet someone so obviously free to express herself without fear of being labelled, pilloried, or prevented from reaching the top through prejudice and bigotry.

Daniels felt like a fraud. She'd taken the path of least resistance, hidden her sexuality in order to further her ambition in her chosen career. The more she thought about it, the more she realized that Fielding was about as far away from her as it was possible to be. And that intrigued her.

'You're with someone.' Fielding looked disappointed. 'Of course you are, why wouldn't you be? That's a real shame, Kate Daniels.'

A smile crept over Daniels' face. *Bloody woman already knew her name.*

Fielding said, 'You didn't mind me asking?'

194

Daniels shook her head. She hadn't felt romantically inclined towards anyone in ages and was about to say something that sounded ridiculous, even in her own head, when a gentle tap on the door stopped her.

The door opened and Jo walked in.

'Oh, sorry, I didn't realize—'

Jo's voice caught in her throat. It was obvious she'd walked in on something sensitive. A deafening silence descended in the room. For a beat she just stood there, eventually telling Daniels she'd catch up with her later. It was a tricky moment. Fielding's piercing blue eyes shifted from Jo to Daniels and back again.

'You are one lucky lady,' she said.

45

Ending the interview, Daniels returned to the MIR hoping to find Jo and explain, but she was nowhere in sight. On the murder wall, a new event had been flagged up for her attention: *Mystery couple found. DC Maxwell on way with further info—ETA 11.30.* Some good news for once. Daniels looked at her watch. Maxwell would be arriving very soon. She pulled out her mobile phone, dialled Jo's number and waited.

Gormley mimicked Bugs Bunny as he arrived by her side. 'What's up, Doc?'

The phone continued to ring out in Daniels' ear. 'Looking for Jo, you seen her?'

'She was here earlier. Looking for you, as it happens.'

'Yeah, I know, but that's not a lot of help, is it?'

Carmichael raised her head from a nearby desk. 'I saw her a minute ago, heading out en route to HMP Acklington, I think she said. I got the impression she'd been called in.'

Their attention shifted as a civilian entered the MIR wearing overalls and a worn leather tool belt round his waist. He was whistling a happy tune, seemingly without a care in the world as he made off across the room. Daniels felt a pang of regret as she watched him unscrew Bright's nameplate, throw it in the bin and replace it with one bearing Naylor's name and rank.

The end of an era . . . but the beginning of a new one.

Gormley had read her mind. 'The king is dead, long live the king,' he said.

The ringing tone stopped. Jo's phone switched to voicemail. Daniels ended the call without leaving a message. But through the window she could see Jo's car where she'd parked it earlier.

She turned her attention back to Carmichael. 'You OK for tonight, Lisa?'

Carmichael nodded in the direction of Naylor's office. 'I've had my pep talk, including the third degree about what will happen to me if I screw up. I know what to do. To be honest, I can't wait to be a student again.'

'You might end up a hooker,' Gormley reminded her. 'Can you handle that?'

Carmichael feigned an edgy look. 'I'll give it a go, Sarge.'

Gormley said something nice about not taking unnecessary risks. Daniels saw his smile dissolve as Carmichael laughed off his concerns. He wasn't being melodramatic. Like many police officers, he was hard on the outside, soft on the inside, fiercely protective of his colleagues who, from the moment they donned a uniform and signed on the dotted line, became part of a second family almost. That was particularly true of his relationship with Carmichael, who had actually been a student not so very long ago. As her direct supervisor, it was his job to look out for her, teach her the ropes, encourage her ambition and give her room to grow. But that also meant he cared about her safety and the danger she'd undoubtedly face by going undercover.

He covered his concern by pulling her leg. 'Well, if you're working tonight, you knock off early, you hear me? Get your glad rags organized, then get some kip before you go out on the game.'

'He's right, Lisa,' Daniels said. 'But before you go, have a dig around in that computer of yours and see if you can pull an old accident report on Beth Finch.'

'Jessica's mum? Don't suppose you've got an FWIN?'

Daniels shook her head ruefully. A Force-Wide Incident Number was the case identifier that would allow Carmichael to call up the relevant file from the database in a matter of seconds. 'No, Lisa—but that's never stopped you before. I can't even tell you where it happened, only that it happened about seventeen years ago. Just do what you can, OK? There might be archived newspaper reports, given that it was a fatal crash. If you find anything, leave it on my desk.'

Gormley raised an inquisitive eyebrow. 'Problem?'

'Dunno yet,' Daniels said, walking away.

Feeling a sudden urge to find Jo before she left the building, Daniels quickly left the MIR and went in search of her. Racing down the corridor, she took the stairs to the floor below and headed for the rear exit. Turning the corner, she spotted Jo signing herself out on the professional visitors' log by the back door. It was a new fad, a health and safety initiative introduced by some nameless, faceless civilian at headquarters who hadn't grasped the concept that police officers had to get a shift on when they were called out. They didn't have time to put their clothes on properly, let alone stand in line to write their names down before leaving the station to attend mayhem on the streets.

Jo pocketed her pen, picked her briefcase up off the floor and slung a Burberry raincoat over her arm, glancing over her shoulder as she heard footsteps approaching.

'Hi!' she said. 'You want me?'

Daniels grinned. *Of course she wanted her.* 'Got time for a chat?'

'Unfortunately not, sorry.'

'I thought you wanted to speak to me.'

'I did, but it'll keep.' Jo glanced sideways. 'Who's your new friend?'

Daniels blushed. 'She isn't a friend, she's a witness.'

'Really?' Jo started walking. 'I'm not blind, Kate. Something was going on in there. But, hey, it's none of *my* business!'

'Damn right,' Daniels said, regretting her words immediately. Why in hell's name did they always end up arguing? They stopped walking as a group of uniformed officers entered the station via the back door. Stepping aside, they faced each other in stony silence from either side of the corridor as the group walked by, a chorus of *Morning ma'am* ringing out as they passed. Daniels waited until the group were out of earshot and then pointed to the exit. 'I'll walk you to your car. Nice set of wheels, by the way. Unusual choice for you, isn't it? Thought you hated gas guzzlers.'

'Times and circumstances change.' Jo took her keys from her pocket. 'You're not the only one with a new friend. I also have someone new in my life, someone energetic, outdoorsy; someone with no hang-ups, no rules or bloody regulations to consider; someone I can have fun with, like we used to, remember?'

A lump forming in Daniels' throat. 'Kirsten?'

'NO!' Jo reacted as if the suggestion was somehow ridiculous. '*Definitely* not Kirsten. You are crazy sometimes, Kate. You really are.'

'Then who? If I'm allowed to ask.'

'C'mon, I'll introduce you. I'd like it if you were mates.'

Whoever it was, Daniels certainly didn't want to meet her. She hated her guts already and didn't want to be mates. She followed Jo across the car park towards something she did like: the profiler's new Land Rover, the biggest, newest and shiniest vehicle there.

It looked great with the sun glinting off its metallic paintwork.

It reminded Daniels of the search team lined up in their Land Rover Defenders in the pouring rain. There was still no word from Weldon, or the geologist come to think of it, but the improving weather was good news. She prayed that it would hold. A horn peeped, interrupting her thoughts, as a jam sandwich swept by. The Traffic car was going too fast for her to identify who was at the wheel, but she waved back anyway. And when she turned back in the direction of the Land Rover, Jo was at the rear of the four-by-four with the tailgate open.

'Meet Nelson,' she said.

Intrigued, Daniels peered inside. Jo's new best friend was a puppy, a brown Labrador of dubious pedigree.

'I named him in honour of Mandela,' Jo grinned. 'Isn't he cute?'

'God, he's absolutely adorable!'

'He was found scavenging for food in the city centre and handed in to the shelter on the twentieth anniversary of Mandela's release from prison. I've been on their waiting list for ages, so they rang me.' Jo's happy expression faded a little. 'I wanted him, of course, but the timing was all wrong. He needed a lot of veterinary attention and I wasn't able to cope with him off the back of my accident, the remand, et cetera. So they found him a home elsewhere.'

'Then how did you end up with him?'

'His new owner died suddenly and they got back in touch.'

'Must've been fate.' Daniels wanted to add, *like us*, but refrained. She reached across to pat the dog's head. Nelson began to wag his tail then peed on the newspaper he was standing on. 'Great way to say hello!'

Jo laughed out loud. 'He's an embarrassment. I can't take him anywhere. Think yourself lucky he's not on the floor by your feet. I've got so many wet shoes I'm considering permanent flip-flops!'

'Am I allowed visiting rights?' Daniels asked.

Jo nodded, a hint of sadness in her eyes. 'I've got to get going.'

Daniels held the door open while Jo climbed in, then watched her drive away. She returned to the MIR, happy they were still friends. When they were more than that, they'd often talked of getting a dog. They had argued over what breed, Jo insisting on a Lab of any colour and description, while Daniels favoured a Border terrier like her nan used to own.

In the end they got neither.

The MIR was buzzing when Daniels entered. Following a leaflet drop, the couple seen acting suspiciously near the crime scene had come forward voluntarily. Ronnie Raine had been a good witness and DC Maxwell was looking pleased with himself as he took off his coat and hung it on the back of the chair.

'Let me guess,' Robson feigned concentration. 'Bet it was a courting couple getting their leg over in the fresh air. There's nowt like a good ol' shag on top of a cowpat or two.'

'Have you been out there at the crack of dawn?' Maxwell asked, rubbing his hands together. 'It's bloody parky, I can tell you.' He sat down at his computer and logged on. 'Not an extra-marital either.'

'Roman soldiers?' Brown suggested, humouring him.

'Border Reivers?' someone at the back shouted.

'Do we look psychic?' Gormley chipped in. 'Stop pissing about and tell us.'

'Hank's right, Neil,' Daniels said. 'Are they in the

frame, or out?'

'Out,' Maxwell said decisively, swivelling his chair round to face her. 'Beverley and Alec Wilkinson are father and daughter, an entrepreneurial couple looking to make a buck by digging up Roman coins using metal detectors. He was keen but she wasn't. They hadn't asked the landowner's permission, hence the row Raine talked about.'

'Didn't he say she was injured in some way?'

'Fell down a foxhole and twisted her ankle.'

'Proof?' Daniels wanted to be absolutely sure.

Maxwell wafted an admission slip in the air. 'Obtained from A&E at Hexham General Hospital, no less.'

'Good work!' Daniels thought for a moment. Something was missing. 'I don't remember any mention of equipment though, do you?'

'That's because they stashed it in a disused byre so as not to draw too much attention to themselves. When Amy's body was found and we turned up in droves, they didn't dare go back for it.'

'Did you check it out?' Daniels again.

'Not personally. I sent the community beat officer who was first at the crime scene—he knows the area like the back of his hand.'

'I remember him. And?'

'It's still there. End of, I'd say.'

'Brick wall more like,' Brown added.

Daniels agreed.

'What do you want me to do?' Maxwell asked. 'We could charge them with trespass, but that's about all.'

'Not worth the paperwork,' Daniels said. 'Write

it up and log it in the system as an NFA.'

Maxwell nodded. A No Further Action from the DCI was what he'd hoped for.

'Boss?' Carmichael put her hand up. 'That stuff you wanted is on your desk.'

'Stuff?'

'Beth Finch accident report,' Carmichael reminded her. 'It was one of ours.'

Daniels thanked her and told her to go home. Then she went straight to her office, made herself a cup of coffee and rang Weldon. The search was now well underway, but so far there was nothing to report. No sightings. Not a whiff of any activity in the mineshafts they'd entered so far.

They agreed to keep in touch.

Daniels put down the phone, took a sip of her coffee, put her feet up on her desk and turned her attention to the report Carmichael had left for her. It was a flimsy document, just two pages long, beginning with Finch's account of the accident as taken by the attending officer at the scene:

Mr Adam Finch, the driver, claims that his vehicle—a Mercedes-Benz 300-Class—left the A696 near Belsay when an unknown vehicle, described as a small hatchback, shot out of the B6544 junction without warning, causing him to swerve violently to avoid a collision. The hatchback drove off without stopping.

Daniels' eyes travelled down the page to a diagram showing the exact location where the accident happened, including the direction it had been

203

travelling in and the position and orientation of the Mercedes when it came to a sudden and disastrous halt embedded in a tree. She knew the road well; an unlit, dangerous stretch with a sharp right-hander that was difficult to negotiate at the best of times.

She read on, noting that a call had come in to the control room at 01.26 on 8 November 1993 with a report of two casualties and an indication of a woman unconscious at the scene in need of urgent assistance. The dispatcher immediately sent one Traffic car, an ambulance and two fire service vehicles. The Traffic car was first on the scene, the officer finding Beth Finch in a bad way and still trapped in the Mercedes-Benz. Paramedics followed soon after. They managed to cut her free and transport her by ambulance to A&E, Newcastle General Hospital.

She was pronounced dead on arrival.

It was an unremarkable RTA report, like many others Daniels had read over the years. She turned the page and found a note: *Driver breathalysed negative*. As her eyes slid over the attending officer's identity—name, rank and number—she felt physically sick.

46

Jessica was drifting . . .

Her father's voice, stern and unfriendly, seemed near and yet very far away. She hadn't meant to disobey him. Not really. But he didn't have the right to tell her what to do any more. She was a grown-up with a mind of her own. Robert popped into her head. She wondered if he was searching for her. Of course he was, they adored each other. They had a future together, no matter what her father said. In her mind's eye, she pictured Robert as he was when she'd last seen him, happy and smiling when she told him of her plans to cut loose from her father and find work abroad.

How long ago was that?

A day?

A week?

Jessica held this image.

She felt good and warm and . . .

She began to cry.

No! She couldn't afford to cry. Tears were no longer an expression of how unhappy she was but precious drops of liquid she needed to stay alive.

'Stop snivelling!' Her father's voice again.

Did the man have no compassion?

'Dad?' she called out into the darkness.

'Dad? Dad? Dad? Dad?'

Please, Dad, find me before it's too late.

Jessica looked down at the rising water, wondering how long it took for a person to drown. She'd read somewhere that drowning was once used to determine if women were witches or not, the suggestion being that the guilty would stay afloat while the innocent would not.

Well, she was innocent and she didn't want to drown.

Not here . . .

And suddenly, all she could think of was water rushing into her body, both her stomach and her airways, pushing out the oxygen and causing untold panic as she tried, at first, to hold her

205

breath . . .

And then?

She would try to draw breath even when fully submerged, setting off a catastrophic chain of events leading to . . .

Asphyxia . . .

Cerebral hypoxia . . .

Myocardial infarction . . .

Death.

Please, Robert, find me.

47

'T893!' Daniels yelled. 'Ring any bells?'

The Toyota was stationary, parked in a place they always used when they wanted to have a rant without fear of being overheard. It was a busy underpass close to Newcastle's central bypass. Rush hour. Cars and lorries flashing past in both directions. Exhaust fumes. Irate drivers. The usual city mayhem. A throwback from her days in the drugs squad. A place to meet her snouts.

The graffiti on Gormley's side of the car was the best he'd ever seen, a flamboyant piece of street art with a tag he didn't recognize. New kid on the block, perhaps? As soon as Daniels pulled in, he could see that something was troubling her. And now he knew why.

'Tango, fucking, eight, nine, three!' she said again, so enraged her face had gone white.

Gormley stopped admiring the wall and turned to face her, curiosity getting the better of him. 'That's Bright's old number from when he was in

Traffic, isn't—'

'Precisely!' Daniels said. 'The RTA report on Beth Finch? Guess who the attending officer was? Only he was a sergeant then and not the head of fucking CID!'

Gormley flinched as she continued to rant. In all the years they had worked together, he'd never seen her so angry. She looked as if she was about to blow a gasket. 'It was a long time ago. Maybe he didn't think it was relevant now, forgot to mention it. Who knows? You said yourself he's had a tough time of it lately.'

His attempt to calm Daniels down by making light of what he knew was a very serious situation only made matters worse. 'That's bollocks! You know it and so do I!' Daniels rounded on him. 'He deliberately kept it from us, Hank. He's been protecting Finch all along. And the only way I get to find out why is by asking him outright.'

Gormley settled back in his seat, defeated. 'Headquarters it is then.'

'He's gone home,' Daniels grumbled. 'Or so he told Ellen.'

'Another one of his headaches?'

'Not yet,' she said caustically. 'Ask me later!'

She started the engine and pulled out into fast-moving traffic, receiving a blast from the horn of the Vauxhall behind. Its driver was red in the face, a man carrying too much weight and far too much attitude for Daniels' liking. He remained glued to her bumper as they sped along the dual carriageway, flashing his lights and yelling like a man possessed.

Daniels was seething. 'You seen this wanker behind?'

Gormley glanced in his wing mirror and caught the whites of a man's eyes. Each time Daniels changed lanes he was right on her tail, weaving in and out of traffic like he owned the bloody road, causing alarm and distress to other motorists forced to take avoiding action.

'He's going to kill someone unless you show him a clean pair of radials.'

'I'll do more than that.'

Daniels floored the accelerator. As her advanced police driving skills automatically kicked in, Gormley relaxed back in his seat and crossed his arms over his chest, a huge grin on his face. Up ahead, traffic lights were about to change. Daniels checked her rear-view mirror again and timed her move just right. Depressing her brake pedal, she slowed the Toyota right down—long before it was necessary—forcing the irate driver into the fast lane. He squealed to a halt parallel with the Toyota, wound down his nearside window and began haranguing her, revving his engine all the while, a hateful look in his eyes.

'You got a road-rage problem, mate?' Daniels said calmly. The man's face paled as she held up her warrant card. The lights changed and she drove off burning rubber as the Vauxhall's engine stalled. She grinned at Gormley, her mood a little better now. 'Maybe he'll wind his neck in next time.'

They drove on, heading east towards Tynemouth, both remaining silent as the miles rolled quickly by. At the end of the coast road, Daniels took the second exit left, passing a school and a swimming pool as the road narrowed, then on to a wide avenue once dubbed 'Millionaires'

Row'. She'd never fully understood why. The houses on either side were big, certainly, each one different from the next, and in their heyday they were probably the dog's bollocks. But now they looked sad and dated, certainly not somewhere *she'd* choose to live.

In what seemed like no time at all they arrived at their destination. Daniels killed the engine but made no attempt to get out of the car. There were no signs of life in Bright's house. No light on in the living room to suggest that he was home. The curtains were drawn back carelessly with no regard for aesthetics, one side more open than the other, a bunch of dead flowers in a vase on the window ledge.

It was a dark, lifeless, shell of a house now.

Daniels swallowed hard, wondering what on earth Stella Bright would have made of it. No doubt she would have clipped Bright's ear and told him to get a grip. Told him to have more self-respect and stop dwelling on the past. But the man was still grieving, unable to accept she'd gone. And Daniels couldn't help him with that.

Gormley's voice filtered through her sadness.

'Want me to come in?' he said. 'I'm thinking you might need a referee.'

He already knew the answer before he asked the question. She shook her head, appreciating his concern. *Everyone deserved a Gormley.* He was more like a cuddly big brother than her DS. Her go-to person in times of crisis, one who would never, ever, let her down. But on this occasion, she considered it unwise to involve him in her fight. And there was a good reason for that. A reason she was unwilling to share with him right now.

She unclipped her seat belt. 'Get a bit of shut-eye. You look like you need it.'

Feeling his eyes on her back, she got out of the car, opened the gate and walked up the garden path. She rang the front door bell. A few seconds later, Bright appeared. He was obviously surprised to see her there.

'Problem?' he asked.

'You tell me,' she said, pushing past into his hallway.

'What the—' Gobsmacked by her rudeness, Bright just stood there, holding the door ajar, breathing alcohol fumes all over her. 'Well, come in why don't you?'

As he began to shut the door, he glanced at the Toyota. Gormley stared back at him, a grim expression on his face. Acknowledging the DS with a nod, Bright shut the door and followed Daniels into his living room, his face flushing up with embarrassment as she scanned the untidy room. The TV was on, the volume turned up loud. A number of empty beer cans lay on the floor, along with a pizza box and the remains of last night's evening meal.

'So this is how you spend your half-days.' Daniels sounded more like a whingeing ex-wife than a subordinate colleague. She picked up the remote and killed the TV, a disappointed expression on her face. 'So tell me about Beth Finch.'

'What about her? She's been dead for years.' Bright held up a can of beer.

Daniels shook her head. 'Water, bottled if you have it—tap water if not.'

Bright left her and went into the kitchen. She waited for a moment, her eyes finding a

210

photograph of Bright and Stella in happier times, his arm round her waist outside a stunning lodge in New Zealand at the world-famous Treetops resort where they'd spent their silver wedding anniversary.

The sound of glass breaking made her start.

She walked into the kitchen to find Bright on his hands and knees, sweeping away the remains of a glass tumbler with a dustpan and brush. The last time she'd been in the room, Stella was still alive. *But only just.* He wasn't coping and had asked for her help. The place was an absolute mess then, as it was now: cluttered and disorganized, dishes piled high in the sink; empty bottles for recycling left on benches waiting to be put out; unpaid—in some cases unopened—bills on the work surface; a fridge it seemed with little in it.

God help us. This is the head of CID!

Bright stood up. He emptied the broken glass into the bin, then took another tumbler from a cupboard and turned on the tap. He ran the water until it was cold, then filled the glass and handed it to her. Daniels had the distinct impression he was going to ask for her help again, only this time it wasn't to clean the house or advise on the best way to care for a sick wife.

'I know you were at the scene, guv.' She never took her eyes off him as she sat down at the kitchen table. Placing her glass on the crumby surface, she pushed a pile of last week's newspapers aside. 'There's no point in denying it, I've seen the report.'

Bright's right eye began to twitch. He took a swig of his beer and then sat down too. Supporting his head in his hands, elbows on the table, he began

211

massaging his temples, clearly a man under great pressure. Whether it was self-imposed or not, Daniels wasn't qualified to say. But he didn't get the sympathy vote. Not this time.

'And don't come over all poorly with me, because it won't wash!'

'You wouldn't understand if I told you,' he said defiantly.

'Damn right I won't. You blew in the bag for him, didn't you?'

48

It wasn't Daniels' finest hour, watching her boss cry. The floodgates had finally opened, his grief and pain pouring out, as she knew it would have to sooner or later—and not before time—triggered by the memory of another man's wife bleeding to death on a cold winter's night. Trapped by her legs under the bonnet of a Mercedes, Beth Finch had suffered a ruptured spleen due the impact of hitting the tree. An unfortunate twist of fate, Daniels thought, to die from an injury to a non-essential organ when urgent medical treatment would almost certainly have saved her life.

The luck of the draw didn't quite cover it.

Daniels had left Bright in a bad way, neither admitting nor denying that he'd taken the breathalyser for Adam Finch. He wasn't so stupid as to compromise her professionally, but she knew in her heart that offences *had* been committed. An offence of perverting the course of justice for him, one of death by dangerous driving for Adam

Finch, who would almost certainly have gone to prison had he been found drunk at the wheel of his car, irrespective of third-party involvement.

Gormley knew it too.

He wasn't asleep—just pretending to be—when she got back in the car. He opened one eye for a millisecond and then closed it again when he saw her glum face. He was good at that, knew instinctively when to talk, when not to. And he'd learned a long time ago not to ask a question when he didn't want to hear the answer. Would that she had also learned that lesson and kept her big mouth shut instead of storming in there, all guns blazing, looking for a fight and finding one too.

And now?

Now she had knowledge she should disclose, and that made her feel very uncomfortable. Bright had done the wrong thing for all the right reasons, acted out of loyalty to a man who'd once saved his life when they were in the military together. He'd made a split-second decision that night, a mistake that was catching up with him nearly two decades later, threatening to bite him on the arse when he was at the very pinnacle of his career.

Daniels asked herself what purpose would be served if she were to drag up past indiscretions seventeen years after the event. Bright was already on the floor; losing his job would crush him totally. The revelation would sully that impeccable reputation Adam Finch was so keen to hold on to. Two men would be destroyed. Good men, on the whole, who'd already lost so much. And then there was Jessica. Poor, dear, Jessica. What would such exposure to do to her if she was ever found?

IF was such a big word.

It was dark already. The road was busy with people heading into the city for a night out. A taxi shot by in the outside lane, a couple of scantily clad women in the rear, already half-cut, by the looks of them. Daniels could do with a stiff drink herself. She nudged Gormley's arm as they pulled into the station; he grunted, looking around him as she waited for the barrier to lift.

Stretching his arms above his head, he yawned. 'You got time for a quickie or you heading straight home?' he asked.

'You want to rephrase that?' Daniels managed a grin, unclipped her seat belt and opened the car door. 'I'm checking in first and then I'm out of here. I want a long soak in a hot bath and three fingers of whisky. And that's just for starters, the day I've had. What about you?'

They got out of the car and walked towards the station's rear entrance.

'I'm going to ring Carmichael. Then Julie wants me home.'

'Good plan.'

It sounded as though things were improving for him at home. Gormley was giving it his best shot and his wife could ask for no more. Daniels swiped her warrant card at the back door. They made their way upstairs and along the corridor to the MIR. She was about to go inside when Gormley hesitated, forcing her to turn back.

Looking deep into her eyes like a concerned friend would, he said: 'You want to talk, you know where I am. But don't do anything hasty, yeah?'

She knew what he was getting at but made no comment. Once inside, Gormley peeled off in the direction of his desk while she checked the murder wall. There were no new events listed, so she went straight to Naylor's office, knocked gently on his door and waited. She heard his voice calling her in and caught Gormley's uneasiness loud and clear from across the room.

He didn't want her in there.

She let go of the handle and turned away.

49

Fuse was the club of choice: the place to be if you happened to be a Durham university student. A supporting group were up on stage playing to an appreciative crowd, three guys on their feet and a young Asian girl on the drums. DC Lisa Carmichael's head was thumping as the music kicked its way around the room. She couldn't hear her own voice as she ordered a vodka and tonic, let alone the barmaid's response as she leaned across the bar towards her.

Superintendent Naylor's instructions had been quite clear. 'Blend in. Make friends quickly. Stick close to the girls without much cash. Eyes and ears open. Don't get waylaid or involved in anything other than what you're there to do. And keep talking to your backup. You're there primarily for the prostitution racket, but if you happen across *our* man, no heroics. *Capiche*?'

Capiche.

Carmichael smiled.

Naylor was nice, *really* attractive, sexy even—in the way that all powerful men were sexy. Or was that rich men? No rich men were ever ugly, wasn't that the way the saying went? Not that she believed it. Besides, there were more ways of being ugly than in the mug department. Celebs nowadays had big egos. When they ponced around the world with lookers half their age, did they seriously think these women were in love with their personalities? And what about the women themselves? Waking up with some wrinkly old git lying by their side, then spending hour after long hour hanging on their every word. It was prostitution, plain and simple, as far as Carmichael was concerned.

As she climbed down from her high horse in the form of a bar stool, Carmichael accidentally spilled the drink of the middle-aged man sitting to her left—an altogether more pleasant man than the wankers she'd just been thinking about.

'Oh, bugger! I'm so sorry. Let me get you another.'

He told her not to worry about it, ordered another drink and asked her to join him. She held up a full glass and shook her head.

'You a mature student then?' Carmichael said.

'Lecturer, actually.'

'Letch. . .urer?' Carmichael felt decidedly odd. 'Of what?'

'Anthropology.' The guy held out his hand. 'Steve Curtis, pleased to meet you.'

'That's humans, yeah?'

'Sort of.' The man grinned. 'You new here? Don't think I recognize you—'

'Opted for Bristol. Couldn't hack it . . .' Carmichael stopped talking, urging him to fuck off and let her have her hand back. Her lips felt rubbery. There was so little saliva in her mouth, her tongue stuck to the roof of it and her words

216

came out all wrong. There were now two Steves sitting next to her and she couldn't remember her script. 'Missed my mates . . . family'n stuff . . . sooo, I rang up . . . binned my course . . . here now.'

'What are you studying?'

'Same ol' bollocks.'

Carmichael felt clammy. Dizzy. She mumbled some ridiculous convoluted excuse and left her new friend at the bar, affronted and in mid-conversation. Wending her way through the gyrating crowd to the ladies' she found several other students there and caught snippets of gossip about someone called Steve. Her ears pricked up as she realized this could be the same man she'd been talking to. One of the gossiping girls was in a worse condition than she was. Very, *very* drunk. Bryony, they called her, a skinny blonde who was trying unsuccessfully to reapply bright red lippy while asking the others what she should do.

Carmichael tried hard to focus on the girl, but the more she stared at her the fuzzier she became. Pushing to get nearer, she accidentally bumped the arm of the big bugger standing to Bryony's left and received a mouthful of abuse in return.

'Hey! Watch what you're doing, ya minger. I was here first.'

Momentarily, Carmichael thought about taking her on, but didn't think she stood a cat in hell's chance in her condition. Then Naylor's words popped into her head. 'Don't get involved in anything other than what you're there to do. And keep talking to your backup.'

Andy! Shit!

Carmichael backed off, apologized and went to

217

the wash basin. Dumping the vodka, she replaced it with water and took a long drink. She set down the glass, turned on the tap and lifted a pool of cold water to her face. The person facing her in the mirror didn't look at all familiar. She had gaunt features, dilated pupils and her hair stuck to her head as if she'd been outside in the rain.

'What's wrong with you?' a dark shadow said. 'You using?'

Carmichael waved it—her—away. She glanced again in the mirror. Despite having washed them off, beads of sweat had reappeared on her brow.

The shadow doubled in size.

A muffled voice.

'Jesus! You got aids or sommat?'

Another voice. 'Leave the skanky tramp alone, Bry. She's so wasted she can't even see you, let alone hear you. C'mon, let's go.'

The dark shadow moved away, taking the strange voices with it. Carmichael had to get out of there too and made a heroic effort to follow it out of the door. It was nearly midnight as she staggered on to the dance floor. The main act were giving it their all on stage, a tune that sounded like recordings of whales and dolphins she'd heard on wildlife programmes on TV—strange elongated calls from somewhere deep under the sea.

Carmichael fought her way to a particular table. Her backup was no longer sat there. Was it that table? Or that one? *Jesus!* She forced her eyes to open wider and looked around her, unable to focus properly. The whole room began to revolve around her, slowly at first, then faster and faster, the coloured clothing of the dancers merging into a psychedelic vortex which then stopped abruptly, sending her reeling off to one side.

A man's hand caught her elbow and pulled her to one side. She struggled to get free but it was no use. Suddenly the floor came up to meet her.

Then everything went black.

50

The chirp-chirp tone and the vibrating buzz of a mobile got louder and louder as it rang out. Daniels slowly opened her eyes, trying to drag herself from sleep. She lay motionless in the darkness, trying to make sense of what she was listening to.

A light was flashing . . .

The noise persisted . . .

And suddenly she was wide awake.

Turning over in bed, she reached out for her mobile as it disappeared over the edge of her bedside table, falling to the floor with a solid thump. Pulling herself up on her elbows, she turned on the light, wondering who was calling at ten past three in the morning. The control room usually called her landline.

Carmichael!

No. According the display it was DC Brown.

'Boss, we have a problem. Lisa's in a bad way . . .' He sounded frantic as he rattled off an address not far away. 'That's her new flat. You need to come now!'

'On my way,' Daniels hung up.

She'd forgotten that Carmichael had moved. She'd been brought up by an aunt after her natural parents died, swept off a mountainside by an avalanche while on a skiing holiday in France when she was only three years old. She'd recently taken advantage of a dwindling housing market and—as a first-time buyer with a steady job—had seized the opportunity to strike out for independence.

Please God, let her be OK.

Daniels jumped out of bed, heart racing and imagination in overdrive. Pulling her hair into an untidy ponytail, she dressed quickly, a pair of old jeans, the first sweater she could find, trainers. Grabbing her biker's jacket from the seat of her motorcycle, she left the house glad she'd refuelled the Toyota on the way back from the coast. The tank had been that low she'd been driving on fumes.

At the top of Osborne Road, she turned left at the T-junction and floored the accelerator, then straight on at the Blue House roundabout skirting the Town Moor. There were few vehicles about aside from the odd taxi and just one pedestrian, from what she could see. Traffic lights up ahead were on green. She turned right, passing a row of very posh houses, a parade of shops, then took a left up Kenton Lane, putting her foot down, checking the speedo all the while. Thirty, forty, fifty, fifty-five. . . Heading slightly uphill now and still accelerating, a vehicle displaying blues and twos suddenly appeared in her rear-view mirror.

Shit!

The patrol car overtook at speed, its blue light flashing. It slowed down in front of her, its POLICE STOP sign illuminated on the roof. Daniels pulled over, hoping it was someone she knew, trying to think of a plausible excuse for having exceeded the speed limit in a built-up area. Not finding one.

She sat there despondently, drumming her fingers on the Toyota's steering wheel, staring at the brake lights of the patrol car.

Carmichael.

'Get a move on then!' Daniels whispered under her breath.

The Traffic officer didn't get out of the patrol car. He was obviously doing a vehicle check. Daniels leaned forward and took her police radio from the glove compartment. She turned it on, just as an urgent call for assistance in the vicinity came through.

'Control to all units. Police officer requires assistance, Stamfordham Road.'

Two units responded immediately: '3398, Byker . . . 3467, Gosforth, on way.'

'Control to all units . . .' The radio again, repeating the call. 'Police officer requires assistance, Stamfordham Road.'

The Traffic man heard it too and responded, '5547 . . . Kenton Lane.'

Daniels did likewise: '7824 . . . Kenton Lane also.'

In the car in front, the Traffic officer quickly checked his mirror, then turned on his siren and sped off. Daniels followed suit, hanging on his tail past the Crofters Lodge public house. They shot across a busy roundabout, Daniels adding her own blue lights to his. Cars gave way as they continued at speed to the location given, concern for a fellow officer taking priority over everything else.

Carmichael would have to wait.

The radio crackled into life again. '3398, stand

221

down. All other units proceed until advised otherwise, over.'

Daniels kept driving. The control room were now satisfied that enough officers were en route and had stood down the car the furthest distance away. She continued to follow the patrol car but was forced to take avoiding action when a car shot out from a side street. It too was being pursued.

It was all happening tonight.

The control room again: '5678 on scene . . . one person under arrest. Officer requires ambulance attention but everything under control now. All units en route to assistance call, Stamfordham Road, can now stand down, over.'

The Traffic officer ahead was first to respond: '5547, that's received.'

'7824, copy that,' Daniels said.

The patrol car stopped at the side of the road, allowing Daniels to overtake him. A little further along, she did a U-turn and drove back towards him, stopping as she pulled up alongside. She smiled at him through the window, lifted her right hand off the wheel and slapped her left, acknowledging her wrongdoing.

He smiled back.

Daniels drove on, bloody lucky to escape a fixed penalty ticket. Arriving back at the busy roundabout where the emergency call came in, she thought about ringing Brown. But she was now only half a mile away so she pushed on instead. Turning left on to the airport road, she took the third exit towards Kingston Park. Three minutes later, she reached the address Andy Brown had given her, a 1930s semi-detached on the main road at Kenton Bank Foot.

Brown's blue Honda was parked, nose in, at a slight angle on the steep driveway, the lights still on, the passenger door wide open. Daniels pulled up behind it and got out. Finding the control switch for the lights, she turned them off and made her way to the front door. But before she had a chance to ring the bell, it was yanked open by a hassled-looking Brown.

'What the hell happened?' she said as she entered the house.

'Either she drank too much or someone spiked her drink.'

'Not good enough, Andy! Which was it?'

Brown looked at the floor. 'I dunno . . .'

'Either way she fucked up . . .' Daniels said. 'Where is she?'

Brown nodded towards the stairs.

Daniels took them two at a time, arriving in a bedroom at the front of the house where a light was on. Carmichael was splayed out on a double bed, completely out of it. Her shirt was up around her midriff where Brown had dumped her, having struggled to carry her up the stairs. Her pulse was racing slightly but her temperature appeared normal. Daniels sat down next to her and lifted one of her eyelids. The DC moaned but the eye underneath failed to register.

'She just looks like she's off her face to me,' Daniels said. 'What happened?'

Brown sat down on a chair near the window. He looked worn out. He was wearing a navy shirt, sleeves rolled up, sweat patches clearly visible under his armpits. He desperately needed a shave and a change of clothes. From the look of him, a stiff drink wouldn't go amiss either.

223

'I had the eyeball the whole time, boss. I promise you. One minute she was fine, sitting having a drink at the bar—'

'Was she talking to anyone?' Daniels interrupted.

'Yeah, this guy.'

Brown dug out his mobile, accessed the image gallery and handed the phone to her. Just then, Carmichael moved her arm across her chest, her eyelids twitching. Daniels watched her for a moment and then zoomed in on the image Brown had captured on his phone. The man in the photograph was smartly dressed, middle-aged, of slim build with dark hair flecked grey at the sides. He had perfect shaped eyebrows, was a man who obviously looked after himself. He reminded her of BBC television football commentator Alan Hansen.

'Who is he?' she said.

Brown shrugged, glancing at Carmichael. 'You'll have to ask Lisa.'

Yeah right. 'So, one minute she was fine. Then what?'

'She went to the ladies' loo. I thought she looked a bit spaced out so I kept an eye on the door. She was in there a while. When she came out she'd lost it completely. I had to bring her out, boss. Believe me, I had no choice.'

'You did good, Andy. Don't beat yourself up over it.'

Daniels was silent for a while, studying the Hansen lookalike.

'There are more photos,' Brown said.

Daniels scrolled through several images, some close-ups, others taken further away. He'd managed to catch the man from a variety of angles.

They were good enough to make a definite identification.

'He wasn't the only one who could have spiked her drink.' Brown's eyes found Carmichael again, concern for his colleague written all over him. 'The place was heaving all night, three deep at the bar at times. There were several changes of staff too. Should I have taken her to A & E?'

'Only if you wanted to ruin her!'

Daniels was being ironic, but she knew he understood. If a serving police officer arrived at hospital under the influence of drugs, it would hardly sit well on her personnel file. At best, it would throw doubt over her chances of promotion if it became common knowledge. At worst it would end her police career.

And no one wanted that.

'You did the right thing, Andy.' Daniels tapped her DC's arm. 'Now fuck off home and leave Lisa to me. She's going to feel like shit when she wakes up and she won't want you here. It's best if I look after her.'

Brown hesitated. He didn't look happy to leave.

'Go on, get out of here. If she gets worse, I'll call a doctor.'

Brown began to walk away.

'And, Andy . . .?' Daniels waited for him to turn round and face her. 'This goes no further, you hear me? I'll tell Hank in the morning, but nobody else needs to know about it. Agreed?'

Brown forced a weak smile. 'Agreed.'

Daniels gave a reassuring nod. She knew he'd keep his word. Brown and Carmichael were great friends. They'd joined MIT together and a healthy dollop of competitive spirit had developed between them, a strong bond and a camaraderie that would stick with them throughout their service.

It was clear from his glum expression that he felt responsible for not having protected her. He was her backup, put there specifically to watch her six. No matter what Daniels said to him now, nothing would dissuade him from the belief that he'd failed spectacularly in that regard. But there was only one person to blame for what had happened, and *she* was lying flat out on the bed.

51

Carmichael's kitchen-diner was at the back of the house: a light, airy room, ripe for entertaining. It had been two rooms once, knocked into one in order to maximize the available space. It had an island in the centre separating the eating area from newly fitted kitchen units and enough electrical gadgets on show to put John Lewis to shame: microwave, digi radio, three iPods no less, docking station and a huge, flat-screen, high-definition TV mounted on the wall at the far end.

Using a remote, Daniels turned it on.

The picture was crystal clear, the sound quality superb; hardly surprising, given Carmichael's interest in all things digital. The DCI listened to the headlines while making a pot of coffee and some toast. She'd woken up in a chair in Carmichael's bedroom with a very stiff neck and a paperback book on her knee: *The Giant Book of Dangerous Women*, edited by Richard Glyn Jones.

An intriguing read she'd dipped in and out of during the night, a book about the most murderous women in the world—including Ma Barker, Myra Hindley and Ruth Ellis—a woman the author claimed had killed in an emotional frenzy but was hanged for premeditated murder. The resultant outcry had led to a majority vote in the House of Commons to abolish hanging in 1956.

Daniels wasn't opposed to capital punishment per se. An eye for an eye seemed fair and reasonable to her. But miscarriages of justice *did* happen and—even though Britain's prisons were bursting at the seams—one innocent person put to death was more than her conscience could stomach. No. On this emotive issue the law makers had got it right.

For once.

Daniels' wristwatch bleeped. She'd set it to go off at fifteen-minute intervals in order to keep a close watch over her young DC, make sure she didn't choke on her own vomit during the night. But Carmichael had slept peacefully, occasionally stirring, but never fully waking up. Daniels felt suddenly fatigued. Her eyes were sore, gritty, the way eyes felt when you had to get up at some ungodly hour to catch an early flight with a ridiculous check-in time. Or, worse still, travel during the night.

No wonder they called them red-eye flights.

Lisa Carmichael looked no better than Daniels felt when she appeared in the doorway fresh from the shower. She was barefoot, dressed in a navy towelling robe, her hair in a turban to match. The cocktail of drink and drugs had taken its toll on her appearance. Her skin was sallow and dehydrated and she could hardly stand up on her pins. From the look of her, she wanted to curl up in a ball and die.

'Sit down,' Daniels said.

Obediently, Carmichael pulled a chair out from the dining-room table, grimacing as it scraped across the hard wooden floor. Flopping down on it, she made no attempt to speak.

'Here, drink this,' Daniels said.

Placing a mug of steaming coffee on the table, she walked back to the kitchen area to get toast. She had no interest in giving her young protégé any sympathy. Carmichael had fucked up big style and deserved all that was coming to her. Question was, would she get back on her bike and start pedalling, or would she fade away like a puff of smoke?

Daniels had known it happen before.

Walking back to the table with a plate of toast, she sat down too, trying to keep her temper in check. She was boiling up inside, angry with Carmichael for making such a mess of things, for allowing a man who may or may not be of interest to them to slip through her fingers.

Carmichael looked up expectantly, waiting for the tirade.

It didn't take long to arrive.

'You never do that again. Do I make myself clear?' Daniels didn't wait for a reply. 'I take it you've heard of Rohypnol? ANY woman with ANY sense watches her drink in a club, doesn't she? Jesus, Lisa! First rule: you buy a drink that comes in a bottle with the top on. Second: you open it yourself and never, EVER put it down!

Third: you keep your finger over the mouth of the bottle the whole time.'

'Don't go on, boss. I feel bad enough.'

'And so you bloody should! Andy had no choice but to pull you out. Fortunately for you, everyone in there took you for a pisshead. You're not a pisshead, are you?'

'No! Of course not, I—'

'You sure about that?'

Carmichael didn't reply, just sat with her head in her hands. Daniels pushed the toast across the table towards her and she immediately pushed it back.

'You going to tell Naylor?'

'No. But don't think for one minute it's to protect your arse, because it's not! Your mistake could have cost you—not only your livelihood, but your life. Hank will have to know, obviously. But I don't want your cock-up reflecting on Naylor, not on his first day with us. He doesn't need it and, frankly, neither do I.'

'I'm sorry, boss. I never had much to drink, I promise you. Two vodkas, that was it. Someone definitely spiked my drink and I've a good idea who. Trouble is, I just can't picture him.' Carmichael shut her eyes, trying hard to remember. But it was no use. She opened them again, her face a sickly shade of grey. After a few minutes, she said: 'He was an older guy, I think. Smart, I think—'

'You think? You're going to have to do a damn sight better than that!'

'I'm not sure.' Carmichael met Daniels' steady gaze across the table, fiery eyes that could cut through steel. 'Maybe it'll come back to me.'

Without saying another word, the DCI stood up and went out into the hallway. She leapt up the stairs two at a time, turning left when she reached the landing. Her leather jacket was hanging untidily over the back of a chair in Carmichael's room. In the right-hand pocket she found Brown's mobile. Returning to the kitchen, she accessed the photographs he'd taken at Fuse, found a particularly good one, zoomed in on the man's face and showed it to Lisa.

'Is that him?'

Carmichael gave a little nod, her eyes misting up. She turned her head, suddenly interested in the patio doors and a well-tended garden beyond, a greenhouse, a little shed and fruit trees on the boundary fence. It was a dull, grey day outside. Depressing, much like the mood in the room.

'Get dressed,' Daniels said. 'We've work to do. And by the way, you'd better eat that bloody toast. I don't make breakfast for just anybody!'

Carmichael managed a weak grin. She pointed to the living room, asking Daniels to wait there while she went upstairs to get dressed. Daniels got up. Taking her coffee with her, she wandered through into a pleasant room with a wooden floor, an open fireplace with a rug in front of the hearth. Two comfy red sofas sat at right angles to one another and there was a second, even bigger, plasma television screen fixed to one wall. On either side of the fireplace, floor-to-ceiling bookshelves housed a massive collection of DVDs—the biggest she had ever seen outside of a shop on the high street.

It was like a mini cinema.

Carmichael's movie taste was diverse: everything

from romcoms through to sci-fi, horror and all drama in between. One DVD stuck out slightly from the rest. Assuming the disc was in the player, Daniels pulled it down. The cover featured Russell Crowe, Ben Affleck and Helen Mirren. It was one of her favourite thrillers: *State of Play.*

The muffled buzz of Carmichael's hair drier reached her through the ceiling. A few minutes later it stopped, replaced by the sound of feet running down the stairs a lot quicker than they had gone up. Carmichael entered eating cold toast, made up and ready to go, her hair tied back now, no longer hanging loose around her shoulders.

A Herculean effort in anyone's book, Daniels thought.

Carmichael just stood, waiting for Daniels to make a move.

'Sit down, Lisa.' The DCI's tone was a little softer now. She wasn't angry with Carmichael. Her outburst had been more akin to that of a caring mother scolding a child and hugging it at the same time for running out in the road, a mother overcome with relief that she had come to no harm. 'I want to find the man who drugged you, and to do that I'd like to take you through a cognitive interview. It's vital we find the bastard.'

'Will that work? Given the drugs, I mean?'

'You still have a memory. All we have to do is access it.'

'S'pose.' Carmichael sounded unconvinced even though she had been among the first batch of detectives Daniels had trained in cognitive interviewing, a technique proven to enhance eye-witness recall by up to forty-five per cent.

'OK, you ready?' Daniels asked.

Carmichael nodded. She knew the drill. Taking off her jacket, she sat down and made herself comfortable. Daniels did likewise and spent the next hour mentally walking the young DC through her encounter the previous evening, going over and over it until they were both exhausted. Carmichael's recollection was understandably patchy. But she remembered that the man she'd met was a lecturer called Steve and vaguely recalled a girl named Bryony somewhere along the line.

She wasn't sure where.

Or even how.

'No good?' Daniels sat back.

Carmichael shook her head, visibly disappointed with the results of their efforts.

'OK, let's knock it on the head.' Daniels yawned. The heat in the room was getting to her. If she didn't make a move soon, she was sure to nod off. 'It's a good start, Lisa. You did really well.'

Daniels yawned again and stood up.

Carmichael did likewise. 'Boss?'

'Uh-huh.'

'I have a question. I know what you're going to say—'

'Oh really? Then why ask?'

'I can get him. Just give me another chance and I won't let you down this time, I promise. You said yourself, people didn't bat an eyelid when Andy pulled me out of there. Let them think I can't hold my drink. Let me at least try.'

'No,' Daniels said doggedly. 'You talk a good job, Lisa. But you just proved you're not ready to go it alone. My fault for believing you were.'

Carmichael looked as if she'd been slapped. She

232

swallowed hard, her eyes filling up. She tried to get Daniels to change her mind but she was having none of it.

'Boss?' Carmichael was almost begging. 'Will you at least hear me out?'

'I said no! So don't be an even bigger pain in the arse.'

Pulling on her leather jacket, Daniels stuffed Brown's mobile phone into her pocket and made a move to leave the house. Carmichael followed her, reaching the front door first when she paused to pick her car keys off the hall table where she'd stashed them the night before. But Carmichael's attempt to block her exit was futile. The DCI stood firm, waiting for her to move out of the way, a steely expression on her face.

'You're wasting your breath, Lisa. I won't let you do it, it's too risky. Besides, you need time to recover from your ordeal, physically as well as mentally. You're in no condition to go back in there.'

'That creep was coming on to me, I do know that much. If he's involved in either the prostitution racket or the murder of Amy Grainger, I'm still your best shot at catching him. Nothing's changed since yesterday. At least think about it.' Daniels took a step forward but Carmichael didn't move. She was frantic. As a parting shot she added, 'You know it makes sense. You can do background checks on him, but we both know that takes up a whole lot of time. Meanwhile he could be back there, preying on another girl tonight. If not for me, then do it for Jessica.'

Even Daniels found that one hard to argue with.

By now Jessica Finch would be in a very bad way.

52

Jessica *was* in a very bad way.

Still alive.

But deteriorating rapidly.

He knew she would be.

A lesser person would have copped it by now.

She hung there, zombie-like, her lips blue, her cheeks striped where black mascara had run down her face. Blood from her wrists had travelled in tiny red rivers down her forearms, staining the sleeves of Amy Grainger's skimpy mini-dress. Her eyes didn't respond to the torch-light. But he was taking no chances. With gloved hands, he blindfolded her before forcing a bottle of water into her mouth. She gasped suddenly, nearly choking as the liquid gushed into her gullet, her mouth chasing the neck of the bottle like a baby trying to find a nipple.

He let her drink, knowing that she'd be doubled up with stomach cramps if she took too much at once. They'd never find her. He'd watched them trying, but they didn't have a clue. Give Daniels her due though, she'd made the connection to his hiding place and that was impressive. Smart cookie, she was. Less than an hour ago, she'd faced the local media in order to find the girl alive. He'd watched her striding confidently to the podium, blinded by flashbulbs as she made her appeal.

She was wasting her breath.

'Please let me go,' Jessica whimpered.

He slapped her hard.

His voice was low pitched and venomous.
'Blame your father,' was all he said.

53

Daniels rapped on the door and waited. Two hours ago she'd left Carmichael to get some rest and gone home. She'd taken a quick shower and changed her clothes before driving to the station in no condition to face a press conference scheduled for ten o'clock. Press conference? Media scrum, more like. The nationals were using bully-boy tactics, muscling in on the action due to a lull in newsworthy stories to report. Television and newspaper journalists were like vultures picking over the bones of the dead, sensationalizing her murder case and trading on people's misery in the name of public interest.

The flash of cameras had hurt her eyes. She had been seated at a table next to Naylor, the force logo carefully positioned on the wall behind them for the world to see. Such blatant self-publicity made her blood boil and she had decided there and then not to play ball. She kept the conference short deliberately, feeling Naylor's concern as she sidestepped questions from the floor.

And afterwards he'd come right out with it. 'Kate, what's wrong?'

Not wanting to dob Carmichael in it, she'd sidestepped that too.

Still thinking about her ordeal, Daniels rapped on the door again. The music coming from Bryony Sharp's flat was loud enough to wake the whole neighbourhood. Gormley raised his eyes to the ceiling and tried the door handle. It didn't budge, so he knocked as hard as he could, then got down on his honkers and shouted through the letterbox:

'POLICE! OPEN UP!'

But there was no reply.

Gormley stood up again. 'I'm still uncomfortable with your decision,' he said.

Forced to concede that she too had reservations about using Carmichael undercover again, Daniels locked eyes with him. 'What choice do we have, Hank? I know you're worried about her. So am I. But you've got to admit, she has a point. If Stevie-boy is our man, we don't have time to fuck around. And this girl may be able to tell us more, if she ever answers the bloody door.'

'Use someone else undercover. Someone more experienced—'

'And what would that do for Lisa?' Daniels said. 'I don't want to pull rank here—'

'But you're going to anyway.'

'Hank! I've made my decision.'

Gormley was sulking now, but before he had time to argue, a girl opened the door. She was dressed in frayed denim hotpants over black leggings, and a skimpy purple ribbed T-shirt that hadn't seen a washing machine in weeks—let alone an iron.

Daniels held up ID. 'Bryony Sharp?'

The girl studied Daniels' warrant card, a look of panic on her face.

'She's gone home for the weekend.'

'I'm Detective Chief Inspector Kate Daniels. And you are?'

'Vanessa . . . Bry's flatmate.'

'Vanessa?' Gormley waited.

'Wilson, Vanessa Wilson.'

Daniels said, 'Well, Vanessa Wilson, I need to contact Bryony right away.'

'What for?'

'None of your business.' Daniels looked past her into the flat as a young man poked his head around a doorway. Their eyes met and he made a hasty retreat. 'Just as it's none of my business what you and your mates are doing in there. I could make it my business, if you insist.'

'You could try her mobile,' Vanessa suggested.

Daniels waited for her to reel off a number, confident that Bryony Sharp *was* the girl she was looking for. In a rare stroke of luck, a member of the university admin staff had confirmed that there was only one student presently on campus with that name. But Vanessa just stood there, leaning against the door stanchion, too spaced out to realize what further assistance she could possibly be.

'Er . . .' Gormley pulled a face showing his irritation '. . . a number might help!'

His words took a moment to register. Then, realizing what he was getting at, Vanessa wandered off, leaving them standing on the threshold. There were sounds of whispering from inside the flat. Then she reappeared with Bryony's number scrawled on a scrappy piece of lined paper.

Daniels took it from her, thanked her and turned away.

'Chief Inspector?'

Daniels swung round.

Vanessa paused. 'Look, she'll kill me if I tell you this, but Bry had a bad experience last night—like creepy, y'know. I told her to ring you guys, but she wouldn't. She should though, because she's in a *really* bad place right now and she needs help.'

Daniels wanted more. 'What do you mean, creepy?'

'She thinks she was drugged by a bloke she met at Fuse last night.'

'Thinks?'

'She was pissed, we all were.'

'This bloke wasn't called Steve by any chance?'

Vanessa's reaction was her answer.

'That's why we're here,' Gormley said. 'Did you meet him?'

'Briefly. I went home early.' Vanessa paused again, pointing over her shoulder. 'My boyfriend, Nick, stayed over. Bry seemed to be having such a good time when we left. Anyway, she didn't come home until mid-morning. Says she woke up in some park in Newcastle in the early hours, freezing and on her own. Doesn't remember getting there, doesn't think, y'know, he *did* anything to her. She was scared to death. Just showered, grabbed her stuff and went home to be with her folks, get her head round it.'

*　　*　　*

Gormley followed the DCI back down a concrete stairwell and out on to the pavement of a busy street. As they walked, Daniels keyed in Bryony Sharp's number, but there was no answer and the phone switched to voicemail:

'The mobile you are calling may be switched off. Please try again later.'

Daniels left a message and rang off. She checked

her watch—twelve fifteen—then guided Gormley along a narrow street, eventually turning left into the cobbled courtyard of an office block housing the university HR department. They'd rung ahead for an appointment and were already ten minutes late.

Daniels' phone rang: Carmichael calling.

She took the call. 'Thought I told you to go back to bed and sleep it off.'

'I did.' Carmichael sounded upbeat. Switched on. Back in business. 'The creep is a lecturer of anthropology. It jumped into my head as I woke up thinking about him. It just came out of nowhere. His name's Curtis, Steve Curtis.'

'You sure?'

'Absolutely! Want me to chase him up?'

'No, stay put, Lisa. Hank and I have it covered.'

There was a brief pause.

'Is he pissed at me?' Carmichael sounded anxious.

Daniels glanced at Gormley. He was smiling, preoccupied with something off to their left, not remotely interested in their conversation. Daniels followed his gaze, a broad grin developing as she saw what he was looking at. A no turning notice fixed to the wall in the yard had been cleverly altered to read: no turn on.

'He's fine,' Daniels said. 'Concerned about you, obviously, but otherwise fine.' A door squealed as Gormley held it open. Daniels walked through. 'Look, I've got to go, I'll catch you later.'

She pocketed her phone.

They had reached an unmanned reception window. Gormley stuck his thumb on a bell-push to call for assistance and then stood back, waiting for someone to appear.

'If I get my hands on that weirdo—'

So he had been listening. 'You'll treat him with professional composure, right? For Christ's sake, let it drop, Hank. Just be thankful she's all right. It won't happen again, I can assure you. Lisa won't make *that* mistake twice. You should've seen the clip of her this morning. I've seen better-looking dead people.'

A wry smile spread across Daniels' face.

Gormley stared at her. 'What?'

'She stirred during the night and called me a *legend.*'

Gormley grinned. 'She was pissed—she meant lesbian.'

Punching his arm, Daniels laughed out loud.

A middle-aged woman arrived at reception, a curious look on her face. She was obviously wondering what they were finding so funny. As wide as she was tall, she was wearing what could only be described as a tent over leggings and saggy flat pumps on her feet that weren't quite coping under the strain of her bodyweight. Daniels had to work hard to keep a straight face, concerned that she might think they were laughing at her.

'I'm Detective Chief Inspector Kate Daniels.' She pointed at Gormley. 'And this is Detective Sergeant Hank Gormley. We have an appointment with Patricia Conway.'

'That's me.'

She indicated a door to her left and buzzed them through. On the other side of it, a dreary, well-used corridor stretched off into the distance for quite a long way. It had green doors on either side that reminded Daniels of the police station.

'Please follow me,' Patricia Conway said.

As she waddled off in front of them, Gormley stifled a grin. 'I know I'm a bit on the beefy side, boss. But aren't her legs on upside down?'

Daniels stifled the urge to burst out laughing, telling him to behave. About halfway along the corridor, the woman stopped in front of a door bearing her name, black lettering on a white sign, the sliding sort, easily replaceable. She invited them inside, offered them tea, which they both declined, then took a seat behind her desk.

'So,' she said, 'how might I be of assistance?'

'I'm trying to find a man called Steve Curtis who works at the university. I have reason to believe that he may be a lecturer or professor of anthropology here.'

'I don't think so.' The woman frowned. 'Unless he's *very* new to us. I'm not long back from the Far East—unpaid leave. My sister lives in Singapore.'

'Nice.' Gormley smiled. 'Could you check your records, just in case?'

Ms Conway nodded, put on a pair of specs and logged on to her computer. After a few keystrokes she leaned forward, peering at the monitor, two tiny white screens reflected in the lenses of her glasses, before looking up, shaking her head.

'There's no one named Steve Curtis in that faculty.'

Daniels wondered if Carmichael had got her wires crossed. And who could blame her, after what she'd been through? But she seemed so clear on the phone. So certain of her facts. Daniels dug deep into her pocket. Earlier in the day she'd asked Brown to send his photographs of their mystery man to her phone. She called up the best one and passed the phone to Conway.

'Do you know this man?'

Recognition flashed across the woman's face. 'This is a wind-up, right?'

54

It felt good to be back in the MIR among friends.

The room was almost deserted now. Earlier, Detective Sergeant Robson had taken the unprecedented step of calling the squad together to tell his fellow officers the truth about his problems, explaining how and why he'd fallen from grace in such spectacular fashion. It was a painful and bruising experience, but they'd reacted positively on the whole, applauding his honesty and appreciating the courage it must have taken to face them head on.

Robson knew they wouldn't forget what he'd done, but drew some comfort from the fact that they'd forgiven him. Daniels had been especially supportive. She'd gone out, leaving him in charge of the incident room; her way of telling the others to let bygones be bygones and drop the cold-shoulder treatment. Robson took a deep breath and wiped his eye as DC Maxwell lifted his head and glanced inquisitively in his direction. Thankfully, his prying didn't last long. He went back to his work as the internal phone rang on Robson's desk.

Robson lifted the receiver. 'Incident room.'

'Yo, Robbo. How goes it?'

'Living the dream, mate.' Robson lied. 'And

you?'

It was Sergeant Eddie Veitch. He worked downstairs in the front office. They'd been friends for many years, played poker occasionally with other guys at the station. A few quid once a month. A laugh. A few beers. No big deal. *Until now.* Their wives had gone to school together and had remained friends ever since. But lately they'd drifted apart, another reason for Robson to feel guilty.

He took a deep breath, hoping Veitch wasn't going to ask them round.

'What's up?' he asked.

'Package for you. Hand delivery. Urgent report for the attention of the SIO.'

Robson relaxed. In Daniels' absence, that meant him. 'Be right down,' he said.

He hung up. Seconds later, the phone rang again, before he'd even risen to his feet. Probably Veitch again. He hesitated before answering, raising his voice to regain Maxwell's attention. 'Neil, nip down to the front office while I take this, will you? Eddie's got something for the boss. And don't hang around down there. Whatever it is, it's urgent.'

Maxwell's mouth twitched, almost a smirk.

It probably didn't mean anything, but Robson instantly felt anxious—nauseous—his new-found confidence taking a dive. Were his colleagues *really* ready to accept him back into the fold? Or were they just pretending to forgive him? Maxwell didn't look at him as he pulled on his jacket and headed out of the MIR.

Robson watched him go, the betting slip he'd purchased in his break time from the bookies around the corner burning a hole in his pocket. He wanted—no, needed—the rush of another big win. He wanted it now. And nothing else would do. Beads of sweat broke out on his brow. He wiped them away on his sleeve, his stomach in knots, his heart thumping. And still the caller demanded an answer.

He reached for the phone. 'DS Robson.'

'This is Laura Somers. Please may I speak to DCI Daniels?'

'I'm sorry, she's out of the office. Can I help?'

'That depends.'

'On what?'

The woman faltered. 'I don't know quite how to put this . . .'

'I know who you are, Mrs Somers,' Robson was trying to help her out. 'And I've a good idea why you're ringing. I work for DCI Daniels on the murder investigation team. Is your daughter there?'

'Yes. She arrived home safe and well about ten minutes ago. I thought I'd better let you know immediately.' Laura Somers paused. Robson could hear shouting in the background as an argument sprung up. A man's voice, he thought. Then a young woman's; Rachel, maybe? Then Laura Somers' voice, yelling in his ear: 'Will you two keep it down!' After a moment of silence, she said, 'Sorry, Detective. As you can imagine, things are a little difficult here at present. I should've been honest with them years ago. It seems I've a lot of explaining to do.'

Robson's mouth had dried up. He too had a lot of explaining still to do. His gambling had split his family apart—not just his immediate family but his extended family too. They'd all piled in. An opinion here. A warning there. So much fucking advice he felt he was drowning in the stuff. He couldn't find words.

Laura Somers' voice again. 'Hello?'

Robson cleared his throat. 'I'm still here.'

'Look, you're obviously busy. I wanted to apologize to all of you for wasting your time, that's all. I genuinely thought my Rachel was missing at first. I certainly never meant to mislead or deceive anyone. I know you have a difficult job to do and I hope you catch the bastard that murdered that poor girl. I'm sure you will. Your DCI sounds like a really good person.'

Robson swallowed hard. Deceit was something he knew a lot about. And Laura Somers was right. Kate Daniels *was* a good person, someone who trusted him to do the right thing and turn his life around. Reaching into his trouser pocket, he withdrew a pink betting slip, screwed it up and threw it in the bin just as Maxwell walked back through the door, his warrant card dangling from a cord around his neck.

Robson kicked his waste-paper bin under the desk, praying that Maxwell hadn't noticed. He thanked Laura Somers for calling and arranged for her to bring Rachel to the station to make a full statement, then ended the call.

'You OK?' Maxwell said as he approached. 'You look hot.'

'Bet you say that to all the guys.' Robson forced an uneasy grin. 'That was Laura Somers. Three guesses what she was calling for.'

Maxwell handed over an envelope. 'Her daughter's back?'

'Yep. The boss was right. Harris is in the clear.'

As Robson slit open the envelope, Maxwell perched himself on the edge of the desk in case the report contained anything requiring his immediate attention. It was a fairly lengthy document, a couple of A4 pages of text with a detailed map attached at the back. Robson took his time reading it, an inscrutable expression on his face. But when he got to the end, there was a distinct look of optimism in his eyes.

He held out the report and said, 'The geologist came up trumps. Fax this through to Weldon. Tell him to focus his search on the shaded areas marked on this map, the only places where green fluorspar was actually mined. And tell him it changes colour when exposed to light, so we're *definitely* looking for a scene below ground.'

'That'll narrow down the search area significantly, won't it?' Maxwell said.

Robson gave a little nod.

The answer was in the question.

Some positive news at last.

55

Patricia Conway's face paled. She looked down at the image on the phone and then handed the device back across the desk. 'He does work here. But in *this* department. He's an admin clerk, not an anthropology lecturer. His name is Stephen, spelt with a ph, not a v. But his surname isn't Curtis, it's Freek. That's F-r-e-e-k.'

'And does he live up to the name?' Gormley

couldn't help himself.

'I couldn't possibly answer that, Detective.'

'Aw, go on. I can see you're dying to,' Gormley teased.

'Is he at work now?' Daniels asked.

'I haven't seen him. Let me check.' The woman placed her hands on her keyboard and typed a command. A duty roster popped up on her screen. She scrolled through a page or two and shook her head. 'Unfortunately not, it's his day off.'

'What exactly is his role here?' Daniels asked.

'He processes new admissions mainly: verifies qualifications, liaises with individual faculties, that sort of thing. He's a pen-pusher, like the rest of us. Delusional too, by the sounds of it.' Conway glanced down at her computer screen. 'He doesn't actually have a degree himself. In fact, he didn't get very good grades at school. Frankly, I'm amazed he ever got a job here.'

Like many people Daniels had interviewed over the years, Patricia Conway was cautious about offering information at first due to a perceived notion of confidentiality. But then the floodgates opened and they couldn't stop talking. What was even more exciting, from Daniels' point of view, was the fact that Conway didn't like Stephen Freek, not one little bit.

'. . . Freek by name, freak by nature, if you want my honest opinion.'

Daniels felt a sudden rush of adrenalin. Goosebumps crept over her skin and the hairs on the back of her neck stood to attention. Was this the turning point they'd been praying for? She lifted her hand, stopping the woman in her tracks. For a split second they locked eyes, staring at one

247

another across the desk.

'Are you telling us he has access to student records?' Daniels asked.

'Of course! The whole damned database. Why?'

Gormley fired off another question. 'Does he share an office with anyone?'

'No. He works alone, along the corridor. We passed it on the way in.'

The air was suddenly charged with electricity. Daniels looked at Gormley with hope in her eyes. If his expression was anything to go by, they were both thinking the same thing. Freek could be guilty of a number of offences, some of them even more serious than administering a noxious substance to Carmichael: ABH, living off immoral earnings, the abduction of Jessica Finch, murder of Amy Grainger—all or none of the above.

'I could show you, if you like,' Conway volunteered.

'We'd appreciate that,' Gormley said. 'It's rare to get this level of cooperation.'

'Oh, I can't give you access,' Conway backtracked, suddenly becoming defensive. 'I'm afraid I don't have that much clout. But I'm happy to show you where he hangs out.'

'That's not good enough,' Gormley bit back, disappointed now.

Daniels couldn't help wishing they were dealing with Maria Wilson, Jessica's personal tutor, the bubbly woman who'd been so keen to assist with their enquiries. *If there's anything we can do, anything at all, just ask*, she'd said, *and meant it*. Showing her frustration with a sigh, she thought of lying to Conway, telling her they already had authorization, but that wouldn't work. Devoid of a better idea, she glanced at Gormley for inspiration. He pulled his chair a little closer to Patricia Conway's desk, placed his elbows on it and clasped his hands in front of him, looking deep into her eyes. She probably thought he was going to say something nice, pander to her better nature.

She was wrong.

'Thing is,' he began, 'we're investigating a very serious matter here and we really could do with your help. We need Freek's details urgently and, while we appreciate you'll have concerns about divulging personal information, legitimate exceptions to the Data Protection Act do exist for good reason, as I'm sure you know. Exceptions that supersede all that bollocks—'

'He means for the prevention or detection of crime.' Daniels cut him off before he said something they'd both regret. It wasn't a good idea to put the woman's back up. They weren't going to get anywhere without her help. 'I won't lie to you. We need to examine Freek's computer before he gets wind of the fact that we're on to him.'

Conway thought for a moment. Then she sat up straight, typed another command on her keyboard. 'I need to pop out for a moment, would you excuse me, please?'

The administrator left the room.

Daniels turned the monitor round so they could view it. On the screen was a page displaying a picture of Stephen Freek: middle-aged, well-groomed, but so obviously posing for the camera. It was *him* all right and he looked like a complete twat. Underneath his photograph were all the details they were after: full name, address—which Daniels noticed was a stone's throw from her

249

own—an NI number and phone numbers too. Gormley made a note of them. Then the door opened and Patricia Conway re-entered.

Daniels thanked her. 'We won't divulge the source of this.'

'We'd like to see his office now,' Gormley added.

Conway nodded.

'Why do you dislike him so much?' Daniels slipped the question in casually as they left the office. They turned left, walking back down the corridor towards reception. Conway didn't answer immediately, just lumbered along in front of them, her slack shoes flip-flopping on the lino, her tent dress wafting as she walked. Stopping short of an office a few doors down, she reached for the handle and turned to face them.

'Off the record?' she said.

Both police officers answered with a nod.

'Freek thinks he's God's gift to women. He's a creepy little git who makes my skin crawl, and I'm not the only one to say so. He's not very well liked around here, especially, though not exclusively, among female members of staff. Are you going to tell me what this is about?'

She waited.

'In a word, no,' Gormley said. 'Data protection's a bummer, isn't it?'

'Very funny!' Conway grinned at Daniels. 'Your friend here should try stand-up.'

'He's not that funny.' Daniels returned the woman's smile. 'We can't tell you why we need to speak to him. But, put it this way: if he were here now, we'd have locked him up. If we're right about him, you'll read about it in the newspapers soon enough.'

The comment seemed to satisfy Patricia Conway. Trying to conceal her delight, she glanced at her watch, opened the door and stood back to let them in.

'Would you let me know when you're finished? I'll be in my office.'

'Actually, I'd like you to stay.' Daniels beckoned her inside and shut the door, blocking out the noise of passing traffic in the corridor beyond. The office was unremarkable, except that it contained two desks but only one chair. 'Is Freek the only person who works in here?'

Patricia Conway nodded. 'Yes, I told you, he works alone.'

'So nobody else has access to that—' Daniels pointed at the computer on Freek's desk. 'If he shares the computer with anyone, we need to know.'

'He doesn't. It's not password-protected, exactly . . .' Conway held up the ID tag hanging on a ribbon round her neck. 'Our system is ID sensitive, much the same as yours, I imagine, the only exception being the System Administrator, who has the power to override an access code.'

'And who might that be?' Gormley asked, pen poised to record her answer.

Patricia Conway grinned.

56

'Can you do an audit trail? Tell us what he's been looking at lately?'

They were still in Freek's office, door locked, blinds down. Patricia Conway nodded, sat down in front of the computer and logged on. At times like this, Daniels preferred to have Carmichael with her. She was MIT's in-house technical expert. What she didn't know about computers wasn't worth knowing. Still, this woman looked like she knew a thing or two also.

'You think he has a virtual life as opposed to a real one?' Patricia Conway asked. Pulling at the neck of her dress, she switched on a desk fan but it made little difference to the heat in the room. She tapped instructions into the keyboard, then sat back reading the data on screen. 'He doesn't appear to have accessed any dodgy Internet sites, if that's what you're after. I'll pull up the files he's been working on most recently.'

She closed down the page, pushed more keys and brought up a history log, enabling her to view by date: three months ago, a month ago, a week, a day. Today's date was on the screen. Thursday, 13 May. It was blank. Conway changed to a week's view, but nothing on the screen rang any bells with Daniels. She hoped she wasn't wasting precious time.

Jessica Finch was still missing.

'That can't be right!' Conway was scrolling again, her eyes flitting across the screen, her brow set in a frown. 'What the hell has he been doing? I don't under. . .'

Her voice trailed off.

But her concern had sent a tingle of excitement down Daniels' spine. Something was very wrong. With Gormley looking over her shoulder, she leaned in closer, eyes firmly focused on the screen. More specifically on a page showing several columns of names, each with a date next to it indicating when it had last been viewed on the system.

In the distance, a siren screamed.

'They're playing our song,' Gormley said.

Ignoring the one-liner she'd heard a million times before, Daniels tried to make sense of the data facing her. It struck her as odd that the list was in alphabetical order, using Christian rather than surnames. The word 'familiarity' popped into her head.

Conway's eyes were like saucers as she stared at the monitor. More tapping. Different pages. It seemed to take for ever for her to look up. 'Some of these are *second*-year students,' she explained. 'He has absolutely no business looking at them! His remit is new intake only. He's even accessed their financial status. Why on earth would he want to do that?'

Why indeed?

A number of possibilities whirred round Daniels' head. Was Freek sorting out the rich from the poor here? Targeting girls he could get into bed? Or was the fuckwit grooming girls from poorer backgrounds, enticing them to make easy money to subsidize their studies? It seemed likely he had something to do with Durham's prostitution enquiry, but she needed more proof than this.

'Maybe someone from within the university instructed him to access these names,' she said. 'Couldn't he have been collating information to assist someone else?'

Conway's eyes flashed. 'No way! At least, not without clearing it with *me* first—'

'But you said yourself you've been away on extended leave. Isn't it possible he was given a task to do in your absence, one outside of his normal remit?'

'It's possible, I suppose, but not likely. We have floating staff whose job it is to do that sort of thing. I can easily check with the person who covered for me while I was away, but I'm sure I'd have been told if that was the case. Otherwise he'd have got it in the neck when I carried out my next check.'

'You check his system periodically?' Daniels asked.

Conway nodded. 'Certainly do.'

'The last time being . . . ?'

'The day before I went on leave. Just over a month ago. I flew out on Easter Monday, the fifth of April. I wasn't at work on the Friday, obviously, so my last day was Thursday the first.'

'And that was the day the system was last checked?'

'*Definitely* . . .' She pointed at the screen. 'There'll be a record of it in here somewhere, if you want to see it.'

'Maybe later.' Daniels thought for a moment. Had Freek taken the opportunity to trawl the database for information while Conway's back was turned? Slipping off her jacket, she pulled up a chair and sat down. 'Can you go back one calendar month, take a copy for me, then tag the students he shouldn't have accessed in the normal course of his duties and take a copy of that also?'

'No problem.'

Conway did what was necessary. Seconds later, in the corner of the room, a printer burst into life. Gormley left them and walked over to it, collecting hard copies as they spilled out, face up but the wrong way round: two files; four pages each; one tagged, one not. He turned them round so he could read them, confirming with a nod that they were what Daniels had asked for. Casually scanning them as he made his way back, his step suddenly faltered and his eyes grew big.

'Fu—' He nearly swore.

'Hank?' Daniels leapt from her seat, her pulse racing. Grabbing the document, she speed-read to a tagged name on the first document: Amy Jennifer Grainger. Daniels' eyes flew down the page, to the second name with a tag against it: Bryony May Sharp. It was a eureka moment. She looked at Gormley, a lump forming in her throat. 'I think we've got him.'

Not entirely sure what they'd got him for, Conway beamed up at them proudly.

'Warrant request, NOW!' Daniels said. 'Phone it through to Robbo.'

Thanking Conway, they excused themselves and left the building. Outside, Gormley walked off to find a quiet place from which to make his call. Daniels checked her watch: one forty-five. She pulled out her phone and dialled a number, suddenly re-energized, ready for anything, a lost night's sleep of no consequence now. Naylor answered right away. She told him what had

255

happened and asked him to cover the briefing at two.

'That's if you're not busy, guv.'

'Hmm . . . hold a second, Kate.'

Daniels watched Gormley sit himself down on a low wall surrounding the courtyard. She caught snippets of his telephone conversation as traffic passed by on the main road out of Durham: *extensive enquiries . . . his place of work . . . he has accessed information . . . examining a database unlawfully . . . a serious offence being investigated . . . his arrest and the search of his premises.*

Naylor was back. 'Consider it done. I just cancelled a handover with Bright. You two been arguing again? He's in a right strop.'

'Nowt to do with me!' Daniels hated lying to him, but Bright had been good to her and she couldn't report him. She just couldn't. This would be the last time, though. From here on in, she told herself, her loyalty was to Naylor. No question. ' 'preciate your help, guv. I'd ask Robbo, but he's got something else on. Hank's dictating a double-u as we speak.'

'You sending the report over electronically?'

'Yeah, by fax in the next few minutes.'

'I'll cross-check the names with the prostitution enquiry and get back to you.'

'Thanks.' A million things were going through her mind, questions she needed answers to. The most prominent of all: would they catch the bastard? 'Guv, I need that warrant like yesterday. Can you make sure it's delivered to Freek's premises as soon as it's signed? And not in a marked car, we don't want to lose him.'

'Would you have suggested that to Bright?'

Naylor made like he was insulted but he was only pulling her leg. 'I'm wounded, Kate. What d'you take me for?'

Daniels could almost hear him grinning.

57

Freek lived on an elegant terrace of Georgian villas close to Jesmond Metro station. Daniels drove along slowly, checking door numbers as she went. The terrace was not as green and leafy as it once was. Many of the gardens were now gravelled or flagged, professionals who lived there too busy to care. High-end vehicles lined the pavement, wing mirrors inverted to avoid damage from passing traffic. Stephen Freek's home was a converted maisonette occupying the ground floor and basement of a three-storey house. It had a separate entrance from the main residence. *No surprise there then*, Daniels thought, as she parked across the road and turned off the ignition.

Checking the street from the car before getting out, she checked her watch: two ten. Robson should have secured the warrant by now. So where the hell was he? She pulled out her mobile and called him, but there was no reply. Maybe he was still with the magistrate. She left a message and rang off. Returning to the Toyota, she gave a little tap on the passenger window.

'No joy?' Gormley opened the door.

Daniels shook her head. 'C'mon.'

They crossed the road, entering the garden through a wrought-iron gate. At the end of the path, a few steps led down to a newly painted black front door. At night the area would be hidden from the quiet street above, perfect for whatever depraved acts its owner had in mind. Particularly if unsuspecting victims happened to be unconscious as he carried them inside.

She rang the bell.

Nothing.

She rang again.

Still nothing.

'Guess that's it then, 'til the warrant arrives,' she said.

Lifting his right forefinger to his lips, Gormley silenced her. 'You hear that?'

'What?' Daniels listened with her best ear but couldn't hear a thing. Not a sound. Zero. Zilch. Total silence. 'Must've been next door.'

'No, it definitely came from inside!'

'No, Hank!'

With a solemn expression on his face, Gormley held up an imaginary bible. His tone was deferential. 'We believed that a serious offender was attempting to resist arrest, Your Honour. Unfortunately, we had no choice but to break into the premises.' Grinning, he stepped back and took a running lunge at the door, smashing into it with his shoulder. Once. Twice. Third time lucky. The door swung open, rebounding on the interior wall, causing a chip of white plaster to fall on the wooden floor.

'Now did you hear it?' he said.

Daniels punched the shoulder he was still rubbing.

'Ouch! That hurt!'

'Don't be such a wuss!'

Looking behind her, Daniels checked the street, making sure the break-in hadn't attracted unwelcome attention. Leading the way into the hallway, she noted the lack of any mail on the floor. Freek had either been home since his encounter with Carmichael or he hadn't received any fan mail that day.

'He must have a cleaning lady,' Gormley said, walking in.

There was very little natural light in the basement, but Daniels could see what he meant. The apartment was well cared for. The wooden floors were so clean you could eat off them. What looked like a bijou basement flat from the outside was a Tardis on the inside. The hall opened out into a large, open-plan living area, distinctly Japanese in style. They stood for a while taking it in: black lacquered furniture, very low seating; hanging lanterns; free-standing sculptures and oriental art—original paintings as well as prints.

Freek was living way above his means.

To their left, a free-floating staircase led up to the floor above. Directly ahead, a giant sliding screen with a subtle cherry blossom tree design hid a small kitchen at the back of the house.

Daniels had to admit it was beautifully done.

Jo Soulsby would love it.

Gormley didn't.

'Christ!' He grimaced. 'The fat lady was right. This guy is an utter weirdo. Confucius he say: sad man with design on girls need to get a life.'

'Serve life might be more appropriate . . .' Daniels glanced at her watch. 'Try Robbo again, Hank. I'll check upstairs.'

She left him to it, her heels clattering on the

259

stairs as she climbed to the floor above. There were two large rooms up there; a study on the left, a bedroom on the right. She chose to look in the latter first. A solid wood super-king faced her on the far wall. It had an intricate lattice-work headboard, a black duvet cover, a black-and-white throw and several white cushions with a bamboo design picked out in black silk thread.

It wasn't a bedroom.

More a stage.

A door to her left took her into an en suite bathroom with a loo, a bidet, his and hers wash basins and a huge, sunken, circular bath. Fresh, tumble-dried linen hung over a heated towel rail and the toilet roll was brand new. Bizarrely, the ends were folded into a point and held there with a sticker bearing some kind of Asian symbol, like you sometimes saw in hotels. Tiring of the Japanese theme, Daniels wondered what kind of sad bastard she was dealing with. She checked the toilet cistern, then peered into the bathroom cabinet and found men's toiletries, all of them expensive, along with a carton of hair dye and, curiously, a tin of smoker's toothpaste.

At least, that's what it looked like.

The tin struck her as odd. It was old and worn when everything else in the apartment was spotless and new. Why? She removed the top and found a white powdery substance. Sedative maybe? Drugs? Definitely not something that would clean his teeth. The stairs creaked on the landing behind her. Daniels spun round. Peering through the crack in the door, she saw Gormley walking into the bedroom, waving a warrant in the air.

'Now all we have to do is find him,' she said.

He joined her in the bathroom. 'It's clean downstairs. And I mean *clean*. There are no personal effects down there. Not a bill, letter, nowt. No books, magazines or videos, despite the flat screen on the wall. That's odd for a bloke living on his own. You?'

She showed him the white powder posing as toothpaste.

'You want a full search team down here?'

'I want the whole place stripped eventually: loft, drains, the works. But we can't afford to spook him. If he gets a whiff of forensic suits he'll know we're on to him and go to ground. This may not be his only pad. It's hardly been used, by the look of it. Probably has another, much closer to his work. Once administered, Rohypnol-type drugs only last a few hours. He'd be cutting it fine getting back here from Durham with an unconscious, dead-weight shag in tow, even if he drives. When we get back, check for any parking permits registered to this address. Unless . . . I dunno, maybe he doesn't screw the girls—'

'You mean, he gets his kicks just looking?'

'Wouldn't surprise me . . .' Daniels gestured toward the adjoining room. 'That bed look like it's been slept in to you? You find any cameras?'

Gormley shook his head, his attention drifting off somewhere.

Daniels tapped her forehead. 'What's going on up there, Hank?'

'Dunno . . .'

'Something is.'

'I was thinking about Amy's underwear not being swapped. Maybe Freek can't get it up. Maybe that powder you found isn't a sedative or date-rape

261

drug. Maybe it's speed.'

'Dutch courage, you mean?'

Gormley shrugged his shoulders. 'Who knows?'

Daniels felt like a kid with pieces of several different jigsaws, frantically trying to fit them together and failing every time. She couldn't decide if Freek was a serious sexual predator or a creep running a prostitution racket in order to finance a flashy lifestyle. He'd accessed the financial records of a number of students. She only needed to look around her to see that he was money-driven, a self-obsessed egomaniac and conman to boot. If he *was* responsible for Amy's death, then he was also to blame for Jessica's abduction. Could he have abducted her to get his hands on her father's cash? Make it big? Live the dream? But in that case, why Amy? That didn't fit. Her parents were poor by comparison.

Nothing made sense.

Moving away from the bathroom, Daniels crossed the hall into the study and stood in the centre of the room checking it out. It was much the same as the rest of the house. Clean lines. No clutter. Gormley followed her in, began a cursory search of the desk. Daniels watched him get down on the floor and run his hands along the base of the desk drawer, making sure that there was nothing taped to the underside.

He shook his head—nothing doing—and went on with his search.

The desk itself was completely bare, apart from a landline that looked new and unused. Daniels picked it up, checking for a connection, replacing the receiver when she heard the dialling tone.

'Smart move,' she mumbled under her breath.

'I'm good, aren't I?' Gormley said, getting up off the floor.

'Not you, you idiot—him! No computer, Hank. Strange for a man who works on one all day long, don't you think? Probably carries it with him. We need to find it before the bastard deletes any stuff he might have on it. Get Brown over here. I want this apartment under surveillance round the clock, starting right now! On second thoughts, get Maxwell. I want Brown to play minder tonight for Carmichael. He knows what this guy looks like. Hopefully we can take Freek off the streets before he does any more damage.'

58

Maxwell's unmarked police car arrived outside the maisonette just as Daniels and Gormley were leaving. He parked the vehicle in shade across the street, staying with it as instructed. Daniels acknowledged him with a nod as she drove away and then called him on the radio, telling him what action to take should the man himself make an appearance.

On the way back to the station, she made a number of other calls: arranging to meet Carmichael at the MIR at seven o'clock sharp; asking the Technical Support Unit for a covert listening device for an operation she was planning in a few hours' time; and lastly to Dave Weldon for news of Jessica.

Still no joy.

It was depressing news. But Daniels' despair

didn't last long. Pessimism was not in her nature. She couldn't allow her concern for the girl to cloud her focus, even for a short time, or the investigation would stall. Her team were counting on her leadership and she had to stay strong.

'What you thinking about?' Gormley asked.

Daniels kept driving. He'd always been able to read her, just as Jo had done. And, like Jo, Gormley had the wisdom to know when not to push it if she didn't feel ready to answer his questions. She smiled to herself as he crossed his arms, settled back in his seat and shut his eyes.

The MIR room was buzzing with news of the day's events when they arrived. The murder wall had been updated: *Arrest Imminent* was all it said. Naylor appeared to be in complete control: all officers were focusing on their assigned tasks; HOLMES was being updated with new intel; every member of the team—civilians included—were doing their bit for the cause.

Leaving them to it, Daniels went straight to her office, intending to ring Carmichael and check that she was feeling well enough to work later. There had been a hint of something untoward when they'd spoken a few minutes ago, something deeply troubling, a slight tremor in Lisa's voice that put Daniels' guard up. The phone rang out. But this time, Carmichael failed to pick up at the other end.

Probably in the shower, Daniels thought.

At least she hoped so.

Gormley was in a strop when she returned to the incident room, the office phone stuck to his ear. 'So how come it's taken four separate members of staff to answer one simple question then? It's

264

hardly a matter of national security.' There was a short pause. 'Yeah? Well, may all of your problems be big ones, mate.' He ended his call abruptly as Daniels approached. 'Jesus! These council officials boil my piss!'

'Oh, really?' Daniels laughed. 'I'd never have guessed.'

'There's no parking permit allocated to Stephen Freek's address.'

Daniels was quiet for a second, still stewing over Carmichael, whether she was up for another bout with Freek. With that worrying thought persisting, she pulled Gormley's phone towards her, took a business card from her pocket, dialled Patricia Conway's number and waited.

She answered right away.

'This is Detective Chief Inspector Daniels. Sorry to disturb you, yet again. I need to ask you one more thing: does Stephen Freek have a car?'

'Yes, he does. A BMW three series convertible. I know that because I'd die for one myself. Well, I'd prefer a Maserati, but a beemer would do.' Conway giggled. 'Sadly, my salary won't stretch to either.'

'You wouldn't happen to have a registration number, would you?'

'It's personalized, I know that much. Hang on . . .' The phone went down at the other end. Daniels could hear the clicking of a keyboard. A few seconds later Conway was back on the line. 'Got a pen, Inspector?'

'Yep, go ahead.'

Daniels scribbled in the air. Gormley gathered up a yellow post-it pad and a pen. As Conway read out the registration number, Daniels repeated it back to her, 'Foxtrot Romeo Echo Three Kilo.'

Gormley looked at the number he'd written on the pad: FRE3K.

'You have got to be kidding!' he said.

59

Carmichael ran the wire along the underside of her bra and taped it to her skin, nestling the microphone in her cleavage. She pulled down her shirt and took a good look in the mirror, making sure it wasn't visible. Bending over the basin, she ran the tap and washed her face, fear of failure creeping over her as it had done all day.

Patting her face dry, she took a long, deep breath.

'Testing,' she said, keeping her voice at the level of a normal conversation, mindful of Daniels at the other end. 'Boss, can you hear me?'

Seconds later, her phone rang.

Daniels' voice: 'Affirmative, Lisa. Meet me in the MIR as soon as you're ready.'

Carmichael put on her jacket. She left the women's restroom feeling nervous but also thrilled at the prospect of catching Stephen Freek.

If only she was up to it.

Andy Brown was waiting outside, lolling against the wall in the corridor, arms folded, feet crossed over one another. Carmichael blushed. It was the first time she'd seen him since he'd extricated her from Fuse and she didn't quite know what to say to him. Daniels had been good about her fuck-up. Gormley, too, considering. But Brown might take

266

the piss, and that she couldn't bear.

He smiled when he saw her. 'Boss wants to brief us asap.'

Carmichael didn't stop. 'Yeah, I know.'

'You all set?' He fell in step.

She kept walking. 'Why wouldn't I be?'

'Just asking.' He was practically running to keep up. 'Hey! What's wrong?'

Carmichael swiped her warrant card at the entrance to the MIR. She opened the door, her stomach churning as she walked into the crowded room. She was behaving like a complete bitch. Not talking about last night wasn't going to make it go away. But she had nothing to apologize for. Did she?

Of course she fucking did.

Brown was her oppo and she'd let him down.

Badly.

She'd reached her desk. 'Look, Andy, 'bout last night—'

'Forget it, man.' Brown's gentle Geordie accent seemed more pronounced than usual, not a hint of one-upmanship or triumph in his eyes. 'We're mates, right?'

'So?'

'So, it didn't happen.'

'What didn't happen?'

Carmichael managed a half-smile, a lump forming in her throat. Brown was a top bloke and a good colleague. She should've known better than to doubt his integrity. Patting his upper arm, she thanked him for his support, wanting to tell him she was still feeling rough, confide in him about the flashbacks she was experiencing. Weird images had come and gone all day in her waking hours as

267

well as when she slept: Freek standing too close for comfort; threatening shadows she didn't understand moving towards her, then fading away; spinning faces turned in her direction disappearing into a black hole. Before she managed to utter one word, Gormley's voice cut through her thoughts:

'You two ready to rock 'n' roll?'

Brown and Carmichael nodded in unison.

'C'mon, the boss is waiting to brief you.'

Carmichael didn't move. Another flashback. They were coming thick and fast now. She should tell someone. No. She had to do this. Had to show them she *could* be trusted. She couldn't let them down again.

'You coming or what?' Gormley asked.

'Sorry, I was miles away.'

'Yeah, well, get your shit together, Lisa. You need to focus.'

Sheepishly, she followed him to the DCI's office. He was pissed at her. It wasn't like him to be sharp. She'd let him down. She'd let them all down. And if the freak didn't turn up tonight they might have lost their one and only chance to nick him.

*   *   *

Brown had gone ahead. He was already in Daniels' office when Carmichael arrived, standing by the window. Behind him, driving rain splattered against the windowpane. It was almost horizontal and very bad news for Weldon, his search team and Jessica. Brown looked more confident than Carmichael felt. A smile of encouragement crossed his face as she followed Gormley in.

She was about to close the door when Naylor appeared, walking towards her with an urgency in his step. Suddenly feeling anxious, she stood back and held the door open. Thanking her as he walked by, he perched himself on the edge of Daniels' desk and nodded at her.

As Senior Investigating Officer, it was her job to brief them.

'Right, you two . . .' Focusing first on Brown, then on Carmichael, Daniels picked up on the tension they were feeling. With an almost imperceptible shake of her head she put their minds at rest. She'd kept her word: Naylor hadn't been told. 'I've put a stop-and-search marker on the PNC so Freek's vehicle is already on the radar of every force in the country. Assuming we don't pick him up in the next hour or so, Fuse nightclub is our next best bet. The object of the exercise is to locate and engage with him in order to arrest him. Is that clear?'

Carmichael and Brown were like a couple of nodding dogs.

'We'll be listening the whole time to both of you.' Daniels' eyes found Carmichael. 'Andy has a receiver as well as transmitter. It's safer that way, Lisa. That means we'll be able to communicate with him if necessary. Just in case you start talking to someone else called Steve, i.e. not Freek—and it does happen, believe me—we need to know from you that you have the target in sight. The words *target in sight* would be good. Or, *I've got the arsehole*, if you prefer. Or any other form of words, so long as it lets us know we can move. Keep talking to us so we know exactly where you are at all times. Let's be *absolutely* clear about this: we're

269

not interested in implicating him. We haven't got time for that. Our sole objective is to lock him up. Understood?'

Carmichael backed up Brown's nod with a: 'Yes, boss.'

'Good. Any questions? If so, spit 'em out.' None were voiced. 'You both sure? We don't want the nine o'clock shudders in the morning.'

Carmichael frowned, unsure what she meant by that.

'Shudda done this . . . shudda done that.' A broad grin spread over Gormley's face. He'd never been able to stay pissed for long. 'Keep up, Lisa. You must've heard that one or I'm losing my touch!'

Carmichael laughed, her anxiety easing a little.

Naylor looked at his watch. 'It's time for the freak show.'

Daniels stood up, pulling her jacket from the back of her chair.

'By the way, I rang my opposite number in Durham,' Naylor added. 'She's fully aware of our intention to mount an undercover operation on her patch. She's instructed officers working the late shift to steer clear of Fuse unless it's *absolutely* unavoidable, so you shouldn't have any problems in that respect.' Fixing on Brown and Carmichael, he said, 'You two take care. Good luck. And Hank, I want Freek back in one piece!'

'Right!' Daniels said. 'Let's go get him.'

*   *   *

They left the station and piled into the Toyota: Daniels and Gormley in the front, Carmichael and

Brown in the rear. Newcastle city centre was extremely busy with late-night shoppers heading home on buses, trains, in taxis. Daniels engaged her blue flashing light in order to cut through the traffic and soon they were crossing the Tyne Bridge heading south to Gateshead.

Carmichael stared out of the window as lamp posts flashed by on her left, the strobe-lighting effect hurting her eyes. Beyond the railings, further downriver, the illuminated Millennium Bridge changed colour. Ruby red clashed with the amber haze of street lamps and blue lights flashing from the roof of the Toyota. And, suddenly, Carmichael was back at Fuse, the psychedelic vortex of lights spinning round her. Faster. Faster. Ever faster.

Daniels glanced in her rear-view mirror. 'You OK in the back there, Lisa?'

'Can't wait,' Carmichael lied, trying to calm herself.

Focus.

No one seemed to have much to say as the miles flashed by and they crossed the force border into neighbouring Durham. The hiatus allowed Carmichael time to get her head together. She wondered whether Freek would show. Her guts were telling her he would and she was desperate to be there when, *if*, they made an arrest.

The radio suddenly interrupted the silence: 'Control Room to 7824.'

Everyone in the car recognized Brooks' voice.

'7824 to Control,' Daniels answered. 'What you got for me, Pete?'

'A sighting of Foxtrot, Romeo, Echo, Three, Kilo parked up in Durham. You've got a stop and search on it.'

There was a burst of *Yes!* from the back seat.

'Don't get too excited, boys and girls. Officer on scene says there's no driver present.'

'You got a location for me?' Daniels asked.

'Certainly do.' Brooks tapped a few keys and read from his control-room monitor. 'It's parked on North Bailey. The vehicle is locked and secure.'

'The bastard's at the club,' Gormley told the others.

'Tell the reporting officer to maintain contact with the vehicle from a covert location until I arrive at the scene. ETA five minutes, no more.'

Daniels turned off the A1M on to the dual-carriageway and picked up speed in the bus lane. Soon after, the yellow glow of Durham City was visible in the distance. She glimpsed the top of the Cathedral through the trees. Flooring the accelerator, heading downhill, she sped through a couple of roundabouts, forced to slow down as she neared the city centre. There were more pedestrians here.

Thursday night was a popular night out in Durham.

Back on the radio: '7824 to Control. Tell the officer if the driver shows, it's still a stop and search. He's to detain him 'til I get there.'

'That's a roger. Anything else I can do for you this end?'

'Maybe later, Pete.' Daniels drove up the hill through the market square. 'Just thank the officer for his assistance. I'll speak to him on arrival.'

The radio went dead.

Turning left into Saddler Street and on to North Bailey, the Castle grounds and Durham's magnificent cathedral were on Daniels' right, Hatfield, St Chad's and St John's Colleges on her left. She stopped the car, exchanged a brief glance with Carmichael in her rear-view mirror.

'Looks like we're on, Lisa. Get your student face ready.'

60

In dim light and shivering uncontrollably, Jessica peered towards the black hole, her only escape from the chamber. The water level had dropped quite a bit in the past few hours and she felt calm.

So calm.

Way beyond terrified.

She called out. But nothing came back except the echo of a rasping voice that no longer sounded like her own. 'Hello, are you there? Are you there? You there? There?'

Who was he? And what the fuck had he meant? *Blame your father.* Blame your father for what? She'd been blaming her father since she was a little girl. Now she'd do anything—anything, to see him one more time. A chance to tell him she forgave him. *For everything.* He wouldn't survive another loss, not after Mum. Losing Mum had turned him into a heartless monster she hardly recognized from before—if 'before' even existed outside of her imagination.

She felt drowsy again, began talking to Robert about their hopes and dreams for the future, the only way she'd been able to stay awake. Sleep now would signal the end. But she was tired, so very, ve-ry tired.

Drifting . . .

Floating away . . .

Sucked into a warm tunnel that took the pain away . . .

Jessica woke with a start as a draught of air, barely noticeable, kissed her face. Was she dreaming? Hallucinating?

No.

There it was again.

She wept hysterically as hope bubbled up inside her, choking her to the point of exhaustion. Either the wind outside had changed direction and she wasn't far from the entrance to the mine, or there was a ventilation shaft nearby.

Either way she might be heard.

Please God, let it be true.

61

Thankfully the rain had stopped. Daniels didn't need her wipers on. Freek's red BMW three series was parked twenty metres away in a line of cars, directly beneath a street lamp. From her position, she could observe both the car and the front door of the club they called Fuse. Her first and only priority was to preserve life. She was desperate to examine the BMW, make sure that Jessica wasn't tied up in the boot.

'Hank, get the jemmy out,' she said.

Gormley got out. He went to the rear of the Toyota, opened the tailgate and took something from the back. Then he walked nonchalantly across the road and popped the boot of the BMW. He shook his head, jammed the boot shut as best he could and then returned to the others.

'There's all sorts in there,' he said as he got back in the car. 'Laptop, few boxes, other stuff I couldn't make out. But no rolled-up carpets with girls inside.'

'Good. Now keep your bloody eye on it.' Daniels didn't mind his black humour. It was his way of coping. Self defence against the things that concerned him most. His emotional connection to the case was as strong as hers. She never doubted that. Pushing a button on her radio, she began to transmit. 'Pete, we're now in position, keeping obs on target. The vehicle has been examined in situ. Jessica Finch is not inside. I repeat, Jessica Finch is *not* inside. Relay that to the MIR for me, will you? No sign of the driver yet. As soon as he's been located I'm going to need a low-loader here to uplift the vehicle forensically. Might be advisable to give the CSIs the heads up on that.'

Gormley began grumbling about the name change. When they had joined the police, Crime Scene Investigators were known as scenes of crime officers, or SOCO. A poncy new name didn't change what they did and wasn't required in his opinion. CSI Northumbria was hardly CSI Miami, was it? Sexing up departments was the wrong way to go, incurring an expense the force could utilize to better effect elsewhere.

'Stop bleating, will you?' Although she agreed with him totally, Daniels had more pressing matters on her mind. She depressed the button on her radio. 'Any chance you could ask the reporting officer to identify himself and stand by until we're

275

done, Pete? The BMW is no longer secure.'

'That's a roger,' Brooks came back.

Seconds later, a car further down the street flashed its lights once.

Daniels did likewise, then cut her ignition.

She swivelled round to face her DCs. 'You ready to make a name for yourselves?'

Brown and Carmichael both nodded, eager to get going.

'Off you go then. You first, Andy.'

Brown got out and made his way along the road past Freek's BMW. From the Toyota, three pairs of eyes watched him until he disappeared inside the nightclub. A few seconds later, Carmichael followed him in.

*   *   *

The place was heaving when she entered, even more so than the night before. Carmichael made a beeline for the bar, bought a bottle of water, and turned to face the throng of bodies already on the dance floor. Stephen Freek was not among them, as far as she could tell, but directly opposite the bar she spotted Brown's distinctive pink Superdry T-shirt that, it had to be said, clashed spectacularly with his red hair.

Carmichael's eyes followed Brown to the nearest table, where a skinny kid was sitting on his own without a drink. He was wearing ripped baggy jeans, a short-sleeved shirt that was far too small for him and tats on his arms he couldn't quite pull off. As Brown was talking to the lad, an equally skinny girl joined them, carrying a beer in both hands. She exchanged a few words with Brown,

276

who pulled up a chair and sat down.

'Can I buy you a proper drink?' a voice behind Carmichael said.

Feeling Brown's eyes upon her, Lisa Carmichael swung round on her bar stool and came face to face with a pair of steely blue eyes.

*   *   *

'Here we go.' Gormley's hand froze over a bag of cheese-and-onion crisps. Daniels tilted her head, listening, as Carmichael's voice arrived in the car.

'No, I'm all right, thanks.'

'Go on,' the male persisted. 'Let me get you one in.'

'Fuck!' Daniels glanced at the road as an old man walking a dog stopped by Freek's BMW. She nudged Gormley's elbow, worried about the stuff in the back. He opened his door, was about to get out and intervene, when the dog lifted its leg and relieved itself on the back wheel.

The man walked on and Gormley shut the door.

Daniels wondered what evidence, if any, the car might contain. Forensics? Hopefully not just the dog's. Everything? Nothing at all? Freek's flat had given them zilch and she figured a man that careful would probably have another vehicle in a lock-up somewhere. The question was: where?

Carmichael's voice again, only this time more forceful. 'I said no! Now get lost.'

'You tell him, pet!' Gormley spoke with his mouth full.

His crisp packet was now empty. He crushed it in his hairy hands and threw it on the Toyota's dash. Daniels picked it up and stuffed it in his jacket

277

pocket.

The male talking to Carmichael wasn't taking no for an answer.

'You want something a bit stronger than that, surely?'

'Typical bloke!' Daniels' eyes switched from the BMW to the front door of Fuse where a number of students were now queuing to get in. 'She's given him the brush-off and still he's coming back for more. What part of "get lost" did he not understand? You think he'll get the message anytime soon?'

'Thought no really meant yes!'

Daniels gave Gormley hard eyes but said nothing: her sexist comment deserved his irony.

'Look, I'm sorry, OK?' Carmichael again. 'Got really pissed last night. Still feeling the effects. Been chucking up all day.'

Silence.

'Thanks for the offer though,' Carmichael added politely.

The male again: 'Oh, I get it. You bat for the other side, right?'

'Aaargh!' Daniels clattered the dash. 'The arrogant fuck!'

Gormley stifled a grin.

*   *   *

Carmichael felt hot. And not in a good way. She watched Blue Eyes wander off, wishing to God she wasn't on duty. In her own time she'd have decked him there and then. Glancing back over his shoulder, he smiled at her. He had the face of an Adonis and an extremely fit torso: wide shoulders, footballer's legs and a seriously sexy smile. A nice change from the uniform bods she was used to looking at day after day.

Shame he was such a nob.

She gave him the finger.

'Keep walking, dozy!' Carmichael was still watching him when out of the corner of her eye she saw someone she thought she recognized. Dropping her head, she made like she was looking in her bag. 'Boss? Pretty sure I just saw Robert Lester. My twelve o'clock. Jeans and a yellow T-shirt.'

* * *

Daniels was straight on the wire to Brown from the Toyota.

'Andy? Lisa's twelve o'clock. Black guy, jeans and a yellow T-shirt. Could be Jessica's boyfriend. Keep your eye on him. But Lisa is your priority, understood? *Lisa* is your priority. You do *not* let her out of your sight, you hear me?'

'Affirmative,' Brown came back.

'Is that soon to be Doctor Robert Lester?' Gormley exhaled loudly, filling the Toyota with cheese-and-onion breath. 'Well, it didn't take him long to get over Jess's disappearance, did it? Thought you said he was gutted, unable to sleep, about to cut his throat over it.'

Daniels didn't answer. She was thinking the same thing.

'Not your type?' a new voice said. A man's voice, lower than the first.

'Something like that,' Carmichael snapped back. 'Arrogant prick.'

279

'Christ, she's popular!' Gormley said. 'Never happens to me.'

'Me either.' Daniels shushed him.

'Who was it said "Youth is wasted on the young"?' The man laughed.

'George Bernard Shaw,' Carmichael said. 'And I'm beginning to think he was right. I much prefer older men. Come to think of it, all my best friends are older than me.'

'Cheeky bitch!' Gormley said. 'You think she means us?'

'I'm pleased to hear it.' The man again.

Carmichael giggled.

The man: 'Weren't you in here last night?'

Carmichael: 'Yeah, only then I was the one behaving like an arse.'

'She doesn't like this one,' Daniels said.

Gormley turned to face her. 'What makes you say that?'

'Trust me, I know.'

Daniels was beginning to feel drowsy. She opened the window and then closed it again as a bedraggled group of youths walked past the Toyota, their smoke as well as their laughter and chatter drifting into the car, making it impossible to listen in to Carmichael's conversation.

'Can't take my drink, can I?' Carmichael's voice again. 'Thought I recognized you.'

Gormley looked at Daniels. 'Is that a signal?'

'Shh . . .' Daniels held up a hand. 'She'll tell us when she's ready, Hank. She knows what to do. We trained her, remember?'

'Bet you weren't so proud of her last night.'

Daniels' retort was drowned out by a crackling on the wire. People in the club began cheering and whistling, their whoops of applause followed by a continuous, ear-splitting screech that made the detectives grimace in pain.

Removing his earpiece, Gormley shook his head. 'What the hell was that?'

'Microphone not tuned in properly.'

'Main act coming on stage?'

'We've lost Lisa.'

Seconds ticked by without further exchange between Carmichael and the man she'd been talking to. Gormley's anxiety was palpable. 'Why doesn't she tell us what's happening. I think we should go in.'

'No, Hank! Let her do her job. Andy has her covered. I told her I'd wait for her signal and that's exactly what I intend to do. If it is him, he could make a run for it and seriously hurt someone trying to get away.'

'Not with my foot on his neck he couldn't,' Gormley said.

And meant it.

*   *   *

'One, two . . . One, two.' The lead singer's voice boomed out from loudspeakers above Carmichael's head. 'Testing. One two, one two.'

The band began tuning up and suddenly the dance floor was awash with people wanting to get closer to the action. For a moment, Carmichael lost Brown in the crowd and that made her really nervous. She smiled at Freek, pretending she was enjoying herself. He smiled back in a way that made her stomach perform a somersault. She was still feeling unwell and the moving spotlights were

281

doing her head in. She didn't think she could take him down on her own. Brown was still not in her eyeline.

It was time to call in the troops.

'They any good?' Carmichael pointed at the stage. The band were ready to play. 'I didn't think much of last night's shower, did you?'

Freek shrugged. 'Were you at the 3D disco last weekend?'

Carmichael shook her head. 'No, I missed that. Stuff, y'know.'

'I tell you, it was audio-visual heaven.' Freek glanced at the crowded room. 'You think tonight's busy? Believe me it's empty by comparison. You just couldn't move. It was truly awesome.'

'Really?' *Awesome?* Coming from the mouth of a middle-aged man, the word sounded ridiculous. Carmichael finished her bottle of water. Freek held up a shot glass, offering to buy her one.

'Vodka, thanks, but only if you join me. What was it you said you lectured in again? Anthropology?'

*   *   *

Daniels and Gormley were out of the car and running towards the club. At the front door, they showed warrant cards. A few girls in the queue stood back. Others scattered, fearing trouble. The detectives pushed their way in through the crowd, still listening to Carmichael. She seemed to have everything under control, but they needed to get to the bar at the far side of the room and that was proving difficult.

Fearing they might lose the target, Daniels

282

grabbed Gormley's jacket sleeve and hauled him back towards her. 'I need to cover the exit. Why don't I wait outside and you try your usual on him? He's so materialistic, it's bound to work.'

'You reckon?'

'I reckon.'

Daniels turned on her heels heading back the way she'd come. Gormley pushed his way further into the club, twisting his body to get through the crowd. As he neared the bar, he saw Carmichael sitting next to Freek. She remained in character as he approached. Gormley had to yell in order to be heard above the din as the music started up.

'Excuse me, sir. Do you happen to own a red BMW convertible?'

'Yes, why?' Freek clearly resented the interruption.

'Registration number, Foxtrot, Romeo, Echo, Three, Kilo.'

Freek bit his lip, a thin film of sweat visible on his brow. 'That's right.'

Gormley showed ID. 'I'm sorry to inform you, but it's been broken into.'

'Bloody *hell*!' Freek put down his glass.

'Don't worry, sir, madam.' Gormley glanced at Carmichael, clearly having fun now. 'We've arrested the individual concerned.'

'Is there much damage?' Freek asked.

Gormley nodded. 'I'm afraid so. I think you should secure the vehicle, just to be on the safe side. Please step this way.'

Freek was already off his seat and walking towards the exit.

62

Gormley led the unsuspecting criminal damage victim out of the club. Freek didn't realize it, but DC Brown was tagging along close behind. As they neared the BMW, Daniels stepped from the shadows holding up ID. 'Stephen Freek, you do not have to say anything. But it may harm your defence if you do not mention when questioned something you later rely on in court. Anything you do say may be given in evidence. I am arresting you on suspicion of abduction.'

'What are you talking about?' Freek craned his neck towards his damaged BMW. He glared at Gormley, who was now holding on to him in a vice-like grip. 'You bastard! You told me—'

'Never mind what I told you.' Gormley cuffed his hands behind his back. 'It's what you're going to tell us that matters. I just wanted to be sure we had your undivided attention, sir.'

They were drawing the attention of clubbers making their way down the street. Brown told the crowd to move away. Daniels thought about contacting the control room for backup when it duly arrived in the form of two panda cars with Durham insignia on the side. They screeched to a halt at an angle, effectively blocking off the whole road, allowing her space to do her job.

The Durham officer?

Daniels smiled.

Peering along the wet road, she held up a thumb of thanks. Car lights flashed, acknowledging her courtesy.

She turned away. 'Check his pockets, Hank.'

Gormley frisked the suspect, seizing a number of items: his wallet, some loose change, a BlackBerry, a set of car keys. He lobbed the keys to Daniels, who radioed in, asking the control room to send a team of crime scene investigators to search Freak's address, and let them know they could also uplift the BMW for examination back at base.

Brown and Gormley put Stephen Freek in the back seat of the Toyota, flanking him on either side. Daniels walked along the road to thank her Durham colleague for his help, asking him to arranged a lift for Carmichael who would stay with the vehicle until Northumbria officers arrived to take it away.

Daniels gave him the keys and went back to the Toyota. Pulling out her mobile, she dialled a number.

Maxwell picked up on the first ring.

'We've got him, Neil. CSI mob are on their way. You can stand down as soon as they get there.'

Maxwell yawned down the phone and immediately apologized. He sounded relieved to be ending a boring duty keeping obs. She knew the feeling. It would be nice to go home and crawl into a warm bed, but that was hours away for both of them.

'Meet you back at the station?' Maxwell said.

'No. I want someone brought in for questioning. We're going to need her statement asap.' Daniels had reached the Toyota. She timed her words perfectly as she opened the door and got in. 'Tell him it's urgent, OK?'

'Tell who?' Maxwell was puzzled. 'Boss? Did I miss something? You haven't told me who I'm supposed to be picking up!'

'That's right, Bryony Sharp,' Daniels said casually. With her mobile between cheek and shoulder, she pulled her seat belt across her chest and caught Freek's shocked reaction in the rear-view mirror.

'That's assuming she'll agree to talk to us.' Maxwell still hadn't twigged.

'Yep, she's been really helpful.'

Daniels rang off, leaving Maxwell to work it out. She drove back to the station making no further comment. After lodging Freek in a cell, she headed straight upstairs to the MIR to debrief the team over a much-needed mug of steaming hot tea. When she'd finished, she picked up the phone, rang the custody suite and asked the duty sergeant to arrange an interview room.

'IR3's empty,' he said.

'Fine, we'll be there in five.' Daniels put the phone down, turning her attention back to the squad. 'Right, this is what we do. Andy, as soon as the CSIs are finished with the car, I want you to go through the contents with a fine-tooth comb. Log everything in the system and let me know if you find anything that'll take us any further. Tell Lisa, when she gets back, same goes with his computer. Investigate the contents, let me know what gives. C'mon, Hank, we've got an interview to conduct.'

They drained their teas. Gormley grabbed his jacket from the back of the chair and followed Daniels out of the MIR and along a corridor where the two-to-ten shift were about to go off duty.

'Sodding part-timers,' Gormley mumbled, loud enough for them to hear, smiling at the jeers he got in return. He glanced at Daniels. 'Still, looks like we're on the home straight now, eh, boss?'

'I'm not sure.' Daniels entered the stairwell and went down two flights to the cell block underneath. She didn't know why, but something didn't feel right. 'He's not what I was expecting, Hank. I thought he'd be pretty switched on, organized, confident.'

'You sound disappointed.'

'I am in a way.' She stopped short of the door to the interview room and dropped her voice a touch. 'He hardly fits the profile, does he? I'm not feeling excited about him. I'm just not.'

'He seems pretty confident to me.'

Gormley wasn't fooling anyone. He looked every bit as underwhelmed as Daniels was feeling. He'd been thoughtful during the debriefing session and she could see the doubt in his eyes as he stood in the dingy corridor. Maybe it was tiredness. They were both bloody exhausted.

'OK, I admit it. He's not what I imagined either. The twat can sense we've got very little on him— and we don't, unless of course you've changed your mind about keeping Carmichael out of this.' He paused for a second. 'Have you?'

'No. I'm not having that.'

'Well then, if Bryony Sharp won't talk, we're up shit creek without a paddle.'

Daniels looked at the ceiling and sighed.

'I'm right, aren't I?' Gormley didn't wait for her reply. He pointed at the door to IR3. 'He looked at a few names on a computer. Big deal! We've all done it and, on its own, it's not enough to convict him. We know it and so does he. So he's got the upper hand.'

On that grim note, they entered the interview room.

*　　　*　　　*

Freek was sitting at the table, a uniformed male officer standing to attention a few feet away. Daniels made eye contact with him, flicking her head towards the door. As the constable left the room, she sat down opposite the suspect. Gormley took his seat, the one closest to the wall where he could operate the recording device. Switching it on, he made sure it was working before getting down to business.

'This interview is taking place at the city centre police office. The time is ten-o-five p.m. I am Detective Sergeant Hank Gormley. Also present are Senior Investigating Officer—' Daniels gave her name. 'And you are . . . ?'

Gormley pointed to the suspect.

'Stephen Pretoria Freek.'

'I must remind you that you are still under caution.' Daniels' eyes travelled over the man, taking in his expensive clothes, a good watch, his relaxed body language: feet apart, hands clasped loosely in front of his genitals, no visible hint of stress on his face. Given the serious nature of the charge he was facing, she found that really disconcerting. She placed a thick document file on the table in front of her with Freek's name clearly written on the front. There was nothing inside except blank sheets of paper. 'Do you understand?'

Freek said nothing.

'Do—you—understand?'

'I'm—not—stupid!' he said.

'I'm pleased to hear it.' Making a cradle with her hands, Daniels put her elbows on the table and gave him what was commonly known in these parts as the Scotswood stare. 'You have the right to have a solicitor present, but you've declined—is that correct?'

'I've been arrested for abduction and I'm entirely innocent.' The suspect met her gaze obstinately. 'I want to hear what you've got to say first.'

Daniels pushed a rogue hair behind her left ear with her right hand. 'We have reason to believe you've been accessing information from a university computer system for your own ends.'

'I haven't.'

'You're absolutely sure about that?'

'Positive. I'm an admissions executive. It's my job to access student records.'

'I agree with you.' Daniels paused. 'Can you tell me why you accessed the records of Bryony Sharp, for example? She isn't a first-year student.'

He shrugged. 'Don't recall.'

'How convenient.' Gormley put on the bifocals his colleagues called his sincerity specs. For effect, he glanced at the file with Freek's name on it. 'Maybe I can help you out. You see, we have not *one* but *two* girls who swear they were drugged by you at the Fuse nightclub in Durham City only last night.'

'I take it you can prove that.'

'You're forgetting something—'

'Am I?'

Grinning, Gormley held up a bag of white powder they had found in his wallet.

'Oh that.' Dipping his head to the tabletop,

Freek covered one nostril and hoovered up an imaginary line of cocaine. He shook his head, tutting. 'What you found was stuff for my own use. So charge me with possession. First offence, I might even get a caution. What d'you reckon, DCI Daniels?'

'For the tape, Mr Freek has just gestured that the white powder found in his possession is some kind of illegal drug.' Daniels picked up the internal phone. 'DC Carmichael, bring the package to IR3.'

Seconds later, Carmichael arrived in the room with a black bin liner. As soon as she walked through the door, Freek recognized her. He tried desperately to hide his discomfort but failed.

Carmichael left the room again.

'What do you think we've got in here?' Daniels tapped the bin liner.

Silence.

'It's your computer. And we've done a check on it,' Daniels lied. The laptop inside was her own. 'Not so cocky now, are you?'

Freek glanced at the tape deck embedded in the wall. 'Turn that thing off and I'll tell you everything I know in exchange for immunity from prosecution.'

'That only happens on American TV,' Daniels said. 'Unfortunately for you, this isn't *24* and I'm not Jack Bauer. It's a bummer, I know, but we don't do bargains—do we, Sergeant?'

'She means you're in deep shit!' Gormley took off his glasses. He always did that when they were interviewing. On. Off. On. Off. His arm going up and down like a fiddler's elbow. 'You're going to have to do a lot better than that to convince us you've done nothing wrong.'

Daniels stared at the prisoner. There was little doubt that he'd administered noxious substances to Carmichael and Bryony Sharp without their consent, terrifying at least one of them in the process; two, if she were being honest. Carmichael still wasn't right. Daniels had known that from the moment she came on duty. But she would be. Eventually. Using her in a covert operation so soon after Freek had dropped her a Mickey Finn had been a calculated risk; one worth taking, as it turned out. In their job, the stakes were high. The ends justified the means. Her DC had done her proud.

But now Daniels was facing the really hard yards: cracking a suspect who had everything to lose and nothing to gain by talking to them. How would Bright handle him if he were here now? Bully him? Wear him down? Maybe try a different tack, one guaranteed to put the fear of God into him. Really make him sweat.

A different tack.

She decided to up the ante. Stop pussyfooting around. 'You want to thank your lucky stars you haven't been charged with murder,' she said.

'Yet!' Gormley followed her lead.

And it was working.

Freek's jaw dropped.

'Did I tell you that one of the names you accessed on your work computer is now dead?' Daniels pushed her chair away from the table. She slid down in it, leaning back, crossing her feet, then her arms, her eyes planted on the suspect. 'Amy Grainger was murdered. But I guess you already know that, don't you?'

Freek sprung to his feet. 'Now look here—'

'SIT DOWN, Mr Freek!' Daniels waited.

Freek stayed right where he was. Gormley stood up quickly, his chair making a noise as it scraped across the floor. He moved towards the suspect with an intimidating look on his face, almost daring him to kick off. Probably hoping he would.

'Why don't you both sit down.' Daniels kept her eyes focused on the man in custody. 'That's better. Now, why don't you stop buggering about and tell us what you know. You've got ten minutes before I put you in a cell for the night. We've got homes to go to.'

Silence.

'Have it your own way . . .' Daniels gathered up the file in front of her.

'OK! I was being threatened—'

'Course you were.' Gormley shook his head.

Freek ignored the dig.

'Who was threatening you?' Daniels set the file down again. 'And why?'

Freek locked eyes with Gormley. 'You think *you're* hard? Do me a favour. You want to see the guys I've been dealing with. They'd kill—' He stopped mid-sentence, realizing what he'd just said. 'They're running a brothel in Durham. They leaned on me, wanted details of girls. Nice *educated* girls with nasty bank balances. Girls they might get on the game. All I did was provide a few names and addresses. That was it. I never did anything more than that, I swear.'

'That's not what Bryony Sharp says,' Gormley reminded him.

Freek looked down at his hands.

'We know all about the prostitution racket,' Daniels said. 'Why d'you think we were in the club? But, as I just told you, we've got bigger fish to fry. One of the girls your friends were interested in is now dead.'

'They're not my friends, I told you.' The suspect was starting to get really agitated. 'You're not pinning that on me! I want a solicitor now.'

'Assuming we accept your story, how come these . . .' Daniels made inverted commas with her forefingers, 'heavies picked you?'

'They saw what I was doing in the club. They threatened to dob me in if I didn't cooperate. I figured the girls whose names I gave them would tell them to sling their hook anyway, so what was the harm? I never would've done it if I thought they were going to be in danger.'

'Take him back to his cell, Hank.'

'No wait! Please, I'll tell you anything you want to know.'

Daniels took an A4 notepad from the table drawer. It landed in front of Freek with a solid thud. She gave him a pen. 'You've got half an hour. I want times, dates, names, descriptions, everything you know about the people who approached you. After that, who knows? Just don't figure on getting out of here anytime soon.'

63

They left Stephen Freek to sweat. A little worry time. Telling him they'd be back to see him at exactly eleven o'clock, they returned to the MIR and sat down with a depleted team. Nothing much had happened in their absence. Crime scene investigators were still processing Freek's belongings and would hand them over as soon as they could. Whatever that meant.

Daniels looked up as Maxwell entered looking dishevelled after his marathon shift in the car: his navy strides all creased at the crotch, shirt stained with the remnants of a makeshift dinner, eyes on stalks from watching the front door of an apartment not a million miles away. She was surprised to see a wide grin on his face.

'Bryony Sharp's downstairs. She just gave me chapter and verse on her dealings with Stevie boy. She needed no persuading either . . .' Maxwell slumped down in a chair, handed over a statement form. 'She's prepared to follow that up in court if necessary. She's a nice lass, actually. A quiet lass, pretty shaken up. She's terrified he'll do it again to some other poor sod.'

'You didn't raise her expectations of a conviction, I hope.' Daniels looked up from the document. 'The CPS will probably knock this on the head before it gets to first base. Any number of people could've spiked her drink, Lisa's too, for that matter. *We* all know he's guilty as sin, but so far the evidence is circumstantial, even if Bryony did wake up around the corner from his home.' Daniels took in the clock on the wall: ten fifty-five. 'Lisa, Andy, you may as well call it a day. Neil, thank Bryony Sharp on my behalf and make sure she gets home before you go off duty. And I don't mean fob her off on someone else. Do it yourself, then you can knock off too.'

Maxwell nodded. Hauling himself off the chair, he sloped off looking decidedly unhappy. Brown picked up his jacket and followed him out, looking

294

back over his shoulder as he approached the door.

'You coming, Lisa?'

'No. I'm going to hang around, wait for the CSIs. I've been in bed most of the day and I'm wide awake. To be honest, I feel pretty wired.'

*   *   *

They resumed the interview with Freek at exactly eleven o'clock as planned. He'd written down a long list, including detailed descriptions of two men he claimed had pressurized him, times, dates and locations where he'd met with them.

'Aren't you forgetting something?' Daniels asked.

'No names, no pack drill . . .' Freek said. 'We were hardly bosom buddies.'

'Why didn't you send the information electronically?' Gormley asked. 'I'd have thought it would've saved you a lot of grief.'

'Why d'you think?' Freek wasn't laughing.

'Humour me,' Gormley pushed.

'Because computer trails are irrefutable evidence, that's why. Ironic, isn't it . . . but now I *am* under arrest, the goalposts have shifted somewhat. I'm not going down alone, I can tell you that. I had nothing to do with that girl's death. Nothing.'

Daniels studied him for a moment. His information may well prove of interest to the Durham force but, as far as her own linked incident was concerned, it gave her very little. The connection between the man she was looking at and Amy Grainger was extremely thin. It was a difficult call, but she decided there and then to hand him over to others, freeing herself up to concentrate on the murder enquiry itself.

'I'll be keeping a close eye on you, Mr Freek. You'll be given eight hours' rest, then someone will come and interview you in the morning when we've had the chance to check this out. Until then, you stay put.'

Daniels' phone rang. Curiously, it was Carmichael. 'Lisa? What's up?'

'You will not believe what I just found,' she said.

64

The MIR always looked eerie at this time of night: the main lights switched off, work stations empty, computer screens dead—the smell of floor polish lingering, courtesy of the office cleaner. Carmichael was tense. She was standing directly in front of the murder wall in an area bathed in a pool of light from spots mounted on the ceiling. She'd cleared two desks and pushed them together to form a long counter. A shallow exhibits box sat on one end with Freek's laptop still inside. A second, empty box lay discarded on the floor, its contents laid out methodically: magazines in one pile, photographs, posters, and so on.

Picking up the photographs, Daniels sifted through them, studying each one carefully. They showed sportswomen in various stages of undress, athletes who seemed totally unaware that their activities were being captured on film—rowers, runners, hockey and rugby players, to name but a few. She was no expert, but the style and print quality led her to believe that they hadn't all come from the same source, much less been printed in the same lab. Some looked professionally done, others were much more amateurish.

Many of the images had holes or traces of dried-up Blu-Tack in the corners, evidence that they'd once been pinned to something else. Daniels picked up the posters. Same here. They were old copies of advertisements for events dating back several months—the type seen on any noticeboard.

'Is this what got you all fired up?' Daniels turned to Carmichael.

Carmichael nodded.

'We knew he was a voyeur,' Daniels said.

'She means perv,' Gormley said. 'That's how she made DCI.'

Carmichael grinned, handing Daniels an A4 sheet. 'I found this with the other stuff.'

It was an advertisement for a flying club based at a local aerodrome:

Jump for your life!
Parachuting and Skydiving
Beginners Welcome
Student Concessions with Union Card.

Reference to an extreme sports organization Daniels had found in Jessica's belongings—an unexplained payment of five hundred pounds— shot into her thoughts, awakening the detective in her. It was too soon to say whether the investigation was about to take yet another unexpected twist. It was all too easy to let your mind run away with itself when you were scratching around in the dark, which was all they'd been doing since the whole team—herself included—had Mark Harris fingered for an incident he had absolutely nothing to do with. And that was only a couple of days ago. Wanting the evidence to fit was very different from actually producing it.

'I couldn't wait to show you.' Carmichael's eyes shifted to Daniels. She certainly wasn't jumping up and down. *Yet.* 'It's a link with flying, yes?'

Daniels conceded that it was. 'I don't want to stifle your enthusiasm, Lisa. But it's very late. I think we should all go home and sleep on it, discuss it with the rest of the team first thing in the morning.'

But Carmichael was resolute.

Still smiling.

Triumphant even.

She knew something more . . .

'What?' Daniels and Gormley said simultaneously.

'What if I told you that flyer has been altered?'

'In what way?' Daniels' heart was thumping now.

'Look at the contact number,' Carmichael said.

They read the flyer again.

Daniels looked up. 'So?'

'It's a mobile number and it doesn't correspond with the flying club's current website—I checked.' Carmichael pointed at the only live computer in the room. It was sitting on a nearby desk and had gone into hibernation, the screen saver showing a floating force logo. 'Take a look for yourself.'

They all moved towards it. Carmichael sat down and ran her finger over the touchpad. The screen saver disappeared and was replaced by the flying club's Internet site, which was open at the home page: *MAC Flying School, Skydive and Parachute Centre.* The club boasted a small fleet of fixed-wing aeroplanes, two helicopters and four qualified flight instructors—two of whom were CAA-appointed examiners. Various numbers were listed for the flying school and the sports activities, but—Carmichael was correct—none of them matched that on the A4 sheet in Daniels' hand.

Daniels looked at Gormley, then at Carmichael. 'I'm assuming the number isn't already on the system?'

Carmichael shook her head. 'The club itself is listed in relation to the general enquiry you instigated in the early stages—i.e. airports within a fifty-mile radius—but this number isn't linked. It isn't registered at all, according to the service provider, so it could belong to anyone, including the bastard that pushed Amy from that plane.'

A ripple of excitement ran between Daniels' shoulder blades. She looked at her watch. It was close to midnight. Too late to ring and ask the Graingers if their daughter had ever expressed an interest in extreme sports. But not too soon to congratulate her brilliant young DC. *Carmichael was definitely on to something.*

65

Daniels slept badly, haunted by girls falling through the air, girls trapped underground, girls coerced into the sex trade. Unable to get back to sleep, she hauled herself out of bed at five a.m., showered and got ready. Downstairs, she made toast and ate it in the kitchen, thinking about the skydiving flyer Carmichael had found among the items crime scene investigators had seized from Freek's vehicle. Jessica Finch certainly had the means to pay for such a course, not so Amy Grainger. Or did she? According to her father, she shared an independent streak with the missing girl. Not content to live off her parents or get sucked into a loan, she'd worked hard in order to pay her way through university. But still . . . was it likely she'd saved enough spare cash to finance the adventure that had ultimately led to her death?

Stranger things had happened.

Deciding to keep her mind open to that possibility, Daniels couldn't get to work fast enough. Dawn was her favourite time of day. She could get into the major incident room before it resembled a circus. Time to think, to mull over the previous day and plan for the day ahead, list what had to be done, by whom and in what order. From the start of this murder investigation there had been few scene issues going forward. No known forensics on the dead girl. Nothing meaningful thrown up in the house-to-house. No bloody witnesses. A recap on the sequence of events that led up to the disappearance of both girls was called for. That way Daniels could pin down the timeline before re-interviewing Freek, an event she suspected would result in God knows how many other follow-up enquiries.

Trace.

Implicate.

Eliminate.

She was still thinking about TIE actions as she let herself into the MIR. Pulling up sharply, she checked her watch, genuinely believing she'd misread the time. Core team members were already there: Gormley, Carmichael, Brown and—*heaven forbid, even Maxwell*—were huddled round a desk discussing the previous night's covert op and Carmichael's subsequent discovery of the flyer.

Gormley began snoring loudly, insinuating that she was late. Daniels grinned, took off her coat and flung it on a chair, telling everyone how pleased she was to see them, adding that they had a shitload of work to do, explaining what she had in mind. Fetching herself a coffee, she invited everyone to get comfy and direct their attention to the murder wall.

Jabbing a button on the remote control, she brought the digital screen to life and scrolled through a number of options before finding what she was after: a split screen containing detailed analysis of the last-known movements of Amy Grainger and Jessica Finch, together with a map plotting the geographical areas where they'd both gone missing.

'I'd like to begin with Amy, who, as you all know, was seen by her parents at seven thirty on Wednesday the fifth of May, just as *Coronation Street* was coming on TV. She was heading to Durham City to meet friends . . .' Daniels used a pointer on screen as she spoke. '. . . So she'd have used this bus stop, just round the corner from her home, less than five hundred metres away. Now,' Daniels took a breath, 'the 15A arrived at the bus stop on time at seven forty-two. CCTV on the bus confirms that only one elderly man got on. Paul Palmer was traced and spoken to during the house-to-house very shortly after the discovery of Amy's body. He knew Amy well enough to speak to her, and claims she didn't arrive at the bus stop that day. Furthermore, he didn't see her while he was standing there, nor did he see anything untoward that he can remember. She could've phoned for a taxi, but local firms say not. At seven thirty-nine, Amy's phone was switched off. In all probability, that's when she was taken. My guess is she turned right, not left, when she left the house.' The room fell silent. 'What? You didn't lie to your parents when you were her age? I bloody did, all the time.'

Daniels used the pointer again. 'There's CCTV on both sides of the road here and here. She wasn't picked up on either camera. But she wouldn't be, would she? Because she was waiting for the bus here before the parade of shops—'

'For a bus that could take her to Sunderland, twenty minutes away,' Carmichael said. 'It's obvious she was taken off the street in a vehicle of some description within minutes of leaving her house.'

'A fingertip search found no signs of disturbance or struggle,' Maxwell reminded her.

'So what?' Carmichael bit back. 'If she responded to the flying club's advert, doesn't mean she ever actually made it there. Or maybe she did and she'd got to know someone there well enough to accept a lift. Her killer, for example.'

'At eight o'clock at night?' Maxwell queried.

Carmichael nearly spat out her tea. 'You think they let you jump on the first lesson? They have to pass the theory first.'

'Lisa's right,' Daniels said. 'Amy accepted a lift from someone she knew. It's the most plausible explanation. I want to move on to Jessica now. A day earlier, on Tuesday the fourth of May, Robert Lester took Jessica home at around eight p.m. CCTV at the entrance to her flat confirms that. They entered at eight-o-six, Lester left on his own at eight thirty-four. About half an hour later, captured on the same CCTV, Jessica leaves the flat at nine-o-seven. She turns right heading towards this Nat West cashpoint where she makes a withdrawal of twenty pounds at eleven minutes past nine. Unless she climbed up the fire escape— and there's no earthly reason why she should— Jess never made it back to her flat. In my view, that's a fair assumption to make, and is supported by the fact that her cashpoint receipt wasn't found there. This is unusual in itself because she was meticulous about keeping her records straight. In fact, it's the only missing receipt, according to the statement supplied by her bank. Jessica's phone goes dead at nine thirteen and I'm certain that's when *she* was taken. Now it gets interesting . . .'

Switching her attention back to the murder wall, Daniels changed screens. Again, the screen was split: one side displaying a detailed map, a network of phone masts stretching the entire length of the country, on the other, a smaller version, spanning an area from Adam Finch's Mansion House in the south to Housesteads in the north.

'On sixth May, both girls' phones were switched on again within seconds of one another directly above the centre of Newcastle at three-o-three in the morning. Together, they pass between several phone masts and from that we are able to calculate that they were travelling in excess of a hundred and forty knots.'

'The journey to Housesteads?' Carmichael was

thinking aloud. 'That's grim.'

Gormley shook his head, a look of pure loathing on his face.

'Both Amy's phone and Jess's were switched off again directly over Housesteads presumably when he . . .' Daniels could hardly bring herself to say it out loud, '. . . when the killer threw Amy to her death. That is where her phone record terminates.'

'It's as if he's pinpointing the spot for us,' Carmichael added.

'Sick bastard,' Gormley mumbled.

'And Jess's phone?' Brown asked.

'Is switched back on at around quarter to eleven on Thursday the sixth of May just hours after Amy's body was found. It makes a journey by road . . . we can tell that from the speed it was travelling . . .' Daniels picked up a road map and superimposed it over the phone mast grid. 'As you can see here, it travelled from a position very close to the Mansion House to Newcastle along the A1. It's my opinion that whoever had it was following Adam Finch to the mortuary where he met myself and our former guv'nor to view and identify our body—'

'Which we later discovered was Amy and not Jess,' Carmichael said.

'Exactly.' Daniels scanned the faces of her team. They were utterly focused, no sign of their enthusiasm waning. She moved on. 'Jess's phone was next used at three thirty p.m. on Thursday the sixth of May when Adam Finch received a text from it.' Daniels took a breath. 'I was standing right next to him at the time, so I know he didn't make that call. I remember thinking that it ruled him out altogether, unless he had an accomplice.

304

He's an objectionable prick, I know. But none of us believe he's involved any more, do we?'

Heads shook but nobody actually spoke.

It was nice to know they were on the same page.

'What we need now is to check the cameras on the A1 northbound to find out whether Freek's BMW or any other car was following Finch during his journey to the mortuary and back. Neil, get on to traffic management. Have them pull the relevant tapes. I want them handed over asap. Andy, call Robert Lester and tell him I want to see him. Don't be specific. Just say I want to ask him some more questions. When you've done that, give the Graingers a call. I need to know if Amy ever expressed an interest in skydiving. On second thoughts, go round and do it in person. You OK with that?'

Brown nodded.

'Good. Lisa, get me everything you can dig up on that flying club. As soon as Hank and I are finished with Stephen Freek we'll be paying them a visit.'

66

Freek had not engaged a solicitor, despite his wobble the night before, so Daniels reminded him that he was still under caution and asked him again if he wanted one present. The suspect shook his head. Then, realizing he was required to speak for the benefit of the tape, he gave his answer verbally.

'Right then . . .' Daniels began. 'Where were you between six p.m. and midnight on the evenings of

Tuesday the fourth of May and Wednesday the fifth?'

'You have my iPhone. It'll tell you all you want to know.'

Carmichael had already examined the phone. He was supposed to be in Manchester on the fourth. All the same, Daniels wanted to hear it from him.

She waited.

'I was at a Foals concert at the Ritz in Manchester on the Tuesday, I know that. I'm into alternative music . . .' Freek's grin was more like a sneer. 'Ask your mate, the cute one I met at Fuse.'

Daniels glared at him. A night in the cells on a hard mattress had done nothing for his appearance: he was sporting a heavy growth of stubble flecked with more grey than his ego could possibly bear; his clothes were rumpled and sweaty; his gelled—normally slicked back—hair stuck out at odd angles. What he might have done to Carmichael had Andy Brown not intervened was anyone's guess. Daniels noticed Gormley's fingers close in a fist around his pen, his knuckles going white as he tried to keep his temper in check.

'Can you produce any documentation to support that?'

'Probably. I bought my ticket online. Fifteen quid or thereabouts—'

'That doesn't mean you were there,' Daniels interrupted.

'No, I don't suppose it does.'

'Anyone go with you?'

' 'fraid not.'

'You drive down in the BM?' Gormley asked.

'No, as it happens I went by train.' Freek yawned,

fed up with their questions. 'I hate motorway driving. I've got an extremely low boredom threshold, as you can probably tell.'

'And on the Wednesday?' Daniels pushed. 'Where were you on the fifth?'

'As far as I know, I was at home.'

'Let me guess . . .' Gormley said. 'You were washing your hair and then you watched TV and there's no one able to verify that.'

Freek smirked.

Daniels wanted to punch his lights out, wipe the supercilious grin off his face. She opened his file, took some pictures and posters out and slid them across the table, spreading them out in front of him. He glanced down at them, totally unconcerned.

'So I like sporty girls!' he said. 'There no law against that, is there?'

Daniels produced the MAC flyer and slid that over too, studying his face for a reaction. There was none. Just the same arrogance he'd shown all along.

'This particular flyer has been doctored,' she said.

'Nowt to do with me.' He didn't flinch, simply pushed the flyer back towards her. 'It didn't belong to anyone, so I took it. I collect stuff like that, as you can see.'

Either he was a very cool customer, or he was telling the truth and had nicked the poster for his own gratification. Daniels suspected the latter and let it go. For now. She was keen to get out of there, pass the bastard into the custody of her Durham colleagues for further questioning. She didn't give a fat rat's arse about what happened to him after

307

that. She had more important things to do. Deciding there and then to bail him, she hesitated for a moment, considering the effect of her actions on Bryony Sharp. Maxwell had said she was a nice kid, terrified at the prospect of this fuckwit drugging someone else. If Daniels let him go now, how could she square that with her?

Carmichael.

Lisa understood what the girl was going through. She'd help Bryony understand the bigger picture, convince her that the police had their eye very firmly on Freek's offending behaviour and promise that something would be done about it, maybe not directly relating to *her* case, but there would be consequences nevertheless. The squirt would lose his job for a start, especially if Patricia Conway at the university were to find out what he'd been up to. And find out she surely would. By the time Durham were finished with him, he'd end up with a custodial for his part in the prostitution racket. Whatever Daniels said to him now, she'd make damn sure of that.

She smiled—an assassin's smile—feeling all warm and cuddly inside.

'I'm a reasonable person,' she said finally. 'In a little while, I'm going to bail you. But before you get too excited, detectives from Durham will be here shortly to have a good, long chat with you. You come up trumps for them and they get the people they're looking for, then who knows? I might think of all sorts of ways to be lenient. You fail to cooperate with them and I'll come down hard on you when you return to the station for a decision. Do you understand?'

'Perfectly.' Freek crossed his arms. 'Do I have a

choice?'

'Of course you do.' Daniels stood up. 'You can take it or leave it.'

The DCI ended the interview and went back upstairs. She called Carmichael into her office and briefed her on the outcome of the interview with Freek. Her young DC looked at the floor, too choked to speak. Daniels gave her a second to compose herself. When she looked up, the stress of recent days had all but disappeared.

'Thanks, boss.' Carmichael dropped her voice. 'Can't tell you how relieved I am that my undercover cock-up isn't going to form part of a public court case.'

'That was never going to happen, Lisa.'

' 'preciate that.' Carmichael then added, 'Robert Lester's in reception.'

'Oh, good.' The internal phone rang and Daniels picked up. It was Brown. Asking him to hold on, she said to Carmichael, 'Find an interview room and make Lester comfortable. Get him a cuppa and tell him I'll be along in a minute.' Carmichael walked away and Daniels went back to the phone. 'Yes, Andy.'

'I've just come from Amy's parents. Your instincts were right.' Brown had a slight tremor in his voice. 'I have in my hand a photograph of Amy parachuting in Australia prior to her degree course—a gap year, so her father tells me.'

Daniels put down the phone in a daze. She left the incident room without speaking to another soul and went down two flights of stairs to the interview rooms below. Robert Lester looked up anxiously as she opened the door. He was extremely jumpy, not at all comfortable in

309

unfamiliar surroundings.

'Have you found Jessica?' was the first thing he said.

'Not yet.' Daniels pointed to the cup in his hand. 'How's the coffee?'

'Bloody awful. I was told you wanted to speak to me?'

'I need more background information, that's all. Something has come up during our enquiries; something I'm hoping might shed light on Jessica's disappearance.'

'Like what?' Lester began to ramble nervously. 'I told you everything when I saw you on Monday. I don't see eye to eye with her father. Well, that's putting it mildly—he hates my guts. I suppose you think he's just an overprotective father. But it's more than that, DCI Daniels. Honestly, the man's a complete racist! You wouldn't understand discrimination. Why should you? Bet nobody ever made up their mind about you at a distance of a hundred metres.'

'That must be really difficult to cope with, for you and for Jessica.'

'She doesn't let him get to her. Sometimes I think she only goes out with me to get right up his aristocratic nose.'

'I'm sure that's not the case.'

'I hope not. I'm mad about her.'

'You must hate him a lot.'

Lester bristled, unhappy with the way the conversation was going. He took a pack of Marlboro Lights from inside his jacket, saw the no smoking sign and put them back again. Daniels found it curious that someone entering the medical profession would choose to smoke. Maybe

310

it was the stress he was under.

No maybe about it.

They could both do with a fag right now.

She decided to back off and get to the point. 'Did Jessica ever mention skydiving or parachuting to you?'

Lester gave a little nod. 'She loves that shit.'

Daniels tried not to react. But he must've seen a flicker in her eyes. His face paled as he misread the gravity of the situation. His hands flew to his mouth. For a moment, Daniels thought he would vomit. Fiona Fielding had told her that Lester and Jess were very much in love. The DCI wanted nothing more than to reunite the couple. But it had been nine days since Jessica's abduction and she was beginning to fear the worst.

'You have found her, haven't you? Please tell me she's not dead.'

'No, we haven't. I promise you we're doing all we can, Robert. And when we do find her, you'll be the first to know.'

'After her father, you mean?'

'Of course.' She could see he resented that.

'Why did you ask about the skydiving?'

Daniels couldn't answer him.

67

Don Fairley looked good in his Aviator flying suit: a lightweight, flame-resistant affair in NATO green with multiple pockets on the thigh and upper sleeves, the logo of the MAC Flying School stitched into the breast pocket. He was standing outside a hangar next to a Piper Tomahawk aircraft, a pair of reflective Oakley sunglasses on his head, a Bose headset in his right hand, a flight plan in his left.

'Is this going to take long?' he said. 'I'm due to take off in ten.'

Daniels stepped forward, showing him photographs of Amy and Jessica, asking if he recognized either girl. She watched him carefully as he put on a pair of reading glasses and scanned the images closely.

'She looks familiar . . .' Fairley tapped the photograph of Jessica. 'The other one I don't recognize. You'll have to ask my partner. We work with different clients. I'm mostly involved with pilot training. He organizes and runs the skydive centre. D'you guys mind telling me—'

'Your partner's name, sir?' Gormley interrupted.

'Stewart Cole.' He pointed towards a single-storey building. 'Try the ground school or, failing that, the office. I've not seen him yet today.' He shifted his gaze to the small car park. 'His car's not here. He might still be on his way in.'

The sun came out from behind a cloud and the wind picked up a little. Taking off his reading specs, Fairley dropped his sunglasses down on to the bridge of his nose as a young woman walked towards him also wearing a flying suit. He smiled at her, tucked his flight plan under his arm and held up his hand, spreading his fingers to let her know that he wouldn't keep her waiting long.

'Can I ask what this is about?' he said, turning back.

'First things first, Mr Fairley.' Gormley pulled out a pen. 'We need to talk to you and I'm afraid it's not something that can wait. Could you accompany us to the office?'

'No, I bloody can't!' Fairley raised his voice, swept his free hand towards his waiting trainee. 'This young woman has paid a lot of money for my time. I told you, I'm working.'

'So are we, sir,' Daniels said. 'We won't keep you longer than is absolutely necessary. Do you have your advertising flyers printed here on the premises?'

'No. A local printer does them for us.' Fairley was beginning to worry. 'He's a friend of mine. Why d'you ask?'

'So you have no objection to providing his details?'

Fairley shook his head. 'Why would I? Look, the office staff can help you with that. Now, I really must go.'

Daniels held out a copy of the flyer the CSIs had found in the boot of Stephen Freek's car. 'Could I ask you to look at this and confirm whether or not it is genuine?'

He almost snatched the flyer from her, looked at the A4 sheet briefly and then handed it straight back, confirming that it was genuine. Daniels looked away as an Audi TT raced through an automatic barrier and pulled up in front of the ground school next to her Toyota. A guy about forty years old, also wearing dark glasses, got out carrying a flight bag. He locked the car and hurried into the building. If this was who Daniels thought it was, she knew he had form.

Carmichael had done some digging before they left the MIR.

'Is that Stewart Cole, sir?'

313

'Yes.' Fairley bristled. 'Can I go now?'

Daniels nodded. 'But we may need to ask you further questions.' She handed over a business card with her name, rank and department on it. When he saw she was Senior Investigating Officer in the murder investigation team, a look of horror flashed across his face.

She smiled. 'We'll be in touch.'

Fairley said nothing as they walked away.

They crossed the tarmac towards the ground school. Two plaques were attached to the wall on either side of the main entrance proclaiming *British Parachute Association Approved Training Centre* on the right; *CAA Approved Flying School* on the left. They found Stewart Cole inside, writing stuff on an old-fashioned blackboard for a lecture they presumed was about to take place. He turned around when he heard them enter, an inquisitive look on his face. He was really good-looking with deep-set eyes, chiselled features and a nice smile. His flying suit bore the logo of the club.

'I'm Detective Chief Inspector Daniels, sir. Northumbria Police, murder investigation team. This is Detective Sergeant Gormley. We'd like a word, if we may.'

'Of course.' Cole examined her ID as if he'd heard wrong. Then he reached out and picked up the phone. 'First, I need to make a quick call.'

He dialled a number and turned away, looking out over the runway as he waited for an answer. Gormley made a face at Daniels. She knew what he was thinking, but he was wrong. Cole wasn't calling his brief, just letting someone know that he had unexpected company, telling the person on the other end to apologize to his trainees for the delay.

He said he'd call again when he was ready to begin his class. Ending the call, he turned back towards them, pointing at a vending machine in the corner of the room.

'It's not wonderful,' he said, 'but it's all we have here, I'm afraid.'

The detectives declined to use it.

They were keen to get on.

Daniels showed Cole the same photographs of Amy and Jessica she'd shown his partner. 'Can you confirm whether or not either girl has visited the club?'

'Yes, they both have. Is there a problem?'

'Can you take a look at this, sir—' she handed him the flyer—'and tell me if it is one of yours.'

Cole spotted the discrepancy almost immediately. Daniels was sure of it. He flushed up, pulled the zip of his flying suit down to his waist, exposing a khaki special forces T-shirt. A link with his army career, she wondered, or just boys being boys, clothing to fit the image? Her father had once owned an SAS-issue knife he'd acquired somewhere on his travels. Loved showing it to folks, but as far as she was aware he'd never pretended it was his. He'd handed the damned thing in when the police had a knife amnesty. Worth a bloody fortune it was too.

'Mr Cole?'

'Sorry, yes, it's one of ours.'

Daniels thanked him. 'Could you take another look, please?'

'A good look this time,' Gormley added.

'What more do you want me to say?' Cole met Daniels' steady gaze. 'OK, it's been tampered with. But not by me!'

'What exactly do you mean, "tampered with"?' Daniels asked.

'The phone number's different. I'll show you.' He walked to a three-drawer filing cabinet and looked inside. From it he produced an identical flyer and brought it to them. Daniels noted that it was for the same course, on the same dates, but on this one the contact number was correct. 'Is someone going to tell me what the hell is going on?'

If she'd had money on it, Daniels would have said he was telling the truth. She glanced around the room. Six rows of chairs faced the blackboard on the rear wall. Either side of it were posters for the Private Pilot's Licence (PPL) Syllabus, medical and safety procedures, navigation, radiotelephony and Met Office charts covering almost the entire wall. In one corner, a picture gallery showed ex-students skydiving, all with smiling faces, some in tandem, some brave enough to jump alone.

Goosebumps covered Daniels' skin as Amy Grainger's dead body popped into her head.

'You don't like the police much, do you, Mr Cole?' Gormley said.

Cole ignored the wind-up. For a long time he didn't answer. Then he took a deep breath, his eyes on the more senior of the two detectives. 'Do you believe in rehabilitation, DCI Daniels?'

Good question. One Daniels didn't answer.

But Cole had her undivided attention.

'I don't know what you think I might've done. But I run a legitimate business here and I've nothing to hide from the police. I've been in trouble in the past, I admit it. But then, I guess you already know that.' The pilot paused. 'Look, I paid for my mistakes a long time ago and I've moved on. My business partner doesn't know of my history and I'd like to keep it that way.'

'I bet you would.' Gormley kept up the pressure. 'Three months' imprisonment in 1999 for Affray, kicked out of the Army Air Corps in 2000. That's not something I'd be proud of either.'

'We haven't accused you of anything, Mr Cole,' Daniels reminded them both.

'Yet,' Gormley said, hellbent on the final word.

On this occasion, Daniels didn't give him the satisfaction. She thanked Cole, deciding to leave it there . . . *for now.*

68

Driving was one of the pleasures of Daniels' life. She never tired of it. But there was stuff she had to do and even she couldn't work and drive at the same time, at least not on a laptop. So she took the unprecedented step of asking Gormley to drive down to the Mansion House as fast as the Toyota would carry them, calling Naylor from the car to give him an update and receive one in return.

'Lisa's squared things with Bryony Sharp,' he told her. 'And she's also been doing some digging into the MAC Flying Club. They are up to their wings in shit, within an inch of being wound up—there's possible motive there.'

'Except there's been no demand for a ransom and no further contact from Jess's abductors since the very first day—'

'According to Finch!' Naylor reminded her.

'Bright tells me he's a bit of a maverick. Always was. Maybe he's going it alone.'

'Don't think so.' Daniels went quiet, reminded of her conversation with Finch in the early stages of the case. *Even if they continue, I will not be blackmailed!* He refused to be intimidated, didn't strike her as the sort who'd submit to the demands of others, under any circumstances. No. He'd see that as a weakness, something to resist at all costs. 'The note he received was never about money, guv. It was designed to torment him. Think about it: he didn't have the best relationship with Jessica and I gather she was pretty headstrong. So when she disappeared he wouldn't have known whether she'd gone off of her own free will or not.'

'So if it weren't for the note, he'd never have known that someone had taken her?'

'Precisely! Receiving that note—and the text sent from her mobile—guarantees ongoing pain and suffering. Mental torture, if you will. His imagination will be working overtime for as long as she remains missing. Is she alive? Suffering a horrible lingering death? What do these people want from him? You get what I'm saying?'

'Seeing as you put it so eloquently.'

Daniels dropped the subject. 'Is there any other news?'

'The Durham lads interviewed Freek.'

'Did they get anything from him?'

'Maybe. They've gone back to Aykley Heads to mount an operation of their own. He's still in custody, but he's their problem, not ours.'

Daniels shook her head in frustration as Gormley was forced to slow to a crawl in a long line of cars stuck in roadwork hell. The mention of

Durham HQ reminded her of the last time she was there, at a Bike Wise event run by the constabulary's motorcycle section. A great day out, one of few she'd had in the past twelve months. If she was on her bike now, the roadworks she was staring at through the window would melt away.

Sensing her irritation, Gormley pulled on to the hard shoulder and shot past the line of cars. Unadulterated road rage contorted the faces of the other drivers as they sped away.

Daniels liked his style.

'Did Andy manage to get hold of Finch's army records?' Daniels asked.

'He did, but only after a monumental battle with the MOD.'

'Pearce and Townsend's too, I hope! Did Lisa tell him I wanted Cole's too?'

'I believe so. How's it going your end?'

'We've interviewed Cole and Fairley, guv.' Daniels felt awkward calling him guv. Somehow it sounded wrong. Bright would always be her guv'nor, despite his bad temper, his bad manners and latterly, she'd learned, his spectacular bad judgement in relation to Adam bloody Finch. She was still really angry with him. 'I have to say, the business looked to be thriving to me. I'm on my way to see Finch right now.'

'Because?'

'I wanted to run their names by him and see the whites of his eyes when I do.'

'Interesting.' Naylor's voice was drowned out by an internal phone ringing somewhere close by. 'Kate, I've got to—'

'Damn!' Gormley swore under his breath. 'We missed him.'

319

Putting his foot on the brake pedal, Gormley glanced in the rear-view mirror. Daniels asked Naylor to hang on. She swivelled round in her seat, just in time to see a Jaguar XJ Portfolio disappearing round the bend.

'Want me to turn around?' Gormley asked.

'Sure it was him?'

'Positive.' Gormley smacked his hand on the dash in anger. 'What a bloody waste of time! Told you we should've phoned ahead!'

'Push on, Hank.' Daniels was calm. 'There's method in my madness. It's Brian Townsend I'd *really* like a word with.'

Gormley's brow creased. 'Why?'

'Let's just say he's a bit more truthful and lot more pliable than the rest.'

'Kate?' Naylor was back in Daniels' ear. 'Is everything OK?'

'Everything's fine, guv. I'll catch you later.'

Naylor told her to take care and she hung up.

69

Mrs Partridge opened the panelled front door before they had a chance to ring the bell. From the look on the woman's face as she peered out from within it was clear she was expecting someone else. 'Oh, it's you, Inspector!' She smiled. 'I heard a car. I thought Mr Finch had forgotten something. I'm afraid you just—'

'Missed him. I know.' Daniels pointed into the house. 'Could we ask you one or two questions while we're here?'

'Of course, come in.'

The housekeeper stepped aside, inviting Daniels and Gormley to go through to the library and make themselves comfortable. Daniels felt anything but as she walked into the room with Jessica's eyes looking down from the portrait, her confidence so powerfully portrayed by the equally scary lady, Fiona Fielding. *Scary, in a nice way,* Daniels thought guiltily, those enigmatic eyes still following her as she took a seat by the cavernous fireplace.

'Do the names Donald Fairley and Stewart Cole mean anything to you, Mrs Partridge?' Daniels said. 'Either recently or in the past.'

The housekeeper shook her head. 'I don't think so.'

'Mr Pearce is out with Mr Finch, I take it? I couldn't tell who was driving the car when it passed us on the road.'

Mrs Partridge nodded. 'Can I get either of you something to drink?'

'No, thank you,' Daniels said.

Gormley just shook his head. 'You told my colleagues that Mr Pearce wrote to Mr Finch begging for work, is that right?'

'I never used the word "begging", Sergeant. But yes, that's about the gist of it. It's not easy, starting out in Civvy Street when you leave the forces. I think it's terrible how the government expects servicemen and women to fight for our country and then won't support them afterwards, don't you? At least Mr Finch is doing his bit. He employs ex-service personnel because he knows he can trust them.'

Daniels remembered the coldness of Finch

towards his housekeeper on the first occasion they'd met and thought it odd that she was so loyal to a man who not only delighted in putting people's backs up, but was downright bloody rude if the mood so took him.

'Are you happy here, Mrs Partridge?' she asked.

'Confidentially?' The woman took in Daniels' nod. 'I wouldn't stay if I didn't need a roof over my head—'

'You live in?' Gormley interrupted.

'A condition of the job, I'm afraid. Ensures I'm at his beck and call round the clock in case he needs anything. The work isn't a problem, but sometimes Mr Finch and I don't see eye to eye.'

'I'm not hearing *The Sound of Music*!' Gormley joked.

Mrs Partridge giggled. 'He *can* be a little difficult on occasions.'

'Tell me about it!' Gormley flicked his eyes in Daniels' direction, teasing them both and putting the housekeeper at her ease. 'Do you see Mr Townsend up at the house often?'

'Not really. He's been keeping himself to himself lately.'

'Any particular reason?' Daniels asked.

'His wife's very poorly—malignant brain tumour. Inoperable, sadly. It's unlikely she'll last out the summer.' The woman looked upset. 'Forgive me, but I have work to do. You'll find Brian in the garden.'

They left the house via the front door and wandered round the back. Skirting the gable end of the mansion, they spotted Townsend about forty metres away. He was edging the lawn with a sod cutter, the like of which they'd never seen before.

About halfway across the lawn, one of Daniels' high heels stuck fast in the turf and she almost toppled over. The gardener stopped what he was doing and stood up straight.

'Steady on, lass, you'll do yourself an injury.' Retrieving the shoe, he smiled as he handed it back. 'My missus is always doing that. I've told her, lawns aren't made for fancy footwear.'

Lifting her foot, Daniels slipped the shoe back on. 'I was sorry to hear from Mrs Partridge that your wife's not at all well.'

Townsend went quiet.

'Cancer is a terrible thing . . .' Daniels felt a wave of grief crashing over her.

Townsend picked up on her heartache. 'Someone close to you?'

Daniels nodded. 'My mother.'

'Then you have my sympathies, ma'am. I just can't come to terms with the prospect of life without Joyce.' Upset now, he bit down on his lip, his eyes darkening. 'My employer lost his good lady a long time ago, but I haven't had an ounce of sympathy from him. A compassionate man, he is not. But he's paying for it now, isn't he? Reaping what he sows.'

'I'd be careful what you say, if I were you.' Gormley's tone was sharp, warning Townsend that he'd overstepped the mark. 'People might get the wrong impression. Nobody deserves what your boss is going through. Jessica's his only child—'

'He stood by and—' Townsend stopped himself going any further.

Daniels said, 'Stood by and did what exactly?'

The gardener looked at the wet grass, then took a tobacco tin from a torn jacket pocket and opened it up. Inside were several pre-prepared rollies. He took one out and lit it, inhaling the nicotine deep into his lungs. He was angry and Daniels wanted to know why.

'Brian?' She used his first name, hoping to prompt an answer from him. 'Please, finish what you were going to say.'

Townsend stared at her. 'He stood by and let it happen to a mate of mine and didn't bat an eyelid. Is it any wonder nobody gives a shit what happens to him? It's the young lass I feel sorry for.'

'How do you mean, "stood by and let it happen"?'

'I've said too much already.' Townsend looked away.

'On the contrary,' Gormley said. 'If you know something, tell us. Only a callous man would refuse to cooperate. You might be the only hope we have of finding Jessica alive, Brian. Please help us.'

Townsend carried on smoking.

Sick of waiting, Gormley told him to stop dicking around. The gardener spat a rogue piece of tobacco on to the lawn at Daniels' feet. It was a gesture she considered deliberate, designed to tell her exactly how disgusted he was with his employer. Then, suddenly, he relented.

'A bunch of us were on special ops in Northern Ireland—V Regiment. Finch was our Commanding Officer. An urgent message came through for a guy in my unit whose daughter was critically ill in hospital with meningitis. She was his only child and Finch ignored the request for repatriation on grounds that it could jeopardize our mission.'

'Maybe it would have. I've had to make tough decisions for the greater good—'

'Nah . . .' Townsend shook his head. 'Jimmy was good, but he wasn't that good. There were other guys in our unit who could've stepped in.'

'She died?' Gormley asked.

Daniels held her breath.

Townsend nodded.

70

Weldon stared at the muddy footprints at the entrance to the mine. The gate was secure enough, a hefty chain wrapped several times around both uprights. But on further inspection he noticed that the padlock was relatively new.

He raised his head.

On the horizon, he could see a line of cars parked on the top road, cameras and binoculars trained on police and civilian search teams as they went about their business. The operation to find the girl had turned what was normally a desolate and beautiful landscape into a day trip for some, attracting a level of interest he personally found repugnant. Morbid curiosity of that kind was something he could not comprehend.

Nor did he wish to.

Pushing his anger away, Weldon studied the footprints again and got straight on the radio: 'Weldon to TSG. Harry, get over here with the cutting gear.'

Within seconds, a stocky guy arrived by his side with a couple of tactical support officers in tow.

They were wearing reflective jackets and one was carrying a large set of bolt cutters. Weldon pointed out the footprints, then stood back and waited somewhat impatiently while they called for tread plates in order to preserve them. It was a dull, windy day. Dusk would arrive in only five hours and he was keen to get going.

The bolt cutters sliced through the padlock with ease. Weldon switched on his cap lamp and led the way as he had done countless times for the past few days, this time hoping for a more fruitful result. The roof of the mine was less than the height of an average man. With water sloshing around his feet, he guided the others by torchlight into the pitch darkness.

Light bounced off wet walls casting shadows in the eerie space as they moved, one slow step at a time, being careful where they placed their feet as they picked their way in. After about fifteen minutes, the tunnel widened and it was possible to stand up straight. Directing torchlight around the dank walls, one officer's sudden intake of breath made Weldon turn around.

What he saw was gut-wrenching, even for the most hardened of professionals. Rooted to the spot, he had only one focus: a set of shackles hanging loose from the wall. Nobody moved or spoke as he examined them more closely, careful not to touch anything, his former police training kicking in. He turned to the others, frustrated with their gruesome find.

'Keep searching,' he said.

Nobody moved.

'Well, go on! What are you waiting for? I'm heading back. The radio's fuck-all use down here and we need a forensics team to examine this lot.'

Leaving them to it—with instructions to stay together should they come to a fork in the tunnel—Weldon made his way back to the entrance. As soon as he reached the surface, he called in the CSIs, then pulled out his mobile and dialled Daniels' number. She answered almost immediately—from a vehicle, by the sound of it.

'What is it, Dave?'

'We have ourselves a crime scene,' was all Weldon said.

'And Jessica?'

'The bastard's moved her. We've got fresh blood here. Your forensics guys are on it. TSG are searching the remainder of the mine in case she's still down there . . .' He paused but Daniels was silent. 'I'm sorry, Kate. I know it's not the news you wanted.'

'No.' The DCI sounded more upbeat than Weldon had expected. 'This is a positive development. If Jess were dead, why move her body at great risk of being seen? Whoever's got her is methodical, make no mistake about that. He'll have thought this through and left nothing to chance. In my book, that means two sites to hide her—in case we got close. With you lot crawling all over the place I don't think the second will be too far from the first. You've got to keep searching. You can find her in time, I know you can.'

*   *   *

Jessica had heard a voice, her father's—clear and strong—telling her not to give up. And now she had a plan . . . of sorts. But would it work?

One chance.
Only one.
Fight, Jess!
Dig deep.
Deeper than ever before.

Manoeuvring her skinny left leg as far downstream as it would reach, she tucked her chin into her chest until the strap of the hard hat she was wearing worked free. Then, tilting her head to one side, she pressed it up against the wet wall with a view to dislodging the hat. Then, at the very last moment, she pulled back. She just couldn't do it, just couldn't bear the thought of the lights going out completely, ending her days in a cold wet chamber, alone in the dark. She wailed, terror overtaking her for a moment.

You must.
It's the only way.

She tried again and this time went through with it. The hat slid sideways and fell—in what seemed like hours of slow motion—glancing off her bony right shoulder, landing in the murky water beneath. Instantly taken by the current, it sailed off and Jess jerked her leg towards it, flailing around in the water, catching the chin strap just right. Hooking it on to her foot, she was amazed to see that the bulb was still illuminated. Sobbing with relief, she rested a while. She said a little prayer, in case there *was* a God.

Maybe He was calling her?

Well, I'm not fucking listening!

It took all the effort she could summon to lift her leg, let alone swing it back and forth using the hard hat to tap out an SOS. It was a pathetic attempt, a stupid idea that had little chance of success.

328

Stealing herself, she took a break and tried again: three sharp knocks . . . three longer ones . . . three sharp knocks.

*   *   *

Less than a couple of hundred metres away, a chill wind whipped across the open moorland. Discovering the crime scene had shaken Weldon. But hearing Daniels' take on things had given him hope. To the right of his search area, another casualty of the operation was being stretchered away to a waiting ambulance, having dislocated a shoulder in a fall below ground. A fractured leg had already claimed one of his team that day, no doubt keeping the voyeuristic day-trippers satisfied on the road above.

He looked on as the ambulance drove away, taking the noise of its siren with it. As it disappeared over the brow of a hill, the area fell silent again. Weldon went rigid. He could've sworn he'd heard something, although he couldn't quite place exactly what it was or where it had come from.

Tilting his head, he listened . . .

Silence.

Only the wind howling through the brush and the distinctive sound of the wing beats of red grouse rocketing up from the heather, their habitat disturbed by a member of the search team. The creature was the bane of every motorcyclist this side of the Isle of Man; one Weldon had come across far too frequently while riding round the countryside.

Then the sound was back.

Weldon held up a hand and blew his whistle.

Those of the search team within hearing distance froze.

*   *   *

Inside the mine, Jessica's heart leapt as she heard the whistle. But her throat was so dry she wasn't able to call for help. The hat was still strapped to her ankle but it was now full of water, dragging her leg downstream like a lead weight. She couldn't find a way to empty it and repeat her SOS.

*   *   *

Outside, police and civilian teams had stopped what they were doing and were maintaining search protocol, their ears pinned firmly to the ground, a call on the radio eventually breaking the silence.

'TSG Leader to Weldon. Was that a *definite* shout, over?'

Weldon looked up, two dozen pairs of eyes turned towards him.

'Not sure,' Weldon radioed back. 'Could've sworn I heard tapping.'

'TSG Leader to all units. Anyone else hear anything?'

Several calls of *negative* came back. One smart arse said the only call he'd heard was one of nature and was told, in no uncertain terms, to fuck right off.

They listened for a few seconds longer.

Weldon shook his head. 'Must've been the wind.'

71

Daniels drove back to the flying school with a sense of urgency, hoping Stewart Cole might know, or at least know of, Jimmy Makepeace. Brian Townsend had told her they were from the same unit and had left the forces at about the same time. Army regiments tended to be close-knit communities, so chances were high.

Besides, she was due a lucky break.

Right now, however, something more tangible than luck was forming in her brain. Last night, when Carmichael had shown them the flying club's website, Daniels had noticed that there were four flying instructors. So far she'd only met two. Gormley had also picked up on this and they couldn't wait to check it out. Pushing the button on her hands-free, leaving it on loudspeaker, Daniels called the incident room.

The phone rang out several times before DS Robson picked up.

'Robbo, you've got work to do. Contact Jo Soulsby and ask her to get to the MIR—within the hour, if that's possible. I also want a full background check on a man called Jimmy Makepeace. Tell Lisa he's ex-army, last known address Newton Aycliffe area. Tell her to drop everything else, I'll explain later. And let Naylor know we're definitely on to something. Tell him we'll be back soon and ask him to stick around if he can.'

'Consider it done. Anything else?'

'I'll let you know later. You any further forward

with the tapes from Traffic?'

'Yes we are . . .' He sounded chuffed to be imparting good news for once. 'A stolen Ford Escort was tailing Finch when he made the journey from his home to the mortuary. Problem is, we can't make the driver. I've put a stop and search on it, but we're probably wasting our time. Most likely it'll be in the river or else burnt out somewhere.'

Daniels thanked him and rang off. She made another call. This time, it was taken straight away, before it had even had a chance to ring out.

'Detective Chief Superintendent Bright's office.'

'Ellen, it's Kate. Is he in?'

'Am I glad *you* called. He's been like a bear with a sore head since you two last spoke. Sorry, no pun intended. What the hell did you say to him?'

Daniels felt guilty for not calling Ellen before now to check on Bright, his medical status at least. It was true she'd been busy. But that wasn't the reason.

'Long story, Ellen. Is he there?'

'I'll put you through.'

There was a short pause and a click on the line.

Then Bright picked up. 'Yes, Kate? Something I can do for you?'

Daniels bypassed small talk and got right to the point. 'Guv, when you were in Northern Ireland did you ever come across a soldier called Jimmy Makepeace?'

'Doesn't ring any bells.'

'Townsend told us that he and Makepeace were in the same unit over there and that Finch was their CO. Knowing he was yours, I was hoping you might've known the name.'

'Who is he?'

'I'm a bit pushed for time, guv. Can you meet me at the MIR in about an hour? It'll save me explaining myself twice over.'

'You think it's him?'

'That's what I'm trying to find out.'

'You have a bad feeling about him. I can hear it in your voice.'

'Let's put it this way, guv, if he has any connection with the flying club then you can bet he also had access to the school register, the lot. He could easily have tampered with the flyer.'

'Have you spoken to Finch about him?'

'Not yet. He's incommunicado.'

'Speak to his driver. Ask him to come in.'

Daniels turned off the main A1 at a sign pointing to Sunderland. Gormley suggested that Bright should be there when Adam Finch eventually came in and Daniels put that to him.

'I'd appreciate that,' Bright said.

There was an awkward moment of silence on the phone and in the car. Gormley glanced at Daniels, probably wondering which of his superiors would blink first. Daniels seemed lost for words and Bright wasn't helping her out. It was the first time they had spoken since their confrontation at his home.

'Give him a break,' Gormley whispered.

Daniels scowled at him.

'Catch you later, guv.' She rang off abruptly. 'What are *you* looking at?'

'Someone with a bit of common sense, I guess.' Fixing his eyes on the potholed road ahead, Gormley ignored her stare. 'Is that the end of it then?'

333

'The end of what?'

'You know what.'

'I'm still pissed with him, if that's what you mean.'

'So, he's no saint! Who the hell is?'

Daniels didn't answer. Slowing down, she turned left. As luck would have it, the barrier to the MAC Flying School was up and she didn't have to stop. Cole's Audi TT was still parked in the same spot. She pulled up alongside and cut the engine, staring straight ahead.

'Wanna talk about it?' Gormley said.

'No, I bloody don't.'

'That's what I love about you. You're such a great communicator.'

72

Cole was not at the ground school so they went to the office instead. A young receptionist informed them that he wasn't at the hangar either. She'd just come from there and had no idea where he was. Asking them to wait in Cole's office, she offered to locate him.

'He's probably done a runner,' Gormley said drily.

Daniels glared at him. 'You don't like him?'

'Not over much.'

'Why?'

'Dunno. Maybe for the same reason you do. Could it have something to do with his exceptional good looks? His toned physique? His thrill-seeking, shit-kicking lifestyle? His fuck-off job?'

Daniels turned away smiling. Through the window she could see the receptionist walking briskly towards a small plane parked on the tarmac, a helicopter with the registration number G-1TWA standing next to it. Wondering if there were other flying schools affiliated to this one but working from the same premises, she sent Gormley out to investigate.

When he'd gone, she glanced idly around Cole's tidy office. There were no personal pictures on his desk but there were lots of souvenirs, including a paperweight bearing the emblem of the Canadian Air Force, a maple leaf in the sky with a vapour trail encircling it. Next to it sat a miniature Sopwith Camel biplane, the fuselage of which was actually a small box containing a pile of Cole's business cards.

Picking one out, she casually slipped it into her pocket.

There was a storyboard on the wall, a photographic record of Cole's exploits over the past ten years. Crossing the room to view it more closely, she observed that the images had been shot at recognizable landmarks all over the world: Ayers Rock, Great Wall of China, the Grand Canyon, to name but a few. Inevitably, a lot of the photographs featured the cockpits of aircraft, both fixed-wing and helicopter. In others, Cole stood beside various aircraft with his arm round the shoulders of other pilots, posing for the camera with a smile on his handsome face. And it was these that sent her heart rate up as she noted four men in total, one of them too old to have been Makepeace.

But the other?

Shit!

The door behind squeaked as it opened.

'Come and have a look at this, Hank,' she said, without turning round.

In the absence of further movement behind her, she turned. Stewart Cole was standing in the doorway, his hands and one cheek covered in engine oil, his flying suit a little grubbier than when they'd first met.

He pointed at the storyboard. 'That's the best part of being a pilot, we tend to get around. I've had some amazing adventures in my time.'

He was being friendly, not conceited. The fact that she was a police officer who might regard him with a certain amount of suspicion because of his past didn't seem to affect his attitude towards her. Daniels didn't know why, but she felt drawn to the man. All morning she'd found herself mulling over his question about rehabilitation, unable to shake it off.

'Who's this?' Turning her back on Cole, she pointed to the older man in the photographs, a man with white hair and a winning smile, his eyes covered with wrap-around sunglasses, a man she estimated to be mid-to-late sixties.

'That's Mac,' Cole made his way towards her. 'Don's father-in-law. The guy who founded the company. Sadly he's no longer with us.'

'And this?' Daniels pointed at the fourth man.

'Ex-army buddy of mine. He used to be one of our freelance instructors.'

Daniels turned to face him. 'Used to be?'

'He left us around a month ago.' Cole's face grew serious as he picked up on her tension. 'He hasn't gone and done anything stupid, has he?'

73

It was gone five, later than expected, when they arrived back at the MIR. Bright and Naylor were both there waiting for news, ready to swing into action with a full murder investigation team and the promise of more resources if required. The atmosphere in the room was one of real hope and expectation: Carmichael, Brown, Robson, Maxwell, all keen to do their bit.

'No Jo Soulsby?' Daniels said, looking round.

'Ladies' room.' Carmichael's eyes looked past her. 'Oh, speak of the devil.'

Daniels turned round.

Watching her former lover walk into her place of work had always been a little awkward, more so in the past few months because both Gormley and Bright had knowledge of their relationship. Even though they were now just colleagues, Daniels felt her temperature rise. She waited for Jo to take a seat, then turned her attention to the task in hand, the hastily arranged briefing.

Cole had cooperated fully, providing vital background information on Jimmy Makepeace, his ex-army pal. Makepeace was a first-class pilot with special operations training who'd taught survival techniques in the military. Daniels was at pains to point out that he also fitted the profile Jo had given them: organized, methodical, a risk-taker . . .

'. . . a good man, but highly volatile. Not switched right, according to Cole.'

'Then that makes him very dangerous,' Jo said.

Robson said, 'I guess that means we're ruling out

Cole.'

'We're ruling out no one,' Daniels corrected him, although she didn't really believe Cole had any direct connection to the murder case. 'But Jimmy Makepeace has history with Finch and that gives *him* clear motive. The thing is . . .' she hesitated, her eyes finding Jo, '. . . it's been several years since he lost his daughter to meningitis. I'd have thought that was too long, if we're talking revenge here.'

'I'd have thought so too,' Jo said. 'But it's not entirely beyond the bounds of possibility. The criminal mind isn't that easy to predict.'

'It wasn't too long for Forster,' Gormley reminded them. 'Twisted bastard waited twenty years to exact *his* revenge.'

Daniels felt an ache in her shoulder. She yearned for the day she could rid herself of the connection with the notorious serial killer. But that wasn't going to happen anytime soon. Jonathan Forster's name and hers were inextricably linked now, whether she liked it or not. Everyone she met, in and out of the job, wanted her to tell them what he was really like.

Scum, that's what.

'Forster had no choice but to wait that long,' Jo said. 'He was incarcerated, don't forget. He passed away his years inside planning his revenge on his mother.'

Naylor was looking directly at Jo now, putting her right on the spot. 'Is it possible that a traumatic event so far in the past could trigger violence in the here and now?'

'Yes, but there has to be a flashpoint, something catastrophic that would send a sane person over

338

the top.'

'Like what?'

As Jo began to explain, Daniels glanced at Bright. In the past he'd not seen eye to eye with Jo, despite her reputation as an exceptionally talented criminal profiler. His attitude to her job was belittling and Daniels was pleased to see that Naylor was including Jo in his plans as a full and valued member of the team.

It boded well for the future.

Carmichael raised her hand, apologizing for interrupting Jo mid-flow. 'Makepeace lost his daughter—that sounds pretty catastrophic to me.'

'Yes, but that was years ago.'

'No it wasn't! It was just last month.'

The room descended into silence.

'What do you mean, last month?' Daniels said. 'Sally Makepeace died in '95!'

'Different daughter,' Carmichael said. 'I spoke to neighbours at his last known address. Soon after they lost Sally, Makepeace split from his first wife, Susan. I'm still trying to trace her. The woman I spoke to said Susan stayed for a while but he left without saying goodbye to anyone. No one had an inkling he'd gone until months afterwards, not even his closest friends and neighbours. Then she ups and leaves the very same way, there one minute, gone the next . . .'

Daniels opened her mouth to speak, but Carmichael was on a roll.

'Since Makepeace wasn't high-ranking ex-army like Finch, I figured he wouldn't be particularly well off. In order to live he'd need money: social security if he was unemployed, a national insurance number if he wasn't. Anyway, I tracked him down to an address in Sunderland and found out he remarried three years ago and had a child, Hattie. Sadly, she also died.'

'Died how?' Naylor asked.

'Also of meningitis, believe it or not.'

'There's your trauma trigger,' Jo said.

'Brilliant work, Lisa!'

The comment had come from Bright. He'd always had a soft spot for Carmichael and had taken a personal interest in her career. She was dependable and industrious and he'd make it his business to see that she progressed through the ranks.

Daniels agreed with him.

'Right,' she said. 'Drop *everything*. I want a concerted effort to bring Makepeace in. Run a full background check: houses, haunts, vehicles, friends, family—whatever it takes. And I want it *yesterday*. I also want covert obs of the North Pennines search area overnight in case he turns up to move Jess again. I want a doctor standing by, briefed on her possible condition, should we find her, with full access to her med history, blood group, et cetera.' Daniels paused, wondering if it was possible to requisition the police helicopter. 'Can you sanction India 99 for our sole use, guv?'

Bright and Naylor looked at each other in a moment of confusion.

Everybody laughed, including the two of them.

'She doesn't want much, does she?' Bright said, just as his mobile rang.

There was a brief hiatus as he took the call.

Pocketing the phone, he nodded to Daniels.

'Adam's here,' he said.

74

They left the others and went downstairs to meet with Adam Finch, making polite conversation on the way, mainly about the enquiry but also about Bright's recent health scare. The MRI had found no tumour or anything else that could have caused his violent headaches. He was no longer undergoing tests and his neurologist had signed him off, ordering him to take it easy.

'Fat chance, eh?' he said.

It was the news Daniels had been praying for. Not that there was any chance of Bright heeding the consultant's advice. He picked up the pace, asking her to do the same, not wanting to keep his friend waiting. She caught up with him as he turned the corner, heading for reception.

Her wry smile was beginning to irritate him.

'OK, so you were right. *Again.* Christ Almighty, are you ever wrong?'

It was nice to see the return of the grumpy bugger Daniels knew and loved. She was relieved that they'd faced one another after that awful row. They needed to pull together, now more than ever. Opening the door to a quiet room off reception, she stood back, allowing him to enter first.

Adam Finch got to his feet and shook hands with them both. He was immaculately dressed in a charcoal-grey suit and a black tie as if he'd come from a funeral.

A bad omen?

Daniels hoped not.

Finch looked tired and drawn, his dark clothing

accentuating this. His hopeful expression faded as she shook her head slowly. As Senior Investigating Officer, it was down to her to take the lead. She asked him to sit down and took the only other available seat in the room, leaving the guv'nor standing.

'We still haven't found Jessica but we've made some huge strides forward today. Why didn't you tell us about Jimmy Makepeace?'

Finch went a ghostly white when he heard the name. He hung his head, struggling for composure and for words with which to respond. When he looked up there were tears in his eyes. He said nothing.

'That's ex-Army Air Corps, Captain James Makepeace, in case you're in any doubt.' Daniels' tone was deliberately harsh. 'You *were* aware that his young daughter died?'

It was more a statement than a question.

Finch nodded. 'He was like a man possessed when I refused his application for repatriation. The man was desperate. Now I know how he felt. But under the circumstances—'

'I'm not interested in your justification, Mr Finch. I have only one goal and that is to find your daughter. Why didn't you tell us this before?'

'After all this time?'

'I specifically asked you who might have a grudge against you.'

'I know—'

'Kate!' Bright's eyes sent a clear message: *What the fuck do you think you are doing?* 'I think Adam's been through enough, don't you?'

'Yes—and so has Jessica!' Daniels carried on. She was far too angry to show compassion. 'We've

342

wasted precious time!'

Bright raised his voice. 'I said, back off!'

Daniels met his gaze stubbornly. 'Fine,' she said, getting to her feet.

'No. Please . . .' Finch turned to face Detective Chief Superintendent Bright. 'She's right, Phillip. We've wasted time and any delay is down to me, not your DCI. To be honest, it really never occurred to me, until . . . and afterwards . . .' He broke down, unable to finish his sentence. His words hung in the air as he choked back the tears, his face wracked with regret, his eyes pleading with them. Finally he said, 'All I ask is that you find her.'

It was difficult to watch a grown man beg. Daniels looked away, giving Finch a moment to compose himself. She felt guilty now for having badgered him, couldn't imagine what the man was going through or how he'd coped in the past nine days. She wanted, needed, to find his daughter. Take his pain away. Make things right for him and for Jessica.

It was too late to help poor Amy Grainger.

Finch cleared his throat, interrupting her thoughts.

What he said made Daniels shudder.

'If it *is* Makepeace after all these years, Jessica's never coming home.'

75

By the time they reconvened in the briefing room, Carmichael had made further headway, discovering that Makepeace had experienced a

343

complete mental breakdown after his daughter's death, another after his marriage collapsed. At one time, he'd been found wandering the streets and was sectioned under the terms of the Mental Health Act.

'He was discharged into the care of the local authority in September '97,' Carmichael said. 'Disappeared soon after.'

'Any psychiatric records available?' Daniels asked.

'Already requested.'

'Good work, Lisa. When they arrive, have Jo take a look. I'm not saying it'll make any difference, but it might provide useful insight into his mental state. I'll give Jo the heads up.'

Back in her office, Daniels sat down at her desk, lifting the phone from its cradle intending to call Jo, aborting the call when someone knocked gently on her door. At the height of any enquiry her office was like Kings Cross at rush hour. It was something she'd had to get used to, work round, and sometimes just ignore.

Robson stuck his head in. 'Got a mo', boss?'

'Is it about the case?'

Gormley pushed past him into the room.

Robson clammed up.

'Then there's your answer,' Gormley said. 'I take priority, now clear off.'

He closed the door, shutting Robson out.

'That was a bit harsh, wasn't it?' Daniels said.

Gormley gave a little *do-I-give-a-shit?* shrug. He made a big smiley face, his eyes like saucers, his teeth exposed like a toothpaste advert. Daniels grinned. She hadn't seen him this excited in a long time and that only meant one thing. He knew something she didn't. Something big, by the look of it.

She sat back as he approached her chair, lifting her feet from the floor as he wheeled it away from the desk so he could better access her computer. After a few keystrokes, data she hadn't seen before suddenly popped up on screen. Her eyes followed his index finger as he pointed to a section relating to the deceased child, Sally Makepeace. Shuffling closer, Daniels stared wide-eyed at the screen.

The revelation hit home immediately.

The date Sally died.

May fifteenth.

Tomorrow.

Daniels checked her watch to be sure. If Makepeace was their man—and they both thought he was—it was Sally's death that drove him. He'd not miss the anniversary.

And if he so much as breathed near that cemetery, they'd be ready for him.

76

Rain hammered on the roof of the Toyota. A landslide overnight had dominated local news all day. A sloping parcel of Northumberland had become destabilized and had dumped itself with some force on to a railway line below it. This weather-related event did not bode well for Jessica Finch or Daniels' team, who had been waiting all day to make an arrest.

It was already eight p.m.

Staring through the misted-up windscreen of her

345

Toyota, Daniels felt thoroughly depressed. But she wasn't finished yet. If she had to sit there until midnight, then so be it. She was sure Makepeace would show.

He just had to.

Naylor's voice broke the silence: '7824, what's your status?'

'No change, guv.'

'Is the surveillance team still in position?'

'Affirmative. Target area secure.'

'On way,' Naylor said. 'Happy to do my bit, over.'

'Unit One,' Robson's voice responded. 'Make it quick, guv. I'm bloody soaked.'

'Dickhead! He wants to think himself bloody lucky,' Gormley said. 'Jessica will be feeling a whole lot worse. That's assuming she is still feeling, poor bugger.'

Daniels stared straight ahead. The rain was relentless, no let-up in sight. The few people daft enough to be outside on such an awful night were either running or shivering under umbrellas. Heavy snow in March. April showers in May. Typical British weather. She leaned forward and grabbed her radio from the dash.

'7824 to Unit One. Maintain radio silence unless you have news to report, over.'

A good ten minutes passed before Robson contacted them again. And this time he wasn't whingeing.

'Unit One. One person in sight, approaching the west gate, over.'

Daniels sat up straight, pushing her transmit button. 'Is it the target?'

There was a long, tense silence.

'I'm too far away to see . . . He's wearing a jacket

346

with the hood up, I think. He's just a silhouette, backlit by a street lamp. Can't make him out, boss.'

Daniels took a deep breath. 'All units, hold your positions.'

*   *   *

In the churchyard, Robson crouched down as the figure walking straight towards him stopped, looked around furtively, and then moved off again.

Robson spoke quietly into his radio. 'Subject acting suspiciously.'

'All units stand by,' Daniels' voice came back.

Up ahead, the figure took a diversion from the main path. Robson could feel his excitement growing, the adrenalin pumping through his veins. A bird flew up out of a bush, startling him.

Robson took a deep breath. 'Boss, he's approaching target area.'

'Hold your position,' Daniels and Naylor both said at the same time.

*   *   *

In the Toyota, Daniels and Gormley could hardly contain themselves. Naylor came on the radio and gave an ETA of a few minutes.

'7824 . . . that's received, guv. Unit One, what's he doing now?'

'It's not him!' Robson's disappointment was obvious. 'This idiot's just taking a piss.'

Daniels smacked her hand against the steering wheel in frustration.

'Taking *the* piss more like,' she said.

347

The radio intercept device was working perfectly. Just as he knew it would.

'For fuck's sake!' the DCI said. 'Unit One, get him out of there. If the target arrives, he'll scare him off.'

Makepeace smiled to himself, started the ignition of his VW Golf and pulled out from the kerb, narrowly missing Naylor's car coming the other way.

*   *   *

Swerving to avoid a collision, Naylor got a good look at the whites of the driver's eyes. It *was* Makepeace. The guv'nor did a sudden U-turn, his brakes screeching on the wet road, and sped off again burning rubber.

'Naylor to all units. I have the eyeball. Suspect identified as James Makepeace on Coldstream Road heading south in excess of sixty miles an hour. Black VW Golf: November-Lima-Five-Nine-Mike-Oscar-Delta. He's turning a left-left on to Kelso Gardens. Any traffic in the area please respond.'

*   *   *

'Yahoo!' Gormley yelled, rubbing his hands together. 'What do you reckon, boss? Dangerous or reckless?'

Daniels ignored the question. She was too busy turning round to give chase. '7824 to Naylor. He's probably heading for the old sports fields, guv.'

348

A Traffic car responded, letting them know his position: 'Tango 3856, heading south-east on Whickham View.'

'Naylor to all units. He's turned right on to Gretna Road, travelling south.'

Gormley was forced to hang on to the grab strap as Daniels shot round a corner in an area they knew well. 'Can't remember the last time I did this, but it's about now my fish and chips used to slide off the dashboard!'

Daniels picked up speed passing a row of old semi-detached houses. In pursuit mode, she floored the accelerator, looking at the vanishing point in the road trying to get the eyeball herself but also watching for unexpected hazards appearing in the foreground. She could see the VW now, weaving from side to side to prevent Naylor from overtaking, clipping wing mirrors of cars parked along the road.

'7824: I'm travelling south on Gretna Road. Right behind you, guv.'

'Tango 3856: I'm going to wait at the junction of Whickham View/Ferguson's Lane.'

'Good move!' Gormley said as they closed in.

'Target vehicle turning left-left into . . .' Naylor hesitated for a second.

'St Cuthbert's playing fields, guv,' Gormley said, helping him out, not bothering with a call sign.

'Jesus!' Naylor said. 'Pedestrians look frightened. They're jumping out of the way. I need to pull off him.'

Another Traffic car joined the hunt: 'Tango 3275: Fox and Hounds Lane.'

Daniels kept her foot on the accelerator. '7824 to Tango 3275. Wait-wait on Fox and Hounds Lane.

He could exit the playing fields.'

'Tango 3275. I'm aware of that location. Standing by.'

'Tango 3856, now on route to Pendower way.'

'He's doing a reciprocal, doing a reciprocal,' Naylor said.

'7824: blocking his exit with my vehicle.'

Arriving at the entrance to the playing fields, Daniels pulled up sharp as the Golf suddenly altered direction. He was now driving straight at her.

'Brace! Brace!' she yelled.

Raising their arms in front of their faces, Daniels and Gormley braced themselves for the impact. A split second later, there was an almighty bang and the sound of debris hitting the front of the Toyota. Then . . . deathly silence.

An alarm went off.

Gormley spread his fingers and peered through them.

'We're still alive then.' He sounded more shaken than he was letting on.

'Oh shit!' Daniels was staring straight ahead. Steam was coming from the bonnet of the VW and Naylor's car door had been flung open on impact. 'All units, he's crashed into the guv'nor. Possible casualties. Ambulance required. We've got a runner! You OK, boss?'

No response.

In the darkness, Daniels' eyes fixed on Naylor. He was out of his car and running after Makepeace. She and Gormley jumped out of the Toyota in hot pursuit. They needn't have bothered. In a move that an England full-back would've been proud of, Naylor tackled Makepeace to the ground. He sounded out of breath as his voice came over the radio.

*   *   *

'One arrest . . .' Naylor cuffed the suspect. 'All units stand down.'

Moments later, Daniels and Gormley arrived at his side. They were both grinning at the state he was in. He'd rolled in dog shit and reeked of the stuff.

'Yeah, OK, I'm too bloody old for this.' Naylor turned his nose up at the appalling stench. 'All I could see was you two covering your eyes. It didn't exactly fill me with confidence.'

'We didn't want to be witnesses, guv,' Gormley said. 'Too many forms to fill in.'

Daniels helped him to his feet. 'Nice to see you haven't lost the edge.'

77

Booking someone in at the charge room is normally a doddle: justify detention to a custody officer, create a custody record, offer representation, search your suspect, lift any forensic samples, seize clothing if necessary and bang them up to await a formal interview.

Job done.

Only today wasn't normal. The suspect was having none of it.

Following his arrest, they had taken Makepeace to the nearest police station, which happened to be

351

the West End nick. But he declined to confirm his identity—refused to accept or reject a solicitor—in fact refused to speak at all. He didn't fight, kick, scream, do or say anything, simply stared straight ahead like they weren't even there, his non-cooperation slowing the whole process down.

Frustrated with his antics, Naylor had gone off to take a shower, leaving Daniels to it. But watching the clock was complete torture for her, so she called Jo Soulsby asking for help.

'Is there any way you can join us, give an opinion on the best way to handle him?'

'Give me half an hour.' Jo's voice sounded thick, as if she'd just woken up.

As they talked on the phone, Daniels made notes, her eyes straying occasionally to the awful weather outside. Questioning Makepeace was going to be a painstaking process, and one she had little enthusiasm for. 'No comment' interviews always left her feeling impotent, the letter of the law tying her hands very firmly behind her back, tipping the scales in favour of the offender. At times like these she wished she could 'fire up the Quattro', drive Makepeace to a remote location and kick the living shit out of him like her 1980s politically incorrect television hero, Gene Hunt, might do. He was a DCI with no such restraints. And those he did have, he chose to ignore.

Would that she could do the same.

But this wasn't life on Mars.

Putting down the phone, she picked it up again and made another call asking the police surgeon to examine Makepeace to ensure he was fit to be interviewed. Bearing in mind he'd been involved in an accident, albeit of his own making, it was best to cover every angle to avoid problems later on. Daniels then contacted the duty solicitor who agreed to offer her services on the off chance Makepeace would accept them. But after only a few minutes she left the cell shaking her head.

Same silent treatment: there was nothing she could do.

At five past eleven, Daniels received a call to say that Jo was in the building. This made her feel really emotional. She didn't know why, it just did. Probably the result of tiredness. Fatigue often did that to her. It was a wonder she didn't spend her whole life in tears.

'Tell her I'll be right down,' she said.

Planning an interviewing strategy for a wilful suspect was a nightmare. Daniels was glad that Jo was going to be involved. She'd assisted them before and her insights were spot on. But as she hurried to reception, Daniels couldn't help feeling that Makepeace was in a league of his own.

A case too far, even for Jo?

She smiled at Jo as she walked through the door, then took her straight to the observation suite, a brand-new, purpose-built facility with viewing rooms where they could observe suspects covertly via CCTV. No sooner had they sat down together than Jo delved into her bag and produced a flask of homemade soup.

'It'll keep you going through the next few hours,' she said.

Daniels took it from her. 'Since when did you turn into a domestic goddess?'

'Hey!' Jo made a face. 'There's more to me than meets the eye.'

Daniels unscrewed the top of the flask. The lentil

soup smelled good. She poured some out and took a sip, feeling it warm her from the inside out. Eyeing Jo over the top of her cup, she felt sad. They had once made such a great team and still maintained a strong bond, invisible to others, but there all the same. She'd almost forgotten how considerate a person she was.

'You look exhausted,' Jo said.

Daniels stifled a yawn. 'I am a bit.'

'How long since you've been home? Twelve, fourteen hours?'

Daniels glanced at her watch. It was actually nearer seventeen. She'd left the house before dawn, had been on duty ever since—as had the rest of her team. Even at this late hour they would still be hard at it, waiting back at the incident room for news, keen to see Makepeace charged. But even keener to find Jessica Finch alive.

'You can't keep this pace up indefinitely, Kate. You've seen what it's done to Bright. Believe me, you'll go the same way. When did you last have a decent meal?'

'Bright doesn't take care of himself.'

'And you do?'

'Maybe not this week,' Daniels conceded. 'But generally, yes. You know I do!'

'But the job comes first.'

It was a definite dig. Daniels looked away. It was the job—*her job*—that had come between them. Always had. Probably always would. No matter how hard she tried, she was incapable of putting anything before it. Even her personal happiness had taken a back seat.

Feeling the intensity of Jo's stare, she turned back to face her.

'What?' Daniels said, defensively. 'Let's not go there, eh? My job isn't nine to five and it certainly isn't easy. But this isn't just another murder enquiry, Jo. A young girl's out there somewhere, waiting to be rescued. Every minute away from the office is a minute wasted as far as I'm concerned.'

Jo studied her, any resentment she may have felt giving way to understanding. She was there to assist the murder investigation team and to support Daniels, even though she didn't think she deserved it.

'To be honest, I've not slept well when I *have* been home.' Daniels said. 'I've been having this weird recurring dream which ends with me firing a gun. It isn't Forster, or at least I don't think it is. I'm firing into the darkness and I don't understand why.'

'It's a dream, Kate, that's all. A sign of unrest. You've had a lot on lately.'

She was probably right.

Daniels finished her soup and felt better for it. Turning her attention to a large flat-screen mounted on the wall, she saw that it was presently showing four images of areas under close observation. But, in this instance, she was only concerned with viewing one in particular: cell number four. She pressed a button on the handset and the split screen changed to a single image. Bizarrely, Makepeace was not sitting on the bed provided. He was lying on the concrete floor, staring unblinkingly at the ceiling. Daniels zoomed in for a close-up on his face: not a flicker of emotion visible.

Having observed him for several minutes, Jo eventually broke the silence. 'You can have all the interview strategies you want, Kate. But if I'm reading him right, he'll continue his wall of silence until you're blue in the face. Psychologically, this isn't affecting him at all.'

'Well, I'm going to have to try! He's been detained for the purpose of interview and that's what he'll get, like it or not. The question is, how do I go about it, what methods do I employ? The Police and Criminal Evidence Act doesn't allow me to pull his fingernails out with pliers, more's the pity. An AK-47 might do it though, if you have one in that bag of yours.'

But Jo wasn't laughing.

'Frankly, I don't know what to advise.' Jo looked back at the screen. 'He's a professional soldier, highly trained in anti-interrogation techniques. Guys like him are taught how to resist, how to shut down in order to protect themselves. They're used to sleep deprivation. Cold. Hunger. Unfortunately, you've put him in a nice warm cell and probably given him something to eat.'

'You're telling me I won't get near him, is that it?'

'I'm telling you it won't be easy to break him down.'

Makepeace hadn't moved an inch.

Deep down, Daniels knew Jo was right. From day one, the man's sole purpose had been to cause alarm and distress, pain and suffering, to Adam Finch—and he'd achieved that in spades. The longer he could go on inflicting that pain, the better he would like it. Jo's words had only served to confirm what Daniels was already thinking.

'I'm sorry, Kate. I doubt he'll tell you anything that'll lead you to Jessica, dead or alive,' she said.

'Because he knows if she's not found it will eventually drive her father insane.'

There was a knock at the door.

Naylor came in looking refreshed from the shower. He greeted them both, letting them know he was ready to interview the suspect. Daniels punched numbers into the handset and the image switched from cell number four to an empty interview room: IR2. They left Jo to observe and took a short walk along the corridor. They had barely sat down when Makepeace was brought in by a PC. Daniels waited for the uniform to clear the room and then switched on the recording device, her eyes settling on the man sitting opposite.

'This interview is being conducted in interview room two at the West Road police office. I am Detective Chief Inspector Kate Daniels of the murder investigation team. Also present is Detective Superintendent Ron Naylor. And you are . . . ?'

Daniels gestured for Makepeace to speak next.

He remained silent.

'Mr Makepeace, would you answer the question, confirming your name, date of birth and current address?'

Makepeace was staring not *at* her but *through* her. It was as if he'd fixed his cold, dark eyes to a point on the wall somewhere behind her and there they remained for the next few minutes.

'The suspect has declined to answer,' Daniels said for the benefit of the tape. 'Where is she, Jimmy?' She waited for a response. But Makepeace chose silence. He didn't even blink. 'OK, tell us where you were between six p.m. and midnight on the evening of Tuesday, fourth May.'

Makepeace said nothing. The only sound Daniels could hear was her own desperate thoughts.

If Jessica is still alive, she can't possibly hold out much longer.

'Can you account for your whereabouts between six p.m. and midnight on the evening of Wednesday the fifth of May?' Daniels continued her line of questioning. But still there was no reply. She tried a different tack. 'What were you doing outside the crematorium?'

Nothing was touching him.

Makepeace was clearly in the zone.

78

An hour and a half of interrogation and not a single word had left the suspect's lips. After the excitement of the arrest, Daniels and Naylor walked away from the interview feeling as if they were right back where they started.

'He gets minimum rest,' Naylor said. 'Then we try again.'

'We're wasting our breath, guv!' Daniels snapped. She wanted to punch something. Scream. Yell. But what would be the point? 'Did you see those eyes? Cold as ice. You could stick pins in them, he wouldn't even flinch.'

'He's a hard-arsed bastard, I'll give you that.'

'Yeah, Jo nailed him as soon as she looked at him. As she said, he's had all the right training. Well, we've had all the right training too and we've been in the job long enough to know when we're beaten. Let's face it, if we're going to find Jessica Finch, alive or dead, we're going to have to do it without his help.'

They walked back to the observation suite to collect Jo, then organized coffee and found somewhere comfortable to sit and plan their next move, knowing that it was important to regroup now rather than leaving it till morning.

It was getting on for two thirty a.m.—and several coffees later—when they finally agreed on the best line of attack. They were about to call it a day when a deafening alarm bell rang out in the building, getting louder and louder the longer it went on.

Daniels shot out of her seat and poked her head round the door to see what was going on. Several officers came tearing down the corridor, heading in the direction of the cell block. With a sinking feeling, she took off after them with Naylor and Jo right behind her. The moment she turned the corner, her worst fears were realized.

The door to cell 4 was gaping open. A huddle of bodies crowded around the entrance, visibly shaken by what they could see. Daniels rushed towards them and pushed her way through. Makepeace was lying unconscious on the floor in a pool of his own vomit, a small plastic bag smeared with human faeces next to him. A custody officer was kneeling beside him, his face frozen in disbelief, completely clueless as to what to do next. A pair of latex gloves dangled loosely from his right hand. Grabbing them, Daniels shoved him aside and snapped them on. Yelling for a defibrillator, she lifted Makepeace's eyelid.

359

The eye underneath was unresponsive.

Tilting his head back, she listened for breath.

There was none.

Someone handed her a resuscitation aid, a plastic valve-like tube designed to fit into a casualty's mouth. Wiping away vomit from Makepeace's airways, she put it into his mouth. Pinching his nose between forefinger and thumb—trying to ignore the stench of vomit—she took a long deep breath and blew twice into the tube. He still wasn't breathing, so she began chest compressions.

'One, two, three, four . . .' Tears were rolling down her cheeks, sweat running down her back. 'Don't you *fucking* die on me you *bastard*!'

Naylor and Jo looked on helplessly as she tried for fifteen minutes to revive him, both manually and by delivering a shock with the defibrillator when it came. She hadn't figured on him topping himself, shafting them completely in the process. The evil sod had prepared for his arrest and, if necessary, his death, right down to the very last detail, concealing poison he knew wouldn't be found without a full internal body search.

Daniels was faintly aware of Naylor's voice as he cleared the room behind her. And, seconds later, felt his presence near her as she continued in her quest to restart her suspect's heart. Deep down she knew that her efforts were in vain. A strangulated wail escaped from her mouth, a demonstration of distress so upsetting it made Jo shiver.

'That's enough, Kate,' Naylor said softly.

And still Daniels continued to ram her balled hands into the centre of the suspect's chest. 'One, two, three, four . . .'

Her voice broke off, exhaustion taking over.

'Kate, he's gone!' Naylor's tone was more forceful than before.

Stopping the heart massage, Daniels sank back on her heels, head bowed in defeat, a mixture of grief and anger washing over her. She was sobbing now, not for Makepeace but for Jessica. Getting up, she pushed her way past Naylor without another word, ripping off her gloves as she went. Jo followed her out. Leading her into a nearby office, she shut the door behind them and held Daniels close until her rage began to subside.

'I'm so sorry, Kate,' she whispered. 'If it's any consolation, I don't think he was *ever* going to tell you where he'd hidden Jessica.'

Daniels withdrew, choking back the tears, a look of pure anguish on her face.

'I hope he burns in hell!' she said.

The search team were now her only hope.

79

When Daniels was a little girl, her father had told her that mist was made up of clouds that dropped out of the sky and landed on the ground with a bump. And she'd believed him. She believed everything he said back then.

They were inseparable.

A lifetime ago.

She'd been thinking about him a lot in the past hour, watching as the sun came up over the horizon of North Pennine minefields, tiny droplets of water clinging to the landscape as she waited for

Weldon to arrive. But it was another estranged father–daughter relationship that was really on her mind, one that now had little prospect of survival.

A slim chance was all Daniels could realistically hope for.

The suicide had come as yet another blindside for her to deal with. She felt guilty that she hadn't seen it coming. Why hadn't she? Hadn't his actions since day one suggested that Makepeace was sick of living, or at the very least that he had nothing left to live for?

Daniels sighed, her eyes scanning the landscape. The murder investigation team had come close. But not close enough. And now they faced an impossible task, searching this dangerous and difficult terrain with its potholes, tunnels and boggy streams stretching as far as the eye could see. She feared that the search could go on for years as another had done at the southern end of the Pennines. She couldn't help but wonder if this would be *her* Saddleworth Moor.

Her phone rang, pulling her away from that depressing thought.

'Kate?' It was Hank Gormley. 'You OK?'

He sounded worried.

'I'm fine. Thanks for asking.'

'I just swung by your house. Couldn't raise you.'

'I'm not in.'

'You don't say.' Gormley chanced his arm: 'You at Hartside, by any chance?'

A wry smile formed on Daniels' lips. He was referring to her fuck-off destination, the place she always fled to on her bike when things were grim at home or at work. An area not so far away—less than thirty miles from where she was now standing—where she went to think things through.

'Close,' she said. 'I'm waiting for Weldon.'

'You sound like I just chucked you.'

Daniels laughed.

And then cried.

No one spoke for a very long time.

'You want company?' Gormley said eventually.

'You need to ask?'

'Meet you back at the office then. And don't be too long or I'll need another shave.'

He hung up.

*   *   *

Gormley knew that choosing to take a ride up there so early in the morning was Daniels' way of holding back the despair. Others might throw a sickie, hit the shops, max out their credit card or drink themselves into oblivion. But solitude was *her* way. And when she'd spent enough time alone, organizing her thoughts, she'd move quickly on, take positive steps and get back on track without dwelling on the past.

What other choice did she have?

She couldn't allow the actions of a deranged man to overwhelm her.

*   *   *

Daniels wiped her eyes. In the early hours she'd telephoned Bright to tell him what had happened. He'd taken it upon himself to contact Adam Finch, giving his friend the devastating news that Makepeace had topped himself. Knowing her former boss, she wouldn't put it past him to have

363

done that in person at the Mansion House first thing. And for that she was very grateful. She wanted to be the one to let Weldon in on events overnight. The news would hit the rescue effort hard. Morale would plummet and heads would go down. She'd have to work hard to build them up again before the search resumed.

Dismounting the Yamaha, she took a long, deep breath. Patches of mist were blowing along on a soft breeze, an eerie sight when you were the only one about. Taking a few steps off the road into wet grass, she listened, watched, wondering if she would somehow sense if Jessica were alive or dead. Not that she really believed in ESP, but she could at least *hope* that it existed. Besides, while she'd been sitting there, she'd had the distinct impression that this desolate landscape was actually talking to her.

*   *   *

The miner's helmet slipped from Jessica's left leg and was gone. Sailing away on the current, taking her only source of light with it, it bumped off the side of the tunnel as it left her behind. Jessica watched it go, but had no energy to care. Fear didn't grip her any more, nor regret, or even pain.

She was beyond that.

Her heart, weakening with every second, would eventually slow to a point at which it would cease pumping blood around her body. She was fading fast, unaware that her temperature was about to drop below a critical thirty-five degrees. Like the current, her mind drifted. She was hardly able to remember who she was any more—or even where

364

she was—as the moving body of water swirled waist-high around her frozen, emaciated body.

If it was to rise any further, she could bow her head and drink.

Any further than that and she would drown.

Either way, there was now little chance of rescue from her living hell.

*   *   *

'This is strictly for your ears.' Several pairs of eyes bore down on Daniels. 'Suffice to say he's gone to his grave taking our only hope with him. It's over to you guys now.'

She was surrounded by TSG officers and Weldon's group of civilian volunteers. It was bright sunshine now. They had pulled their utility vehicles off the road, parking them in a circle; protection from the weather, should it change again for the worse—which, in this part of the world, it frequently did.

Each member of the search-and-rescue team had listened intently and without interruption as she delivered her account of the previous night. A stony silence descended, followed by cries of: *bastard, selfish twat,* and a whole lot worse—all sentiments Daniels agreed with. She did her level best to lift their spirits. Then, reassured that they would carry on regardless, she left them to get on with it and rode back to Newcastle as fast as she could.

The atmosphere in the MIR was just as bleak as the one she'd left behind. And here too she had work to do to boost her flagging squad. Gormley was standing in front of the murder wall, a look of resignation on his face. He hadn't noticed her come in and, despite his earlier attempt at humour, she hadn't seen him look this glum since . . . she couldn't remember when.

He'd shown resilience even on the worst cases they'd worked together over the years. But this one had really got to him, and Daniels knew why. Finding a dead body was awful—informing a loved one of a death by homicide, even worse—but they dealt with that every day. No. It was the not knowing that was eating him up—eating them all up. Unless they could give closure to Adam Finch by finding his daughter, dead or alive, he would remain in limbo for the rest of his days.

Now that *was* hard to take.

Carmichael looked miserable too. Sitting at her desk, one hand supporting her chin, she was flicking aimlessly through a psychiatric file on Jimmy Makepeace obtained too late to do them any good. She didn't seem to be looking for anything in particular, just leafing through it for something to do. In fact, she was so disinterested it could easily have been the *Beano* for all the attention it was getting.

Daniels wandered over to take possession of the file. The enquiry into a death in custody was guaranteed to get messy. Not that she was in any way to blame. Nevertheless she wanted to prepare herself in case she was called to give evidence to the Police Complaints Authority. Makepeace had been *her* prisoner and she was the SIO.

She was about to ask for the file when something in it caught her eye.

But the pages had already slipped through Carmichael's fingers.

'Jesus!'

Daniels ran a hand through her hair. She didn't know if she believed what she'd just seen or if it was a case of wishful thinking. She asked Carmichael to skim the file again. Slowly. Reacting to the urgency in her voice, the young DC turned back pages until she was told to stop.

Raising her head from the file, Carmichael locked eyes with Daniels. 'What is it, boss?' she said.

Daniels heard footsteps behind her, but the file was her only focus. Carmichael's words and the manner in which they had been uttered acted like a magnet, drawing the gaze of detectives working nearby. Within seconds, Gormley, Brown and Maxwell had gathered in a huddle around her, making her the centre of everyone's attention, all of them steeling themselves for the bombshell they knew was coming.

'We can no longer interview Makepeace . . .' Daniels said. 'But we can interview his first wife, Susan.'

'If we ever find her,' Gormley said.

'I think I just did.' Daniels pointed at a photograph of a young girl in the file. 'If that is his daughter, I know exactly where I can find his ex.'

80

'She's gone,' Adam Finch said.

He looked tired. Not surprising, given that he'd been woken in the small hours to receive the distressing news that the only person who knew

367

where his daughter was had committed suicide. Daniels was sensitive to the fact that the murder investigation team generally, but she in particular as SIO, might not be welcome at the Mansion House right now. Jimmy Makepeace had been captured, arrested, and remanded in custody. But they might as well have given him the keys to his police cell for all the good it had done.

But Finch was curious. 'Why do you want to see Mrs Partridge?'

Daniels stepped forward. 'It's vital we speak to her. What do you mean "gone"?'

'She resigned. After ten years, she suddenly ups and leaves! No explanation.' Finch rolled his eyes. 'My employees are a bloody ungrateful bunch sometimes. You'd have thought she'd have shown enough loyalty to work her notice at least.'

'How long ago did she leave?' Daniels asked.

'Why do you need to know?'

'I'll explain later. How long?'

'Twenty minutes, half an hour, no more than that. Assuming she hasn't called a taxi, it'll take her at least that long to walk to the village.'

'Could she have taken the bus, sir?' Gormley asked.

Finch looked at his watch and shook his head. 'No, she'll have missed it. There's only one an hour I believe, the next one's due at twenty past. Jessica used to get it when—'

He broke off as Gormley caught Daniels' attention and tapped his watch. It was already five past twelve. They had time to catch up with Susan Makepeace, but they needed to move fast. Leaving Finch in the study, they practically ran back to Carmichael's car and got in.

'Step on it, Lisa,' Daniels said.

Carmichael drove away so quickly she sent plumes of dust high into the air as the gravel gave way beneath the tyres of her three series BMW, a car she'd recently acquired with money her aunt had given her. She shot down the drive, sending geese running for their lives. At the main gate, she turned right on to a B road and floored the accelerator for about half a mile, slowing less than a minute later as she reached the outskirts of the village of Kirby Ayden.

The BMW inched along, three pairs of eyes glued to pavements on either side of the road as they passed a row of quaint, olde worlde shops on the right: a tea room, a bakery, a newsagent, a barber shop sporting an old-fashioned red-and-white striped pole outside. No unisex salon here.

'Pull in!' Daniels said sharply.

She waited for Carmichael to stop, then pointed across the road to a market with more visitors than any of them expected to see in a village this size. Individual stalls were selling anything and everything it was possible to cram on to half a dozen trestle tables pushed together in two parallel lines with a walkway in between.

'There she is!' Carmichael was pointing through the front windscreen.

Straight ahead, Mrs Partridge was trudging along the street, head down, pulling a large bag on wheels. Carmichael checked her rear-view mirror, eased out on to the road and put her foot down.

'Pull up short,' Daniels said.

Carmichael did just that and her boss jumped out.

'Susan Makepeace?' she yelled.

The woman struggling with the bag on wheels stopped dead in her tracks. She didn't try to run, just turned towards Daniels, smiling like butter wouldn't melt. A couple she obviously knew approached her. Then, following her gaze, they hesitated a moment before walking by, deciding not to get involved.

Sensible.

'The photograph, Susan.' Daniels held out her hand. 'Where is it?'

Susan Makepeace didn't respond.

'Here, let me take that from you.' Carmichael took possession of the woman's bag. 'It must be heavy.'

Susan Makepeace didn't resist. She let it slip easily from her grasp.

As the bag was searched, Daniels made a quiet plea for information as to Jessica's whereabouts, playing the sympathy card at the same time. But her efforts were in vain; Susan Makepeace wasn't listening. Carmichael found what she was looking for: the framed photograph the DCI had first seen in the kitchen of the Mansion House just six days earlier whilst her young DC was cramming her face full of home-made scones.

Delving into her pocket, Daniels pulled out a second photograph, the one of Sally Makepeace and her father that she'd found a couple of hours ago in his psychiatric file. Placing the two side by side for comparison, she saw that they were identical, the only difference being that on Susan's copy, the photo had been trimmed so that Jimmy Makepeace didn't feature.

A small group of inquisitive onlookers were now staring over in their direction from the market square. Daniels put Susan Makepeace in the rear of the BMW and climbed in next to her. The woman began to sob. Handing her a tissue to dry her eyes, Daniels nodded to Carmichael, who started the car and drove off at speed.

'It's over, Susan,' Daniels said gently. 'Jessica will die if we don't find her soon. If you ever cared for her, you must tell us where she is.'

'I don't know, I swear. I'd tell you if I did. It can't have been Jimmy. I've not seen or heard of him for years, but I know he'd never harm a child. He loved our Sally so much. He was a good man, a brilliant partner, in spite of his problems.'

'He was, Susan. But he changed after Sally died, didn't he?'

The woman nodded.

'He was ill. We all understand that,' Daniels said softly.

Susan Makepeace let out a heartbroken sob. 'He was so unhappy. In the end, I couldn't live with him any more. I changed my name so he wouldn't find me. I know how it looks, but I had nothing to do with Jessica's disappearance, you must believe me. We were so close. As I told you, she was like a daughter to me.'

Gormley's phone rang loud in the car.

As he took the call, Susan Makepeace carried on talking.

'My daughter died in my arms, Inspector. One minute she had a mild headache, the next she'd turned into a medical emergency. She didn't have a chance. I know Jimmy blamed Mr Finch for not allowing him home, but it wasn't his fault, really it wasn't.' She wiped a tear from her eye. 'As it turned out, he'd have been too late anyway. It was

371

that quick.'

A tale so desperate would normally have brought a lump to Daniels' throat, except that the woman was lying through her back teeth. Or if she wasn't now, she soon would be.

The DCI played along. 'It must've been a very difficult time for you both.'

'When Sally was little, Jimmy was never there. He was down the pub with his mates. That's the truth of it. And afterwards, well, let's just say he projected his guilt on to Mr Finch because he couldn't bear to live with it.' Susan Makepeace sighed loudly, seemingly a little calmer now. 'No, Inspector. Mr Finch didn't make him turn to drink. Jimmy had done that long before Sally got ill. He'll never change.'

'So why were you running away?' There was no compassion in Daniels' tone.

'Brian told me what he'd told you, more or less confirmed what I'd been thinking for this past week or so. I couldn't face Mr Finch after that. I'm sure you understand.'

Clever answer. 'Townsend knew who you were?'

Susan Makepeace shook her head. 'Nobody did.'

'He was good mates with your husband, wasn't he?'

'Army buddies yes. We never saw them socially. At least, I didn't.'

Gormley twisted in his seat. 'Boss, you need to hear this. It's Robbo.'

There was a message in Gormley's eyes as he held the phone out to her: *This is really important.* Daniels apologized to Susan Makepeace. But the woman had already turned away and was staring blankly out of the side window as the countryside flashed by.

Daniels lifted the phone to her ear.

Robson sounded excited. 'Someone rang Makepeace's phone at around two a.m. I only discovered that ten minutes ago when I was taking possession of his property. It's a number he calls regular.'

'Do we know who?'

'No.'

'It's not on the system?'

'Not registered either.'

'Hold on.' Daniels clicked her fingers. 'Pen, please, Hank. On the dash.'

Gormley grabbed the pen she was pointing at and handed it to her along with a scrap of paper he took from his pocket. Daniels went back to her call, writing down the number as Robson reeled it off. She thanked him and hung up. Looking sideways, she stared at the back of Susan Makepeace's head, wondering if she was on the level, almost sure she was not. The woman had her face pressed up against the window, looking out, and didn't turn around when the phone call ended.

Daniels still had Gormley's phone. Catching his eye in the rear-view mirror she keyed the number she'd just written down and waited . . . Seconds later a phone rang in the car. Now Susan Makepeace turned around, her expression stone cold.

She knew she'd been rumbled.

81

Contemplating her next move as the BMW sped northwards, Daniels felt bereft of energy. Another 'no comment' interview back at the station was more than she could bear to think about. Susan Makepeace sat quietly beside her, no longer the unassuming housekeeper. Something in her head had switched the minute she knew they were on to her, a malevolent smirk appearing on her lips that led the detectives to believe she would follow her ex-husband's example and refuse to co-operate.

Think, Kate! Get your act together.

It was time to press some buttons, provoke a reaction. Daniels didn't care how she got the information from Susan Makepeace, so long as she got it. Just then the car passed a sign—motorway service station, half a mile—which gave her an idea. Leaning forward in her seat, she tapped Carmichael on the shoulder.

'Pull into the garage, will you, Lisa? Get me some water and twenty tabs.'

Carmichael indicated her intention to exit the A1M. 'The usual, boss?'

'Please, I'm gagging for a smoke.'

Feigning a yawn, Gormley looked at Carmichael. 'I'll come with you, I could do with some air and I need the cashpoint. My lass is going out on the hoy tonight with some lasses she went to school with. She'll have my guts for garters if I come home empty-handed.'

Daniels stifled the urge to grin, grateful that she had such an alert couple of detectives with her.

Both Gormley and Carmichael had picked up on her ploy to get them out of the car. She hadn't smoked in a long time and just wanted a private chat with the former Mrs Makepeace.

Having cautioned and arrested her on suspicion of aiding and abetting an abduction, to question her before she was properly represented would constitute a technical breach of protocol. But it was a judgement call. Daniels was acting on instinct. Any court in the land would forgive such a small indiscretion. Her primary duty was and had always been to preserve life, protect the public, and keep the Queen's peace. If she were being honest, right now it wasn't the sovereign's peace on her mind. It was the nasty piece of work sitting right next to her in the car.

Carmichael slowed as she passed the familiar blue countdown markers to the start of the deceleration lane: three slashes . . . two . . . one. She left the motorway on the slip road. The service station was busy, parking at a premium, no spaces close to the shop and restaurant. There were fewer cars parked near the perimeter fence in a quiet spot overlooking open fields.

Carmichael used her initiative and drove in that direction.

Stopping the car, she killed the ignition and got out, taking her keys with her. Gormley followed, telling Daniels they wouldn't be long. Susan Makepeace watched them go and then met the DCI's gaze with a look of defiance. There it was again. That same malicious, mocking smirk that said: *Can't fool me, I know what you're up to.*

'Where is she, Susan?' Daniels saw no point in wasting precious time. 'We know you're involved now, so you may as well tell us. It'll save us all a lot of aggravation back at the station. Your ex didn't like it much last night, that's for sure.'

Susan Makepeace didn't even flinch. Just sat there tight-lipped. She'd been a good-looking woman in her time. But the years had taken their toll, adding fine lines to her face, particularly around her mouth. She looked away as a car drew up alongside with a couple of kids in the back, a boy and a girl. The little girl smiled at her and received a weak smile in return. The chance encounter came at exactly the right time and was like manna from heaven to the DCI. She'd been due some luck. The girl was of similar age to Sally Makepeace at the time of her death.

Daniels seized the moment. 'Was it the stress of losing Sally that turned him, Susan?'

Makepeace swung round. 'Off the record?'

'Of course,' Daniels lied.

'Do you believe in fate, Inspector?'

'I think certain things happen for a reason, if that's what you mean.'

'When I went to work for Finch I had *absolutely* no idea who he was.' She hesitated. 'I can see you don't believe me, but it's true all the same. In fact, everything I told you earlier was true. Finch wasn't to blame for my daughter's death and my Jimmy was a big drinker who couldn't reconcile himself with his . . . his lack of interest in Sally when she was alive. By the way, I'll deny everything if you repeat it. I won't be saying anything in a formal interview. I know my rights. You can't question me without a solicitor present, if I choose to have one. And I *will* have one. You can be sure of that.'

'I'm not asking you anything, Susan. You're

telling me, aren't you?' The car next to them moved off again. The little girl in the back seat waved. Susan Makepeace didn't wave back so Daniels did it for her, prompting further conversation, trying not to sound confrontational. 'You were saying, Susan?'

Makepeace studied her hands. 'All the time we were separated, I still wore Jimmy's rings. That was one of the first things he noticed when I bumped into him in Kirby Ayden about a month ago, quite by chance. He was very unhappy, said he wanted me back. Shortly afterwards he told me who Finch was. He asked me to help him teach the bastard a lesson. No, I'm wrong there. He begged me. Got down on his hands and knees and cried like a baby, he did. He promised not to harm Jess, though—'

'That's total bollocks and you know it. Jimmy left nothing to chance. He'd been watching Finch and planning his revenge down to the very last detail.' Daniels ran a hand through her hair. 'Jesus, he must've thought all his birthdays had come at once when he saw you! Make no mistake, he *has* harmed Jess, and killed another girl—all so he could have his revenge on your employer.'

'I don't believe you.'

'Believe what you like, it's true. He used you, Susan. Played you like a fiddle, can't you see that?'

'He loved me.'

Daniels thought for a moment. 'He never told you he'd remarried, did he?'

That one hit her hard, Daniels could see it in her eyes. Only the faintest flicker of emotion, but it was there nevertheless. And when vindictive people get hurt, their first reaction is to hurt back.

'That's clever, Detective Inspector, but it won't work.' The smirk returned. 'I won't tell you where he's keeping her *or* where he's living.'

'He's not.' Daniels stuck the knife in, oh so gently. 'Living, I mean.'

Absolute silence.

'Oh, didn't I mention? Jimmy poisoned himself in the cells last night.' Daniels waited for a reaction. None came. So she turned the knife, a little further this time, twisted it as it reached the woman's heart. 'He's dead, Susan. That's how much he cared about *you*. So, if you know where Jessica is, now's the time to tell me. Unless you want to spend the rest of your life in Durham's notorious She Wing. That's where they send all the pathetic women like you. Myra Hindley. Rose West. They were besotted with men too, for all the good it did them.'

'You're *lying*!' Anger had taken over now.

Daniels reached into her pocket and withdrew a photograph of Jimmy Makepeace, the official one taken in the cells following his suicide: vomit, snot 'n' all. She handed it over and braced herself for the woman's rage. Only she wasn't quite quick enough. Screaming like a woman possessed, Susan Makepeace swung her left arm across the back seat, catching Daniels full in the face with the back of her hand, her diamond engagement ring embedding itself in her lip, splitting it wide open.

It stung like hell.

Momentarily stunned, Daniels lifted her arm to fend off a second attempt. It never came. Susan Makepeace was struggling with the door now, trying to get out of the car. But Carmichael had been one step ahead; she'd had the good sense to

378

put the child locks on. Daniels leapt across the seat, restrained the woman, forcing the snips on, making sure they were good and tight. She slumped back into her own seat just as the front passenger door opened and Gormley's head appeared through it.

'OK, boss?' He pointed to the blood on her lip. 'Been at the Jammy Dodgers again?'

'Where's the fucking fags?' Daniels yelled.

82

Susan Makepeace refused to cooperate with Daniels after their tête-à-tête in the car, so Gormley and Carmichael were interviewing her instead. Not that it would do much good. She'd said fuck-all since arriving at the station and that's the way it would stay, if DCI was any judge of character.

Naylor ordered her to get herself checked out at the hospital then go home and get some rest. Well, she'd see about that. Sliding her arms into the shoulder straps of her back protector, fastening it with a belt around her waist, Daniels pulled on her leathers and went in search of her motorcycle with no intention whatsoever of stopping at A&E on the way home.

Thankfully the seat wasn't wet despite leaving her bike exposed to the elements all day. Pulling on her helmet, she winced as it squashed her cheeks together, pushing her fat lip forward and jamming it between the soft inner lining and the teeth she was grateful she still had. Then she

379

pulled on her gloves, mounted the Yamaha, flipped her visor down and rode off out of the car park.

As she turned on to the main road, she smiled to herself and waved at Naylor, who was, or so he thought, surreptitiously gazing down from his office window on the second floor making absolutely sure she'd left the station.

He knew her so well.

Arriving home ten minutes later, Daniels let herself in with the intention of a quick turnaround: shower, change of clothes, ice pack on that lip, then business as usual. She'd slip in under the radar and be back at her desk within the hour. If she kept her head down, Naylor would be none the wiser. That was the plan, anyway.

Setting her helmet down on the bottom stair, leaving her keys inside as always, she made her way along the hallway to a kitchen she'd hardly seen in three days. Picking up the phone, she rang Weldon. But the news wasn't good: the search team were flagging and there'd been no sign at all of Jessica, or anyone else for that matter. She hung up and slumped down on a chair. It was then that she spotted the business card on the kitchen bench where she'd left it, a little helicopter motif in the left-hand corner.

She called the number on it and waited.

The phone rang out only twice before he picked up and gave his name.

If a voice had a feel, his was like velvet: warm, soft, no edge to it.

'It's DCI Daniels here, Mr Cole.' Her hand went to her mouth as she caught sight of her reflection in the polished steel toaster on the kitchen bench:

an ugly bruise and dried blood visible on her upper lip. She wasn't sure what possessed her to say what came out next, but from the moment she'd met Cole, she'd had the feeling he was one of the good guys. 'I need your help,' she said.

'You can have all the help you want, Inspector.' He sounded intrigued. 'It'll cost you, mind. You call me Stew, I call you Kate. How's that?'

She took no offence, surprised that he'd even remembered her name. Dropping the formalities, she explained about the frantic search to find Jessica Finch. Then, without going into detail, she broke the news that his former friend, Jimmy Makepeace, was dead. There was a pause at the other end; a long, awkward pause while Cole digested the information he'd been given. Then he was back with her again, asking what it was she wanted him to do.

She told him about the search area. 'Don't know if you're familiar with the North Pennines, but it's *really* rough ground up there: shaft mounds, spoil heaps, old mine workings and not a lot else. The place is riddled with hidden rocks and streams. When I first saw it, I have to tell you, my morale took a dive. I can't imagine why he chose it. There'd be easier places to hide someone.'

'Sounds like Jimmy,' Cole said. 'Told you he was a nutter! If there was a hard way, he'd find it. That's the kind of guy he was. He was a good pilot, though. The best. I know it's a bit of a cliché, but flying, or should I say, landing a helicopter really isn't rocket science. It's just a question of doing your homework.'

'Homework?'

'We call it the five S's: size, shape, surface,

surrounds, slope. In other words, is it big enough? Is it long, wide, or flat enough? Are there tree stumps, rocks, any kind of bogland? Anything at all that might affect our ability to land? In your case, there obviously is.'

'Pylons, obstacles, that sort of thing?'

'Exactly. Slopes are tricky. You need at least twelve degrees nose up, nine from side to side, otherwise you're in trouble. We're trained to pick natural markers in the landscape: trees, rocks, any sort of visual that might aid an approach—one forward, one lateral—but even in the most difficult territory you can usually find somewhere to land. That's why we complete two orbits before we give it a go.'

Give it a go?

Daniels didn't like the sound of that.

'In my time in the military, I saw guys do amazing things in conditions you wouldn't wish on your worst enemy.'

'Like Jimmy?'

'Yeah, like Jimmy.' A hint of sadness crept into his voice. 'It's hard to believe he's done something like this.'

'You said he was a good pilot.' Daniels cut him off, trying to keep him focused. She didn't want him to dwell on the whys and wherefores of the case, just help her to solve it. 'Better than you?'

'Maybe,' Cole said honestly. 'Why don't you show me the site. We can take a look now, if you're up for it.'

83

Cole was confident but not arrogant, which was just as well because Daniels didn't fancy a trip in a flimsy bloody flying machine with some egomaniac at the controls. She thanked him, gave him the geographical coordinates for the search site, then hung up, agreeing to meet him there as soon as was humanly possible.

Before she left the house, she rang Weldon, letting him know they were on their way, asking him to keep quiet about her unofficial help if Naylor happened to make contact in the meantime. It was probably best if *she* was the one to tell him she'd commandeered a private aircraft at God knows what cost—five, six hundred pounds an hour?—while off duty on sick leave.

That *would* go down well.

'I'm supposed to be resting,' she said.

'Has something happened?' Weldon sounded concerned.

'Tell you later.'

Minutes after that conversation, she was back on the Yamaha, speeding to the same coordinates she'd just given Cole. He was waiting for her when she arrived, standing beside what could only be described as a Smart car with rotor blades on top and a couple of insubstantial skis underneath. Two wheels or four Daniels was happy with. Helicopters were something else. But this case had started with a journey in one and she was hoping that's where it would end.

Cole's eyes slid over her as she dismounted her

motorcycle, took off her helmet and shook her hair free. He grimaced when he saw her lip.

'That's quite a pout,' he said. 'Where'd you get it?'

'Long story . . . c'mon let's go.'

She was nervous as they got into the helicopter. The cockpit was a mass of dials, switches and levers, none of which made sense to her. Cole handed her a Bose headset like the one she'd seen his business partner carrying at the flying club. She put it on as he prepared for take-off, the sound of revving engines reverberating inside her chest.

Cole checked her out. 'You ready?'

'As I'll ever be.'

'Hey, get your shit together. This is no time for wimps.'

Daniels made a face, an extremely pale one. Cole took hold of the aircraft's cyclic, a joystick-type instrument for controlling directional movement: pitch and roll; side to side; forwards or back, any which way—or so he was telling her. She wasn't really interested, so long as he could fly the damn thing.

'Don't worry, Kate. I used to fly the Lynx.'

Brilliant, Daniels thought. *What's one of those when it's about?*

Cole smiled; a handsome smile she could've fallen for not so very long ago.

'Everyone in my unit wanted to be a pilot.' He lifted off, his eyes all over the place, checking various instruments, his main focus being the primary flight display which incorporated an artificial horizon, air speed, vertical speed, altimeter. He pointed at an Army Air Corps badge that was dangling above their heads: an eagle inside a wreath with a crown at the top. He looked sideways at her, grinning. 'Wanna know what the euphemism is for a pilot's wings?'

'No, but I'm sure you're going to tell me.' Daniels felt her stomach turn to mush as he banked steeply before levelling off again.

'They used to call 'em "the great golden leg spreaders".'

'Course they did,' she scoffed. 'Because women love to shag pilots, right?'

'Works for me,' he said, flirting with her.

'Only in your case it backfired,' she reminded him. 'Spectacularly, as I recall.'

'You read the file.' It was a statement, not a question.

'You kidding me? I'm a police officer! Of course I read the bloody file!'

Cole's expression hardened with the memory of a fracas that had drastically altered his life and robbed him of his career, a fight in a bar over a woman witnesses were clear he was trying to protect. The man he'd wounded was her ex-boyfriend, who'd just stuck a glass in her face after she dumped him in favour of Cole.

'I was a mug,' he said eventually. 'She went back to him while I was inside.'

'Doesn't surprise me.' Daniels meant it. 'Some women are their own worst enemy when it comes to domestic violence. They want their heads read.'

Cole's shrug was an admission that he was better off without her.

They flew around for half an hour or more, hardly speaking. Daniels was bloody exhausted, and tense—not because she liked her feet on the ground, either. The enquiry had taken its toll on her. Not once, but twice, events that had nothing to do with the enquiry had led her in the wrong direction. Blind alley syndrome was not uncommon in her line of work. Mark Harris was merely trying to get to know the daughter he never knew he had. He was an innocent man. Freek, on the other hand, was not. Durham had him bang to rights for passing information to the prostitution ring. He'd get what was coming in due course. But that didn't help in the search for Jessica.

Cole pointed.

Something had caught his eye.

Daniels couldn't see what he was looking at.

Her spirits soared as he altered course in order to check it out. It seemed to take forever to get there. Then, as the helicopter hovered in mid-air, blowing grass and debris around beneath it, the focus of Cole's attention turned out to be nothing more than an abandoned picnic blanket, flapping wildly in the wind.

Again, the aircraft banked sharply.

Holding on tight, Daniels felt her stomach somersault. She waited until the aircraft tipped the other way before letting go, her hopes plummeting as she spotted members of the search team making their way towards their vehicles, parked on the main road off to her left. Dusk was descending fast now; high time they called it a day—a situation not lost on Cole.

'It'll be dark soon,' he said. 'We don't have a lot of time.'

Daniels made no comment. She didn't need telling that it was madness risking life and limb out here in the wilderness on a doubtful outcome. But she couldn't bear the thought of leaving yet.

Neither could she accept that Jessica Finch was dead. She wouldn't abandon the search until Cole told her it was too dangerous to continue.

He kept flying.

But for how much longer?

And then . . .

Nothing.

Daniels was seeing things that weren't there.

Seconds ticked by.

Anytime now, Cole would utter the words she didn't want to hear. Sense would dictate that he put safety first, and he'd insist that they turn back. She watched his concentration, willing him to keep going for a few minutes more.

He did.

She was grateful for that.

Daniels blinked. On the ground beneath her she could've sworn she saw torchlight. One minute it was there, the next it was gone. She swung round. Weldon's rescue vehicles had formed a caravan, a moving chain of lights on the main road. Search teams were on their way back to base. So whose torch had she seen? One of her TSG's? Or had she just imagined it?

Reacting to her behaviour, Cole said, 'The light plays tricks sometimes.'

Looking over her left shoulder, Daniels scanned the ground again.

Cole followed her gaze. 'I can't see anything. Hang on, I'll go round.'

The helicopter shot forward and upwards, before banking sharply to the left. Cole put it into a steep descent, but the wind was causing him difficulty. Daniels watched him struggle with the controls and held on nervously as he brought the aircraft back to a hover. Even with the headphones on, the thwacking sound of the rotor blades was deafening.

'There! See it?' She pointed to a spot directly ahead. 'White object, near the sluice gate of the mine. Can't make out what it is, can you? Can you get us down?'

Cole looked below. The ground was uneven, covered with boulders and streams. There was only one possible area where he could land.

'I can . . . but in this wind it might not be pleasant. How's your stomach?'

Daniels blew out her cheeks. 'Just get us on the deck.'

'You want me to come with you when we get there?'

'Not sure?'

'You need to *be* sure,' he said with conviction.

Daniels had lost the white object. 'What the *hell* difference does it make?'

'A shitload.' Cole looked at her. 'There are different limitations for landing and shutting down in a confined area. Trust me, I'm a pilot.'

'OK, yes then.' Daniels braced herself for a bumpy landing, subconsciously checking her safety harness and making sure it was good and tight. 'Whoa! What you doing?'

'Sorry, rapid change in wind direction. I've got thirty knots up me chuff. I'm going round again. You want me to radio the tactical support team?'

'We can't wait for them. We'll lose the light. You get us down there. I'll radio in.'

Cole nodded. 'Suit yourself.'

'Daniels to Tango, Sierra, Golf, over . . .' She waited. But there was no response from the TSG.

Cole was struggling to manoeuvre the helicopter, which was bouncing around in the wind. Checking the map on her knee, she tried again. 'Tango, Sierra, Golf, come in. If you can hear me, I want a team over to search coordinates: Hotel, Alfa, Seven—Golf, Foxtrot, Two asap. And alert the doctor please. Suspicious item on the ground. I'm going to investigate.'

With great skill and much difficulty, Cole managed to move into a relatively clear area. Fixing the helicopter's tail, he moved the body of the aircraft round, checking if he was safe to land. Aware of the dangers of blade sail, a situation that could technically chop off the tail—a not-so-comforting gem of information her police pilot had imparted on their descent to Housesteads Roman Fort—Daniels shut her eyes, hating every second they remained in the air.

For the first time in a long time, she prayed.

84

Cole shut the chopper down and put the rotor brake on. When the blades stopped turning they jumped out, grabbing a backpack of emergency equipment on the way out the door. At the entrance of a disused mine they knelt down. Reaching in through the sluice gate, Daniels took hold of the white object she'd seen from the air, her hopes fading to nothing as she stared at her find, an unremarkable hard hat—the type a potholer or miner might use.

A tear ran down her face as her frustration

spilled out. Sinking back on her heels, she was about to discard the hat when the cap lamp flickered faintly . . . then the battery died.

'Oh my god! We found her, Stew!'

Time stood still for a second as they stared through the bars of the sluice gate. Then Cole dragged Daniels to her feet and searched her backpack. Locating an axe, he smashed the butt end against the lock on the gate, which flew off, narrowly missing her head. Switching on their torches, they waded into the mine, knee-deep in icy water, forced to bend double by the low ceiling, stopping every few metres or so to take a breather.

Daniels called out to Jessica.

They listened.

No joy.

And pushed on . . .

A hundred metres further in, the worst possible scenario presented itself. There was a fork in the tunnel ahead, each offshoot as ominous and terrifying as the other. This was no time to admit that they weren't keen on enclosed spaces. Even less keen to separate, but driven on to find Jessica, Cole peeled off to the left, the DCI to the right.

Daniels had been alone in some difficult situations in her time but the walls of the tunnel seemed to close in around her now. Fear gripped her, a claustrophobia so overwhelming she had to fight hard to go on. She'd rather have confronted her nemesis, Jonathan Forster, again than face this unknown threat underground.

Go on, you can do it.

It's just a tunnel!

How on earth her father, or anyone else for that matter, ever managed to work below ground was beyond her comprehension. She wished he was here now to guide her. He would take her by the hand—like he used to when she was a little girl—and tell her some cock-and-bull story about the magical interior world she was entering. It didn't feel magical. It felt as close to Hell as a person could get. A place of evil and suffering: remote, totally petrifying and spine-chillingly creepy.

As fear wrapped itself around her and tightened its grip, Daniels lost her footing and plunged headlong into the icy water, gashing her right hand on the wall as she went down, dropping her torch in the process. In blind panic, she scrambled around on all fours trying to retrieve it. For once, luck was on her side. Although submerged, the torch was still lit and heavy enough not to have been swept too far away in the current. She managed to get a hold on it but, just as she did so, the light suddenly went out.

The icy water had taken her breath away. Hyperventilating now, she was sitting in water, chest high, in unimaginable darkness. Jessica Finch was dead for sure. It was inconceivable that she could survive captivity down here for more than a few days.

As panic set in, a million spiders crawled over Daniels' skin. Imaginary they may have been but she brushed them away as if they were real, yelling out in desperation and conscious of the terror in her voice.

'Stew! Stew!'

Nothing: just the plink, plonk of water falling all around her.

Daniels shook the torch violently.

Suddenly the light came on.

Thank you, God!

She could breathe again.

Cold and disorientated, she shone the light first one way, then the other, again and again. Both looked identical.

Fuck! Was she facing in or out?

'Stewart!'

Come on, Kate. Think!

'JESSICA!'

The stress in her voice was bloodcurdling as it echoed back at her.

She shot against the wall as her flashlight caught the eyes of a rat.

Kicking out with her feet, she thrashed around in the water until the bastard thing disappeared. Taking a long, deep breath, she urged herself to keep going. But first she had to calm herself down.

A few more deep breaths and her brain began to function once more:

Water runs out of a mine, not in.

She peered down the tunnel the way she'd come. Turning back was a temptation but not a serious option. She'd gone there to find Jessica Finch, dead or alive, and she wasn't about to give up. She'd come too far to abandon her now. With her bearings once again intact, but with no idea how far the mine extended, she set off with renewed determination, the backpack getting ever heavier with the weight inside.

'Jessica!'

She stopped to listen once more. But it was no use. Up ahead, a huge black hole beckoned. Whatever it contained, the sight of it alone raised the hairs on the back of her neck. Like an enormous mouth threatening to swallow her whole, it appeared to be some kind of chamber cut into the rock. Thinking she'd heard someone behind her, Daniels swung round, hoping to see Cole wading towards her. She was mistaken. There was nothing except pitch darkness.

Jessica *was* in there though, Daniels could sense it, just as she had that morning when she'd sat astride her bike, scanning the landscape from the main road. All she wanted now was to find her and get the fuck out of there as fast as she could. Scrambling forward, straining to see, her eyes scanned the wet walls for evidence of recent activity, anything at all that might lead her to believe she was on the right track. But the place looked as though no human had passed through in decades.

Hanging on to the straps of her backpack, she set off again, wondering how Cole was doing, hoping he was having more luck than she was. Her heart was thumping with sheer exhaustion by the time she reached the chamber. It was now or never. Dipping her head low, she went in.

On the far side, she was able to stand upright for the first time since entering the mine. It took all her resolve just to haul her wet, aching body off the floor. But as she raised her head and lifted the torch, her blood ran cold.

She let out a gasp.

No!

Taking a small step backwards, she sank to her knees, effectively blocking off the entrance. A whimper echoed in the chamber. This was not Jessica calling for help but the sound of her own voice.

Two rats paddled by, their beady eyes glowing in

the darkness. This time Daniels didn't flinch, flail around, or scream. She was too traumatized by the sight facing her to pay them any mind.

'Kate!'

A faraway voice called out to her.

It was calm, not unduly alarmed, a man's voice, she thought. Cole maybe? The TSG? Whether it was real or imagined, Daniels couldn't tell. She didn't care anymore. Caring for people hadn't turned out well up to now: Mum, Dad, Jo, Jessica . . . all the victims who'd gone before. In different ways, she'd cared for them all, some personally, others in the course of a so-called dream job.

Being a murder detective occasionally gave her an adrenalin rush but most times not. If she was being honest, the majority of the time it was gross—pitiless, vicious, repulsive—and totally unbearable. Right now she ached to turn in her warrant card and walk away.

'Kate?'

She turned and looked over her shoulder.

In the tunnel, Cole stopped dead in his tracks when he saw her, tears unashamedly running down her face, the torch shaking in her bloodstained hand.

'You don't want to go in there,' she said gently.

85

'She's breathing, just.' Daniels wiped her nose on her sodden sleeve and stopped snivelling. 'We need to get her out of here now!'

'You want me to go back and radio in?'

'No time. Get the axe out. Quickly!'

Turning her back on him, Daniels hung on to the mouth of the chamber, obscuring its interior from Cole, wondering if she ought to let him in there. It was a crime scene after all. *A major one.* She dismissed that thought. Keeping Jessica alive was her only priority and she needed his help. She'd preserve life over a crime scene any day of the week and worry about recovering forensics later.

Refastening her backpack, Cole blew on his hands.

Daniels turned round. 'You ready?' she said.

He didn't look ready, but he nodded anyway.

They crawled into the chamber, the DCI going first.

She shone the torch against the wall as they stood up straight.

Cole's reaction was predictable for a civilian who'd never before witnessed a scene this horrific. Sadly, Daniels had. For a moment he stood there, unable to draw his eyes away from what was, to all intents and purposes, a macabre crucifixion. Shaking both from cold and shock, his purple lips looked black in the darkened chamber. They turned down at the edges as he fought to stay in control of his emotions. Observing at first hand the level of cruelty one human being could inflict on another was always the hardest part to endure.

Averting his eyes, he focused his torch and his attention on Daniels.

It took a moment for him to verbalize thought . . .

'I saw some shit in the military, but I have to tell you . . .'

His voice trailed off.

An eerie silence prevailed, save for the drip, drip of water from the roof above. Sickened by what he'd seen, Cole hung his head a second, then looked up and let out a tirade of swear words, enraged that the man responsible for Jessica's incarceration had taken the coward's way out and would not face justice. Daniels agreed with him, but didn't comment, merely pointed at the axe in the crook of his arm.

'I'll protect her hands, you get her down.'

'No wait! I need to do something first.'

Cole swung into action then, dispelling all thoughts of Makepeace from his mind. They had a job to do and there was no time to waste. Handing her his torch, he slipped his arms out of the straps of his own rucksack. Daniels didn't argue, just trained the torch on him and moved towards the girl.

Jessica's emaciated body hung from the chains that bound her, head lolling to one side, a tortured expression on her face. She looked as though she was dead. Putting two fingers gently on her neck, Daniels felt a weak pulse and spoke a few words of encouragement, hoping she heard them. Coma patients had reported hearing the voices of loved ones. If Jessica knew she hadn't been abandoned it might make the difference between life and death.

'I hope he burns in Hell.' Cole had the bag open now. 'Can you hold this?'

Daniels left Jessica's side to help. With enormous difficulty, she took the bag from him, her injured hand almost collapsing under its weight. It must have weighed in excess of twenty-five pounds. How he'd managed to lug it all the way from the entrance was anyone's guess.

Removing what looked like a sturdy waterproof bag, Cole opened it up. Inside was a folded block of heavy duty plastic material—orange, yellow and black—and some strange looking bellows. He began working hard, inflating what Daniels now realized was a floating stretcher, complete with zip-up survival cover, insulated to keep their casualty warm.

A lump formed in her throat. 'You steal that piece of kit from your employer?'

Cole pretended he hadn't noticed she was close to breaking down.

'Nah, picked it up at Waitrose on my way to meet you. Wanna see the receipt?'

Blinking back tears of relief, the bedraggled SIO managed a weak smile. Cole had been her very last hope of finding Jessica in time to save her life. He'd stepped into the breach when others would have hidden behind excuses. She could never repay him for that.

Cole took a much-needed breather. Soaked through and shivering uncontrollably, the effort required to work the bellows had taken its toll on him. He looked into her eyes and then started pumping his arms again.

'How the hell do you do it, Kate?'

Daniels' tone was hard. 'Someone has to.'

She knew then why she did it. Because no one else wanted to, was the short answer. Now back in command of her emotions, she pushed her doubts away. This was no time to wallow in self-pity or make decisions on her future career. The police force was her life, the only life worth living, as far as she was concerned. She was bruised by it often. But bruises heal . . . eventually.

She hoped Jessica would too.

Cole was now done.

In silence they released Jessica from her restraints. Cole lifted her up and laid her gently in the stretcher, wrapping her up securely, like he was putting a child to bed. A few last words of encouragement from Daniels and they began the journey back down the tunnel. It was touch and go whether Jess would make it. But at least they were taking her home.

86

Daniels parked her bike at Hartside Pass, switched off the ignition and lifted her visor. From here she could see right across the Solway Firth to Scotland as well as Helvellyn, Great Gable and Skiddaw in The Lakes. Taking off her leather gloves, she studied the scarring on her right hand and recalled the terrifying, rat-infested tunnel where she'd gashed it.

Any shred of sympathy she might have felt for Jimmy Makepeace had quickly turned to rage that day. He had, as Cole said, taken the coward's way out, leaving Jessica to die a horrible death in a chamber of unspeakable horrors, shackled to the wall without a hope in hell of escape and little chance of being found. A suicide note found at his house suggested he'd acted alone and offered a muted apology to the parents of Amy Grainger. Detectives treated it with the contempt it deserved. The irony of leaving another couple childless had obviously passed him by.

Even though it hadn't always felt like it, in their search for Jessica the murder investigation team had never lost sight of the fact that they were simultaneously investigating the death of another young girl. Amy Grainger had been a happy and vibrant young woman with everything to live for; a young woman who loved the countryside and who, it seemed, had paid with her life for bearing a likeness to someone else. Her parents had since returned to the place where she died, comforted by the beauty and solitude of the Roman Wall and its surroundings, a wondrous place Amy would've loved to explore, had she lived long enough to see it for herself.

The investigation into her death had lasted eleven days. But it had touched so many people's lives on the way. Mark Harris and his daughter, Rachel Somers, were now reunited. Durham Constabulary had smashed the prostitution ring that had preyed on impoverished students from the city's university and had charged two men with living off immoral earnings. Stephen Freek had also been charged, with aiding and abetting, along with offences against Data Protection. Daniels had made it her business to instigate charges of her own: a count of administering a noxious substance and one of abduction in the case of Bryony Sharp, which would undoubtedly lead to a consecutive term of imprisonment. And that was good enough for his other victim, DC Lisa Carmichael, who'd learned a valuable lesson in the course of her dealings with Freek.

Even with the weight of the law behind her, there were some cases where Daniels had no choice but to accept that she might never know the whole truth. Susan Makepeace was one of those cases. She had lied to police about her involvement in her ex-husband's wicked revenge; it was likely she supplied him with information about Jessica. But the former housekeeper would not stand trial because, in their wisdom, the Crown Prosecution Service had decided there was insufficient evidence to obtain a conviction. In Daniels' mind, no questions remained: why else had the woman cut Jimmy out of the photograph of her daughter, if not to conceal it from her employer? Susan Makepeace was guilty, all right, of that she had no doubt.

The investigation had thrown up many issues for Daniels: the innocent had been under suspicion, the guilty had escaped justice and along the way she had learned that sometimes rehabilitation *was* possible. It certainly was in the case of Stewart Cole, who received a commendation for the assistance he'd given the murder investigation team. He was indeed one of the good guys, and Daniels would remain forever in his debt.

A few weeks after the case was finally closed, she began receiving curious postcards from abroad, all unsigned, all bearing the same simple message: *Are you hungry yet?* Each time one dropped into her in-tray, Daniels thought about Fiona Fielding and wondered what might have been. Who knows? Maybe they would meet again . . . someday.

Maybe not.

The complexities of the human psyche are many. Some people are for ever stuck in the past. Jo Soulsby was Daniels' past, just as Mark Harris was Laura Somers', Makepeace was Cole's, Finch was Bright's. But critical to the case was the relationship between Jimmy Makepeace and Adam Finch. And, because of that final connection—a decision made many years ago that had nothing whatsoever to do with her—Jessica Finch had very nearly died in that chamber. And would have done so, had Cole not floated her out of the mine and airlifted her to hospital.

Another hour and they'd have been too late.

Her captor, Jimmy Makepeace, had taken his secret to the grave. So in the end it was down to one minute piece of forensics and Jessica's own resilience that she survived at all. When Daniels found her—unconscious, head bowed and chained to the wall, an emaciated, torn soul—she'd wept tears of anger that a person could treat another so cruelly. But later there were tears of joy when word came through from the hospital that she was sitting up in bed with her father by her side. Her injuries were more psychological than physical. She'd managed to suck water from strands of wet hair in order to survive. The rain that Daniels had been so desperate about had, in a twist of fate, saved her from certain death.

Within a few days, she was out of the high-dependency unit. Doctors were confident that, in time, she would make a full recovery. Now, more than ever, Jessica was determined to complete her studies and enter the medical profession. Whether or not her father would relent and accept Robert Lester as part of her life . . . who could say? But even Adam Finch had shown his good side, bankrolling the MAC Flying Club out of gratitude to Stewart Cole.

Daniels took a long deep breath and flexed her hand. Thankfully her scars were only superficial.

Today, tomorrow, next week, there would be another case to solve, other families looking for justice, revenge, closure.

Her phone rang. The display read: Hank.

'Where you at?' Gormley said.

Daniels grimaced, hesitating a little too long.

Gormley didn't wait for a reply. 'How's the view up there?'

Smiling, she looked over the stunning countryside. The Amy Grainger case had pushed her and her team to the limit. But Jessica Finch had survived, and so had they. Today was a day without a cloud in the sky.

A happy day.

'Perfect, Hank . . .' she said. 'The view's just perfect.'